Return to Dust

Books by Andrew Lanh

The Rick Van Lam Mysteries
Caught Dead
Return to Dust

Return to Dust

A Rick Van Lam Mystery

Andrew Lanh

Poisoned Pen Press

Copyright © 2015 by Andrew Lanh

First Edition 2015

10 9 8 7 6 5 4 3 2 1

Library of Congress Catalog Card Number: 2015932051

ISBN: 9781464204265   Hardcover
      9781464204289   Trade Paperback

Poisoned Pen Press
6962 E. First Ave., Ste. 103
Scottsdale, AZ 85251
www.poisonedpenpress.com
info@poisonedpenpress.com

Printed in the United States of America

To Eric Minh Ky Tang
bo ming oy

Prologue

The First Congregational Church down on Main Street tolls its ancient bell in the high clapboard steeple whenever there's a funeral. No matter what I'm doing, I freeze, hunch my shoulders, flooded with melancholy as I struggle to catch my breath. I am back in old Saigon, leaning against the chapel wall, out in the dusty street under a tropical sun, and the awful peal of bells in the small La Vang Chapel—creaky and broken at the edges—makes me shiver. At that moment I know I have to run away.

Maybe I'm ten years old, I'm not really sure, but the good Sisters toll the bell when one of the boys in the ramshackle orphanage dies. The heavy hand of Sister Do Thi Bich, the severe nun who calls me "Satan's bastard." Scared, I run.

But there's nowhere to run, really. I need to be in bed when they walk through the corridor, counting bodies in a singsong voice: *mot hai ba bon.*

Nam. Five.

Five was Diep, the boy who died in the morning.

Sau bay tam chín. Six seven eight nine...

Muoi. Ten. I am number ten in the decrepit wing at the back of the building. The end of the line, in the dark corner, shuttled there, next to the sewer pipe, where the smells from the black water gag me, make me heave.

Good night, Vietnam. Goodbye, old Sai Gon. Hello, Ho Chi Minh City.

I run away for the day, though I know I'll pay a price. One more beating. It doesn't matter anymore. The good Sisters with the bamboo switch or the other boys who hate me—they shove, trip, or batter me. Slap me in the face.

Bui doi. Dust boy. Impure. Mongrel. American blood.

I run.

I run away from District 4 where the Most Blessed Mother Catholic Orphanage is, that grubby quarter of the city, an island, isolated, the squalid streets where the conquering VC shepherded all the Southern army fighters, the rejects, the poor, the defeated—shacks and makeshift hovels and polluted water. On the main street, Nguyen Tat Thanh, folks push and jostle, curse the motorbikes and *cyclos* and sputtering cars jockeying for space. Food vendors cook noodles and rice over low flames, kneeling in the hot dust next to the black sewage that seeps into the river. Green-bottle flies swarm and bite, and an old woman, her face hidden under a *non la*, a conical straw hat, sells durian and dragon fruit in the shadow of a crumbing brick wall built when the French ruled the land. I sneak across the Saigon River, listen to the groan of a water bull. When a vendor turns away, I grab a chunk of stale bread, gobble it down. I run.

I go to find the only friend I have. Tranh Xan Vu most likely is working somewhere in District 1, the land of the rich Viet Cong, the victors, five years after a war that ended on April 28, 1975. Vu will be near the square across from the Rex Hotel on Nguyen Hue Street. The hotel where the American military ran operations. Where the lipsticked taxi girls winked and loved all night long. Here now dark Cuban women with heady perfume and harsh eyes mingle with the blustery Russian tourists who smell of sweat and motor oil and anger.

I like my friend Vu, I suppose, because he likes me. Perhaps fifteen years old, a stringy, skinny boy, dark as old wood, a tiny boy with a pushed-in face, he found me months ago when I'd been sent by the nuns to the marketplace to carry back bundles of lemongrass and a bag of rice. He'd been lounging under the shade of a banyan tree, sitting on the *cyclo* he used to make money, waiting for some insolent VC to nod at him, sneer a destination, and hop onto the three-wheeled machine. He'd seen me walking past, loaded down with bundles, sweating, the boy always chosen for the horrible task, and he'd yelled, "Hey, America."

That had startled me. I ignored him.

"You, America." Again, but with a laugh. "You, American boy in blue and white." The uniform of the schoolchildren: white shirt, blue shorts.

He'd spotted me as a forbidden boy with American blood. Perhaps the deep blue eyes that glanced at him. The rigid chin. The wavy hair. A pureblood Vietnamese, someone who should have shunned me, instead he sought me out—because he was all about America. "And of the freedom," he'd stammer in thick English.

Mockingly, he sputtered his familiar line to potential customers: "Where are you off to?"

Ban muon di dau?

It was a time before Tet, the New Year, and the Buddhist monks shuffled in the streets. People sat and communed with the ghosts of their ancestors. Bowed, honored, prayed to.

I didn't answer at first, but finally, weighed down by my weekly load, I climbed in, and he shuttled me to the orphanage. After that first time, we watched for each other.

There were times when I sneaked out of the orphanage, late at night, alone, miserable, running through the alleys, scrounging for food discarded by the street vendors—food that the wild dogs hadn't found. Vu, it seems, was always out and about, hanging against a post with a cigarette bobbing in his mouth. That is, the stubble of a discarded cigarette from one of the Russian tourists—a few intakes of smoke left.

He lived with his father and grandmother in District 4 in a shack with a corrugated tin roof and twisted boards. I met his father once because he demanded I do so. I bowed to his grandmother who sat on a wobbly chair by the doorway, an old shriveled woman noisily chewing betel nuts. Her few remaining teeth were stained dark red, which told me she'd wanted to be a beauty as a young woman—those dark teeth a mark of loveliness then. She barked at Vu but he bowed, smiled at her.

Vu's father, Tranh Kan Tan, frightened me: a hard-muscled little man, all sinew and bone, he'd been a soldier for the defeated South, and after the surrender he'd been sentenced to a re-education camp. Re-education: prison. *Nha Tu Chi Hoa.* Beaten, starved, recorded propaganda blared into his ears day and night, weakened by malaria during *bao*, the monsoon season, he'd been dumped back home, and tried to pick up a life as a *cyclo* driver. His stony silence alarmed the Soviet tourists he met at the Rex Hotel, or he'd lose his way, stare off into space. He'd throw up his hand as though to fend off attack. Vu told me he machine-gunned birds in the sky. He ducked from showers of napalm as he hid in the elephant grass. At night he heard B-52s circling overhead.

So the *cyclo* remained unused until Vu appropriated it, though the few cents he earned barely paid for joss sticks needed to honor the ancestors.

I could never get Tranh Xan Tan's haunted face out of my head. He was what was left when the American helicopters sailed off for good from the roof of the American Embassy.

He was the dead country, labeled *ke phan boi*. Traitor.

I met these men all over the city. Frozen men, I called them. Men whose inner clocks had stopped and their faces told you they'd lost the will to live. Ice men. Blocks of stone.

Today I find Vu sitting on the *cyclo* near the Ben Thanh market in District 1. A policeman is yelling at him, telling him he is not allowed there. But Vu stares him down, defiant, his lips trembling. I've seen him in such moods before—dangerous, scary. The policeman has a deep Northern accent that especially jars, and Vu answers back, imitating the blunt demands. Infuriated, the man strikes him in the face. I watch from a corner, nervous.

Then I realize what is happening. Vu sometimes wears an American army fatigue shirt he's found, some tattered military issue remnant with torn sleeves and a hole in the shoulder. A soldier's nametag on the breast—*Johnson*—the words *U.S.*

ARMY, and a patch of stripes on the sleeve. Taboo, this shirt, of course, and cursed. The policeman demands Vu remove it, but Vu doesn't move.

My eyes travel to a poster on the wall behind him—Ho Chi Minh at his most imperious: that awful stare. Revered Uncle Ho. His signature words are emblazoned across the top, though the VC has tattooed them to all our souls: Independence and Freedom. *Doc lap va Tu do.*

One afternoon I'd been forced to hand out leaflets in the marketplace. Freedom and Independence. Over and over. The cheap broadside printed poorly with smudged ink, Uncle Ho's face slightly contorted so he looked even more menacing.

Now, looking up, Vu spots me. He starts to mouth the word *America* as a greeting, but stops, frightened. He looks away. He cannot save himself but he can save me.

Immediately a couple of soldiers appear and Vu, surprising them, pedals away like a madman, though they try to block him. He breaks through, sails past me, a triumphant look on his face, and disappears. The soldiers look angry but they start laughing.

I will never see Vu again.

Late at night as I roam the streets, stealing food from bamboo baskets in the stalls—there is never a time when I'm not hungry—he is nowhere around. One afternoon after I am beaten up by the other boys who call me the son of a whore mother and an American cowboy, I run away. My left eye is bloodied, throbbing, already black and blue. I have nowhere to go, so I seek out Vu's shanty.

The grandmother sits out front, but she refuses to look into my face. I call out, "Vu." Nothing. I want to hear him call my nickname, "America." I like that. The land of everybody's dreaming.

His father steps from the shack. Tranh Xan Tan stands still, eyes squinting against the sun, a man who has taken a vow of horrible silence. The frozen man I have trouble looking at. He watches me closely. I wait.

"Vu?" I ask.

Nothing. But his eyes shift toward a narrow space alongside the home, and there, mangled and twisted, is the *cyclo*. He disappears back into the shack.

I start to back up, my throat dry, my eyes wet. But the grandmother mumbles something and reaches behind her. She hands me a tight bundle wrapped in old newspaper. I take it.

The American army shirt. I can tell by the hint of khaki color, the buttons on a sleeve.

Back at the orphanage while I wait for the beating from the nuns for running away again, I open the package. There it is, that precious shirt, but the front is bloodied now. I jump back, cry out. Nearby one of the boys, not at his chores because he's ailing, looks up, and smirks. He sees the shirt.

"Are you crazy?" he yells.

I will hide it under the cot, but of course it will be gone soon. But I want to keep it a little longer, cherish it. Vu and the dream of a land he would never see.

As I tuck it away, I feel something in the breast pocket. A folded over, crumpled handbill. The same one we all see in our nightmares. Uncle Ho, whose features are now wrinkled out of recognition. I spread it open. There is that mantra to our defeat: *Doc lap va Tu do.*

Independence and Freedom. But Vu had scribbled one word after the line, though he'd misspelled it:

"Amrica."

Chapter One

When I sent flowers to Marta Kowalski's funeral, I considered it the last contact I'd ever have with her. It was my way of paying my respects to the woman who'd cleaned my small apartment twice a month. I'd even skipped the funeral. After all, we'd never been friends. Friendly, yes, because she knew people I knew in the small town. And she also dusted my furniture with a loving hand. A chatty woman, a little too perky for my tastes, she was small and round, with too much powder, too much drugstore perfume, and too many jangling bracelets. Worse—a smug church-going gossip who reveled in the vices of folks I'd never met. When she straightened my messy apartment, I made sure I was out. When she ran a cloth over the leather-bound books on my shelves, her eyes shone, happy. I liked her, I guess. After all, I did send flowers. That says something, doesn't it?

So I was surprised one night when her niece Karen phoned as I was getting ready for bed.

"Rick Van Lam?"

A good beginning. Not Rick Lam or even Mr. Lam. Not even the way some souls mispronounced it—as *lamb*. My full name—the way I like it.

"I know we've never really talked but we *have* met. I don't know if you remember me." She stopped, drew in her breath, waiting. "Do you remember me? I'm sorry. I'm nervous. I'm Karen Corcoran."

I did remember her because, well, I remember people. That's what I do. Pretty, almost waiflike, blond and slender, with razor-thin lips, she was probably in her mid-thirties. I remember that she was wearing a peasant-style dress, too baggy, unflattering, the kind of dress women wear to avoid being looked at.

We'd been at the same party, but some time ago. Somebody's birthday. An instructor at the college. We'd talked for a minute—she was a little flirty, I thought—and before she drifted away, she'd said we should get together for coffee. I never answered her. Later on, at one in the morning, lonely and a little desperate, I thought I'd approach her. But something kept me away. She stood in a corner, arms folded over her chest, head tilted. Her eyes darted about, unsettled and edgy. Those dusty blue eyes looked pale as old faded paper flowers. She wore her hair long, straight, uncomplicated, and, as I watched her, she pulled at a strand, nervous.

I'd seen her around town, of course. Sometimes when I saw her at a convenience store at night, picking up milk or pumping gas, or when I spotted her driving down Main Street, she wore her hair in a casual ponytail, almost sloppy, with strands flying loose. Even careless—especially careless—she was pretty. Crossing paths, we usually said "hi" or nodded at each other—but that was it. I was always planning future conversations with her, but I held back, afraid I'd be disappointed.

"I remember you." I was smiling, waiting, happy to hear her voice. "Of course."

"It's business." Matter-of-fact, blunt.

I kept smiling. I felt a flush of pink rush to my cheeks.

"Business?"

"I want to hire you."

That surprised me. So late at night for such a call. "You need an investigator?"

"To investigate my Aunt Marta's murder. Marta Kowalski." A melodramatic pause, calculated. "Murder," she whispered.

The rawness of her voice alarmed, chilled. I glanced at the clock on my desk. Midnight. Maybe she'd waited all night to get the courage to call. But midnight?

I could hear her suck in her breath, a small cry escaping from the back of her throat.

When I still didn't answer, her voice gained urgency. "I want to hire you to find her murderer."

Marta Kowalski, the woman who cleaned my carpets.

"You don't think it was a suicide?"

A thin laugh, almost mocking. "No, I don't."

"Why?"

"Can we have lunch tomorrow?"

Chapter Two

The next day, at one o'clock, I nursed a potent espresso in a little sandwich shop across the street from the strip-mall shopping arcade where Karen Corcoran operated her small art and gift gallery, Corcoran's Treasures, a cubby-hole store where tourists and visitors to the Farmington Conference Center at the Marriott down the street bought her own oversized, garish abstract canvases as well as the cookie-cutter pastel landscapes executed on Chinese assembly lines. She obviously made a living, though perhaps a slight one, but then so did hectoring, fast-talking drummers on cable TV.

My sidekick, Hank Nguyen, with all the accumulated wisdom of a twenty-three-year-old sage, once joked with me about Karen's artwork when we strolled past the gallery and glanced in the window. "It reminds me of a Technicolor digestive surprise."

"Perfect for over the pull-out sofa in the basement rec room," I'd added.

Now I watched as she strolled through the parking lot adjacent to the arcade. She'd asked to meet at one o'clock—she'd get someone to cover the shop—and it was already fifteen past. She moved quickly, her body half turned away as she tried to shake off an old woman who trailed her, touching her elbow, pointing back to the shop. Karen looked harried, yet her strides were deliberate, purposeful. Her phone voice echoed—hesitant yet determined. A curious combination. But whispered, too.

I stood up as she approached my table. I smiled but she didn't, which made me feel foolish. She was sizing me up—I recalled her stance at that party, her arms folded, that judgmental look in her eyes—and she nodded formally with a slight wave of her hand. Then she reached across the table to shake my hand. Her nails were painted a dark red.

"Hello, Rick."

At that moment the waitress hurried over, but Karen, sitting down and adjusting the sweater she wore, ignored her.

"Two espressos," I told the young girl. Karen nodded.

"Do you want to hear the special of the day?" the waitress asked, hovering. Young, chubby, with cobalt-blue lipstick and matching eyebrows, her hair streaked with blue and gold, she probably was a college girl, maybe even at Farmington College, its stately brick and pilloried buildings standing just down Main Street across from the town green. I didn't recognize her, though. I teach there part-time, but most of my charges are beefy ex-Marine crew-cut guys planning careers in Criminal Justice. When she moved her arm, pointing at a chalk-covered blackboard over the counter, I spotted a run of red and green tattoos down her arm. I told her we'd wait to order.

"I know I sounded odd on the phone last night," Karen began, smiling slightly. "It's just that I had to work myself up to call. At midnight—well, I *had* to then. Or never."

"I was awake."

A pause. "I didn't care. Sorry, but I'd been planning it for days and I kept wondering if I was losing my mind and…"

I broke in. "You said murder."

As I said the word, evenly, stressing it, she started, a small sound escaping her throat. For a second she closed her eyes. I expected her to cry. But when she opened her eyes, I saw hot anger in those pale blue eyes, now grown steely.

"My aunt would *never* commit suicide."

"You sound so sure."

"I am."

"But the police…"

"I don't give a damn." She breathed in. "I just don't."

Marta Kowalski's bizarre death three weeks back had surprised everyone in Farmington, the affluent town outside of Hartford, Connecticut. It was the story everyone talked of for days. Marta was a woman people knew but scarcely thought about. A sensible woman in her sixties, a meticulously neat woman who wore too much makeup when she scoured your bathroom. Moral as all get out—she'd tell you so in case you missed her stellar character. Well, I never considered her as someone who, in the awesome grip of despair or depression, would hurl herself off the old stone bridge that arched over the Farmington River. A widow, Marta had been a housekeeper at Farmington College, retiring a few years back and living on her husband's pension, eventually taking a few cleaning jobs here and there.

"To keep the old hand in," she once told me.

One of the places she cleaned was my apartment.

She certainly didn't need the money. Unsolicited, she'd shared that information more than once with me—and to perfect strangers at Walmart. She carried her elastic-bound weathered bank books with her, tucked into a huge black patent-leather purse, the kind women carry to bingo games at church halls—and she would produce evidence of her modest but comfortable wealth at the slightest provocation. She wore her shallowness like a badge of honor. I rarely thought about her, even as I wrote a check and left it on the hall stand. Like everyone else, I was startled by her sudden death. She left no suicide note. Hearing of her death, I'd felt guilty because I didn't think she had an interior life worth considering. I wasn't happy with my own moral lapse.

I looked into Karen's face. "Is there any evidence of foul play?"

She paused, drew her lips into a thin line. "No."

"Then how...?"

She threw back her head, defiant. "The coroner said she died from injuries from her fall. To her head. Neck. A shoulder broken."

"So you're saying she was deliberately pushed?"

"Well, something like that." She stared over my shoulder.

I waited, but she offered nothing else.

"But Karen…"

The waitress returned with the coffee, determined to take our orders, and we chose quickly. Only designer food was available. I ordered homemade rye topped with oriental-style free-range chicken marinated in sesame oil. Karen pointed to beef drenched in oyster sauce served on watercress from the community garden across town. The chef had too many spices to work with. Everything on the menu was described in long paragraphs with too many adjectives—succulent, refreshing, inquisitive, innovative, startling, exotic, beguiling. Beguiling? I opted for that dish—the running-wild chicken. Few things beguile me. Women, I suppose, and Billie Holiday music. Not food.

"No, listen to me." Karen's voice was hard, metallic. "You gotta investigate her murder, Rick Van Lam." She stared into my face. "What are your rates?"

I sat back, watched her closely. I was most likely the only PI she knew of. After all, there weren't many in Farmington Center, and I was probably the only one whose apartment had been cleaned by the allegedly murdered woman. Talk about your job referrals.

"Slow down, Karen," I told her. But the look on her face gave me pause. Humorless, deadly serious, a pinched tightness around the eyes.

"I guess I have to convince you."

"I'm listening."

"I can't convince you." She took a sip of the espresso. "I don't have a shred of evidence that it wasn't suicide. I can't prove anything. I can't. But I have the money, and you, well, do this for a living, right?"

I shook my head, grinned. "Sort of. Actually I do insurance investigations out of Hartford. But I do get to turn down jobs, you know."

She sat back in the seat, breathed in, sighed. "I'm sorry. I know I'm coming on like a speeding truck here, but, you see, I can't sleep at night."

I tapped the table. "Look, Karen, suicide is difficult to deal with." I knew I sounded a little patronizing, though I was trying not to. "It's shattering, it's…I remember there wasn't a note."

"Yes, no note," she echoed.

I shrugged. "True, not everyone leaves a note—last thoughts to a world they're leaving behind." I stared into her face. "Especially if you hate that world."

Karen's fingers tightened around the small espresso cup. I thought it might crack. "I hate hearing you say it that way. My aunt didn't *hate* the world. She loved life." She looked around the room. "She—that sounds simple but it's true. That's my point."

"What?"

"That's my evidence."

I bit my lip. "That she loved life?"

I panicked. How could I get out of this sad scene diplomatically? I wasn't about to take money from a woman who was hurting, whose dark grief made her suspect foul play. Loved ones left behind, of course, have a lot of trouble with suicide, I've learned—they are being told that death is more beautiful than they are. Not always welcome news.

Karen saw something in my face. "I'm not crazy."

"I'm sorry. I didn't mean it that way."

She was wearing a light blue sweater, a little baggy in the elbows. I watched her body twist under it. She had an appealing way of flicking her head back whenever she finished saying something. I hadn't had a serious romance for a year or more, just bittersweet moments with faculty secretaries that drifted into silence and indifference. I tried to keep romance separate from business, but I sometimes faltered. Now I wanted to avoid looking at that sweater. Her skinny hands with the prominent blue veins, nervous hands—focus on them. Her nails were long, manicured, but painted that shrill red. There were traces of dried paint on her knuckles. An artist's weathered hands, dull with flecks of burnt sienna and white titanium. Out of nowhere I suddenly entertained an image of those fingers around her aunt's neck.

She spotted me looking at her hands and suddenly dropped them into her lap.

"Like everyone else," she went on, "I resigned myself to Aunt Marta's suicide. Not that it made any sense, mind you. Marta was a devout Catholic, you know. But who was I to say? The police report and all..."

"The autopsy?" I assumed there was one.

She didn't answer me.

"What about her state of mind? Was she unhappy?"

"Aunt Marta was really depressed lately. I knew that. You could see it in her face. She never smiled anymore."

"When did you last see her?"

"A week before...maybe. She was bothered by something, but she wouldn't talk about it." She lowered her voice when a couple of older women were seated at the next table. She strained her neck, trying to see them. "I thought that was someone I knew," she said. "I'm a little nervous talking in such a public place about something like—like murder." She whispered the last word, but it still must have startled her. For a second her mouth trembled.

"Karen, depressed people kill themselves."

She leaned into me, her fingers almost touching mine. "I *know* she didn't kill herself. In my bones, Rick. I was going through some of her papers—you wouldn't believe the boxes of letters and coupons and newspaper clippings she left behind—and there was a packet from her travel agent. Two tickets to Las Vegas. Right there. For three weeks after the day she died." She rushed her words. "She'd be leaving this week."

"So what're you saying?"

"I'm saying that she had planned this super vacation to Las Vegas with her friend Hattie. They had tickets and an itinerary and hotel accommodations—all in this little packet from Argosy Travel in Hartford. Coupons for free slot-machine money. That sort of thing. She dies on Friday night, the middle of October. At home there's a ticket to Vegas the first week of November. She was going on a damn vacation. Come on. You see?"

She sat back, triumphant, satisfied. The look on her face saddened me—expansive and smug, the face of a brilliant child who feels she has won an irrefutable argument. Absently I rubbed my palms together. When I'd been on the police force, I'd witnessed so many times when the people who killed themselves—or even killed others—had made elaborate plans for the next day or even the next year—sometimes with the very people they ultimately confessed to murdering. "Karen…"

The food arrived and we delved into understuffed sandwiches and more espresso, which was making me wired. I had never eaten there. I purposely avoided the fashionable luncheonettes—all retro Victorian tinplate advertisement and spit-clean chrome polish—that had become trendy in this part of swanky Farmington, along with exotic crafts boutiques, avant-garde art galleries, gourmet food shops, and fern bars with Peruvian wicker and bitter local wine. Book shops with coffee table books on New England covered bridges and rediscovered Connecticut Indian trails. Surprised as I was that the food was delicious, I noticed that Karen stopped eating after a few bites. I'd already finished half a sandwich, gobbling it down, licking my lips like a comic-strip character, and I got embarrassed. I always ate too fast—the result of being a little boy in a Saigon orphanage. Or so says the beautiful psychologist who used to be my wife.

"Buying a ticket for a vacation doesn't mean much for someone who is really unhappy."

"It's more than that." Karen pushed her plate away so she could fold her arms on the table. "She was gloomy, yes, but she said something that convinced me—when I remembered it later." Karen's eyes got wide, demanding. "She said in three more years she would be seventy and…and…she smiled and said she wanted to travel somewhere—like Europe or California. She'd promised herself. At seventy. Because both of her parents had died in their early sixties. Her husband died in his early fifties. Her brother—my father—died young. Forty-seven. We don't live long—all of us. You see, Rick, she saw seventy as a badge… of survival."

I scratched my head. "Okay, I see that. But what about the depression?"

"Yes, she *was* depressed. A few weeks before, we learned that Joshua Jennings passed away in New York."

"They were friends?"

"She was real close, but...well, I always thought a lot of it was in her head, you know. She cleaned his house, but they *liked* each other."

A strange coupling, I thought. The gaudy woman and the severely conservative old Yankee.

"I knew Joshua a little."

She wasn't listening. "Sort of close." She hesitated. "For years, I guess. You know, this is a small town. Joshua and Marta got friendly when they went on the same tour of Russia a few years back. The college sponsored it."

Joshua Jennings had been an ancient man, as pale and dry as starched laundry, in his late seventies, maybe early eighties, a long-time Farmington resident, a wizened little man, stooped over, always appearing in town with a neat Van Dyke beard, a lion's head cane, and Dapper Dan suits years out of style. He'd been a fixture at the college for a few years after his retirement from teaching at the exclusive boys' academy in the town center. After years spent drumming history and Latin into boys in neat blazers and caps, he'd retired and crossed the street to the college. I'd seen him at college functions. A man who missed the class-room and believed his money made him wanted. He created a lecture series no one attended. Once, dragged to one, I heard him ramble on about a minor Latin poet whose name meant nothing to me then—or now. In recent years he'd become a hermit.

Karen grew quiet. Outside, I noticed, it had started to rain. Light, early November rain, a brisk wind rustling the last dead leaves of the hawthorn trees that dotted the sidewalk. Farmington is a town of old people, I thought, many with tons of old money. Quietly I watched the sloppy end of autumn.

"My aunt had a special place for Joshua. They were friends. Good friends. They had some stupid, mean fight, she told me, and they stopped speaking. He refused to reconcile. He moved away, and then the next thing she knew he dies in New York. She was depressed."

"They never patched up their differences?"

She shrugged. "No, that's why she was so down."

I waited a heartbeat. "What did they fight about?"

She looked away. "Aunt Marta thought they should have a life together. You know, two old people…traveling, laughing…"

"But Joshua was a crusty old bachelor."

Again the shrug. "Marta was a foolish romantic, Rick."

"And he said no."

"Worse—he said to leave him alone. It knocked her for a loop. Then he died."

"You're not persuading me she wasn't suicidal."

"You don't understand. You don't kill yourself because your friends die around you."

"It happens. He died weeks before she did."

"Yeah, so what? You get sad when friends die. Other friends died and she got sad." She looked pleadingly at me. "It's worse when you're older. She was an old lady. You read the obits and remember when you were young. And Aunt Marta liked her little quarrels, her feuds. A hard woman. But you don't kill yourself."

"Nothing else bothering her?"

"No," Karen answered too quickly.

"You sure?"

"I can't be sure, you know." She locked eyes with mine. "We had a good relationship, Rick, but we didn't talk about serious topics. She didn't approve of my life—unmarried, living alone, in my thirties. Sometimes we fought, like families do. But once a week we met like clockwork, usually for lunch."

"You don't sound like you welcomed it."

She smiled. "It was a routine she demanded. She could be, well—imperious. My brother, Davey, and I were her only relatives, you know."

"Davey?"

"Do you know Davey? Works at the Farmington Garden Center."

I did, vaguely, in the way I knew all these people. For some reason I'd never connected Davey Corcoran with Karen Corcoran—brother and sister. Her brother was an irritating man who sometimes parked in the handicapped-only designated spots around town. Or, at least, I'd seen him do it once. That was enough to make me dislike him.

"I know who he is."

Karen ran her tongue over her lips. "My aunt didn't like him, had nothing to do with him. They didn't even talk. I have to tell you that."

"Why not?"

"She wouldn't tell me."

"But you have an idea, no?"

"He isn't doing anything with his life. They used to go to Mass together. He could be like her—passionate about Jesus. Then he stopped. They had some fierce fights, I know." She deliberated, as if considering where her words were going. Her eyes darted nervously, trying to avoid eye contact. "But that doesn't mean Davey would hurt her. I didn't mean that."

The waitress asked if we wanted dessert. Karen, I noticed, didn't even look up because she was staring intently into my face. I waved the waitress away.

"Why are you so sure he's not involved?"

She didn't answer for a while. Finally, a rush of words. "I think I should tell you that Davey was left nothing in my aunt's will. A couple of bucks, I think. Something to make it legal."

"And you?"

Sheepishly, her head dipped into her chest. "I was left over a hundred grand."

"Nice."

"It didn't make me happy. This is the money she got from her husband's insurance. I didn't know she had it. I knew she had some savings because she always waved those damn bank books in everyone's face, but I never thought it was that much."

"Was Davey upset?"

She waited, her finger rimming the espresso cup. "You'll have to ask him that."

"I will."

For the first time she smiled. "Then you'll take the case?"

I didn't answer. I took out my wallet, withdrew some cash, and slapped some fives on the table. Immediately she reached into a pocket. "We'll split it, okay?" She pushed back some of my money, and I picked it up, tucking it into my shirt pocket.

I wasn't through yet. "Karen, there's one thing that's the bottom line. Motive. You say murder. I say motive. Who'd want your aunt dead? The spats you talk about are…trivial. Motive? Help me out."

She closed her eyes for a second. "I can't. My aunt was a simple woman. She cleaned houses, for God's sake. Even yours. She went on trips and cruises with her friend Hattie. She went to the Indian casinos. You know, Foxwoods. She had friends, she went to church. She adored church. She had no enemies." A pause. "I mean, yes, sometimes she could be curt, rub folks the wrong way."

"But somebody killed her?"

She reached over to tap my wrist. "Look, Rick, do this for me. I need a professional eye here. Just look into it for three weeks or four. Promise me that. If, after that time, you tell me it was suicide, I stop. Okay. Okay?"

Suddenly, unexpectedly, she took a check from her pocket and handed it to me. She'd already made it out.

"I don't know anything about rates but this is a down payment, I guess. A retainer? Use what you need to for three weeks or so, and then, if there's anything left, give it back. Okay?"

She handed me the check for five thousand.

I grinned. "My rates are considerably lower."

"Perhaps you should think about that."

"All right."

I told her about my usual rates, about the contract I'd want her to sign, other legal ramifications, and the reports I'd file with her periodically. She nodded through it all, but she'd stopped listening. She'd gotten what she wanted.

"Don't count on anything." I stood up. "I have to tell you that up front."

For the first time she grinned widely, her face bright and sunny. She reached out and touched my sleeve—a casual, uncomplicated touch that I felt through the fabric of the sports jacket I wore.

"I owe her something, Rick," Karen confided. "She raised us. I didn't like her a lot of the time, but I did love her. When my parents died, she was the one who watched over me. Now I have to watch over her. It's something left undone in her life. I have to do it."

I nodded.

Karen's face got cloudy. "Somebody didn't love her. Somebody killed her."

Chapter Three

As I trudged home through leaf-strewn sidewalks, a wispy autumn drizzle made my skin clammy. Fall is my favorite season, but I don't like it when the skies open up. The clever, seasoned PI who didn't check his phone for a weather update. The detective strolling without an umbrella. By the time I got home, I was wet.

I smiled as I recalled words from the little book I carried to America, a tattered volume that once belonged to my mother. The words sometimes came to me unexpectedly, sometimes like my own private jester. *Buddha's words are a large cloud. The rain it gives waters the world.*

It didn't matter because I was still soaked.

I live on Cedar Lane, a quiet street running off Main, maple-shaded and elegant, lined with Victorian gingerbread houses, huge places that evoked days when families were large and played croquet on rolling green lawns. I'm down the street from Miss Porter's School for Girls, the exclusive prep school whose buildings resemble the expensive old homes but with a lot more children, most of them teenage girls with trust fund personalities. My apartment is on the second floor of a wonderful painted lady. Rococo turns and surprising angles, and floor-to-ceiling bay windows with rippled glass panes. Gracie, my landlady, paints the house canary yellow each spring, each season the color a little more shrill. "The cheap blonde on the corner," some folks mocked. I like that. Back home, I changed my wet clothes, lay on the sofa, and stared out into the backyard where the giant oak trees sagged under a wet El Greco sky.

Later I called Liz Sanburn, a criminal psychologist working out of the Farmington Police District. She's also my ex-wife.

She was in her office.

"Sanburn," she said, all business.

I smiled. Her whiskey voice, throaty and low, was so different from Karen's reedy, high-pitched tone. Liz is dark-complected, as slender as Karen perhaps, but athletic, the result of those dedicated aerobic classes at the West Side Y way back when. Her dark raven hair is always close-cropped, hugging her head like a bonnet. That's so the elegant gold-and-diamond earrings she favors stand out, dramatically.

I stopped myself—why this comparison of the two women?

"Liz, it's Rick."

I could hear the smile. "Oh, no, either you need information from the police or you're asking me out to our ritualistic and obligatory ex-wife-meet-ex-hubby dinner."

I hesitated. "Actually, both."

"I knew it. I was looking at the calendar and expecting your call. You are a rigid type, Rick."

"The good nuns drilled obedience into me."

"Not always a virtue."

"It makes my vices predictable."

"But there are just too many to count."

"We can start over dinner tonight."

"What do you need—besides a dose of atonement for sins committed?"

I told her what I wanted—a copy of the Farmington Police report on Marta Kowalski's death. A copy of the autopsy. Any toxicology or serology reports. The usual. I could get them using the circuitous channels of my employer, Gaddy Associates, but Liz is more thorough. She has a veteran detective's research eye. If there was anything else in the files—or anything said informally in the office when she searched out Marta's file—she'd pursue it. She understood the importance of the offbeat suggestion, the random bit of information. She's also a wonderful gossip, though she'd deny it. Gossip, she once told me, is not gossip when it's fact. Then it's information.

"Yeah," I'd told her then, "that's why you subscribe to *The National Inquirer.*"

She's worked with me often enough to understand that trivial detail—albeit dismissed by the police clerk—might solve a crime. She also knows that police stop looking for evidence when they've made up their minds. And having categorized Marta's death a suicide, there was no need to continue looking.

"Be nice to me," I teased.

"I'm always nice."

◇◇◇

Until dinnertime I caught up on paperwork, did some billing on some completed fraud cases, and began a file on Marta on my Mac laptop, where I store my research and notes. I created a new file under Marta's name and jotted notes about the case. I had little except Karen's name and her earnestness, as well as a notation about brother Davey's anger and alienation from his dead aunt.

I dressed for dinner with Liz, donning iron-pressed khaki slacks, a pinstripe tan shirt with an art deco-design tie, and a mustard-yellow sports jacket, finished off with tasseled oxblood loafers. I carried a tan London Fog over my arm.

My look for fall—I looked like a tree waiting for winter.

I knew my clothes made my mocha skin seem even darker and my black hair looked like India ink. My deep blue eyes, a gift from the American soldier who was my father, were lost in the dark face inherited from my Vietnamese mother. I'm a good-looking guy, I know—sort of a vain declaration. But women find me attractive. My slanted lazy eyes can widen suddenly to reveal deep baby blue pupils. People don't expect such eyes, aquamarine and glittery, from an Asian.

My mind wandered to Karen Corcoran. What did she see when she looked at me?

Liz and I met in the parking lot of Cavey's, a classy French restaurant we both like in Manchester by way of I-84. She stepped out of her car and I kissed her on the cheek. She was dressed in a brocaded jacket, vaguely Chinese, a silky brown and lavender mix of shades. She shivered as a slight breeze blew across the parking lot, and she rushed toward the restaurant. She looked over her shoulder and saw me staring. "Shame on you."

We had a curious relationship, the two of us—one we both cherished but…at times difficult.

We'd been married in Manhattan right after Columbia College, and by the time I'd joined the NYPD, our marriage was already crumbling. Three years later, when I left the force and headed to Connecticut, it was over because we couldn't live together. Somehow, though, our love refused to die, and she followed me to Connecticut. She said she needed to be near me—not married, God no, but *near*. The stupid fights, the late-night phone calls, the awful silences, the explosive angers—led to a necessary friendship that most folks would never understand. Sometimes we dreamed of reconciliation, but it never happened. We always found each other when the loneliness set in. Then, suddenly, we remembered that we were divorced. I can't imagine a life without her.

Seated, we made small talk until our drinks arrived. Then she became all business, dipping into her purse and extracting a thin sheaf of folded computer print-outs. She spread them out on the table, leaned back, took a sip of her martini.

"It's pretty cut and dried." She slid the sheets toward me. "I don't know whether there's a murder lurking in these pages."

"Simple suicide?"

"On the night of October 11, around six in the evening, Marta Kowalski called Richard Wilcox, an old friend, to tell him she planned on visiting. He says she was depressed on the phone—crying, incoherent. Wilcox lives in a condo complex less than a half-mile from her house, and she said she'd walk over. She always walked to his house. When she didn't show up, he called and got no answer. The next morning some school kids spotted her body on a rock ledge in the Farmington River. The police suspect she'd jumped off the bridge on the walk to Wilcox's. It's out of the way, out of sight, banked by overhanging hemlocks. The kids screamed until someone called 911. It's not a huge drop but she broke her neck, smashed a shoulder. Enough of a drop to kill, I guess."

"Nightmares for those kids."

Liz thumbed the report. "That's all the info that's in here."

"Any evidence of foul play?" I picked up one of the sheets and ran my fingers down it, rereading what she'd just summarized.

"Not in the report. Everybody keeps saying how depressed she was. I mean—Karen. Wilcox. Others. No one thought to get the old woman counseling. Christ, these people."

I smiled. "Spoken like a true police psychologist."

"That's why they pay me," she shot back, a little irritated.

"Sorry." I waited until she smiled at me. "So everything points to it being a simple suicide. She walks over a bridge high enough for death and is swamped by a wave of despair. She hurls herself over the railing."

Liz nodded. "Well, that's how the police read the facts." She drummed her fingers on the table. "So Karen thinks it's murder?"

"Marta had tickets for Vegas three weeks later."

Liz frowned. "So what?"

"I know, I know, but when you're a family member..."

"I never thought that Karen was all that close to her."

That surprised me. "You know Karen?"

"We're in the same health club. Once or twice we chitchatted. That kind of thing. She mentioned her aunt one time to a bunch of us in the sauna, and it wasn't flattering."

Now I was interested. "What did she say?"

"Oh, I don't know—something about another boring lunch with her. A throwaway remark, but she said it sarcastically. When we all laughed, she said she was sorry—it came out wrong, she said. She babbled, apologetic. Sort of embarrassed, like she couldn't stop talking."

"That all?"

"That's it."

"The autopsy?" I prompted.

"Healthy older woman, in pretty good shape, a little over-weight. Nothing out of the ordinary. Except one surprising thing, though maybe it wasn't so surprising—in retrospect. Marta had an alcohol blood count twice the legal limit. For driving. Of course, she wasn't driving. She was a little bit hammered as she toppled to her inglorious death." Smiling, she took a dramatic sip of her martini and raised the glass to me.

"Karen didn't tell me that."

"Maybe Karen doesn't know."

"She must."

Methodically I rustled through the sheets while Liz scanned the menu, holding it close to her face. Vanity, I thought, smiling. Her reading glasses remained in the purse. She ordered for both of us, while I kept nodding at her suggestions. She knew what I liked. I wanted to read everything she'd brought, but it was as she said. The only new information was Marta's intoxication, but I figured if you're depressed, that's an easy and comfortable route to take. Numb all the available senses.

"Could she have toppled to her death? Not a suicide but a simple accident?"

"That's in there somewhere." Liz touched the report. "The police ruled that out because the railing is too high to simply topple over. You have to climb up a stone partition to get over. And even then—a shallow rockbed below. That would sober me up fast." She frowned. "I can't see this leading anywhere."

"Karen wants me to give it a month."

She shrugged her shoulders. I knew the gesture—it's your call.

"Something else," Liz began. She bit her lip.

"What?"

"Do you know Vuong Ky Do? Willie Do?"

"Yeah, sort of. He used to work at the college. Why?"

"Vietnamese?"

I nodded. "Yes."

"Back in April Marta called the cops on him. I guess they'd had a fight in Joshua Jennings' front yard. She claimed he didn't say anything, but *glared* at her. Her word—*glared*, so much so that she felt in danger."

"He's an old, harmless man."

"Are you sure?"

"No, I'm not. I mean, he's been scarred by the war, a man who always looks hurt. Frozen men, I always call such men, but…"

She broke in. "The cops went to his home just as a precaution. Marta said nothing happened, but they wanted his side. He *had* no side. When the cops questioned him. he folded in, started to shake. He *stared*—a rock. His son rushed in. It went nowhere. Marta, I gather, had yelled at him for tracking dirt onto Joshua Jennings' floor—she'd just polished it. A war of words—from *her* side. No follow-up."

"I can't imagine Willie doing her harm."

"I don't know the man."

"Well, neither do I, but…" My voice trailed off. "I'll talk to him."

Liz didn't look happy. "I hesitated telling you. I know your place in the Vietnamese community is tenuous."

"I'm fine."

"Now you're lying to me."

I grinned. "How can you tell?"

"Please, dear Rick. You're as transparent as a boy stealing apples from a farmer's yard."

I sat back. "Willie Do."

Do Ky Vuong. A casualty of the old war. Stunned by pain.

The few times I thought about Do Ky Vuong—the man everyone called Willie Do—I found myself suddenly back in old Saigon, trapped in a memory of my friend Vu's father, Tranh Xan Tan, the frozen man so traumatized by the Commie re-education camp. Two similar men who rarely spoke, but worse—men whose ravaged faces communicated all the horror of that war and punishment—the hollow eyes, the blank stare, the voice so soft it might be one you imagined. The shell of a man. The man whose face was a clock without hands.

I trembled, remembering.

◇◇◇

I first met Willie Do at Farmington College, where he worked as a janitor. Spotting him as a fellow Vietnamese, though one who hugged the corners, I'd approached him, introduced myself, but was met with silence. Soon I learned that his reticence was more than his dislike of me—the mixed-blood *bui doi* on campus—though that was part of it, perhaps. But Willie Do turned away from everyone. It was as though someone plopped him down into an American landscape, and he awoke to nightmare and fear.

He even looked like my boyhood friend Vu's father—small-ish, tight-muscled, wiry, hair clipped off with kitchen scissors, a work shirt too large for his tiny frame. I'd learned through my young friend Hank Nguyen, someone who had his ear to the Vietnamese tom-tom drums, that he'd been re-educated—a beaten man who escaped with his wife and son and daughter to Hong Kong—and then on to Guam and the States. His little daughter had been raped and brutalized by Thai pirates before his eyes, and she died weeks later in a Hong Kong refugee camp. His vow of silence settled in, horrible, inviolable.

Hired by Goodwill Industries, set up in a small apartment in Unionville, he drifted from one menial job to the next until Farmington College hired him. But shortly after I began working there, he was fired. He chain-smoked Lucky Strikes, inside in winter, in the hallways. Warned over and over, baffled by such a law when utter lawlessness had earlier defined his life, he persisted—until he was let go.

He did handyman jobs around town. A car washer, trash man. And he was Joshua Jennings' twice-a-week yardman.

How did he connect to the story of Marta Kowalski?

"Rick, your mind is wandering."

"I'm thinking of Willie Do."

"I know."

Over dessert we caught up on each other's lives. She'd been back to New York to visit her parents who were still angry she'd left the city. In the warm light of the candles her olive-toned skin looked muted, silky. She was the dark negative to Karen's sunny photograph. If I hadn't been married to her once already, I might have been tempted.

"How are you?" she asked. "I haven't seen you in a while."

"You know, nothing much."

She looked me full in the face. "Karen is a pretty woman." She was watching me closely. "Not beautiful but pretty. Wouldn't you say that's the word for her?"

I thought of Karen—reedy, slender, her eyes the color of a dusty prairie flower. Yes—pretty. Not beautiful. Liz was a beautiful woman—the exquisite coal-black eyes glowing in the dark oval face.

"Yes, she's pretty."

"She's very skinny," she added. "All skin and bones. Don't forget—I've seen her in the sauna. Naked."

I grinned. "Liz, your words are giving me mental pictures that..."

"Be careful," Liz interrupted, unsmiling. "You know how you are around attractive women."

"For God's sake, Liz."

"I know you, Rick."

"What does that mean?"

"Nothing. I know you."

"You're the only beautiful woman I ever chased."

Now she grinned. "And look how that ended up."

Chapter Four

Outside, by the cars, I kissed her, thanked her again for the information. We lingered there, smiling, and she was the first to leave. It was a cool, serene fall night, the sky white with stars. After she drove away, I leaned against the car door, hesitant to go home, pulling in the collar of my fall coat. I wanted a cigarette—I'd stopped a few years back—but I always craved nicotine after dinner with a beautiful woman and French food and wine and strong, kicking coffee.

Since I had to drive home through Hartford, I decided to stop at my office to check in. I do my investigations out of my Farmington apartment—sometimes I even use my office at the college in between Criminal Justice classes taught to eager freshmen who have seen too many episodes of *True Detective* and *CSI*—but I am a partner of Gaddy Associates, Private Investigation, Inc., housed in the historic Colt Building in the south end of Hartford.

When I pulled into the parking lot, I noticed the lights were on in the sixth-floor office. Gaddy was there. Gaddy is Jimmy Gadowicz, a rough-and-tumble PI, a man in his late sixties, a man who took me in as his only associate a couple years back. His firm—our firm—did mostly insurance fraud for the likes of Aetna, Travelers, Cigna, The Hartford, you name it, in the epicenter of America's insurance. We didn't get into murder, Jimmy and I. We played it safe among the white-collar insurance execs.

I took the elevator to the sixth floor. The Colt Building is an old derelict factory building, once owned by Colt Firearms. A decrepit building, it houses cheap, partitioned rents for public TV access shows, fundamentalist religious crusades, starving artists, karate or tai kwon do classes, left-wing political action groups, and fly-by-night business ventures. A world of spirited people living off nothing.

Gaddy Associates—most folks call Jimmy by the nickname Gaddy except close friends—was a straight-arrow firm. Jimmy's a man of incredible bluster, but I've never met a man so honest—and so infuriating at times. He'd fought in Vietnam—a young manhood trial by fire—and that's why he had me around in the first place. Jimmy saw me as part of that past—his past. He's a big pile of a man, unshaven half the time, always sweating, even in winter, mopping a grainy forehead with a gray handkerchief, a man poured into extra-large sweatshirts that ride up a tremendous belly.

"What the hell you doing here?" Jimmy greeted me. The room smelled of thick cigar smoke and old tuna sandwiches and stale breath. He looked me over. "Coming here dressed like a goddamn pansy in that outfit."

I grinned. "So much for politically correct tolerance. And just what's wrong with my clothes, Jimmy?"

"Rick, you look like a...forget it." He shook my hand.

"I'm just checking in—in case you missed me."

He grumbled. "Sometimes you make no sense."

"What are *you* doing here?" I asked.

Jimmy was sitting in front of an old wooden file cabinet. The drawers were pulled out. Papers were scattered across the floor. A wastepaper basket was jam-packed with torn files. He threw his hands up in the air.

"What, Jimmy?"

Silently he handed me a printout. "This came in the mail."

A message from the owner. The decaying building—so loved by the migrant tenants—was under consideration for a sale to a firm that specialized in state-of-the-art urban studios for the young professionals.

"We're gonna have to move."

"Not yet," I told him.

He stopped shuffling papers. "I planned on staying in this hole-in-the-wall."

"We'll find a place."

"It ain't that simple." He pointed to the file cabinets. "I don't know why I saved all this shit."

"A goldmine of cases."

"Yeah, right."

"Jimmy, we'll find a place."

He peered at me. "No, *you* will find a place. I'll just show up to say yes or no." He watched me closely. "You're up to something, Rick." He sat back and lit a cigar.

I nodded. "Do you remember Marta Kowalski's death?"

Jimmy spends a lot of time in Farmington, usually at my apartment or at our hangout, Zeke's Olde Tavern, so he knows the business of the small town. He also has a nose for detail. He'd remember my cleaning lady. I'd certainly talked about her death to him at the time. Now I told him about Karen and her hiring me to investigate her aunt's murder. As I was rambling on, shifting my head to avoid puffs of cloying cigar smoke that I was sure he purposely directed at me, I could see he was anxious to break in.

"Murder?" he barked when I paused. "And you took the case?"

"Yeah, I think…"

"I think you lost your mind. That necktie on too tight, Rick? The money is in fraud, not murder. Murder is messy."

"You sound like a bumper sticker." My eyes burned from his smoke. I got up to open a window and the chill November cold rushed in. He shivered and frowned as though the crisp air would do him in.

He put out the cigar. "Okay, tell me your thinking."

I did, explaining what little Karen had told me, the conditions of our tentative contract, the huge retainer. He liked the amount of the check because part of that would be his, of course. Dollar signs flashed in his eyes.

"I think it's worth a shot," I summed up. "After all, there're some unanswered questions. Maybe I can give Karen a little"—I hesitated—"closure."

He narrowed his eyes. "I hate that goddamn word."

"I know."

"Yeah, then why…?"

"Useful, sometimes."

"Christ, Almighty man."

"I think part of our job is customer peace of mind."

This last bit came out a little too—well, purposely unctuous. I couldn't help it because while I was talking, Jimmy had a simpering smirk on his face—a father listening to a foolish, errant son, dutifully waiting to impart wisdom to the ignorant child.

Suddenly throwing back his head, he laughed so hard he started to choke. "Shit, how you talk. Ivy League PIs." He shook his head.

I laughed, too. Jimmy never let me get away with anything. Sometimes I didn't even know I was trying to. "You got my meaning, no?"

"You goddamn dictionary." He was still grinning. "Motive," he said. "Remember that word—motive."

"I know."

"Motive."

"I know. You taught me that."

"No, you don't remember sometimes. You're a babe in the woods. That's why you need me. I think it's a wild goose chase, but it's your time and it's money in my pocket. You gotta keep this firm afloat." He tapped me on the shoulder. "I'm out of here. Home to bed." He looked around the shabby room. "I'm gonna miss this dump."

"Bette Davis said the…"

He broke in. "Now that was a real actress in the day."

He grabbed his jacket and fumbled for the wooden matches he always uses to light his cigars. "See you." Then, from over my shoulder as I sat in front of a computer screen on my desk, "Is this Karen a beauty?"

I looked up and felt my face get hot. "Yeah, she's pretty."
There was that word again. Damn: pretty. Blond blond blond.
"Be careful." He was grinning. "You know how you are."
I tapped my fingers on the table. "What does that mean?"
He left without answering.

An hour later, driving home on I-84, scooting between two
racing semis who saw my decade-old and rusting BMW as fodder
for late-night, superhighway fun, I swore out loud. In the space
of one hour two people—Liz and Jimmy, ex-wife and resident
yenta—had warned me about beautiful—no, pretty—women
getting in my way. What the hell were these people saying?
Was I that shallow? Or transparent? Stupidly I remembered a
young taxi girl who smoked cigarettes outside a Saigon bar as
she whispered to passing soldiers—I'd watched her when I was
a thirteen-year-old boy. She was pretty, too. Day in, day out—I
mooned over her. Was I merely a stammering immigrant to
these shores? I was in this to solve a murder. I was a professional.
Murder, not mayhem or matrimony. Murder, not matchmaking.
Murder. Or, frankly, was it indeed just a suicide?

Suicide, not, well—sex. Damn.

Chapter Five

I woke up bloated and tired—last night's wine leaving me headachy. I yawned, pulled myself out of bed, and showered. My muscles ached. I really needed to get back to running. I'm not out of shape but in need of muscle on my long, lanky body. The slightest beginning of a paunch because I was no longer a young man. Thirty-nine now, my last birthday—a created birthday, given me when I arrived in America, a thirteen-year-old boy who, till then, had no birthday at all, or at least none that I remembered from the orphanage.

I decided to hit the gym before my ten o'clock class. I teach two days, Tuesday and Thursday, one section of Introduction to Criminal Science and one of Investigations. While swimming laps in the pool after the workout, I was distracted, unable to focus. A horrible image overwhelmed me—Marta Kowalski dropping off that final cold stone bridge. The cleaning lady no one paid any attention to—an old woman dragging a dust cloth over my bookcases. Was it possible Karen's instincts were on target?

At that moment a wave of belief swept over me. But why would anyone kill her? And in so gruesome a fashion? Toppling onto those rocks. A neck snapped. So I stopped swimming, resting on the side of the pool, my hair in my eyes, heart pounding, the veins in my hands jutting out as I gripped the side of the pool.

Leaving the gym, I spotted Hank Nguyen headed to the parking lot with a backpack casually slung over his shoulder, a couple books cradled against his chest. Despite the morning chill, he wore his jacket unzipped, flapping in the slight breeze. Worse, he wore a pair of khaki cargo shorts. November, I thought—why do young people think they're invincible to the elements? Probably because they are. When you hit your late thirties, you realize that nature crouches on the dark horizon, getting ready to trip you.

"Hey, Hank," I yelled, causing him to stop moving.

"Rick," he answered. "I was gonna call you later. I had to be in town this morning. See what you're up to."

"You're just the man I want to talk to."

He grinned. "Ah, you need my help with some mystery."

I paused. "Actually, I do."

That surprised him, so he stopped moving. "Really? Tell me."

"Time for coffee?"

He nodded. "I'm on a break from the academy. Thought I'd use the library at my old alma mater." He pointed toward the College Union. "The coffee is not good here. They use your recipe."

"You'll live." I smiled. "No one has a recipe for making coffee."

"Maybe that's the problem then. Mystery solved."

Now twenty-three years old, Hank Nguyen had graduated with a degree in Criminal Justice from the college and was training at the Connecticut State Police Academy. He wanted to be a state trooper—the first Vietnamese-American, he claimed—and then, a few years down the road, a private investigator. Like me. We'd become close friends after a bumpy start. Pure Vietnamese—part of a big, rollicking family in East Hartford, all fleeing from Saigon in 1975 or thereabouts, drifting on hostile waters to Hong Kong—he had disliked me when he was my student, sitting in my class with a scowl on his face. I'm mixed blood, one of those pathetic lost souls celebrated in Broadway's *Miss Saigon*—to my horror—and the native Vietnamese are notorious in their dislike of such impurity. We also served as grim reminders of the deleterious American presence on that war-torn soil.

Hank and I had some angry moments, even foolishly grappled on a tennis court one afternoon—a lame physical confrontation that was more ludicrous than hurtful—and then, curiously, Hank began to trust me—and to like me. Born in America, he had been raised at home with the blustery old biases carried from Vietnam, but also a lot of love. A bright guy, and funny. Hank—his real name is Tan—became my buddy. I liked him a lot.

"So you got a case you want me to help solve?" Hank asked, walking alongside me.

"Willie Do." I threw out the name of the man who'd supposedly skirmished with Marta Kowalski.

Hank stopped walking, his face hardening, and leaned into me. "Vuong Ky Do."

"The one and the same."

"Willie doesn't bother anyone, Rick." His tone was nervous and dry. "Willie...well, hides from the world."

"So I remember."

"Tell me."

I watched Hank's face closely, animated, twisting to the side but back to me, eyes bright but wary. Ever since we became friends—and especially after he made it his passion to make me a part of his family, the Sunday morning guest for familial *mi ga*, the ritualistic chicken soup—Hank defined himself as my sidekick in my investigations. Most of my endeavors involved mundane and deadly dull insurance investigations that kept me busy and paid the bills. Tedious, granted, but for Hank, with all the fire of a young man who loved mystery and crime and punishment, my wanderings were the stuff of Arthurian quest. Sir Galahad with an iPhone, a Twitter obsession, and a Mac Powerbook. Jimmy Gadowicz found him a little too eager, but tolerated him with a grandfatherly tap on the shoulder. Liz, those times we were together, found him charming, delightful. And he blushed when she smiled at him. I found him good, honest company.

As he tagged along on my fraud investigations, sitting in the car stuffing his face with doughnuts and drumming his fingers on the dashboard, turning up the radio when a Maroon 5 tune came on though I immediately lowered the volume, he had a lot to say about the world I inhabited. So many years my junior, he sometimes assumed a patronizing tone—the cocky

American-born Vietnamese man who felt a need to school the always insecure immigrant boy who chose him as a friend.

We sat at a table in the back of the hall. Hank stretched out, his legs resting on the bottom rung of a cafeteria chair. He was wearing a canvas jacket, vaguely military, and a J.Crew T-shirt beneath it. In his baggy shorts and orange sneakers he seemed ready for a day of surfing at a Rhode Island beach rather than getting ready for autumn and Thanksgiving feasts. A tall gangly young man, dark as nut bread, with narrow, slanted eyes in an intense hard-angled face, all his hair cropped close to the scalp and one discreet earring, he watched me closely.

"Willie Do is a dangerous topic, Rick."

That surprised me. I sat up. "What? For God's sake, why? I remember him from the college. He never spoke but…"

He broke in. "Everybody in the Vietnamese community sort of leaves him alone."

"Because of…"

"What he went through. Christ, Rick. The torture, the escape." A long pause. "But I think the brutal rape and death of his little girl ended his life. He had to *watch* that as it happened. He stopped breathing."

I shuddered. "I can understand that." The frozen man.

Now Hank stared into my face. "No, you don't. I don't think anyone can ever understand that. Yeah, my family…you on those Saigon streets, alone…yeah. But not like that. So you got to be careful when you bring his name into any investigation."

I breathed in. "Which is why I was planning on calling you."

"What could he have done?"

"Maybe nothing." I sighed. "Probably nothing."

"You know his story," Hank stressed.

I nodded. Quickly I filled Hank in on Karen Corcoran's belief that her Aunt Marta had been murdered. Hank knew nothing of the suicide—though he insisted he remembered seeing Marta leaving my home one afternoon, her glare at him unfriendly, a finger wagged angrily at him for some reason—but now, hearing about Karen's hiring me, Hank got angry.

"You don't mean she says that Willie…?"

I held up my hand. "Let me tell you. Wait. You're getting hot under the collar. Marta called the cops on him, I understand. She cleaned for old Joshua Jennings, and he was the yardman on the grounds. Something happened—something stupid. Something about dirty footprints tracked inside, and she lost it, screamed at him, accused."

He leaned into me. "But he wouldn't have fought her. The man has no fight left in him…."

"He didn't. But she claimed his look was—venomous. Dangerous. She felt threatened. So she called the cops."

Hank's anger was growing, the reddish color rising in his cheeks. His eyes flickered. Protective of Willie, he stammered, "She…she had a hell of a nerve."

"But the cops questioned him. I guess they had to follow up, you know, but I guess Willie got really quiet, started to tremble, you know, maybe flashbacks to…the old days, cops…and his son…"

"His name is Toan but everyone calls him Tony…."

"Well, his son intervened. Nothing happened."

"Despicable, all of it."

"Hank, relax. Cops doing their job."

"This Marta was a damn troublemaker."

For the first time I smiled. "She was a bit of that, I agree. A hard woman to like. A woman of strong opinions."

He smirked. "And yet you let her into your apartment."

"I liked the way the woman handled a dust cloth."

"And yet your apartment always looks like the back room of Goodwill."

"Nevertheless…"

He hurled out his words, fierce and unfriendly. "Well, what do you want from me, Rick?"

I watched him. So much confusion. I pointed at him. "Hank, calm down. I'm on your side, remember?"

A thin smile. "Sorry."

"I know the sad story everyone knows about Vuong—Willie." I began. "But that's about all."

"It's more than sad, Rick. It's…it's so raw you wake up sweating about it. That is his only story, really. A quiet man, but a brooding one, so hurt." He hesitated. "My mother says he is just waiting to die."

"I don't know anything about his family. Where does he live?"

"They got a three-family in Unionville, by the railroad tracks. An old company house from the factory days. A little run-down, sagging porches, asphalt siding. The son and his wife live on the first floor—they own the place. They got a fifteen-year-old boy, sort of a wise guy kid, rumor has it, always picked up for things like shoplifting. Kid named Roger but everyone calls him Big Nose. Nice touch. He answers to that. Willie and his wife, Linh, live on the second." Hank smiled. "The third floor is one of my distant cousins, a young guy named Fred, just married last year with a new baby. I mean, no one knows Willie because he stays away from folks."

"Does he work?"

"Not that I know. The college let him go. Handyman jobs. I guess, well, like he cut Joshua Jennings' lawn, that sort of thing. Lives on Social Security."

"So he just stays home?"

"The funny thing is that his wife—we call her Aunt Marie— knows my grandmother, good friends from somewhere, probably back in Saigon. They see each other at New Year's—that sort of thing. Grandma likes her a lot because she's warm, caring, and, I guess, she put up with a life with Willie. I mean, she loves her husband."

"I need to talk to him."

Hank had been sipping his coffee but choked. "God, why?"

"Because I have to follow up on Karen's story."

Fiercely: "Willie didn't murder Marta Kowalski."

"You don't know that."

He sat back. "Yes, I do." He locked eyes with mine. "Because she yelled at him for tracking mud on a floor? Jesus Christ, Rick."

"I know, I know. Crazy, yes. But I need to follow up on everything. Maybe Willie can tell me something about Marta's state of mind, her attitude, what set her off."

"Trouble, Rick."

"How so?"

A deliberate hesitation as he chose his words carefully. "He's old-fashioned."

"Meaning?"

"He won't talk to you. He's—well, like my father and grandfather."

I nodded. "You're kidding me, no? After all this time? He won't talk to me because I'm mixed blood. *Bui doi*?"

A sheepish smile, embarrassed. "Yeah."

An old story, marrow deep. I'm that curious breed produced by the Vietnamese Conflict: an Amerasian, one of the so-called children of the dust, the dirty secret, the *bui doi*. I have no idea who my mother was, except that she was a Vietnamese woman who, in the final days of the war, carried a child by a white American soldier, also nameless and now forgotten. I was dumped off at an orphanage when I was around five. I have dim memories of my mother, whispers of stories, though sometimes I can feel her holding me tight. My real first name is Viet, but in Vietnam I was Lam Van Viet. In America, a young boy, resting in a foster home in the Bronx for a month, I was Viet Van Lam, and then I allowed myself to become Rick Van Lam. I didn't mind—I was thirteen and I wanted to become American. I wanted to fit in.

I still do.

"I still don't fit in," I said to Hank.

"You got a home here." He pointed out the door. "You were lost in Manhattan so you came here. This is home now. And my grandma adores you."

"And I adore her."

Slowly he whispered, "Poor Willie Do."

"I need to interview him, Hank. And I'd like you to come with me. I need you to set it up."

A sigh. "He won't talk." Finally, pushing his coffee cup away, he decided. "Then I gotta get Grandma on it. Call his wife. This isn't going to be good. Willie suffered in the re-education camps.

If he runs from authority—if he trembled and hid when the Farmington cops showed up—that could not be a good sign."

"I gotta talk to him."

"I'll talk to Grandma."

Now I smiled. "She has magical powers."

He rolled his eyes. "So you say. My God, you and her mouthing all that Buddhist wisdom."

"Maybe you should listen to her—and me."

"I do listen, but…" His voice trailed off.

"But what?"

"What would Buddha say about Marta's death?" he asked suddenly, a grin on his face.

I considered the question a serious one, though I knew Hank often got a bit mocking about his roots. After all, he lives in a divided household where his imperious father is a nominal Roman Catholic while his mother is a Buddhist, and his maternal grandmother whispers Confucian precepts in his ear all the time. He'd rather listen to hip-hop dance music or whatever faddish noise is blaring off satellite radio.

I was born a Buddhist. I believe that because the only thing I carried from the Catholic orphanage was a tattered, faded brown-covered paperback, slim as a calendar, that my mother supposedly left with me. It's my only proof—my only family heirloom. *The Sayings of Buddha.* I still cherish it. In Hank's house there is a shrine to the Virgin Mary and Jesus covered with palms from Palm Sunday Mass. But there is also a Buddhist shrine next to it, dedicated to dead relatives—you see it the minute you walk into the kitchen. Sticks of powerful incense, a bowl of blood-red oranges, joss sticks, and bright glossy icons. I always think of my mother when I see it. Sometimes I believe I see her bowing before the shrine.

My unknown but beloved mother.

"Earth to Rick." Hank waved his hand in front of my face.

"Sorry, my mind drifted."

"Back to that orphanage?"

I didn't answer, bothered by his flippancy. But then I said, "As a matter of fact, yes." Those pithy, wonderful sayings come at me every so often. I listen to them. They warn me of danger. They humble me, level me. So now, thinking of murder, I found myself thinking of Buddha. "Always appropriate, let me tell you," I said to Hank. "Buddha would say: 'When you think you are at the beginning, then you are really at the end.'"

"I'm confused."

"I know, but that's all right."

He watched me closely. "I'm starting to think you believe Marta Kowalski was murdered."

The moment he spoke those words, a little mockingly, a boyish glint in his eye, I froze. Yes, I realized—some gut instinct told me there was more to the story than the sad suicide of an old depressed cleaning woman.

Hank was shaking his head.

I told him, "The end of the story is already in my hands. Another quote: 'You start the journey in one place and you at that moment have reached your destination.'"

"So we have to investigate."

"We do."

"I'll talk to Grandma."

"Once again we're partners."

"TV Associates." He sat back, triumphant.

An old joke—perhaps not a joke any longer. Tan and Viet, partners. Blood brothers. The firm he envisioned down the road: TV Associates, Private Investigation. Private eyes on the world of crime and punishment. Superheroes. His dream and, I supposed, mine. Brothers born out of a country of monsoons and banyan trees, the whisper of jasmine always in the air. Tan and Viet. For a new America.

But first—Vuong Ky Do. A diplomatic interrogation of one of the shattered souls who wanted to forget that land of monsoons and banyan trees and the scent of jasmine. What that man had burned onto his soul was the stormy South China Sea and the approaching Thai pirates with death in their hearts.

Chapter Six

Vinnie joined me in the cafeteria for a late lunch. I'd spotted him after my class and asked him to join me. One of my good friends on the faculty, Vinnie is a math professor I met a few years back when we huddled together at a dreary staff meeting that went on too long—he kept nudging me to stay awake—and we became fast friends. I like his blunt manner, the way he deals with garrulous staff members, cutting through their verbiage, and sinking cynical shots at their arguments. He also relishes crime and punishment—not the novel, but the theory. He teaches geometry and pre-calculus, which I consider runic language, and, like Hank Nguyen, he has a keen interest in my lackluster, mechanical investigations. As a mathematician, he claims he can contribute a logical and geometrical approach to solutions.

I was in the middle of mentioning Marta Kowalski—he'd known her and we'd talked of her suicide—when his wife joined us. Marcie taught American literature in the English Department, but she's also Vinnie's bookend. When you see one, chances are great the other will shortly appear. I stopped in mid-sentence, let her deposit her tray of tuna salad and tomato soup on the table.

"What are you boys plotting?"

I laughed. "Why? Do we look conspiratorial?"

"You bet. Vinnie leaning in, expectant. You, wide-eyed with a secret to share. Two little boys without marbles."

"That sums it up," I told her.

I outlined my new case, Vinnie and Marcie leaning in now, elbows on the table. They were fun to be with, and both thought my life as a PI was fascinating. I kept telling them it wasn't. Usually it wasn't—that much was true.

An unlikely couple, this long-married pair. Both a little chubby, both in their late thirties, maybe early forties, eager assistant professors, they often were mistaken for brother and sister: dark, round, with flat, melon faces, big mooncalf eyes set wide apart. They lived for weekends in New York or Boston—and for dining out. I never asked how the two met, but they differed in everything but looks. Vinnie is rock-bottom conservative, not so right wing that he'd thump a Bible or beat up a save-the-whale advocate or dump tea bags off a same-sex marriage cruise ship, but certainly sleeping with real-estate Republicans. Marcie, on the other hand, is a vocal firebrand, an unreconstructed liberal of the old order, resident feminist, part of the rag-tag Democratic mystique of left-of-center radicals born back in the Reagan era. You'd recognize her by the FREE TIBET or PRO CHOICE bumper stickers on her Volvo. How they didn't kill each other I never knew. But they joked endlessly, often ribbing each other in ways others would see as fodder for a wild and wooly episode on TV divorce court. Whatever they did worked—they obviously loved each other to death.

"You both knew Marta," I said.

"But murder?" Vinnie's question hung in the air. "I was surprised and all—what with the suicide—but murder?"

Marcie was shaking her head. "Now that you mention it…"

Vinnie groaned. "Oh, God, not a conspiracy theory."

She punched him in the arm. "Be that as it may, I think we need to look…"

I held up my hand, traffic cop style. "Wait, you two, wait. This is my case. Nobody's talking murder yet. Nobody. And the only reason I'm bringing it up—even though I know I'll regret it since you'll both be rapping on my chamber door—is because you both are on my list of people to interview."

Triumphant, Vinnie said, "I've always wanted to be a suspect in a murder."

"A suspect, all right," his wife added.

"You got a minute to talk?" I asked. I'd already taken my laptop from my carrying case, positioned it on the table—I rarely left home without it—and ran my fingers over the keyboard. Marcie and Vinnie, seemingly startled into seriousness by the presence of the electronic age, stared at it. I detected the natural nervousness that always resulted when questioning anyone about a—well, maybe a murder. I recalled the looks from my days as a patrolman back in New York. The humor abruptly stopped as Marcie decorously folded her hands in her lap, ignoring her lunch, while Vinnie scratched his head, eyes narrowed, as though I'd asked him a perplexing question.

I looked from one to the other. "When was the last time you saw Marta?"

Quiet a second, they looked at each other as though waiting for the other to answer. Vinnie spoke up. "A short time before her death. Late August sometime. Just before classes started, I think. Right, Marcie?"

She nodded. "Yes, we were really busy with school meetings but getting ready for visitors—folks coming for a party for Vinnie's mom. We asked Marta to help us get the house ready. You know, housekeeping."

"Anything odd about her?"

They both shook their heads vigorously. Marcie glanced first at Vinnie. "If anything, she acted the way she always did. I mean, we'd hired her before, of course—sooner or later, everyone in town hired her—but she could be...difficult."

"Difficult?"

"You know—tell you what she thought, even if you didn't ask her. If you left a letter out, she wasn't happy until she read it."

Vinnie added, "A snoop."

"We didn't talk much, but she seemed in a good mood. I remember it made me nervous—she actually sang as she worked."

"In fact," Vinnie added, "I remember she said something about traveling. A trip planned…somewhere."

"No signs of depression?"

They both shook their heads. Vinnie went on. "Far from it. Of course, this was before she learned her old friend had died."

Marcie broke in, "She did mention Joshua Jennings, though. Pissed off that he'd ended their friendship. But I remember now that she said something strange—he would eventually come to his senses and return to Farmington."

Vinnie continued, "Later on I heard she was bothered—really bothered—when Joshua Jennings died. Stunned, in fact. But I didn't see her at all during that time."

"Who told you?"

Marcie spoke up. "I did. I bumped into her friend Hattie, you know, the one she always traveled with. She told me Marta was in the dumps. I think I said I wanted to call Marta for some fall housekeeping—clear some summer stuff out—and Hattie said, well, good luck with that. Marta had slipped into a deep funk because of Joshua dying."

"Did Hattie say anything else?"

"No. Hattie didn't make too big a deal out of it. *She* wasn't depressed, I can tell you. 'You know how Marta is,' she hissed. 'If it ain't a melodrama, it ain't anything on TV.' A week later Marta was dead."

I summarized their comments onto the laptop, while they watched. My fingers stopped. "Were you surprised at the suicide?"

A long silence. Then Marcie spoke softly. "I hoped it was an accident. Frankly, I didn't care for her—too judgmental. She refused to dust my framed letter from Obama…."

"A form letter, autopen signature," said Vinnie.

Marcie frowned. "Whatever." A deep sigh. "She was happy at our house. I can picture her beaming as she straightened out the rec room, getting the beds ready for our visiting nephews. I hate the idea that she chose her death."

"But her later funk…"

"If she got down, it was well—normal. I was sad when I learned Joshua had died. I liked him. We all liked the old man, but he was frail, sick. He'd become a hermit at the end, cranky, determined to recapture a life he'd lived a half-century before by moving to his old college town. Old people die."

"I agree," Vinnie added. "I couldn't see her committing suicide. I always thought she just fell."

"The police classified it a suicide."

"Why would anyone murder her?" Marcie's voice was too loud. "Really? What was there to be gained? Nothing." She took a bite out of her salad, sat back, finished with the subject.

Hearing a voice behind me, I swiveled and faced another young professor, Peter Canterbury, as he approached us.

"This looks serious." He pulled up a chair.

He was sipping orange juice from a container, the straw bent. A lawyer—and proud of it. Peter taught government and pre-law, and was closer to Vinnie and Marcie than to me. A little too chummy, I always thought—that, and a competitive streak that wasn't attractive. Marcie liked him—he'd been a scholarship boy who'd pushed his way up. His father was a disaffected sixties hippie, a potter and weaver who had no loyalty to the woman he'd married. A bright student, Peter earned a Wesleyan scholarship, a law degree from New England Law in Springfield.

We'd started an off-and-on friendship some time back, both of us single and wandering, but most times we just didn't click. He was a grasping man, and I came to see him as a game-player. A lean, hungry man, and you know what Shakespeare said about such souls. In fact, he'd played King Lear in a college production of the classic. We'd applauded him but suggested he stick to law. He wasn't good.

As single guys we sometimes hung out together, going to Wolf Pack hockey games in downtown Hartford. We'd drive to Foxboro for a Patriots game. That kind of thing. He dragged me once to Hooters but I balked—too much raw hunger, beer suds, and stalled pickups in the parking lot.

All this activity happened before he married a woman named Selena. She and I had dated briefly and intensely one long, hot summer, but she threw me over for Peter. We'd been out to dinner during which we probably exchanged five coherent words.

"You'll always be poor," she said to me, dismissing me.

Then she married Peter, which stunned us. Yes, he was good-looking, and a lawyer. But he was ginger ale, and Selena saw herself as champagne. And because of my brief, unhappy fling with Selena, Peter often avoided me—or sniped at me. According to Marcie, he harbored suspicions about Selena and me, convinced we still had a thing for each other. There were no grounds for such thinking, of course. Selena looked through me, and I—well, looked beyond her. Yet Peter was afraid of me. That, coupled with what turned out to be a fragile marriage, spitfire quarrels in public, made life rough for him. When she drank, Selena flirted. She also flirted when she was sober, but not so obviously. A beautiful woman who understood men's weaknesses, she'd even continued flirting with me because it was her way of annoying Peter. It had nothing to do with me. As far as I'm concerned, it was over. I had no feeling for Selena.

"Join us," Marcie told him. I wish she hadn't.

"Nobody's laughing at this table." He was watching Marcie, avoiding me.

Marcie grinned. "This is business, Peter." She lowered her voice melodramatically. I laughed out loud, and Peter squinted, waiting for a punch line. "Rick has been hired to investigate Marta Kowalski's death."

For the first time Peter looked at me, a crooked smile that suggested people were crazy to put their trust in a bumpkin such as myself, but he said nothing.

I closed my laptop, and kept still.

Vinnie abruptly changed the conversation, drifting onto some school politics he was hot about, and Marcie countered him. The sparks flew. I stood up. "I need to leave." I waved good-bye. "I'm headed to meet Karen at her aunt's home."

"Why?" From Vinnie.

"To pick up some papers and to scout around."

Everyone stood up, and Peter glanced at his watch. "I'll walk out with you. I'm already late. Selena's in the parking lot."

We didn't speak for the few minutes it took us to get outside. Once there, Selena looked startled to see the two of us together, but she flashed a broad smile. She was leaning against her car, bundled up, a knit cap pulled over her forehead. Despite the mild chill in the air, she seemed ready for an Arctic blast.

"My, my, dear Rick."

Peter frowned. "Selena." He mumbled the name.

I felt his eyes darting from her to me. Christ, I thought—must every encounter be a test?

"Well, well, well," Selena hummed. "If it ain't Bruce Lee." A pause. "Or the Karate Kid, revisited."

"Hello, Selena," I smiled back.

Saying nothing, Peter climbed into the passenger seat, leaning over to open the driver's door for Selena. She was still standing outside, watching me. Through the glass I could see Peter's face—rigid, disapproving—curious expressions for such a soft, pliant face. Selena's head swerved, catching a glimpse of Peter, and she smiled.

"Looking handsome." She winked at me, but her voice was too loud, almost strident.

Peter leaned on the horn.

"Come on, Selena, for Christ's sake."

Marcie once told me, "They never learned how to get it right—marriage. You can't get married for all the wrong reasons."

I'd thought of my marriage to Liz—wrong, as well, but we never stopped loving each other.

They drove off, but Peter's wild gestures suggested another fight. As the car turned, I saw his face—hot, flushed. Selena, as usual, was rigid, but the twist of her head was violent. And something else now, meanness of spirit. This was not the couple I knew last year. They'd been the charmed couple. Zelda and Scott on the Riviera. Dancing the night away at the Farmington Country Club. The cat's meow couple.

She wasn't always that way. When we dated, back before Peter, she was often difficult, but fun. A warm, lovely woman who craved attention. Yes, I found her crispness annoying some of the time, as well as her blatant envy of others, but she made up for it with surprisingly tender moments, witty chatter, irreverent, spirited, and lots of ribald laughter. At times she got lost in doomed silence, heavy as lead, a faraway look clouding her eyes. She'd had breakdowns as an adolescent, she confided one night, bouts of dreadful panic mimicking a cruel mother given to fits of madness. She'd joke about it.

"They said I wasn't all there. I'm missing a piece."

So I always thought of her that way—a puzzle begging to be completed.

Then she married the cagiest man we all knew, the zealous law professor who was always talking of the Deal to be made. She couldn't help herself, she said—she fell in love like a besotted high-school girl. Okay, the ice queen wed Machiavelli Junior. Inevitably they would have found each other. Somehow, though, marriage changed both. They lived on his meager assistant professor's salary and the scant income from her gift store in town. It obviously wasn't enough. They were invited to all school parties, but everyone hoped they wouldn't show up. She'd become louder now, more domineering, and sometimes when I saw her she looked on the verge of tears. At those times I remembered her stories of breakdowns, failed therapy, and madness in the eye corners. She flared up in public. She was cruel to people like shop clerks and waiters. He, in turn, had lost his steam, that fiery upward-I'm-going passion. I gave the marriage six months. If that.

One time she told Marcie she should have married me. When Marcie told her it was too late, she'd whispered, "We'll see about that. Rick is my destiny."

"Watch out," Marcie had warned me. "You're not free of her."

"Oh yes I am."

Chapter Seven

Karen met me at her aunt's house on Forest Road in the Union-ville section of Farmington. The front door was wide open despite the chilly air, and she stood facing out, her arms folded over her chest. She looked impatient, though I knew I was prompt. I'm always on time. The good sisters in Saigon taught me that trick. It was one way to survive the bamboo rod against my backside.

Aunt Marta had lived in a small, drab house, a simple cookie-cutter Cape Cod tucked behind thick overgrown hemlocks with weeping willows smothering the roof. Perhaps the house had been cared for at one time when her husband was alive, but it wore a look of decay now, the gray clapboards faded and chipped, roof tiles slipping, a gone-to-seed front yard blanketed by windblown leaves and stringy, dead grasses. As I walked in, Karen backed up, sank into a wing chair by the front window.

"I'm selling the house. I don't want to live here. I hate this house."

She looked ready to cry but pulled herself together.

I looked around. A house lacking personality. Faded rose chintz on the sofa, thin blue polyester drapes, dusty plastic flowers on the glass-top coffee table. Glossy religious icons in plastic frames, one after the other, hanging crookedly on the walls, shriveled palms tucked around them. Everything was neat here, but cheap. I breathed in—a hint of mothballs in the air that reminded me of an old closet suddenly opened—that kind of cloying smell. Marta had not wanted to spend money on furnishings, so she froze her settings in some undefined decade long gone.

Karen saw me looking around. "I've already taken some things out. The few things I want to save. Photo albums, old furniture of my grandparents'. A table I remember. Nothing else I want here. I'm gonna sell it all."

She waved her hands again, as though she hoped her gesture would make it all disappear.

Dressed in brown slacks, a little too tight in the thigh, she had thrown a bulky off-yellow cotton sweater over them. With her long blonde hair pulled into a ponytail, she looked self-consciously seasonal. Even her lipstick was a shade of Halloween orange, an eccentricity that jarred—but compelled you to look.

Once, walking with Hank Nguyen through the arcade, he'd commented on her window display of her own art. It wasn't the first time he'd mocked her artwork. "Thomas Kinkaid meets Jean-Michel Basquiet at a potluck supper."

She moved from the wing chair to sit on the sofa next to me, so close her sleeve touched me, and I smelled lavender perfume, the kind her aunt wore. Turning to look at her, I saw Marta's face—the same angular bone structure, the same razor-thin lips, the same wispy blue eyes.

"Here is the list I promised you."

I had asked her for a list of her aunt's last cleaning jobs, the people whose homes she routinely cleaned. I quickly scanned the list. Karen had written their names in neat script, with phone numbers.

"Any acquaintances I should talk to?"

She ignored that. "I copied it from her notebook. She had scaled back her jobs lately—mainly two professors."

I saw the two professors' names, and I saw Marcie and Vinnie's names. She pointed. "One of her last jobs. There may have been others." A quick smile. "You—when you called her."

"I know." It was a small list, but a decent place to begin.

"You asked if I knew folks she had trouble with—like arguments."

"And?"

She shook her head. "Off and on spats with Hattie Cozzins, her old friend. And—that scene with Willie Do. She didn't *like* him."

I nodded and tucked the list into my pocket.

I spent the next hour checking out the house, and Karen left me alone, busying herself in the kitchen, rifling through boxes, selecting items she'd carry to her apartment. When I walked into the kitchen, I spotted her idiosyncratic choices: a stained pot holder, Dutch boy-and-girl salt and pepper shakers, a chipped serving dish, a pie tin. The longer she emptied the cabinets, the lighter her spirits became. I heard humming at one point, a top-ten radio hit I vaguely recognized as an old Michael Jackson song. *The man in the mirror*...She was happy by herself, so I left her alone. Every so often I looked over, said something, but each time she frowned. Obviously I was smashing through some reverie she was enjoying.

A waste of time, this survey. I discovered nothing unusual. A small cubbyhole desk yielded piles of bills and receipts, but nothing out of the ordinary so far as I could tell. Sadly, Marta threw little out, which could be a good thing for someone looking for clues, but not always. In my laptop I jotted down bank numbers and accounts. I entered names copied from letters, some from out of state. Casual acquaintances she met in Atlantic City and Vegas. A number for the bus company that ran tours to gambling centers.

What secrets did this woman have?

I pulled out drawers, ran my fingers across the bottoms, and Karen, entering the living room where the little desk sat, bit her lip. Breathing in loudly, she glared at me as though I were a surprise prowler. Quirky, she obviously had an invisible boundary I was always crossing, something that baffled me. She may have hired me, but she looked unhappy that I was rifling through a dead woman's life. Then she went back into the kitchen and I heard cupboards opening and closing. A dish broke, and she swore.

I walked through the basement, the upstairs bedrooms, the attic crawlspace. Nothing out of the ordinary—no secret vices, no hidden cardboard box sealed with duct tape. This was a conventional lady, by all accounts. She paid her bills faithfully and didn't touch that hundred grand from hubby's insurance. I found a huge carton of Christmas cards from years past, each year's arrival bound by elastic bands and each placed back in the original envelopes. She'd saved them all. Hundreds. The words inside were standard and hardly personal—the platitudinous "Have a great Christmas" sentiment. Yet something bothered me, and eventually I went back to check the addresses—every card was from a man. Not one was signed with a woman's name. Did she know women? Yes, obviously, there was Hattie Cozzins, for one. Her travel companion. But no cards in the pile from Hattie.

On a side table, pinned between two bald-eagle plaster bookends, were a few old books, two volumes of *Reader's Digest* condensed novels, as well as a three-volume *History of the World* from 1897, bound in faded red leather, an American Bible Tract, circa 1850, with broken spine. Slips of paper marked pages. A book on Scripture that contained a pull-out chart at the back, tracing the history of the Christian world from Creation to 1900, a documented span of four thousand years or so. Adam and Eve to—well, McKinley. I found a couple of worn nineteenth-century novels, with mottled gilt edges. *The Wide, Wide World. The Gates Ajar.*

"Aunt Marta's home-correspondence school," Karen noted as she walked by me.

"Bizarre collection."

"Church sales, probably. She didn't like to read anything that disturbed her."

"I collect old books." I examined the thick volume of *The Gates Ajar.*

"Joshua Jennings wanted her to read classic literature." Karen shook her head. "Him, the old teacher and collector. He valued old books over people. Imagine Marta reading, well, I don't know—Plutarch? Lord, Shakespeare? She moved her lips when she read supermarket tabloids. She never did read anything. He would lend her volumes, but she didn't want to read them. She only wanted to impress him. If she returned one with a smudge, he'd flip out. Not that he gave her the collectible ones. God forbid. Books were sacred."

"Books *are* sacred."

"I remember once she told me he was astounded that she'd never read James Fenimore Cooper. His favorite author. She said he yelled 'Natty Bumppo' at her, and she said nobody in their right mind is named Natty Bumppo. He wasn't happy." She chuckled at the memory.

I laughed, too. "She started." I pointed to the dining room table where I'd seen an unopened book resting on some newspapers. I went to get it and held it up. An exquisite volume. *The Last of the Mohicans* from an elegant, leather-bound set from the turn of the century. My hands lovingly handled it. A volume out of G. Putnam's, bound in half-morocco, a silk ribbon market, unfortunately located on page two. A facsimile manuscript page.

"This is classic Victoriana," I told her.

"Whatever."

"She didn't get very far."

Karen glanced at it. "Yeah, she mentioned Cooper to me. 'Impossible,' she said. The first page put her to sleep."

I laughed. "I bet she never returned library books either."

"Joshua realized his home-correspondence school was a bust."

"So she had dreams of a life with Joshua?"

Karen looked into my face. "My aunt could be a foolish woman, Rick. I tell you—she was too fond of Joshua—with that big house on the green, his—his patrician background, his kindness to her. She thought he cared for her, and I guess he did in his own way. She even thought they, you know, might marry and travel. He flattered her—teased." A sigh. "She was foolish."

"That explains her depression when he died."

She shook her head back and forth. "Well, that started earlier when they had that fight. He told her not to come to the house. To stay away."

"That must have hurt her."

She bit her lip. "No woman wants a man to reject her."

"No man wants a woman to reject him."

"It's not the same thing, Rick."

"How so?"

"It just isn't. Men don't get it."

"But…"

She turned away. "I don't want this conversation."

The house yielded no surprises. I found nothing out of bounds in the closets. No hidden men's clothing to suggest secret lovers, no rattling skeletons, no Victoria's Secret catalogs, no taboo sex toys. Hers was a modest, decent life lived simply. No rose for Emily, this woman. There were no exotic foodstuffs in the kitchen cabinets, no international coffee flavors, no low-fat cuisine in the freezer, no food processor. Maxwell House coffee. Dial soap. In a hall cupboard were five bottles of whiskey, rye and scotch, two unopened. The third was nearly empty. She used an old-fashioned coffee percolator, sparkling clean. Technology was ignored here: no answering machine, no cordless phone. She had an old VCR, broken, with a cassette of *The Sound of Music* resting on top of it. She had an old RCA TV in her living room, not a sleek flat-screen. Here was a doggedly conventional woman. There was nothing to break the pattern that caught your eye when you opened the front door—a sort of lower-middle-class life lived redundantly in all the rooms.

But deeply religious. Ivy curled from the belly of the Infant of Prague statue on the TV. Gilded crosses adorned the walls. Glossy Russian icons of Jesus' head, oversized and startling, hung on the bedroom wall. She was, I knew, a church-going Catholic. I'd found canceled checks for payments to the church, regular contributions to Catholic Charities, payments for memorial Masses for her dead husband. A Mass card from his funeral. Pamphlets for pilgrimages to shrines at Lourdes. A book on Our Lady of Fatima. Nothing offbeat here where conservative religion thrived.

Except for a stack of pamphlets bound together with elastic bands. Manifestos from the Brown Bonnets, a vociferous, local charismatic Catholic women's group opposed to abortion, pornography, same-sex marriage, progressive Catholicism, and all-around good fun. A group that marched in Washington at pro-life rallies. They'd picketed Bill Maher when he performed at the Bushnell. These pamphlets bore Marta's address label, with some numbers above it. I recorded the information.

"Nothing to suggest violence hiding in a corner of her life," I told Karen.

She looked disheartened.

"But there's nothing to suggest suicide, either," I added.

No pills. No prescription drugs, no letters chronicling depression. No suggestion of a woman on the edge. It was the undemonstrative house of an old woman decidedly content, someone whose life was defined by periodic trips to gambling palaces with busloads of other women. Yes, a little fanatical when it came to religion, but she was, well—normal.

Karen was in a hurry to leave, snapping lights off before I could gather my jacket. In the driveway she confessed, "The place gives me the jitters." She added, "It's worse with you here."

"Why?"

"With you going through her stuff, well, the smell of murder fills the place."

"No murder yet, Karen."

"I get a little crazy." A long pause. "Sometimes." She smiled an apology. "I feel like she's been staring over my shoulder here, telling me I'm doing something wrong."

"How about a cup of coffee? We can talk."

She turned away. "I have to get back to the shop, Rick. I'm unloading stock later."

Alone, I decided to walk Marta's final route to verify the timing. I checked my watch. Four-fifteen on the dot. I set out on foot for Richard Wilcox's condo, Marta's destination the night she died. I walked down the sidewalk, ambled along the narrow road and through a small park near his home. I walked slowly, trying to approximate the methodical steps of a depressed woman, one nearly seventy years old, a woman with a little too much whiskey in her bloodstream. At exactly 4:37, by my watch, I turned onto the road that crossed the Farmington River. The garden-style townhouses were in sight. It was a short walk, shorter than I'd assumed. That was why she never drove her car.

Standing on the stone bridge, I gazed down into the Farmington River, churning and swelling with the heavy autumn rains we'd had recently. A few huge dark boulders dominated the stream. When she died in September, it must have been a mere trickle of water—after a parched August. I focused on the boulders, a run of sharp rocks and broken branches. From this spot Marta had fallen—or was pushed. Or, I realized, possibly killed elsewhere and dumped here. But that seemed a stretch.

The bridge was old-style masonry, ornate carvings decorating the rounded corners, unscary gargoyles peering out, without menace. A tarnished bronze plaque announced it was dedicated during the Depression. Calvin Coolidge was president. Silas Lowe was first selectman. The bridge arched up in huge carved blocks of dull brown limestone and beige granite. There were no metal railings here as I thought the police report indicated, only elaborate stone abutments, bulky and stolid. I realized the height was easily three-to-four feet of masonry, and a step up from the sidewalk.

No, Marta couldn't have toppled accidentally into the river, even with her elevated alcohol level. She would have had to climb up onto the wall in order to hurl herself over the edge, a deliberate act.

Or, of course, she could have been pushed over.

I looked around. The bridge was shielded from the condo complex by a line of huge evergreens. Low-hanging hemlocks blocked the sky. Behind me was the park. There was a good chance she would be alone in this spot.

It was a good place to murder someone, assuming the victim would die after dropping the twenty or so feet onto the rockbed. An old woman, tipsy, would prove no challenge. But the murderer would have to check to see if the fall killed the poor soul.

My phone rang.

"It's me." Hank's voice sounded far away.

"I just walked from Marta's home," I told him.

"Look," he broke in, "I got Grandma to talk to Aunt Marie—and to Willie Do. Nobody's happy."

"I didn't expect them to be happy."

"You got your wish. Anyway, I'll pick you up at six. We gotta have supper, she said. I gotta be there." A heartbeat. "This is not gonna go well."

"Six it is."

"Don't dress like you fell off a luxury cruise ship."

"I'll…"

The line went dead.

I climbed up the foot-thick rock wall, waist high, and stood there. I balanced, a little nervous in that precarious position. A boy, speeding past on his bicycle, stopped for a second and watched me curiously.

"You gonna jump, mister?" A smile on a wise-guy face.

I maneuvered myself down. "Do kids jump from here into the water?"

He looked at me as if I were stupid. "There ain't no deep water here. It's all rocks and stuff. You smash your head open if you try swimming here." He sped off.

That, of course, was exactly what happened to Marta. A fearsome place to kill yourself. I couldn't see Marta choosing this gruesome, unpredictable place to die, toppling onto the rocks below.

◇◇◇

Back at my apartment I skimmed through my notes on the laptop, jotted ideas and facts on note cards that I pinned onto the pegboard over my desk, and stared. My computer screen won't allow me that wall of real space to intuit connections that might leap out, slap me into sudden recognition of the obvious. One of Jimmy Gadowicz's old-time methods still worked—post it all on a wall in front of you, index cards overlapping one after the other, colored pins suggesting patterns, and if there's a secret there, it will emerge. That's how Jimmy functioned. He was my teacher—I listened to him.

Then it hit me.

When Karen didn't answer at home, I called the store. She seemed surprised to hear from me.

"Did your aunt have an insurance policy? I don't recall seeing one at the house."

A long silence. Then, awkwardly, "I told you I took some of her papers home. I'll show you."

I was impatient. "Was there a policy?"

"Yes."

"Why didn't you tell me?"

"It's for a half-million bucks."

She waited for me to respond. Nobody collected if it was a suicide.

An edge to her voice, unhappy. "I didn't want to tell you because I thought you wouldn't take the job. I'm not in it for the money, Rick. Don't think I'm doing this for the money. I should have told you. I was going to, I mean it."

"You gotta be honest with me, Karen."

"Oh, I am." She made a clicking sound. "I try to be. Sometimes I have trouble telling people things they don't want to hear. "

"But I need to hear things, Karen."

A little pouting. "I know, I know."

"I'm working *for* you."

"Believe me. I already have money from her. She was my aunt…"

She went on and on until, annoyed with my silence, she mumbled good-bye and hung up.

Chapter Eight

Vuong Ky Do lived with his family in a triple-decker home near a busy corner off a small shopping plaza in Unionville, perhaps a half-mile from the modest neighborhood were Marta once lived. They were neighbors separated by two or three tree-lined streets. I noted this fact as Hank pulled up to the curb in front of the building. An isolated house, out of place on the commercial block, a Shell gas station next door with plastic streamers blowing in the wind, and a small discount liquor store on the other side. Across the street a strip mall of beauty parlors, laundromats, a mom-and-pop home-style eatery with a neon sign flashing GOO EATS, the "D" unfortunately missing. Cars buzzed in and out of the parking lot, blasted through flashing lights. A Dutch Colonial at the far end of the block had been converted into law offices and an optometrist's office.

"I wonder how long Willie's home will last," I told Hank.

"The last holdout," he answered. "The greasy wheels of progress."

I sang off-key. "'They paved paradise and put up a parking lot.'"

"Hey, how poetic," he said.

"Hank, I didn't make up the line."

A pause. "I didn't think so."

Each floor held a front porch with low turned railings, and on the first floor—Willie's son's apartment, Hank told me—a dumpy old sofa was pushed back against the clapboard siding. A couple plastic lawn chairs accompanied it, one turned over. What looked like the chrome bumper of an old car was leaning against the wall. Glancing up toward the second floor, I noticed an empty porch—but an old woman stood there, unmoving, staring down at us.

Hank waved. "Aunt Marie."

She nodded and stepped back into the apartment.

As we sat in front of the house, Hank pointed out a chassis of an old Chevy up on blocks at the end of the long driveway that led alongside the house and ended at a back chain-link fence, rusted and bent in. "Probably gets more mileage than your tinker-toy BMW."

I wasn't listening. I was watching an older model Toyota with rusted fenders and a yellow tennis ball bobbing off the top of a wavering antenna. The car bounced into the driveway, disappeared from sight in a lot behind the house. But immediately a young couple walked alongside the house, headed to a side entrance.

Hank yelled out the window. "Hey, Freddy."

The young Vietnamese man looked sixteen, a skinny kid wearing a baseball cap turned backwards. Shifting a grocery bag from one arm to the other, he said something to the woman with him. We got out of the car and Hank excitedly introduced me to his cousin Freddy, his young wife, Mia, and the chubby baby Sarah she cradled in her arms. Smiles all around, Freddy punching Hank in the shoulder, the baby gurgling her happiness.

Freddy whispered, "We heard all about you coming here." He was looking at me. "Aunt Marie told us." He leaned in. "She's unhappy."

"Everyone in this house is always unhappy," Hank offered, but the remark confused Freddy. It also confused me. And it confused Hank himself because he twisted his head to the side, eyes narrowed, as though someone else had made the blanket statement.

Nothing more was said, but we followed the young family up the side stairwell, and waved as they headed to the third floor.

"Tell your mother I love her New Year's rice cakes," Freddy yelled down. Hank squinted up at him. "That's a hint," Freddy went on, grinning. "For more."

Aunt Marie was waiting for us on the landing, her back against the open door.

A small, thin woman with large brown eyes in a smooth face, she looked like an adolescent girl, except for the shock of abundant white hair. Probably in her mid-sixties now, she'd pulled her hair back into a loose bun, a yellow silk ribbon sloppily attached at the back. She bowed to me, and I bowed back. "Welcome." Another bow. But her voice trembled as she looked away, darting back into the room. I followed her nervous gaze, but there was no one else there.

"Vuong is not home yet," she addressed Hank. She waved at the empty table.

For a moment they chattered in Vietnamese, the easy familiarity of family members, and I understood that he would return shortly. A favor to a friend who needed another hand to hold the end of some drywall going up in his house. She looked at me and said in English, "He cannot refuse a friend."

"Of course," I answered.

She held up a finger, as though remembering something, and scurried into the kitchen.

A neat apartment, hard-pressed curtains covering the windows, flowered slipcovers over the sofa, though the hallway into the rooms was cluttered with two large cardboard boxes tied with string, prominent addresses evident: Ho Chi Minh City. I noticed Hank eyeing them.

She laughed. "We send clothes and too much medicine to Vietnam."

Hank looked at me. "In the early days they had nothing there, the family that stayed behind." He addressed Aunt Marie. "But Vietnam is doing fine now—no need for medicine and…"

She shrugged off the comment. "Vuong will never stop sending packages back there. No matter what." She shrugged. "It's what he has to do." She pointed to a small dining room table off the kitchen. It was covered with frayed oilcloth, with old wooden country-style kitchen chairs positioned around it. "Sit, sit. Please."

As she walked by Hank, she let her hand graze his cheek, smiling at him. "I remember you when you were a little boy, Tan." She used his Vietnamese name. "Always had an answer for everything. But adorable."

I almost quipped, "Still does," but such a remark from me would be untoward, rude.

Hank grinned foolishly. "I'm a man now, Aunt Marie. I'm gonna be a state trooper."

"And such a handsome one." She wagged a finger at him. "You give your mother sleepless nights."

She bustled around the kitchen, refusing our help, though she kept glancing back at us, her face worried. When she caught my eye, she smiled warmly. A kind woman, I realized, a beautiful soul. That simple act of letting her fingers graze Hank's cheek communicated so much—and for a moment I was jealous of that familial touch.

The aromas drifting from the kitchen reminded me of how hungry I was: the tang of lemongrass, the rich anise-peppered broth for the noodle soup called *pho*, even the tray of sliced overripe mangoes resting on a table. She placed a pot of jasmine tea next to it, and nodded at Hank. Pour. Sweet to the taste, a hint of flowers, soothing, rich. She placed a dish of *goi cuon* in front of us—thin rice paper wrapped around bits of shrimp, diced basil, and carrots. We dipped the treat into small bowls of peanut-speckled hoisin sauce. Freshly made within the hour, the appetizer was a mixture of textures and flavors. Hank grunted his approval. Then she served us bowls of Vietnamese comfort soup, *pho,* the beef noodle, thin strips of uncooked beef dropped into a fiery broth where they immediately cooked. Flavored with bean sprouts we lifted with chopsticks from a plate and sprigs of green basil we broke from the stem, hoisin sauce drizzled in, warm buttery vermicelli noodles floating at the bottom, I could have wept with pleasure. I watched Hank pour hot sauce into his, which I refused.

"Coward," he whispered.

"This needs nothing but a pair of chopsticks and my appreciation."

Aunt Marie smiled at me. "You do not live in a Vietnamese world," she said quietly.

At that moment, startled, I was conscious of my status as *bui doi*, the almost white man in the room. I also realized why Vuong delayed returning home—or at least I believed I knew. I was a violator in this room, a different sort of ghost from old Saigon—the curse of the American War that took away his life. Generations in America would never forgive. Some folks would never break bread with me. I recalled a friend in college who was Vietnamese and Chinese—most of the first boat people were of Chinese background, in fact, *Viet Ching*—who traveled with a pack of Vietnamese friends in San Diego—until, that is, he told them that his mother was Chinese. He was shunned from the group. Now I squirmed in my seat, conscious of a bloodline I had no control over, and I caught Hank's eyes on me. They twinkled. Relax, the look communicated. Friends here, all of us. Then, a sardonic shake of his head. At least until Vuong arrived home.

And yet I was invited here—Hank's grandma, I figured, and the utter kindness of Aunt Marie. And probably awareness that such an interview was necessary.

"My Vuong," Aunt Marie suddenly began, "is a difficult man."

The words hung in the air, ominous.

Hank spoke up. "Rick knows the story, Aunt Marie."

I murmured my condolences for the death of her daughter so many years before. But of course that horrific death of a thirteen-year-old girl was the morning's news, always fresh, forever raw. Always a wound in the heart.

"He's always waiting for something to happen." She sat still, her hands folded in her lap, watching me.

"I mean him no harm," I told her.

She smiled thinly. "I know that. Hank's grandmother speaks of you with affection. You have her blessing." I bowed. "But this has nothing to do with you, Rick. This is the story of a man who gets up in the morning and waits for the hour he can go to bed." Her eyes got wet, and she turned away. "He carries our little Linh in his heart but she won't speak to him."

"Aunt Marie," Hank began, "Rick just wants information."

She wasn't listening but spoke softly in Vietnamese. "*Thuong nhieu qua.*"

The words hung in the air, awful, powerful. So much love. A love so profound it colors any day of any life.

At that moment the door opened and Vuong walked in, a little sheepish, his jacket folded over his arms. His wife immediately stood up and walked to him, tucked her arm into his elbow.

"Mr. Rick Van Lam," she said.

"Thank you for seeing me." I bowed.

We exchanged some pleasantries in Vietnamese, my own words catching in my throat, but Hank kept sliding us through the formalities, his own voice tense, brittle.

Vuong spoke now. "I remember you from the college."

"Of course."

A sliver of a smile. "A place that does not believe in Lucky Strikes."

"Like a lot of the world, Uncle," Hank said.

Surprisingly, the man walked up to me and stuck out his hand. "Willie Do." His American name. I nodded.

Small like his wife, as slender, but with wired muscles, a bantam rooster of a man, powerful-looking, even in his late sixties, he scratched his balding head. Red blotches covered his scalp. A blood-red scar over his left eye, ragged and broken at the edges.

We sat in the living room, Hank and me on the sofa, Willie in an armchair, his knees drawn up to his chest. Immediately he lit a cigarette and the thick smoke circled his head. He smiled and pointed the cigarette at me. "Here no one will stop me."

I smiled back.

Aunt Marie did not sit but stood behind his chair, hovering, watching, one of her hands resting on the top of the chair. At one point, as he settled back, twisting his head up to blow smoke into the air, she touched the back of his neck. He frowned.

Willie cleared his throat. "I never liked her." Said with a finality, as though he understood he had to have this talk—did he see me as some sort of authority?—and wanted to cut to the chase. The information hurled out there—blatant, strong.

"Marta?"

"Who else? That's why you're here, no?"

Hank broke in. "Why not, Uncle?"

"A woman that looked at you like you don't belong in her world. Like her private kingdom."

"What did you think when you heard she killed herself?"

"I don't think nothing. I won't think about her."

"But you must have wondered why?"

"I know why."

"What?" From Hank.

"Joshua Jennings was dead."

"Tell me about that." I watched him closely.

For the first time he relaxed. "Twice a week I worked his yard. A fussy old man, Joshua. But when he looked at me, you know what I saw there? A man respecting another man. He tells me, 'No one ever touched the flowerbeds like you, Willie. The lawn like a carpet.'" He locked eyes with me. "We understood each other." A pause. "And that was the problem."

"How so?" From Hank.

"Marta worked the inside of the house. But she talked of Joshua like—well…'Joshua and I…We…Joshua and I…' Like she and him was, you know…"

"A couple?"

"You could see it in her eyes."

"You fought with her."

He waved his hand in the air. "Not a fight because I ain't said nothing to her. Joshua kept planning to move away. The house was too big, he was too old, over and over. He had trouble with climbing. Marta fought that—like a dream slipping away."

"But he did move away."

"She screamed and screamed at him. I could hear it from the garden. I never thought he would, you know. Even with his bad heart. One day he says he sold the place. It's done. He said he felt—good."

"He fought with Marta. Told her to stay away, no?" From Hank.

Willie was quiet for a long time. "Because of me, I think. But maybe not. Maybe something else." He shrugged. "Joshua, he knocks on the window for me to come in and get my money. A muddy day, I wasn't thinking. In the kitchen he is laughing with me, happy, but Marta starts to yell at me. She followed me outside and yelled and yelled. She called me a 'lousy foreigner.' I glared at her and went home. Days later she called the cops." He trembled. "They come here."

Aunt Marie spoke up. "We don't like cops coming into the house." She touched Willie's shoulder. "It was like the old days in…"

"In Saigon," her husband finished.

"But they went away," I said.

"A waste of their time."

"But then Marta fought with Joshua?"

He nodded. "Joshua heard how she talked to me. How she called the cops. When I came back to mow the lawns, he told me she would not be coming back. He said—well, never such a way to treat a man…in his house. I mean, he turned red in the face. They had fights, he said."

Willie's comment surprised me. So that skirmish in the kitchen was perhaps only a small part of the reason for Marta's exile and her movement into depression. Another fight with Joshua?

"He never saw her again?" Hank asked.

"I don't know. Maybe. But I think the fights with her made him decide to move away. One day he tells me the house is sold.

He gives me a pile of money. Over five hundred dollars and says, 'For you. Take it.' He laughs and tells me to have a good life."

Willie sat back, finished. He lit another cigarette.

"You ever see Marta again?" I asked.

He grunted. "Once in the aisles of Walmart. She walks by and said I should go back to where they eat dogs."

Hank was readying to say something, but choked, rolled to the side.

"It wasn't funny."

Willie folded his arms over his chest, the cigarette tight in the corner of his mouth. He dipped his head down, and I realized he was through talking. Everything he'd told me had been thought through, planned, out of some sense of obligation. Something he had to do—and now it was done.

Hank said what I hadn't planned on saying. "Marta's niece thinks someone murdered her."

A long silence, as I watched Willie's face harden. Even his eyes got dull. His lips were drawn into a thin line. He glanced through the kitchen door and I followed his gaze to the religious icons resting on a shelf. Once again that curious melding of Jesus Christ and Buddha. A Catholic wife and a Buddhist husband. The joss sticks and the blood-red tangerines. The dried Sunday Mass palms. He looked back at me. "It doesn't matter now. The minute you are born you begin your journey to death. She got there ahead of the rest of us."

The door opened, and Tony Do stormed in. A rough-looking man, short as his parents but thick, barrel-chested, a thin whisper of a moustache above his lip. A narrow head with a high flat forehead. Tony worked in a body shop in town, and he'd once ignored me when I'd stopped in to check on some repairs. Spotting another Vietnamese there, greasy in overalls and watching me from a doorway, a wrench in his hand, he turned away at my friendly nod. Now, glaring at me and then at Hank, he positioned himself behind his father. A curious tableau, I thought—mother and son as guardians of the wounded old man.

"Hey, Tony," Hank began, standing. "We were just leaving."

Tony looked at his mother. "Everything okay?"

She nodded. "Your father has answered all the questions."

Tony breathed in, but he still didn't look happy.

"Did you ever meet Marta?" I asked him.

For a moment he stared at me, unfocused, but finally he answered, though he looked at Hank, whose head was bobbing up and down. "Yeah, once or twice. Maybe more. I don't know. Around town. Sometimes I helped out at Jennings' place. When Pop needed another hand for something. Like to move the lawn tractor onto a rack. She'd be there, looking out the window, frowning."

"Tony…" His mother began. "We are through here."

Tony wasn't listening. "She treated Pop like a piece of shit."

His mother shuddered. "Tony, please."

"And calling the cops. Christ Almighty."

Tony had a raspy, cigarette smoker's voice, and he started to cough, gagged. He wiped his mouth with the back of his hand.

I spoke up. "Your father handled her the best way, Tony. He ignored her."

Snidely, not looking at me. "And still the goddamn cops knock on his door." He swung around to look into his father's face. God knows what he saw there, but it gave him pause. He backed up. "Enough."

I headed to the door. "Thank you."

Tony interrupted. "Old man Jennings respected my father because Pop understood how a job was supposed to be done. Pop took pride in that yard, and Jennings understood that. He valued—order. When he moved away, up to Amherst, he thanked my father."

Willie struggled from the chair and faced his son. "No more."

Tony faltered. "I just want them to understand that you have pride…yes, pride."

His father moved toward the kitchen. I could tell he was embarrassed by his son's declarations. A man does his job and does not need a son to declare how good he is at it.

"Yes," I noted. Then, perhaps foolishly, I quoted Buddha. "A man is the leaf he touches." Then I tried to remember the line in Vietnamese. "*Mot nguoi dan ong la anh cham vao la.*" I stammered, mumbled the last syllables.

A flicker in Willie's eye corner. A quick nod.

But Tony was rattling on. "Christ, even after he sold the place, before he left town, he called Pop and told him to work in the yard before the new owners—you know them, the Canterburys—arrived."

His father shot him a look that I had trouble reading. He disappeared into the kitchen. Tony was oblivious.

"Did you ever see Marta again?" I asked Tony.

"As a matter of fact, I did. She was at the post office one afternoon when I walked in. She was telling someone that Joshua Jennings had died."

"How did she act?"

"She was sobbing out of control."

"That's sad," Hank noted.

"I didn't think so," Tony said. "I hated what she did to Pop."

Hank and I said our good-byes, and left, Tony trailing behind us. On the first floor he turned toward his doorway, but then, rushing back, grasped Hank's elbow. "Come inside for a minute."

We followed him into his apartment. "Pop'll be mad at me for what I said upstairs. He says I talk too much. I don't care. I had to say something."

We stood in the doorway, looking in on a messy apartment. His wife was nowhere in sight, but a scraggly fifteen-year-old boy was stretched out on a ripped sofa, playing some video game off the TV. He glanced up and made no effort to lower the volume.

"Turn that goddamn noise down, Big Nose," his father yelled.

The boy ignored him.

Tony motioned us to a desk near the kitchen. It was really an old maple table, cluttered with bills and magazines and folded plastic bags from a local Vietnamese market named Bo Kien. He reached under some Vietnamese newspapers and pulled out what looked like an old scrapbook. "Here."

In a voice that was soft and gentle, removed from the brutal rasp he'd used upstairs, he flipped open the yellowing pages. He thumbed past slick color photos of his family in America. But at the back he slipped out a black-and-white photograph that was perhaps six inches long. I held it in my palm. Wrinkled, bent, one side water-stained, the other side faded and torn, it was a photograph of his family.

"My father carried this on the boat from Saigon. The only picture we got. Ruined, yes, but every week Pop comes downstairs and looks at it."

A dim photograph of Vuong as a sharp-looking young man, standing next to his pretty wife, whose hand rested on the boy Tony's shoulder. Tony was maybe fourteen years old. But in the faded section on the right was the faint ghost of a young girl, nearly faded out of view. Her father's head was inclined down toward her neck, and his hand rested on her shoulder. A tattered, miserable remnant, this relic that had barely survived the rough waters of the South China Sea, but I noticed Tony lovingly replaced it in the scrapbook.

"Pop won't keep it in his place," he told us. "Every time he holds it he mumbles the same words." And then Tony chanted in Vietnamese: *Kinh cau sieu.*

A prayer that the dead would find peace.

I closed my eyes, a little dizzy.

"He is waiting for her to come to him and say that she is at peace. Every day he waits for her ghost to move through him."

Chapter Nine

Hank followed me into my apartment.

"That didn't go well."

I shrugged. "I didn't expect it to."

"Willie Do is not a cold-blooded killer."

"I agree with you." A pause. "But I was surprised by his son's anger—at Marta."

Hank looked into my eyes. "Everyone's protective of Willie."

I nodded. "Such a sad man." I breathed in. "A frozen man."

Hank eyed me closely. "You know, Rick, we believe our ancestors—our dead—are with us. A breeze, a butterfly, a smell of jasmine—all signs of being touched by a dead loved one. Ghosts wander. *Ma troi*. You look in Willie's eyes—blankness there. There's no energy to kill—no spirit. Nothing there. You know why? Because his daughter's ghost can't find him in America."

"What about the brother who lived?"

"Tony?" His look was sharp. "You think he'd kill Marta?"

"He hated what she did to his father."

"C'mon, Rick."

I said nothing. I took off my coat and sank into a chair.

I thought of something. "What about the wild grandson? Big Nose. You told me he was a boy headed for trouble—shoplifting, thrills, craziness."

Hank thought a second. "*Song voi*, as we'd say."

"Meaning?" I didn't know the Vietnamese.

"You live fast—rush your life."

"That's a house of pain."

He smiled. "Except for the chubby baby on the third floor."

"Another fat American."

Hank looked around my rooms as he sat down. "Dragging more junk off the street?" He pointed to a tattered oriental.

"A church rummage sale."

He frowned at the old sofa, the Victorian magazine rack with too many scratches, a garish lamp with ruby tassels. "Your apartment will never be featured on the...I don't know—Home and Garden Channel."

Hank preferred a sleeker look—chrome and glass. Or, frankly, a room with one huge plasma TV dominating one wall, and a sofa from IKEA in front of it. Bags of potato chips. A six-pack. Girls.

While he rifled through my CD collection, I organized my notes in my laptop, then added material. I worked under a bronze-and-green-glass lamp that might have occupied a store-keeper's desk a half-century back, illuminating someone who might be recording sales figures in a leather-bound country-store ledger.

I ignored the sudden rapping on the door, but then I heard the raised, humorous voice. "I know you're in there. I own the goddamn building."

Grinning, I opened the door to let in my landlady, Gracie Patroni.

"I'm not bringing food this time." She waved empty hands at me. "So you don't have to lie and say you already ate at a restaurant."

"Come in, Gracie." I motioned her to the sofa. "Hank's here."

"I know. I see who walks into the building."

She sank into the deepest end of the old sofa. Gracie is probably in her early eighties, a tall woman, rail thin, her hair pulled back and secured with an elastic band.

"I know I'm interrupting." Yet she wasn't apologetic.

Gracie often stops in, lingering, gabbing, running her fingers over the windowsills to check for dust. Her visits never bother me because she's one of the people I adore. She likes me, too. Gracie's a flamboyant woman, though she can be a serious moralist at times. She'd been a Rockette at Radio City Music Hall, had entertained the troops with Bob Hope in Korea, and then followed a husband to Connecticut. She lives on the first floor, rents out an apartment on the second to me and one on the third to a new guy, recently divorced, a man I'd only talked to a few times. The last tenant upstairs had been an old, retired mechanic who tuned the old car she never drove. He had a heart attack changing the oil. I liked him, too. The new man upstairs was—well, a mystery so far.

"Busy?" she asked.

"Grab yourself a beer," I told her.

I went back to finishing my note-taking on the laptop. Gracie wandered around, made small talk with Hank, spotted my new possession—I caught her eyeing the new oriental with disapproval. Sitting next to Hank, she leafed through a magazine and frowned. It was an industry trade, *Criminal Justice Monthly*. She obviously thought it a waste of a good tree.

Bored, she walked behind me and looked over my shoulder. "Marta Kowalski?"

I closed the top, smiling. "Confidential information."

"Yeah, sure."

I expected her to make a flip comment because she found my role as PI hilarious. Sometimes when she left me a scribbled note pinned to the door, it was addressed to Hercule Poirot or, worse, Miss Marple. Yet whenever Jimmy visited she came knocking on the door with some lame excuse. They baited each other out of some love ritual I could never grasp. Sometimes, I knew, he visited with the hopes of seeing her. If she didn't interrupt us, he'd be disappointed. He's old—she's a lot older. They share war stories that seem some sort of foreplay.

"Yes, Marta Kowalski." I looked at her. "You knew her."

She sat down, finished the beer quickly, wiped her mouth with the back of her hand.

Gracie obviously saw Marta entering my apartment to clean, and for the previous tenant of my rooms, an old professor who'd died. I inherited the apartment—and Marta.

"Yes." A cold tone that surprised me.

"Do you think someone would murder her?"

Silence.

"Were you surprised at the suicide?"

"Yes, I suppose so." She stood up, turned away. "I didn't like the woman."

It dawned on me that we'd never discussed Marta. Gracie and I chatted about so many folks in town—she was filled with anecdotes and salacious gossip. But never about Marta, lumbering up the stairs with her cleaning kit. One time Gracie admitted that Marta did an expert, efficient job. Of course, there was no reason to have any conversation because Marta was hired to do a job. Maybe I assumed the two old women, both long-time residents of Farmington, sat down with coffee for a chat. Most times I wasn't there. I left a check in an envelope on the hall table.

"Weren't you and Marta members of the same church?"

"Yes. St. Augustine's. The Catholic church." She stammered, "I don't sound too charitable here, saying I didn't like her, but you asked me."

"Why?" I was watching Gracie, uncomfortable now.

"When she first started coming to the house to clean the apartments—you guys *are* a dirty, lazy bunch, if you don't mind my saying so—I invited her in for coffee. You know, something simple. We saw each other at the church but never spoke to each other. But she was downright rude to me. 'No time for socializing,' she said. Like I was insulting her. That was horse manure, Rick. Horse shit, in plain English."

I went over to the refrigerator and took out two more bottles of beer, silently handed one to her. She took a couple of sips.

"Maybe she just wanted to get her work done."

"Sounds weird to me," Hank contributed.

Gracie shook her head vigorously, looking at me as though I were a dim-witted child. "Not likely." She nodded at Hank. "She *was* weird. Stupidly, I tried a couple times. I'll tell you, she was not a nice woman. Then I overheard her talking at the church hall once—about me. She mentioned that I'd been an entertainer, like it was something dirty. Real mocking-like. *Entertaaaainer*. Dragging it out like that. 'Lah-di-dah,' she said. Me living in a canary-yellow house I slept my way into. She whispered that I had been a whore. She knew I was nearby, so she did it on purpose. She did me dirt, Rick."

Gracie's words stopped me dead. This portrait clashed with my own image of the old woman, always smiling at me, always a little too prying, that was true, but—harmless. Even sweet. That was the word for it—sweet. Sometimes a little too sweet, little girl coy and cute, a cultivated sugary surface. But I never gave the woman much thought. She dusted my books. She vacuumed the carpets.

"She was always nice to me."

But I recalled the words of Buddha. *She who is born with an axe in her mouth cuts herself when her words are cruel.*

Gracie drained the last of the beer.

"Women didn't like her," she stressed. "Marta wore more than one face in the world. I saw two or three of them."

"So she had enemies?"

"None I knew of. I didn't belong to her world, you know. But generally speaking, if someone murdered her, I'd lay you odds it was a decent woman."

Gracie was in a hurry to leave, especially when she saw me typing some of her reluctant remarks into my laptop. Okay, I was probably less tactful than I should have been. She gave me a withering look reserved for pushy salesmen and religious zealots.

"That's the sum total of my knowledge of that evil woman." But it wasn't her real final comment. Over her shoulder, "And she called herself a Catholic. At least I didn't become one of those *other* Catholics. Like her."

Hurriedly I jotted down that last comment. I'd have to follow that up later. What other Catholics? I made a notation—the Brown Bonnets? Those merry mariological happy campers, the right-wing, anti-porn, anti-choice Catholics whose propaganda I found in Marta's house. What role did they play in her life?

After she left, blowing Hank a kiss from across the room, he looked up from his iPhone where he was happily texting someone. "That was interesting."

I nodded. "A complicated woman."

"Gracie?"

I laughed. "That's a given. But I was thinking of Marta."

He stood over me as I was reviewing the names of people to be interviewed—Marta's short list of clients.

Hank read out loud, "Richard Wilcox, Charlie Safako. Farmington College professors who haven't had sex in years?"

I laughed. "Put me on that list."

He hit me in the shoulder. "Yeah, sure."

Hank always assumed I had more of a life than I did.

"I told you how I met her once, right?"

"Tell me."

"I guess it was her. A cleaning lady. Once, when I came looking for you."

"What happened?"

"She yelled at me—said you didn't entertain students at home."

"How'd she know?"

Hank laughed. "Maybe she didn't. It's just the way she thought it should be."

He read the names off the bright screen, along with my notations. "These guys are weak suspects. Wilcox and Safako."

"Weak professors make strong suspects." A little too glibly.

"Joshua Jennings?" he read out loud. "He's dead. You're listing men who are dead as suspects? He was a hundred years old, at least."

I looked up. "You knew him?"

"When I had work study in the library, he'd hobble in, ask for books we didn't have."

"Maybe you'd misplaced them."

He laughed. "Such a list you have, Rick. People with dirty houses. Dead people." He leaned over me and tapped the

keyboard. Awkward spelling and spacing: "Rikl vamn Lamm."
He pointed. "She cleaned your apartment, too." He grinned.

But then he watched as I made some notes about Karen's
brother, Davey Corcoran, as well as Karen's holding back info
about the insurance policy.

"Think she did it?"

I pressed the "save" key and stood up, stretched. My plans
for a quiet evening at home—alone—were gone. The Jonathan
Kellerman novel sat unread on the nightstand. I punched Hank
to move him out of the way. I wanted to get away from the
screen—and the Marta case. While his company was especially
welcome when I did my tedious and methodical fraud or divorce
investigations—he was great at those long, tedious stakeouts,
scouting out bathrooms, sitting in a car with his phones and
tablets and Twitter feeds, with stale tuna sandwiches on whole
wheat and lots of juvenile humor—a young man who could
sniff out a Dunkin' Donuts from a half-mile away—I had some
reservations about drawing him into a murder case. Of course,
I told myself, I'd already *done* that.

I was always afraid he might get hurt.

Fraud investigation could involve playful strategy, much
like a board game. Hank, ever inventive and resourceful, was a
pleasure to be with. But of necessity and legally he had to stay
on the fringes of my investigations. I had the license—he didn't.
I thought of Joshua Jennings' love of James Fenimore Cooper—I
was Natty Bumppo and Hank was Chingachgook, the Indian
sidekick. Or, as Mark Twain said, we should call him "Chicago."
If Marta was murdered, I didn't want Hank to be in the thick
of it. This case was much more than people secreting ill-gained
money in phony accounts, or people lying about debilitating
injuries to get a measly couple thou from Aetna Insurance. This
was murder. Maybe. I didn't want him to get too close to it.

"Let's go out for a walk," I said.

We headed to Zeke's Olde Tavern a few blocks west of the
town green, about a half-mile from my house. It was surprisingly
windy, the hard night air heavy and wet against our faces. The

streetlights sparkled brilliantly through the last of the translucent yellow and orange leaves stubbornly clinging to the maple trees. I pulled my jacket tighter around my neck. Winter was coming in. It was still early November but the smell and feel were there. Someone was burning wood in a fireplace. The acrid scent tantalized. I shivered.

Hank was dressed—as he would have said himself—for the Alaskan tundra by way of some trendy mall outlet. He'd gone to his car to retrieve a thick woolly parka, a ferocious wool scarf, and a Boston Red Sox baseball cap pulled tight and backwards, hip-hop style, over his forehead. He didn't look chilled at all. The slight boy inside was nowhere to be seen.

Tucked into an old mahogany booth, age-stained and jack-knife hewn, beer marinated, with lovers' initials and dates overlapping and disappearing into the grainy shellac, we quietly sipped long-necked Buds.

"I used to come here years ago," Hank told me.

"When?" I asked.

"College."

"You weren't twenty-one."

"Like that stops anyone these days."

It was a quiet weeknight. Just the usual town drunks, some late-night college kids with bogus IDs—Hank's casual observation—and unhappy husbands and wives. The bar had an awkward mix of town and gown, with the locals hating the college kids who in turn mocked the locals. It had vintage mahogany high-back booths, with original tables with scratched-in graffiti dating back to 1900. But as the elegant mahogany stools at the bar wore out, they were replaced with shoddy plastic-covered ones, stools that clashed with the old-world feel of the place. Sometimes the owners introduced plants—real ones—but within the month they died of inattention. Every so often a local got drunk and was thrown out—then the college kids applauded. When a college kid got ousted, the locals raised their beer steins in salute. It was that kind of a place. Tonight there were a couple of barflies, that's all, the kind with no flesh left on their frames, too much fear in their eyes.

"By the way," Hank began, "my mother says for you to stop over. You haven't dropped in for some time. Maybe Sunday morning?"

I smiled. "She making *mi ga*?"

Hank laughed. "You got it. Your favorite." The Vietnamese chicken soup. His mother's version was about as savory as possible, a far cry from the bland versions I'd discovered in Vietnamese restaurants largely catering to white palates.

"I'll be there."

There was a time when I wouldn't have agreed so quickly to such an invitation. His mother is a sweet woman who accepted me immediately—but she tends to like everyone she meets. The grandmother dotes on me—a highly spiritual woman with her Buddhist prayers and ceremonies. But the men—well, his father fought for the American-Vietnamese forces, a topic he will discuss with me for hours at a time. When he gets drunk, which is often, he attacks the white in me. But the grandfather is the problem—he hates my mongrel guts. He doesn't want me in the house.

"I got to warn you, though," he confided, "my father's on a kick about the United States opening trade relations with Communist Vietnam."

"I won't mention it."

"He's gonna demand your opinion. Be careful."

"I'm always diplomatic."

"Yeah, right."

Hank's fingers circled the neck of the beer bottle. He started to peel off the moist label, flecking it into little balls of paper that dropped like sloppy hail around the base of the amber bottle. With his thumb and index finger he flicked the rolled-up balls of paper at me, like pellets from a gun. They shot across the table and careened off my chest.

"Are we back in grade school?" I asked him.

I had a second beer and munched on stale beer nuts. The Tavern, I swear, kept all munchies in back until suitably stale, then served them. Hank refused another beer. That oddly pleased me. Big brother Rick, all over again. Hank leaned over, speaking confidentially. "You want to know the name of your murderer?" A dramatic pause. "He's here."

Startled, I twisted my head, surveyed the bar as though I knew the culprit by sight.

"Behind the jukebox," Hank whispered. "He just walked in."

I peered through the dim light. I noticed a tall man nearly in shadows. Ken Rodman. I frowned as I turned back to Hank. He was grinning. Ken was the newest tenant on the third floor of my house, a decent-looking man in his early forties. He'd moved in three or four months back. In fact, Hank and I had helped him maneuver an ungainly sofa up the back stairs. Visiting that morning, Hank announced that he always had the bad luck of visiting places when sofas were being lifted up multiple flights of stairs. Though he seemed anxious that we leave, Ken had offered us diet Cokes as a reward. That was my last real contact with him. An insurance exec in Hartford, freshly divorced—Gracie's gossip. I'd since said only three or four words to him as we crossed on the stairwell or in the back parking lot. He drove a sleek black Audi that's always impeccably clean, inside and out. I knew that for a fact because I peered inside one time. I couldn't imagine he'd allow mismatched furniture in his apartment. No, unlike my eclectic lot of dubious origin, his came, I suspected, from some store where born-again bachelors shopped. Pier One, perhaps. Or the Pottery Barn. Everything Scandinavian and Euro teakwood and big off-white linen throw pillows. I shivered at the clinical thought.

Hank was smirking. "Your murderer."

"What the hell you talking about?"

Hank gave me a Huckleberry grin. "You know how you spend all that time typing Marta's cleaning clients into your laptop— your tidy list of possible suspects? Which, of course, includes you, probably the real murderer. I wouldn't be surprised."

I was impatient. "Yeah. What's your point? What are you trying to say?"

"Well, Rick, I know for a fact that Marta cleaned Ken's apartment at least once. I stopped by to see you and you weren't home, but Gracie told me Marta would be cleaning your apartment after she finished with Ken's. So he's your murderer."

I laughed at him. "I already know that." But I cringed—just how many people *did* Marta know? Karen had given me the short list of permanent weekly clients, the old professors Marta knew for years and had become friendly with. Everyone kept saying she didn't do it for the money, that she was loaded, but she certainly kept her dance card full. Have feather duster, will travel. The woman who returned to dust.

My list struck me as a little foolish. How many other cleaning jobs were there? How many possible connections did she make? Was there somebody out there whose apartment she had cleaned only once? Some maniac? Some—what? Motive, motive! Marta kept no orderly accounting of work done. Much of her pay was under the table anyway. She kept no appointment book at all.

Hank was stretching, scratching his head.

"But then again," he yawned, "maybe not."

I got ready to leave, fishing for my wallet.

I wasn't happy. Hank's jesting—he still kept nodding toward Ken Rodman—rankled. There just seemed too many paths now. I liked things orderly, logical. One of my professors at John Jay once lectured our class—a good detective likes things plain and simple, that's natural, but never expects to find things that way. That's because life is illogical—so annoyingly unnatural. Detectives have to sift through messy, random lives so that things become clear. Somewhere in the wet swamp of a murder scene there lies the dry island. A good detective swims to that land. I remember getting confused with all those metaphors and swimming directions, but the message was obvious. If you think you're going to find the murderer behind the first locked, obvious door, you should pursue a less predictable career. You'd have better luck on a TV game show. Door number one? Two?

Hank shoved me as we walked out the door. "Aren't you gonna cuff Ken?" His lips spread into a thin, cynical line. "He's already planning his next murder."

I looked back over my shoulder. In the dim shadows of the bar, Ken had spotted us. Taking a sip from his bottle, he turned away.

Chapter Ten

After midnight, lazy at my desk, my laptop humming, I stared numbly at my feeble list of suspects. Even the word *suspect* now seemed pretentious. Interviewees—that was better. How many more? Idly, I added Ken Rodman's name to the end of the list, most likely a throwaway gesture. Someone whose rooms she cleaned killed her—possibly. If murder it was…My fingers typed: "I understand a pesky Marta Kowalski cleaned your apartment one time. Did you murder her? Did she leave a particularly egregious dust ball that sent you into a fevered rage?" I highlighted the line and pressed *delete*.

It was late. I was punchy, humming with a slight buzz from the beer, a little annoyed at Hank and not certain exactly why, hazy with the uncertainties of the case. Standing up, I slipped off my shirt and rubbed my chest. I yawned. It was time for bed.

The phone rang. I glanced at the clock—nearly one in the morning. I debated letting the machine pick up because the caller ID indicated UNKNOWN, but at that hour the temptation was immediate and welcome.

At first the phone voice was faraway and small, almost indistinguishable, like a small child sputtering into the phone.

"Who is it?"

The rambling went on. A thick voice, a man's voice I could tell now, but a foggy one, as if something were stuck in his throat.

Nothing.

I was ready to hang up when I heard my name. My whole name. "Rick Van Lam." Said sarcastically in a singsong tone.

"Who's this?"

"Like you don't know."

Well, I didn't. So I waited. Someone knew my name, so the call was deliberate. My eyes half-shut with fatigue. I rubbed my chest as I settled into a chair. We waited, both of us, in silence, the sound of tinny laughter in the background. I guessed the caller was at a bar. I heard the twang of a country song playing on a jukebox, the clinking of glass against glass. Someone yelled, an indistinguishable slurring of words.

"It's Davey Corcoran." The voice spoke directly into the receiver, the words now clear and sharp, but spiked with sloppy anger. Davey Corcoran, calling from a last-call tavern, drunk out of his mind. Great, I thought. A good-night bedtime call, so much better than a lullaby.

"What's up?"

He laughed that phony laugh of bitter drunks, a rumble hearty yet cold and deadpan. A laugh with no soul. "You know what's up, man. I just want to tell you one thing." His words slurred into each other so that the effect was breathy and difficult to understand: *Ijuswannatellyaonethinnng*. Like that.

I waited. Silence. "Well..."

"Well, my sister got a fucking nerve hiring you to do this shit about my aunt. She leaves a note on my door, telling me you're gonna talk to me. I don't think you realize that this is a crock of bullshit."

"Davey, it's her money."

That laugh again. "It's my aunt's money."

"Davey..."

"Save the shit, Lam. Little sister sucked her way into that cash, and that's a fact. Not that I cared. Or even had a chance. Good old Marta had no use for me and..." He babbled on, again incoherent.

"Why?"

"Why what?"

"Why did she leave you out of the will?"

"That's not why I'm calling."

"Well, why are you calling?"

"I want this stopped. I don't want you bothering me—or anyone."

"If your aunt was murdered…"

He gasped. "Shit. It wasn't murder. Who'd wanna kill that old bitch?"

"Karen thinks…"

He cut in, furious. "Let me tell you something about little sister. Karen's not the pretty little thing that gets you all itchy between your legs, Lam boy. I know how she works around guys. She always got her way. She hated my aunt—Christ, how could she *not* hate that witch?—but she put up with her shit because she knew I wouldn't. I don't know what this game of hers is, but I want you to think about one thing." A long pause. "You listening?"

"Yeah."

I heard the jukebox music stop. I heard glasses tinkling, someone yelling a man's name.

"She's crazy. I don't mean she's, you know, like, just funny crazy. Oh, that Karen—how wacky. I mean she's certifiable. I don't mean she hears voices and stuff"—he started to laugh again—"but she gets real depressed, and—well, she's nuts. Psychiatrists run away from her, you know. We both belong in a ward. She's cut from the same crazy quilt as dear old Marta." His voice got mean now, gravelly, rich with venom.

"What's that gotta do with your aunt's death?"

"I never said it did."

"Then…"

"Then nothing. I'm just warning you that she and I are not close, and I don't give a fuck about my aunt's money. I don't want you pointing a finger at me, hear? All this talk about duty and respect for Aunt Marta. I don't know what her game is—if there is a game—but she's living in her own little world sometimes…"

"Why didn't your aunt like you?"

He laughed a long time. "Because I once wished the old bitch would die a mean and horrible death."

"Davey, tomorrow morning—if it's okay—I'd like to come to see you before work, and…"

"And I got my wish," he ran on. "A mean and horrible death. Who said there isn't a God?" He hung up.

Chapter Eleven

I had a fitful sleep, nearly toppling out of bed more than once, waking in a sweat, so in the morning I jogged a solid mile or so in the fierce chill before I headed to Davey's apartment. I knew he clerked in an upscale garden shop on the outskirts of the town—a glossy-brochure nursery with pampered potted plants and color-coded Italian patio tile and biodegradable fertilizer for the weekend farmers of town. I wanted to catch him before he left for work, though I didn't know whether he'd let me in—or, in fact, even remember his drunken phone call. His conversation had been unsettling, and I'd dreamed of falling into a jukebox all night, or having it fall onto me, one of those noisy, multi-colored affairs with circus bells and clanging, carnival hoopla—a combination jukebox and pinball machine that kept attacking me. Somewhere on the boundaries of that quirky nightmare was Davey—nasty, sloe-eyed, puffed up and bloated, and I swear I dreamed the smell of alcohol.

I ran and ran, nodded to strangers on my street, enjoying the crisp, clear morning. My breath hung in the air before me like a cloud I ran through, while the sun shone brightly through the skeletal trees, stringy shafts of light, a sky of shimmering birthday party favors. And then I showered, long and hard. My head was clear.

When he answered the door around nine, he was still unshaven, dressed in his underwear—large boxer shorts that had tropical palm trees on them. His T-shirt announced the superiority of left-handed people.

"I told you I was coming before you left for work."

"I should've baked a cake?"

But he was smiling, not some joyous grin, more a cynical slit of humor, the look of someone pleased with himself.

"Funny guy."

"That's why I'm so loved in this little Puritan village."

"Can I come in?"

He half-bowed, mockingly, and I walked past him. "I suppose the only way I'll end my sister's curious obsession is to entertain the questions of her newest boyfriend."

That remark stopped me. "Boyfriend?"

"Not yet? My, my, she's slow. I guess grief has a way of slowing or tempering the body's fires. Or is it money?"

While he talked, he left the room, and I could hear him muttering from another room, drawers opening and closing. He hadn't closed the door, and at one point he glared out at me, the look on his face suggesting he didn't know he had a visitor. He emerged dressed in a plaid flannel shirt and creased jeans, the urban gardener ready for labor, and I realized he'd be going to work unshaven. I supposed it fit his image. The better to sell plaster-of-Paris lawn cherubs to suburban homesteaders, though perhaps, given the season, he'd be selling more—what?—more designer rakes and tulip bulbs from Holland? Half-priced Halloween pumpkins and fresh Christmas grave blankets? The mysteries of outdoor pastoral life.

Davey was different from the image I'd created last night. Of course, he was sober now, but with his seedy, craggy look, he resembled someone who liked the bars too much.

While he was dressing, I surveyed the small, cramped living room. Stacks of paperback books and magazines and newspapers cluttered the room. The *New York Times*, tied in bundles with clothesline rope, rested on the floor. There was accumulation everywhere, stacks of magazines lying under piles of clothing, unwashed heaps of T-shirts and trousers and socks, everything intermingled. He lived a slovenly life, to be sure. Even the few chairs were heaped with unopened mail, junk mail, flyers, brochures hawking sales at retail outlets. Seed catalogs from Burpee's. Sears catalogs. The Home Depot. Lowe's. Barnes and Noble. Did the man throw anything out?

He pushed some papers off a chair and motioned toward it, a grin on his face.

"I live like a packrat, but not always. Things got ahead of me. I spend my days clerking for the rich and at night I read."

"What do you read?"

I removed a stack of catalogues from a fifties-style kitchen chair, all cherry-red vinyl and chrome—and sat down.

"I read everything. It's a bad habit school gave me. Give a kid *Treasure Island*, and he's yours for life." He folded his arms over his chest. "But you're not here to survey the reading tastes of the American loner." A quicksilver smile. "Or, if I read your mind correctly, the American loser. Some article you'll someday write about the predilections—literary or otherwise—of the incipient serial killer."

Abruptly, he swept books off a chair, pushing them onto a littered floor, sat down, and stared straight into my face. Four feet away from me, he made eye contact. Not pleasant. I knew he was attempting to be amusing, his voice was high and animated, his sentences ending with a slight laugh. But he was jittery and unhappy. A thin line of sweat appeared above his thick eyebrows, and the corners of his full mouth were moist. Occasionally he flicked his tongue nervously to taste the escaping saliva, swallowing, and I thought of animals I'd seen doing the same thing on the Discovery Channel.

"Why'd you call last night?"

He sighed, closed his eyes, then smiled. "I have some trouble with demon rum, I have to admit. I was sitting on a bar stool and thought of Karen—we don't talk, you know, a few words now and then—and how she left me that note about you and her lamebrain theories of murder—well, I was thinking about that as I downed one more shot, and I got mad. I get awful mad when I'm drunk." A sly grin. "You really should have an unlisted number."

He couldn't sit still, so he disappeared into the kitchen, muttering about coffee. He emerged with two cups of ready-made coffee, put one in front of me. I don't drink coffee without plenty of milk, so I left it there, untouched. I didn't want it anyway. A grimy cup in a disorderly place.

As he walked back into the room, I noticed how big he was—a huge shock of a man—and the word that came to mind immediately was fleshy. Fleshy—just that. It wasn't solely the puffiness around the eyes, or the bloated lips, or the creased brow—clearly the remnants of last night's drinking spree. Instead, it was the ungainliness, a sort of *lumpen* physique, that of a roly-poly TV buffoon who liked wine and whiskey and Necco wafers. The pinkish baby-face glow of his skin suggested softness, but his languid moves across the room made me think that he had a layer of water moving beneath the surface of his skin. He was blond and blue-eyed, with a wide peculiarly handsome face—but what I noticed was the sheer bulk of him. A package seeping at the corners. He was worlds apart from his slender, wispy sister.

"I gotta leave in a few minutes." He put down his cup. I noticed he'd drained it in one long gulp.

"Tell me what you think."

"Actually I summed it up fairly well while plastered on the phone." He grinned, but I detected a flash of fire in the eyes, anger in the tight corners of his mouth.

"And?"

"And—well, I was mad when I didn't get any money from my beloved aunt, but I wasn't surprised. We didn't talk for a long, long time. She hated me—my life." He waved his hand around the cluttered room. "I didn't see her for months. I mean, I saw her around town, but she snubbed me in that wonderful Victorian way people in Farmington sometimes affect. Like they think they're characters in a Henry James novel or something. Anyway, we didn't talk…"

"Why?"

He shrugged his shoulders, and I knew he wouldn't answer. "There has to be a reason."

"Maybe only in her goddamned mind. She said I was a failure, you know. Working as a clerk. Dropping out of Trinity in my junior year. Living in this less-than-desirable part of town." He kept going, but he wasn't looking at me. He was lying, repeating some fashioned fabrication he'd used before. He took a deep breath. "I didn't even attend the funeral."

"Yeah?"

He narrowed his eyes. "Am I a suspect in her suicide—I mean—murder?"

"You had motive."

"A motive?"

"She left you no money."

He burst out laughing, but it was humorless. His mouth went slack. "That's not motive enough for me. If I wanted money, would I be living like this?"

"But you're still angry."

A long silence. Then he spat out words. "Well, of course, but it's not about the money. Although, as Karen probably told you, I did consider contesting. I was—and am—mad about the very existence of that wretched woman. You see, I didn't *like* her. At all. I know she took us in when our parents died. I give her *that* bit of familial duty. But Christ, she never let us forget it either. 'You'd be out on the streets if I didn't take you in. Foster care—starved, beaten.' How about loved? The missing equation. Tell you the truth, there must have been insurance money from dear old Mom and Dad. She got that. We never heard about that. The woman had very little love in her."

"I'm sorry. Children should be loved."

He eyed me. "Did you hear that on Dr. Phil's infomercial?"

"All I'm saying…"

He yelled out, "I'm angry that she is still in my life, even though she's dead and buried. That's why I called last night. I'm mad because Karen won't let her stay dead. The fact that you're sitting here right now proves it. I can't escape the bitch."

"So you don't think it's murder?" Without thinking I sipped the coffee. My fingers had been around the handle and stupidly I raised the cup. I swallowed stale black coffee, lukewarm and filmy. Davey was watching me as I dribbled it back into the cup. I was not the gracious guest. The good nuns of my childhood would have frowned.

"That good, huh?" He grinned. "Well, to answer your question, frankly no. I have to tell you I was surprised at the suicide. Marta was too greedy to take her own life. I mean, she sucked in other people's energy—she hungered for sensation and life in the most obvious way. Especially after her husband died, that poor bastard, happily free of her, though his early death I think was his escape clause in a bad marriage. No, Marta wanted to live forever."

"But do you think she killed herself?"

"Yes."

"Even though she was a Catholic?"

"She was depressed. Karen said so. Being Catholic got pushed to the back burner maybe."

"Meaning?"

"Catholics kill themselves, Lam boy. I repeat. She was depressed."

"Or so Karen said."

He nodded, smiled. "Depression with a capital D."

"Why?"

"She must have wanted something that she couldn't have. I suspect it was genteel respectability on the arm of Joshua Jennings. The poor Catholic girl hungry for the patrician Yankee. Whatever it was, it was enough to allow her to kill herself. She always got what she wanted."

"But Karen said you were close to her for a long time. She told me you were her golden boy. You and she—religious, going to Mass."

He shook his head. "That was a while ago."

"What happened?"

"She was—unforgiving."

"Of what?"

A long pause. "I told you—failure."

Davey was sailing through his words, singing them out in a practiced voice, but suddenly the head stopped moving as his eyes focused on something behind me. I turned my head but he rustled in the chair, standing up.

"I have to leave now." He dismissed me. "It's getting late."

"One last question. You said Karen is unbalanced...."

Nervous, he waved his hand. "Ask her about the pills she takes for depression. Her own suicide attempt in high school. We Corcorans are not the most stable people. Marta fashioned her into a pesky prig, a little Miss Puritan of Farmington High. Then she let loose, all systems go. She learned about medication. You know, after Mommy and Daddy bought lunch in the interstate pileup, little Davey and Karen lost their way on the path to Auntie's house."

"You enjoy mentioning Karen and her pills."

"I'm giving you clues, Lam boy."

"To what?"

"To why you're wasting everyone's time and money."

"It's Karen's time and money."

He motioned me up from the chair.

"Karen does seem ambivalent about your aunt, Davey. I grant you that."

He laughed. "How perceptive of you. Most of Karen's conversations with me started out—'I had lunch with Aunt Marta today, and she said my lipstick was too bright.' Or, 'I had lunch with Aunt Marta today, and she said I'm drifting.' Ambivalent, huh? No flies on you, Lam boy."

"You can love..."

"Let me sum up my sister for you. Karen runs from everything while she actually believes she is running toward it." He pointed to the door.

I wasn't ready to leave so I resorted to a pathetic ruse. "Can I use the john?"

He looked ready to say no, but hesitated, pointing behind him. But when I went into the tight room, I saw an unflushed toilet, clumps of hair circling the sink drain, the smell of cigarettes and whiskey pervasive. I turned back in time to see Davey hovering in that spot behind where I'd been sitting, tucking something under a pile of magazines. He caught me looking at him, his hands still holding something, and he grinned sheepishly.

He rushed to open the door for me, silent now and frowning. I walked by him and started to say something—to thank him?—but he leaned into me. I smelled whiskey and stale vomit, curiously mixed with some cheap drugstore cologne.

"Please don't come back. Next time I won't be the happy host. You won't even get a cup of bad coffee."

Chapter Twelve

Sitting in my car, I called Richard Wilcox, the last man known to speak with Marta. A retired professor, many years retired in fact, he occasionally wandered through the college hallways, visiting his old department and noisily decrying the rising illiteracy of the newer generations. He was heard to mumble something about Generation X one day as he stood in line in the library and was ill-treated by a mohawk-shaved, blue-haired, heavily tattooed, earring-clad kid. His remark—"X is how they sign their student stipends"—gained instant notoriety among the junior faculty.

He was, he would tell you immediately—an essentialist, though I had no idea what that was. Of course, your puzzled expression allowed him to explain. "An essentialist is one who believes there are certain essentials every student must learn." Those essentials, I learned, did not include my specialty of Criminal Justice—or the newer departments of Business Administration or Computer Technology—programs the failing liberal-arts college quietly established to ensure its life in the new century. Old Richard Wilcox and I had nodded at faculty gatherings, but I always had the feeling he was New England xenophobic—somehow Asians had no place among his sheltered ivied walls.

He was hard of hearing so I had to raise my voice and speak slowly. He kept saying no no no—"No, I'm busy, no, I have no interest"—until I connected the words "Marta" and "murder." He stopped and I heard asthmatic wheezing, a shortness of breath.

"I can see you briefly, young man. I've become ill and need to go to John Dempsey for a checkup at twelve. Come at eleven, and leave by eleven-thirty."

He hung up without saying good-bye.

I waited the dead time at a McDonald's, savoring real coffee, Paul Newman's, in fact, with milk, hot and tasty. I extracted my Mac from the shoulder carryall and set up shop in a corner booth near some old codgers who all knew one another and were territorial about their seats. While I typed in my notes on Davey, including a few suspicions about what he was hiding in that rising tide of yellowing pulp newsprint, a youngster, standing in the next booth, peered over at my machine, burping into my ear. Now and then he'd hiccough and spittle would fall onto my shoulder, so I shifted my position. He kept blinking at the screen and my busy, fast-moving fingers. Finally I asked the mother to remove him from my soggy shoulder, and she got indignant.

"He ain't bothering nobody."

The kid dropped back into his seat, punched his toddler sister, and for some reason, glancing a moment at the two little fidgeting kids, I zeroed in on Karen and Davey, two orphaned children under the autocratic control of Marta.

◇◇◇

When I arrived at Wilcox's condo, the front door was open a crack. I tapped on the door and he mumbled, "It's open," his voice thick.

He was sitting at a small card table near the kitchenette, dressed in an old-style narrow-lapeled suit and tie, an overcoat draped over his shoulders, an overnight bag by his feet. When he told me he'd be leaving for the hospital, he wasn't fooling.

His condo was a sad fifties apartment-complex-turned-condo—tiny rooms with no moldings or sills. Square, institutional windows overlooked Dumpster-lined parking lots. I was surprised to find an old retired professor there, but perhaps he had no money. I knew the pension he'd get from the college was minimal, but still…Well, no matter. He'd lined the narrow walls with deep bookcases and the effect was pleasant, if claustrophobic. Scanning the walls told me he'd been an economics professor in his glory days. After all, how many other people maintain a shelf—near the living room door and in my sight line—containing at least ten different editions of Adam Smith's *The Wealth of Nations*, paperback to hardcover?

He was rushed. "Sit down, sit down. Make this fast. The taxi is coming shortly. This is all foolishness."

I sat across from him at the card table as though getting into position to deal a hand of bridge. A nervous, birdlike man, pale jaundiced flesh on tiny bones, a speckle of a man, someone near seventy or older. It was hard to tell his age because he seemed so frail, anxious, jittery, constantly looking toward the door.

"You okay?"

He ran his tongue over his upper lip. "At my age when I go into the hospital I fear I'll never come out. This is overnight, but I fear it's the cancer coming at me."

"I'm sorry. You have cancer?"

He gave me a slight, bitter smile. "We'll find out, won't we? I am tired, tired all the time. Tired. Weak. And sometimes, lying in my hot sweaty bed, I know it's cancer. Sometimes you don't need a doctor to tell you what the soul already knows. You wake up feeling hollowness in your bones, emptiness in your blood vessels. You know it."

Through most of this he didn't look at me, but at the end of the declaration—for that's how it came across—he stared directly into my face. "I've seen you around. At the college. One of the new people." He glanced toward the door.

"I'll hear the taxi," I said helpfully, but he glared at me. "If you want, I can drive you to the hospital."

He shook his head back and forth. "Oh, no. They *know* me." Again he checked the doorway. "It's amazing that I think of nothing but dying since my doctor suggested I go into the hospital for this battery of tests. I've always fought against negative notions." He chuckled. "You probably find that amusing coming from an economist. We live our lives sugarcoating depression and recession and…" He stopped. "Talk quickly about Marta."

I told him what I was doing, but he got impatient halfway through my explanation, causing me to stop, wave my hand emptily in the air, and wait for him to say something.

He rolled his eyes. "I'll tell you what I know so you can put an end to this madcap adventure of yours, young man. First of all, people like us do not commit murder—nor do we know people who do so. Marta once told me that Karen—a niece she dearly loved, I tell you, and constantly did for—was given to fantasy, imaginings, the preposterous gesture. Marta was not murdered. Her suicide was, if anything, unfortunate."

"Unfortunate?"

"I've given this a lot of thought. Obviously. We were very close, she and I. We talked like old and cherished friends. I say unfortunate because, well, I think she didn't *plan* it. I think it came upon her almost as a whim, although whim is an—unfortunate word here."

"But she was depressed, possibly clinically."

He waved away my comment. "We all are when we get past sixty, young man. Some at fifty. I started at forty." He chuckled. "We've just gone emphatically over the top of the roller coaster. Dame Fortune's wheel." He started to rise, thought better of it, but his eyes fixed on the front door.

I pushed. "But we're talking extreme depression here, maybe so severe that…"

That wave again. "She was deeply depressed because of the death of another friend of ours, Joshua Jennings. They were extremely close. He got really old fast—he'd fallen in his big old house, feared his staircase—and he moved away. She had trouble with that. They hadn't been talking for some stupid reason—she never would tell me what it was—and then he up and died. A great-niece tended to his last days. Death is something old people do." He smiled. "I may indulge myself shortly."

"Any idea why they had a falling out?"

"No, but it must have been a lulu."

"Why?"

"Marta gabbed about everything. If she refused to talk, you knew it was something really serious."

"But then he died."

"I must say, his death seemed to really haunt her, because they hadn't stayed friends. He died out of state, and she never, well, she never said good-bye. Sad."

"Did she tell you this?"

"In so many words." He looked to the door, looked down to check on the tidy overnight bag. He touched it possessively, and then looked at me. "We talked of his death and she was sad. So was I. He'd been my friend, too."

"But depressed enough to kill herself?"

He pressed both hands together, closed his eyes and sighed. When he spoke again, his voice was less affected. "That's the strange part. I didn't think so. That's why I say it was whim. Whim."

I echoed his word. "Whim?"

"Yes. She was walking to my home that night—we'd spoken over the phone earlier—and I think it all came together as she crossed the bridge over the river."

"What came together?"

"The death of Joshua, my increasing weakness—I could do less and less—her own aging, her unhappiness with her pathetic nephew, her reservations about her niece—two ungrateful children, really—and the first chill of autumn. The approach of winter. That would make me kill myself. And she'd been drinking a little too much as the result of all of this. I could barely understand her on the phone. I think she approached that final bridge and caught her breath, looked over to my apartment in the distance, and just let herself fall."

"But she'd told you she was coming over. She wanted to see you."

Richard scratched his neck. I noticed loose dangling flesh, a chicken's jowls, flapping back and forth.

"That's the strange part. We talked on the phone, but briefly, unexpectedly. It was a Sunday, and Sundays are bleak, unreal days for people like us. Killer days. I said come over, she said no, and then, later on, she called and said she would walk over.

But she was panicky, her voice so low I could hardly hear her. She was drunk—never a very attractive side of her, I must say, but she also seemed scared."

"Scared that someone was going to kill her?"

Richard started laughing, then stopped, coughing and choking. He composed himself. "My Lord, you young people watch too many TV shows. No, I just think she was afraid of being alone that afternoon."

"But you said she was scared."

"My interpretation. That's all."

He seemed so frozen, sitting still, packaged for the road, that I needed to move. As I wandered to his bookshelves, he watched me closely. There were no personal photographs in the room. Book-lined shelves, regimented and ordered, and heavy, unattractive furniture hugged the corners of the room. Without the books there would be no personality here. But no popular books, no novels, no magazines. No flashy dust jackets. No, everything had the utter seriousness of an old-time college professor's office and library.

Wilcox followed my movements, my fingers on a dusty book jacket.

"My books miss Marta's adroit cleaning touch. I'm forced to employ an agency that has no love for books. Marta loved the old volumes. She loved my old books."

"That's right," I said, "she was your cleaning lady."

He bristled. "Young man, Marta was hardly anyone's *cleaning* lady in any conventional sense. True, she cleaned houses, but she chose her clientele carefully after her retirement. She didn't need the money, you see. And so she cleaned friends' houses...."

"She cleaned mine," I interrupted, sitting back down.

Wilcox looked angry, whether at the idea of her helping me or at my interruption, I couldn't tell.

"She liked to keep her hand at it, she told me. Cleaning, for Marta, was really part of the social life she maintained with three or four of us. Marta was a serious, careful woman, true, a woman given to inexplicable biases and hardheaded attitudes. Some so childlike—maybe I should say childish—that she came off as charmingly…primitive. Straightlaced, as it were. But, you see, I find myself smiling when I think about it. She was a woman who liked the company of sparkling, intelligent men. I say this selfishly, because I was one of the chosen."

His long reverie had a dreaminess about it that made me fidget. I recalled a junior faculty member referring to Wilcox as a sterile little man. At the time I thought it a cruel, unnecessary remark.

Silence, long and deadly. He smiled mischievously. "You'll discover that Marta loved the company of men. I'm sure you'll discover this as you violate her life. She had little use for the cattiness and foolishness of women her age. One friend, a dreadful boor named Hattie. Doubtless you know that. But Marta, well, I guess you'd say she shone around men. She radiated. She simply liked our company. Now there's nothing scandalous in this, I hope you realize, but simply affection—yes, that's the word—affection, genuine and real and true, for the company of men. That, my young man, is why she cleaned apartments, as you call it. That's probably why she cleaned *yours*." He was grinning now.

"So you were companions, social friends, or…?"

"I looked forward to her visits. I'm alone most of the time. We'd chat and we'd walk for lunch, and she'd entertain me with her nonsensical stories of Atlantic City and slot machines and Don Rickles shows. It was all very amusing. I couldn't stop her once she began."

"That sounds patronizing."

His eyes became steady. "You don't understand."

"Help me."

"We *liked* each other."

There were sounds coming from the street. I talked faster. "You mentioned Marta's problems with her nephew Davey Corcoran?"

He grimaced. "A loser. But I never met him, to tell you the truth. Marta insisted he was charming and handsome in his early days. I told her we were all charming and handsome in our early days." He chuckled. "But they were close back when. Years back. He wrestled with bouts of extreme Catholicism. In and out of church. Madness, really. A zealot, then one who lapsed. He drove her places, flattered her, you know, that sort of thing. But something happened. She wouldn't tell me but I do know that she refused to mention his name. One time I mentioned him and she stormed away, didn't even stay for lunch."

"How'd you meet her?"

He smiled. "I'd seen her around, of course. A woman who liked to be looked at. This is a small town, you know, and I saw her at the college when she worked on the housekeeping staff. I came to know her when we all went on that trip the college sponsored to Russia in 2003."

"You went?" I was surprised. I'd spotted the brochure at Marta's home.

"So many of us from the college went. Joshua Jennings, in fact. That's when he met her. It's when all of us discovered Marta's charming personality. Her gift of—vignette. We had a great time. A bunch of old professors—and Marta. Some students, of course, but God knows what they did." He pointed to one of the cabinets across the room, an elaborate oriental lacquered chest. I walked up to it. One small, almost hidden shelf had a few items spread about, randomly: a black enamel box with a painting of peasants at a well, a white-gold pin shaped like a white-birch tree, a Russian Orthodox icon of Jesus on the cross. Even a tarnished school medal of Lenin. It was a tourist's travel bag of goodies. I reached for the icon.

"Don't touch anything," he yelled. "I saved those idiotic mementos because I am reminded of our beautiful trip, which was also my last one. At one time I traveled a lot."

"Was there any tension on that trip—I mean all you gentlemen and Marta?"

He ignored me, so I shifted questions.

"You mentioned that she and Joshua Jennings had a falling out."

His tongue licked the corner of his mouth and then disappeared. "I don't know what about." Said deliberately, harshly.

"I don't believe you."

The veins on the back of his skinny, speckled hands popped up. His eyes got darker, the craggy face murkier. "That's rude, young man."

Persistent, I corrected, "You must have thought about it."

And then, his eyes closed tight, he talked quietly, circling and recircling his words, bobbing his head into his chest, swallowing his words. "I don't know what happened but I often guessed and when I asked her—point-blankly one day—she got curt and left early. When I asked Joshua, he babbled about her cruelty to a Spanish gardener or something…or a garden man…I don't know. Joshua Jennings was my friend but too—too what? Too manipulative. He flattered her as much as she him. I think she was dazzled by his old money and old New England name and his aristocratic background. He was a snob, but to her it seemed like polish. She was, after all, a little Irish girl who married a Polish nobody. I believe she pressured him for something and he got scared, inveterate old bachelor that he was…"

"Do you think she wanted marriage?"

"With that old bastard?" He looked up at me. "I don't know and I don't care what happened, but I know something happened and I bet she was the instigator. She probably envisioned herself the mistress of the manor. Foolish, no? She drove him out of state, I bet, because she could be forever at you, at you, pressuring you. She was a driven woman when she wanted something. She wouldn't let go of something. Sometimes you wanted to shake her…" He stopped, stunned by his own words, and trembled.

He stared into my face.

"She liked me," he said finally.

"But she didn't like you enough?"

Now he looked at me, his glare hard. "I couldn't understand it." He sounded bewildered. "Not as much as I liked her. But that was true for all of us."

"What do you mean?"

"She started to withdraw," he said. "I'd call and call, and she'd eventually show up. But"—now the words were spoken through tight lips—"she was into other things. Her words: 'into other things.' Things—like I was a thing." His index finger curled around the arm of the chair, and the skin, already pasty white, became translucent.

"What other things?"

"I never found out."

I leaned in closer, bringing my face near his. I was fascinated that this man could move through such a range of attitudes toward Marta in such a small space of time—all the while slumped in that hardback chair, the heavy overcoat slung neatly over his shoulders. He was still talking. Marta had treated him cruelly in the final days. She'd been beautiful and loving and wonderful and funny and sweet. But all this anger was whispered now, his voice scarcely raised, the quiet in the room still there, the muffled street sounds wafting in, as I watched a man waffle back and forth between love and anger. Here, I thought, was an old man who'd been left, felt betrayed, who still loved and was still confused. But as I watched him I realized it would be impossible for this man, so weak, so tired and skinny, to have murdered the robust, lively Marta.

At that moment, in the silence when neither of us spoke, a taxi blared its shrill horn, and we both jumped, startled out of the dim oppressive silence.

"My taxi," he roared. "Out." He pointed. He jumped up, grabbed his overnight case, and pushed me out the door.

As I watched him rush to the waiting taxi, striding ahead of me with sure steps, I revised my simplistic reading of him as feeble and delicate. Here was a man whose moves were deliberate and forceful. The taxi had already pulled away by the time I made it to the sidewalk. Richard Wilcox only looked fragile seated in a gray room. When he had to move, he moved.

Chapter Thirteen

Karen and I met for lunch at a small Vietnamese eatery in the South End of Hartford, a tiny place tucked between an over-stocked Asian grocery and a raucous karaoke club that specialized in top-forty American pop songs sung in Vietnamese. Slick-haired New Wave Vietnamese gang boys sang Lady Gaga and Robin Thicke to their pouting girlfriends. Hank first brought me to the restaurant, where he proceeded to "re-educate" my Vietnamese taste buds, as he termed it. I went there a lot. I suggested it to Karen when she told me she had to be in Hartford for an appointment later that afternoon.

I arrived at twelve and she was already there. I spotted her standing outside the restaurant as I pulled into the lot. Above her head the flashing neon sign read Pho Saigon, and near the door a half dozen little Asian kids played leapfrog with one another, toppling over, bumping, blocking the doorway. Giddy teenaged Asian boys in hip-hop jeans and buzz cuts over blank mocking faces watched everyone. Karen looked nervous, standing there, the little kids brushing her dress, oblivious, weaving around her, their high-pitched mixture of English and Vietnamese jarring and shrill. When she saw me she smiled.

"I've never eaten Vietnamese food."

"I'm your guide." I bowed.

Inside, under a garish overhead light, with the discount store streamers and the gaudy dragon-etched mirrors on stuccoed walls, we tucked ourselves into a booth, and she immediately started fiddling with chopsticks. She was nervous.

"Relax. We're no longer at war."

"I'm not nervous about being here," she said, a little angry. "I'm just nervous about what you have to tell me."

Now I laughed. "Well, we can both relax. I have nothing to tell you yet."

"Nothing?"

"At least nothing along the lines warranted by your generous retainer."

She looked disappointed. But she smiled, sipping the tea that the waiter placed before her. "Good tea."

I smiled. "Buddha says, when you are weak, drink tea."

"He actually said that?"

"Yes."

I ordered bowls of spicy *bun* for both of us, a traditional dish of diced spring roll, thin barbecued pork strips, served over cellophane vermicelli noodles, with a slight hint of mint, basil, enhanced by fiery *nuoc mam* sauce. And I ordered hot French-style Vietnamese coffee, the vaguely cloying concoction with sweetened condensed milk. I loved the smells wafting through the place. At a rear table another waiter named Diep was dicing two-foot shafts of aromatic lemongrass.

While we drank steamy crab and asparagus soup—compliments of the house—I filled Karen in on my activities. The case was too new, I told her. I'd wanted to have lunch because I really wanted to ask *her* questions.

"Karen, I'm having trouble getting a clear-cut picture of your aunt."

"Why?"

"I mean, I knew her as this sweet, older woman, you know, unremarkably middle class, neat as a pin, tidy, with an old lady's blue-tinted permanent, and sensible shoes. A little nosy, yes—judgmental. A—well, cleaning lady."

"She was that." An edge to her voice.

"But Davey portrays her as an intrusive monster, cold and unyielding. You paint her as a nice average aunt, a woman who liked Atlantic City and church. But I sense you had your own problems with her—you loved her, yet you were annoyed by her control."

Karen looked hurt, drumming the table with chopsticks. "She *was* those things. Nobody is just one thing. You know that. What are you saying?"

"If we're talking murder, she had to be something else. Something about her had to trigger murderous intent in someone. Someone willing to *murder* her—possibly to be caught."

She bit her lower lip. "That's true." Said too quietly. "But that's what *you* have to find out. So what's the problem?" Her voice became clipped, brittle.

"Well," I breathed in slowly, "I had a talk with Richard Wilcox and he described her as—well, a woman who liked the company of men. That's how he put it. An aged *femme fatale* running around with a bottle of Windex. She seemed to like her good times…"

Karen cut me off. "Yes, I know that about her. She could be flirtatious and a little forward sometimes. Sort of embarrassing in an old lady, true. She enjoyed dancing and parties. We *talked* about it, she and I. She wanted *me* to go out more to meet people. It was all innocent. After all, a woman her age…"

"But even at her age she wanted companionship. Nothing wrong with that. Maybe a little romance. A liaison." The words stuck in my throat. I pictured Marta scooting around my apartment with a vacuum cleaner. "She could still have wanted a relationship. Did she have one after her husband died?"

A pause while she sipped tepid tea, her hand circling the small cup. "Not that I knew of. Actually we didn't talk about things like that. Anything real personal. We *avoided* stuff like that. It came up now and then, almost by accident."

"What do you mean—by accident?"

"Well, I know that she'd have these little tiffs with the men she worked for."

"Tiffs?"

"She'd get into a snit if she didn't get the right amount of attention, I think. They were all jealous of each other, all those old men. She liked the attention of men."

"Wilcox said she could be mean-spirited and hard."

She nodded, agreeing. "It had to do with Joshua. Everything always came back to Joshua, the old professor." She sat back, sucked in her breath. "Something happened during her last year. I mean she always talked about those old guys in the same way—revered men, educated men who liked her—but suddenly she focused exclusively on Joshua. It was Joshua this and Joshua that. You know. It got a little embarrassing. And scary, I thought."

"Scary?"

"After all, Joshua was eighty maybe. Maybe older. A decade older than her. I know she found him charming and man-nerly—you know. She wanted to be part of that world. He was old guard, old-fashioned prep school finish. Farmington WASP to the nth degree."

"But why scary?"

"Because there was something life-or-death about the way she spoke about him."

I pictured the irascible Joshua Jennings—another small, frail man like Richard Wilcox, but bright-eyed, quick-witted, sprightly for his age. He fancied himself a daring spirit, the cruel old man with the wicked remark, slightly risqué, but he was really a conservative snob. Dressed in worn sport jackets with leather packets, old gray slacks that rode too high on his waist, he watched the world with condescending eyes.

"And rich," I said out loud.

Karen nodded her head. "Yes, very rich. I know that Marta talked of his money. But she didn't need money."

"What did she want?"

"I think Marta thought she might marry Joshua. Travel with him. All that."

"But they stopped being friends."

"They fought. Some nasty fight. Bitter. She told me it was about the gardener, that Willie guy, but I don't know. It had to be something else. I think it was about marriage. He could be a notorious flirt, too—a lecher really. I think it gave her the wrong idea. I don't know for certain but I think Marta pressured him. I'm guessing. Let me tell you, that topic was taboo with us. He was a sick old fool, an old geezer, Marta called him once—but they played off each other that way. I think they loved the game."

"Maybe *he* loved the game, not her."

"Maybe. Yeah, Marta wouldn't."

"But she changed the rules."

"Yeah, maybe. I suppose it scared him. He was an old bachelor with only Marta as a friend. A hermit."

"Is that why he moved?"

We dug into the *bun*, me with chopsticks, Karen with a fork. For a second her mouth puckered at the tartness of the *nuoc mom*. The aroma of sweet basil wafted across the table. The quiet of the restaurant was broken when the door opened and a bunch of kids tumbled in, screaming and running. For a second Karen looked disoriented. Then she looked at me.

"Maybe. Maybe not. He'd been trying to sell that big old derelict house on the green for a while. Off and on. Fickle. For sale—not for sale. He was getting weaker and was afraid of falling down the stairs. I think she said he had trouble climbing to the second floor. He mentioned a retirement village—near a library, back in Amherst where he'd gone to school, a small place for him and his rare books—and Marta fought him. I suppose she thought she would take care of him. They fought, stopped talking for months. Marta thought it temporary—they loved their stormy silences—but then he sold the house, moved away, and Marta fumed."

"It must have broken her heart."

Karen frowned. "Rick, she was angry—not depressed. She got in the dumps when he *died* six months later. She imagined herself living in that big old house, the wife of the sophisticated, respected Joshua Jennings. She'd play lady-of-the-manor for those boring college receptions he hosted there. It was an old lady's stupid fantasy."

"I know. I used to go there. We all did. That's how he met the Canterburys who bought the house. He even loved Liz, my ex-wife."

She wasn't listening. "A foolish woman."

"Karen, his death must've hit her hard. Two weeks later she's dead."

"Well, think about it. She reads it in the paper. He dies in New York City, you see, visiting a relative or something, a niece, and there was the huge, front-page obituary in the local paper. It drove her nuts because she'd always planned on a reconciliation."

"But he'd finally made a decision."

"And didn't say good-bye."

"He was still angry with her?"

Her voice cracked. "He wanted nothing to do with her. She violated some awful rule he had. It had to be more than a simple fight. She would never discuss it."

"Why do you say that?" I asked. I poured her more tea.

Karen fiddled with her napkin, crumpling the paper. "I need to tell you something. She sent at least one letter to him in Amherst, early on, back in May, and he never answered. One letter that I know of. She got his address from the boys' school, and I think she pleaded with him. He got it, of course—he didn't refuse it—but he never answered. I remember she sent the letter certified, on purpose, so he'd have to sign. She saw that signature on the little green card as his ultimate insult to her. She carried it around all summer, steaming. She threatened to go there—to confront him. Tell him off."

"She told you this?"

"Only after he didn't answer her letter. She never mentioned the letter to me—before that, I mean. Then he died."

She started fumbling with some papers. "I have the obituary here." She smiled. "Those papers I mentioned to you. I have them here." She handed me a folder of papers, and I glanced inside. Neatly clipped news clippings, the insurance policy I'd asked about, other personal papers, all bound with elastic bands.

"I can borrow these?"

She nodded. "Of course."

For a while we ate in silence, absorbed in the food.

I caught her looking at me, a whisper of a smile on her face. "You have an interesting face."

I smiled. "Interesting?"

"I mean that in a good way—attractive, I mean." She got flustered. "I mean the Asian and the blue eyes and the..."

I grinned.

She looked down, embarrassed. "Conversation messes me up."

"Thanks." I cleared my throat. "Tell me about Davey."

For a few minutes she told me what I already knew from my conversation with him. They weren't close, but she claimed to love him. Years ago, when their parents suddenly died, they were inseparable, hiding together in the lonely shadows, sheltered by Marta and her husband until he died. But they drifted apart as grownups.

"He's real strange, and Aunt Marta had little use for him."

"Why?" I watched her face. "That bothers me."

"I think she saw him as a bum. At one point he was more... Catholic than she was, if that was possible. At the end I couldn't even bring him up in conversation."

"They had a fight?"

A pause. "Maybe. Yes."

"Your aunt seems to have a habit of fighting on a grand scale."

"She was passionate about things she believed in."

I let it go. "Davey told me something interesting. Marta always got what she wanted. The only way he'd see her killing herself was if she couldn't have what she wanted."

"I said she was—passionate."

"My question is, what did she really want that she couldn't have?"

She frowned. "Are you thinking Joshua?"

"Maybe. But maybe that's too simple. Maybe there's something else. If it's Joshua, there goes your murder theory. Joshua was dead by then. There was no chance they'd ever reconcile."

"And it makes the suicide more realistic." She sighed. "I still cannot see her killing herself. If you were at that last conversation I had with her…"

"Davey and I talked about her being Catholic and all."

"She was devout. Devout people don't kill themselves."

"Yes, they do," I said.

She looked into my face. "This is Davey talking, I think."

I waited. "Davey makes me nervous," I broke in. I deliberated a moment. "He warned me about you. Said you had bouts of—depression. Mentioned medication. Illness."

Karen's face hardened, anger seeping in. Then she forced an apologetic smile. "I knew he'd tell you that. A breakdown in high school. One in college. I went to school in Boston, at Emerson, but the city got to me. I had problems so I had counseling. So what? Bouts of depression come and go, so I deal with them. Marta wanted me to be a carbon copy of her—her bigotry, her rigidity, her fear of different people. Her knee-jerk Catholicism. She bought me clothes like hers—all pastels and matronly stuff. But Davey has made a point of telling everyone I'm nuts. I'm not surprised. It's his favorite story. I can get moody, I know. I get overwhelmed." She looked into my face. "I'm still like Marta in that way. I sometimes want the world to obey my orders, and then I fall apart. I get lost."

She suddenly reached out and touched the back of my hand. "I'm not crazy. My family has problems—I mean me and Davey. We had a peculiar childhood after our parents got killed. We sink low and come back up." She smiled, thin, wistful. "We're not crazy. My family is not crazy. Doctors do let us walk in the streets."

When we left the restaurant, we lingered in the parking lot, for some reason not ready to leave each other. The day was bright with cold sun, those icy shafts of light that spike a lazy November afternoon. She started to leave, but turned back, grinning. "Doctors do let us walk the streets."

Chapter Fourteen

I planned to spend the next day interviewing. I got up at five, jogged for a couple of miles in the early morning cold, bundled in old sweats and a pullover knit cap, and sat at the breakfast table with coffee and dry toast. I leafed through the folder Karen had given me, but nothing jarred. The insurance policy was typical, the other papers were familiar tedious documents from Social Security, federal and state governments, stapled tax returns from H&R Block, the usual conservative and mechanical portfolio of an average wary citizen. Everything in order. The insurance policy confirmed my earlier observation—if I proved Marta was *not* a suicide, Karen got a lot of money.

The only item I lingered on was the obituary of Joshua Jennings, a man I vaguely knew—and liked. I recalled reading that very obit in the local newspaper. The frayed clipping—it looked much handled, and I imagined Marta rereading it late at night—showed an old photograph when he was probably fifty or fifty-five, a head shot revealing bright intelligent eyes in a narrow, patrician face. He had that signature Van Dyke beard, but it was dark then. The last time I saw Joshua it was white—a pale murky white, a little unkempt and poorly clipped.

The article had appeared in the *Farmington Weekly,* so it was front-page and extensive. Jennings was a prominent local citizen, and one of the richest. The article talked of his long, distinguished career as a Latin professor at the equally distinguished

Farmington Boys' Academy off the town green. It mentioned his retirement at sixty-five and his subsequent involvement with nearby Farmington College as advisor, lecturer, and adjunct faculty, teaching German and French courses.

"I like to keep my hand in it," he was quoted as saying.

I remembered how Marta had used the same expression about her housekeeping jobs.

It mentioned his legendary philanthropy, his inveterate bachelorhood, his feisty presence at town council meetings, his membership on the Republican Town Committee, the Masons, and it mentioned his move six months earlier to Amherst, Massachusetts. He wanted a retirement village in the town he remembered fondly. It mentioned a surviving great-niece in New York City, whose apartment he was visiting when the massive stroke hit him. The niece requested contributions to the Boys' Academy where the school was already organizing a scholarship in his name. The article mentioned that all his assets—the reporter talked of a bequest rumored in the amount of over four-million dollars—were left to the boy's school. An endowment in his memory. He wanted a new library wing named in his honor.

I put down the article. Nothing untoward here, the only surprise being the amount of the bequest to the school. That was a hefty piece of change. Had Marta wanted that money? that world? that aristocratic aura? Joshua lived in a huge Federal brick colonial off the green, across from Miss Porter's School, and the old homestead had been filled with family antiques, leather-bound books, and quiet, inherited charm. When he moved out of state, most of his furniture and other possessions had been given to the college to benefit a scholarship fund.

A descendant of early founders, Jennings epitomized old-guard New England, Puritan glory filtered down through the ages into less reverential times. He'd also been an inveterate book collector, whose fine-tooled leather volumes were the subject of my own intense envy during my infrequent visits. He once showed me a volume of incunabula, kept behind lock and key in a document box he claimed once belonged to Thomas Jefferson.

Did Marta imagine herself the *nouveau-riche* mistress of that polished, sleek, understated world?

But Joshua wanted out of it—he'd been talking of quiet retirement villages for years. The house went on and off the market, always with excessively high asking prices, because, someone told me, he was ambivalent about leaving Farmington. He was in failing health. We all watched as he finally sold to Selena and Peter, and we celebrated with them. I'd actually gone to the celebration at the house. Their timing was right because Joshua had fallen, and he panicked. He wanted to get out. Joshua toasted Peter and Selena, who beamed. Joshua looked melancholic, but said he had no choice. A one-level home in Amherst, his bedroom set, the desk in his library, his rare volumes.

"Remember me," he'd asked us, a poignant valedictory.

I phoned the newspaper to talk to the writer of the obit. I left a message on his machine. Could he please call me? I wanted the name of the great-niece in New York.

◇◇◇

Marta's only woman friend, Hattie Cozzins, answered my knocking immediately, halfway through my second knock, as though she'd been standing behind the door. Eleven in the morning, she was dressed for a cocktail hour. She seemed out of breath, speaking in a faint, Marilyn Monroe whisper, her hand against her chest.

"Are you all right?" I asked.

It was a dumb question. Of course she was all right. We were doing old-time Hollywood movies here. *Some Like it Hot.*

"Come in." She pointed to a chair. "I thought you might be late." I'd told her eleven o'clock on the phone. It was five before the hour.

She looked familiar, though I'd never met her. I realized I'd seen—well, her prototype, writ large. Years back on an early Sunday morning in Las Vegas, walking through the glitter casino on the way to the checkout desk, I spotted so many women like her: silver-strapped heels, tight reddish-orange cocktail dresses holding in a little too much flesh, the hair too-many times blonde so that it looked washed out and vaguely like straw, the overly made-up face with the eyeliner too deep and too indigo, the lipstick too coral and too smeared. I realized that Hattie was, alarmingly, a type. I know, if you push it, we're all types, but she was a cultivated *type*, hothouse variety.

"Marta was my best friend," she was saying in a soupy voice. Without asking, she poured me coffee, handing me the cup. She already had her own, a trace of lipstick on the rim, and a burning cigarette in a Trump Casino tourist ashtray next to it. The coffee was hot and amazingly tasty.

I checked out her apartment. Filigreed lace on cascading, white curtains, on the oversized lamps, on walls. Frills, pink and white. Baby's breath clusters in faux-Hopi pots. A fluffy carpet, periwinkle blue, with candy-cane pink-and-white stripes woven through it. It looked as if an errant child had skipped through the room trailing melting, sticky candy. There were dolls everywhere—in cradles, clustered around plants and books and magazines. All of them stared at me with blank, unmoving eyes—the waiting room of a drug clinic. We were not alone there, I told myself.

"More coffee?"

I nodded. She made good coffee.

She was talking in that same breathy whisper, pausing now and then to taste the cigarette. I said very little, but that didn't seem to matter because she'd constructed an agenda, and she was hell-bent on running through it. She rattled on about their deep love for each other, their frequent vacations to gambling resorts—"How we did love those slot machines, we two old biddies on the bus tour"—their dinners together at Red Lobster, their lengthy late-night phone conversations. "Two women who refused to allow old people into our bodies."

"You were supposed to go again."

"What?"

"Vegas. You had tickets?"

She squinted. "Yes, as a matter of fact, we'd be flying out to Vegas right about now."

The sudden realization startled her, though she had to have thought of it earlier. She stopped, and I noticed wetness in the corners of her eyes. Traces of mascara leaked down her wrinkled, powdered cheeks. Any more crying and this would not be pretty.

"I suppose my ticket is still somewhere in her house."

She actually sobbed.

"I'm sorry."

"Thank you."

"Why would she kill herself?"

Silence. Her fingers trembled as she lit another cigarette. "There must have been something she didn't tell me. We traveled together, we were friendly, but we really didn't confide *personal* things to each other. Even if we did talk for hours. Our friendship was, well, not one where we talked about—real things. One of those friendships that old people fashion out of—loneliness. I could see she was depressed…"

"Joshua Jenning's death?"

"Maybe. Probably."

"You're not sure?"

"Well, they *were* friends. Like all of us, though I was rarely invited to his home. Marta made sure of *that*. She didn't talk about it—really. We all buzzed about his dumb move, the stroke, and dying in New York. I mean—New York? Really? But…" She trailed off, her hands in the air, cigarette smoke above her head. She looked so sprayed together I feared spontaneous combustion.

"Karen thinks murder." I said it flat out—to get her reaction.

I expected her to gasp, but instead she laughed, long and uproariously.

"I *know*. That girl can—amuse. Come on, boy. I can accept a suicide because I have no other choice, but murder? *Pull-ease*." She screamed the word out. "Why in the world? Marta? Really? She cheated at cards—her only vice." She stopped laughing. "Ridiculous. Simply ridiculous. Karen is off in her own world. Always has been. She and that Davey. Loopy, she is. Spend any time with her and you'll understand what I mean. Those poor kids have always been trouble."

"Like what?"

"So much psychiatric care."

"Even Davey?"

She leaned in, confidential. "You know, it's real weird. Marta didn't care for Karen, but was close to Davey—he was her favorite when he was a teenager. She doted on him. They were a pair, very religious together, the two trooping off to church. Devout Catholics. And then he goes from nice to nuts, if you know what I mean. And then they have a real blowout."

"About what?"

"She wouldn't say. It was so bad she actually fainted on my sofa." She pointed to the blue velvet monstrosity nearby, covered with spider-web antimacassars, and we both were quiet, as though Marta lay there still, fainting, gasping for breath, a nosegay held to her nostrils.

"No idea?"

"None whatsoever."

"Tell me about the Brown Bonnets," I said.

"The Brown Bonnets? That dreadful group of Catholic nuts. How'd you know about them?"

"I found their pamphlets in her house."

"Nothing, really."

"Marta supported them?"

"I don't think so. I know she mentioned them now and then. It was a recent thing, her interest in them. She was a devout Catholic, as I've said, a regular churchgoer. I mean, the woman liked her good times, don't we all, baby, but she was a prudish woman. A puritan in her own life, let me tell you. She liked to drink with the guys, dance the night away, especially the cruises we took on Carnival. But this was one proper lady." She paused and took a huge drag on her cigarette.

"Like you," I said.

She stared into my eyes—to see if I were mocking her. "Yes, exactly. Like me."

"But she did have an interest in them?"

"About a half year ago she came upon this article in a

newspaper about the Brown Bonnets, and she got their literature in the mail. She went to a couple meetings, but she knew I had little patience with that kind of fanaticism, so we never talked about it because I'd yell at her. They're the ones you see picketing Planned Parenthood in Hartford. They lined up with those placards with pictures of aborted fetuses. Just when you're driving by, headed for breakfast at McDonald's. Good God! Talk about losing your goddamn appetite! They tried to block the Robert Maplethorpe retrospective at Real Art Ways last year. Marta thought they were dedicated. That was her word. They wear these unattractive brown bonnets and carry Bibles, and scream at bishops about queers in the Mother Church. You know. Supposedly the Virgin Mary inspired them—talked to them from a tree in Albany, New York, or somewhere. Incredible." She stared at me, wide-eyed, unblinking.

"A tree in Albany?"

"Maybe Buffalo. You know how the Virgin always appears in a tree—never at eye level. And always in Catholic neighborhoods. Like UFOs always landing in trailer parks. God's sense of humor, I guess. But I don't know if Marta joined them."

"I don't know either. You didn't know? You were her friend."

"I don't think so. She'd never confide *that*. Believe me. She couldn't like such people very long."

"Tell me about Joshua Jennings."

A shift in her expression, her eyes got smaller, her lips razor thin.

"Karen says Marta may have wanted to marry him."

Hattie yelled at me. "They were *just* friends. I told you that. That's all. Marriage? Ridiculous."

"Karen was guessing."

"Nuts."

I folded my hands in my lap, closed my eyes. "Karen thought Marta wanted the life he had. She wanted to be Mrs. Joshua Jennings."

She spoke rapidly, all humor gone now, her spine rigid in the chair. "What life? An old and dying man. Years older. Sickly.

Marta—well, she flirted with him—lord, she flirted with all the old coots—but he was just a friend and employer. We were all friends. Nothing more."

Her voice was rising, and she stood up, turned away. Bothered now, alarmed at the idea that Marta and Joshua might have married, she gripped the back of the chair. Her oversized rhinestone ring caught the light. The fingers trembled.

"She wrote him in Amherst."

Hattie turned to face me. Her chin quivered, her eyes flashed anger. "I know. Well, maybe there was something going on that I didn't know about. But Marta and I—we had an agreement about things. We didn't push over the line…"

"What line?"

"Into romance. Frankly, romance. A confession, Rick. The *one* line we drew in the sand. We knew it would damage all of us. You see, we all met on that college trip to Russia in 2003."

"Who else?"

"Well, the two of us, and Joshua, and Richard Wilcox and Charlie Safako. We bonded together."

"Tell me about the falling out with Joshua."

"I know there was a doozie of a battle between the two of them."

"About?"

"Not sure, darling."

"Ideas?"

"I told you—we didn't talk about things like that."

"But you must have wondered."

"He wanted to move. She'd go on and on about it—to utter boredom. I don't know if that was *the* fight."

"Maybe something else?"

"Maybe. But he wouldn't write to her after he moved. No contact. I knew that." She laughed hoarsely. "I'm not saying she got what she deserved, but she could get pushy."

"Then he died."

"How we cried when we read that obituary. Held onto each other like little schoolgirls."

"She never saw him after he moved?"

She stopped. "I don't know. She even followed him to Amherst to see him. This after he hadn't answered her letter."

I sat up. "What happened?"

"She came back furious. I'd never seen her so mad. She cursed him." Hattie was trembling.

"So they fought?"

"She wouldn't say what happened at all. Refused to talk about it. She kept calling him a bastard."

"Did you ever find out...?"

She interrupted me. "It became one more taboo subject with Marta. Frankly, that list was getting a little too long for me."

Hattie was in tears now, shaking. I got up to leave.

There was a photograph of Hattie and Marta by the door, framed and resting in an ivy planter. I picked it up and stared into the black-and-white graininess. It had been taken at Atlantic City, I assumed. There was a cheap T-shirt stand behind them, a child in a bathing suit standing on the corner. A boardwalk umbrella. Part of the marquee of a casino. But I noticed two other things. Marta was dressed up the way Hattie was now—gussied up with huge costume sequins and a silk dress slit up one side, oriental style. She wore a sequined comb of some sort in her hair, and her head was thrown back, as though she'd been caught in the middle of a once-in-a-lifetime laugh. Sunlight glinted off the sparkling rhinestones on her dress. She shone. Party girl. She looked happy. This wasn't the cleaning woman I knew.

But the second thing was that there was another person in the picture. Standing off in back, turned halfway toward a hotdog stand, oblivious of the picture taking, was a figure I recognized as Richard Wilcox, dapper in a white linen suit.

"Who took this picture?"

She spoke matter-of-factly, dismissing me. "Joshua Jennings. The summer we all got back from Russia. We wanted the party to go on forever."

Chapter Fifteen

Charlie Safako had a shadowy reputation. A full professor of history, a man in his early sixties, he was a man I didn't like. Not that I'd ever spoken to him, other than to argue at faculty meetings when he screamed about the danger of faculty liberals—the "libs"—infiltrating the promotions committee. Charlie had agendas, to use another one of his words. Agendas, as in educational philosophies or personal mandates on living one's life—and people were always getting in the way of his fulfilling them.

Charlie lived in a small red clapboard, center-chimney Colonial tucked into a tree-lined side street within walking distance of the college. Sometimes, late mornings, I'd see him sauntering to his first class, leisurely and unhurried. Unmarried, he was a bulky man who always looked as if he'd been unable to finish his daily grooming. There was usually a spot of dried shaving cream dappling a cheek, or a ragged spot of beard untouched by a razor, or excessive clumps of lint on a rumpled sport jacket. He'd once been described by a student as an unmade bed, and I liked the notion.

With his beet-red spotty cheeks, his small faraway brown eyes, his thinning tuffs of brown-gray hair, he looked like an incomplete animal. A hopeless snob, he viewed history as the blessed bastion of Anglo-Saxon reserve, fearful of the encroachment of Neo-Marxists in the study of history—to gather from his op-ed diatribes to the local press—and probably only took his clothing to the dry cleaners twice a year. Sometimes he smelled like old rags under a kitchen sink.

I rang the bell four or five times before he answered. His doorbell was one of those ersatz medieval chimes that clashed with the plastic, chipped mailbox and the Walmart all-season twigs-and-twine wreath on the door. I had called that morning so he expected my visit. Now, grinning, he waved me into the room, but didn't suggest I take a seat.

Nor did he offer me anything to drink, which pleased me. Inside everything smelled like old professor. Parchment pages, texts discoloring into yellow pulp, dress shirt starch, and dried funeral flowers. Everything was neat, I noticed. It's just that everything looked flaky, decaying. Marta's cleaning touch was sorely needed here.

Late afternoon, almost twilight, though there were no lights on. He was drinking a diet cola from a can. The room was chilly yet I noticed he was sweating. He was nervous.

"I know why you're here," he said suddenly. He was already shaking his head vigorously, dismissing me. "Nonsense, pure and simple." He never once looked at me, and I wanted to leave because the closeness of the room made me dizzy and tired.

"I have nothing to say," he said. "Nothing at all."

"Don't you have an opinion? You were a friend. You traveled to Russia and Atlantic City and…"

He cut me off so abruptly I felt as though he were standing over me, looking down at me. Yet we were both still standing, and I was taller. "Young man, what's your trivial game?"

I didn't answer.

He waited a moment. His eyebrows twitched. "I realize that you need to *make* a living. We continue to pay for that stupid war over and over and over and…"

I broke in, flummoxed. "What? Are you talking about the Vietnamese War like it has something to do with my visit here?"

He sighed. "I'm a professor of history. American history. I am endlessly fascinated by the place of evolving immigrant generations into the scheme of things. The boat people from that unfortunate war have insinuated themselves into the colleges and professions and the culture..."

"Bullshit." I cut him off.

He smiled. "How characteristic! One generation to our shores and you acquire the language of the gutter."

He was baiting me, pushing me away from my reason for being here.

I asked him, point-blankly, "Just what are you hiding?"

He opened his mouth but nothing came out.

"We're here to discuss whether Marta was murdered." I smiled disingenuously. "Did you do it?" A pause. "It stands to reason..."

I swear the man's face went from beet-red to clammy white. The big-knuckled fingers crumpled the soda can.

"What are you hiding?" I asked again, enjoying this. He squirmed, something I'd never seen a human being do. Like a Disney cartoon character. Daffy Duck meets Viet Cong.

"Young man." He took a deep breath. "I have nothing to hide. If you think I'd kill the only person who kept the dust from my coffee table, you must be crazy."

"More than a cleaner, no? She was your friend."

He wiped his brow with the back of his hand, then dried the hand on his shirt. Really attractive, very farm hand. "Yes, she was. Sort of. But I always felt she was closer to Joshua and Richard." He frowned. "Much older men, you know. She and I were closer in age."

"When did you last see her?"

"Do we really have to go through this?"

"Yes."

He sighed. "If I answer, will you leave?"

"Yes."

He nodded.

"When did you last see her?" I asked again.

"Two days before she died." An edge to his voice.

"How did she seem?"

Silence.

"How did she seem?" I repeated.

He rolled his tongue over his upper lip, looking around the room as though for an exit, and said quietly, "All right, if I can get you out of here. She had just finished cleaning when I returned from classes. I asked her if she wanted coffee—we'd often sit and she'd talk and talk. She was very amusing in a way, a domineering woman whom I called my Dollar Store dominatrix as a joke, which she didn't like. She said no. That was unusual. She was in a deep funk. I was in a deep funk—I was hoping she'd amuse me."

"Why were you down?"

"What?"

"You said you were in a deep funk."

He narrowed his eyes. "We're not here to discuss—me."

"It seems…"

He raised his voice. "Marta left, just like that. Walked out. She actually looked pale, like she was sick. I called after her and said, 'Are you all right?' She didn't answer. Something was on her mind. Distracted—Marta was not a thoughtful woman. I don't mean stupid—just someone who left life…unanswered." Charlie paused, stuck out his tongue again. "I always regret that I didn't pursue it. My mind was on something else."

"What?"

Charlie opened his eyes wide, then frowned. He waved at me as though I were a small child he wanted to shoo out of the way.

"You *are* a cretin. Whatever happened to that much-touted oriental behavior of respect the young have for their elders?"

I waited.

"I'll retire in a year or so. I will be free of a generation that includes you—the self-loving egotists of pleasure. And the academic youngsters bouncing to radio waves in their heads while their fingers text inanities via Twitter as I lecture on the Civil War."

I couldn't let that pass. I leaned back against a table, put my weight on one foot. "There was a time when you didn't distance yourself from the younger generation."

It was a cruel jab, said purposely. Charlie Safako may have become the disaffected, seedy professor, but the rumor-mongers insisted he still saw himself as the consummate lady's man. A recurring tale on campus suggested that he'd fathered a child with a coed some thirty years back, when he was newly hired at the college. It had been squelched, as those things were in those days, but the rumor persisted, stayed with Charlie Safako like an old dog, and he always bristled under the tale. No one ever had any proof—certainly no thirty-year-old popped up in U.S. History I and screamed "Daddy, Daddy" like a scene out of a bodice romance—but the story made the rounds every so often. In fact, many undergraduates hero-worshipped him because of it. It gave the old man—famous for his risqué asides in class—a kind of rogue cachet.

He pursed his lips but said nothing. He seemed relieved that I'd taken that low road—as though he could live with the old, dumb rumor. I saw the hint of a sardonic smile that disappeared quickly. He turned away.

I repeated my question. "What are you hiding?"

I waited and thought of one of the precepts of Buddhism: *You must abstain from false speech.* I waited.

But he simply pointed to the door.

People pointing at a door is one of the familiar signposts of the private eye. You learn to nod, smile at times—not this time, I'm afraid—and, well, leave.

Chapter Sixteen

I checked my voice mail when I got back home. The obit writer had left a brief message. He'd never been given the name of Joshua's great niece. He sounded a little peeved. "Otherwise," he added curtly, "it would have been in the piece."

I scribbled a note card and pinned it to the wall: Track down the niece.

The phone rang. Gracie wanted to get an early dinner at Zeke's Olde Tavern.

Just as I closed my apartment door, I bumped into Ken Rodman, headed upstairs. "Hello," I called to him.

"Rick." We shook hands.

I didn't know much about him. I did know that he'd separated from his wife and three kids in nearby Avon, was some sort of insurance adjuster or salesman, and had lived until his divorce was finalized in a dorm room at some religious retreat in Hartford.

We stared at each other, neither moving. "You knew Marta Kowalski."

"Why?"

He was dressed in polyester basketball shorts and a new sweatshirt, a gym bag slung over his shoulder. A tall man with long, gangly shoulders, he had a slight paunch that he scratched.

"Well, I'm a private investigator, following a lead."

My out-of-the-blue question—I obviously take my interviews where I can—didn't seem to faze him.

"Yes, well, she cleaned my apartment twice."

"That's it? You talk to her?"

"Briefly. Frankly, she was too nosy. About my life. So I left."

"Ever see her again?"

"No." He rubbed his stomach again, looked at the stairway. "I was not gonna hire her again."

"Why not?"

"I told you—nosy. Too many questions." A slight smile. "Like you."

"Well, thanks."

"It's nothing," He was already headed upstairs, and disappeared from sight.

Gracie stepped out of her apartment, stood at the foot of the stairs. She was frowning. "Odd one," she whispered. "Secrets."

I grinned. "They're not secrets if he tells them to you."

She smiled back. "Nobody's allowed secrets in my building."

We headed to Zeke's Olde Tavern where we had roast beef sandwiches on rye, with homemade potato salad. The place was quiet, with a couple of college kids playing video games or lost in their cell phones. I ordered her a white wine, but she held up her hand.

"Make it a Bud," she said to the waitress. "White wine, indeed." She smirked. "I was a Rockette, baby. We always drink beer."

Jimmy Gadowicz strolled in, bellowing that he'd called my phone to say he was coming out of Hartford to visit, but it went to message. When I didn't pick up, he knew I was somewhere in the neighborhood. The Tavern was the place everyone checked to find any of us.

"I got my cell phone on me," I told him. "*That* number."

He waved his hand at me. "Hey, I memorized one number for you. That's enough."

Jimmy smiled at Gracie, and I noticed he'd marinated himself in some Walgreen's cologne. Fruit flies could take extended vacations on his round cheeks.

"What did you want?" I asked him.

He ordered a Bud.

"Nothing. Quiet night. Thought I'd check on you. The Case," he stressed, capitalizing it. "The Case." He chuckled.

I smiled—Jimmy was one of the good guys.

I sat back, my hands around a scotch and soda, nice and cold, and sighed. These were my good friends, and I was happy. Gracie and Jimmy. He grinned at Gracie, and she twinkled. Lord, I thought—romance in the age of Medicare.

"What are you smiling at?" Jimmy asked.

"I like being here with the two of you."

Jimmy looked at Gracie. "A lonely boy, this one."

"You do know I'm sitting here, right?"

"That's the point," Jimmy smiled.

Gracie grumbled. "We got to get him married."

"He should marry Liz again. A beautiful woman."

"A good-looking couple," Gracie answered.

"I like Liz."

Me: "So do I." I grinned. "You both know that."

"He's been seen around town with that Karen girl."

"A job," I emphasized.

"The Case." Again, capitalized.

"So how *is* the old case going?" From Gracie.

"Fraud is a lot easier," I said glumly. "It's cut and dried."

Jimmy leaned into me. "Tell me the one thing that bothers you so far? Of them all, the one thing that doesn't fit. Pick one thing—the burr under the saddle."

Gracie leaned in, too.

I thought for a minute. The two of them, each with raised drinks, stared at me, expectant. "She fought with Joshua Jennings—and never made up. Something was definitely on her mind the day she died. Wilcox said she sounded panicky. She was headed to Richard Wilcox's to tell him something."

Gracie spoke up. "Perhaps she made it there after all, told him something, and he had to kill her. He walked her home by the bridge and pushed her."

"Maybe."

"Or," Gracie went on, "that squirrelly nephew of hers might have acted out of drunkenness. You said…"

"Or," Jimmy interrupted, "Karen herself is afraid of something."

"C'mon, Jimmy. Then why hire an investigator? The case was closed." Gracie blinked her eyes.

"The obvious is wrong, the least expected is true, and…"

"Spare me," Gracie turned to Jimmy. "Is he spouting that Buddha bit again?"

"…the insurance money," Jimmy concluded. "Karen has to prove it was murder to collect, even though she is the murderer."

I interrupted, smiling. "Excuse me, beloved duo. Whose case is this anyway?"

"But you're so young and—untutored." From Gracie.

"Ah, Gracie, my rock 'n' roll friend."

I ordered another round of drinks for us.

"You know what I also find alarming." I sat back. "I've learned that Marta, admittedly an attractive woman for her age…"

"—Of her age," Gracie interposed, frowning.

"Of her age. Sorry. I mean, she was a real flirt, vivacious. She liked the company of men. She had a way with men…."

Gracie made a groaning sound.

Jimmy grinned. "She probably flirted with me."

I jumped in. "You never met her, Jimmy."

"But if I had, she would have."

"Which," said Gracie, "would be like flirting with a Disney character."

He made a face. "That makes no sense."

Gracie went on. "Men found her charming. People talked about her behind her back."

"The only person she *never* flirted with—is me. She was a little coy but…"

Jimmy punched me in the arm. "He's feeling insecure because a dead old lady never came on to him."

At that moment Ken Rodman walked into the bar, spotted us, and looked ready to flee. He caught me watching him, so he walked over, said hello, nodded at Jimmy. But he was jumpy. Of course, the three of us were perched there like the Spanish Inquisition. He stammered a quick I'll-see-you-I-was-just-gonna-get-a-beer-but-it's-really-too-late, didn't wait for a response, and hurried away. We watched him stumble out. He was dressed in a muted flannel shirt and a buckled bomber jacket, black boots and jeans. Everything looked spanking new, as though he were rehearsing a new look for a new season during a new lifetime. It was a little sad to see those sharp store-bought creases and shiny military boots and careful, unblemished leather. A catalog photo come to life, something out of the winter Eddie Bauer mail-order brochure.

Gracie laughed low and hard, purposely throaty. "We ruined that man's plans for the evening."

"Which were?" Jimmy asked.

"Being anywhere we three ain't."

"But why?" I asked.

Jimmy spoke. "Looks like he wants to be where nobody knows him."

"But why?" I repeated.

"Some people are private."

"But why?" I said again, grinning.

Gracie examined a broken nail. "I knew I shouldn't have rented that third floor to him. I'm better at screening folks."

"You rented to Rick," Jimmy told her.

"He was too good-looking."

"Thanks. But Gracie, come on. The man is innocent until proven guilty."

"For God's sake, Rick," she laughed, "who the hell still believes that?"

Chapter Seventeen

Two days later, a Saturday, I drove to Amherst, about an hour's drive up the highway from Hartford. Marta supposedly had gone there to visit Joshua, at least once, and had been rebuffed—if I could believe Hattie's description of a pale, stricken Marta freshly returned from her brief, futile trip. I wanted to find someone who'd talked with her—or seen her that day. I'd called Hattie back for any other memories, and over the phone she remembered that Marta's visit took place after Labor Day. It was the weekend after the holiday, she remembered, because they'd gone away—"We went to Atlantic City for a quick breather"—and had just come back.

"She ruined the whole long weekend," Hattie said, "talking about Joshua moving away from us like that."

"Were you surprised she went to Amherst?"

"Well, I didn't know it till she got back."

"But why did she wait until September? After all, he'd moved the beginning of April."

Hattie said she had no idea, but then added, "Marta was angry all summer. She was downright *mad* at him. Then she got real down. She always expected him to apologize. Or forgive her."

"But that didn't happen."

"No, it didn't."

Hank came along for the ride. He'd called the night before, checking in. "Aunt Marie called Grandma—said you behaved yourself."

I smiled. "I am trainable."

A ripple of laughter. "I haven't seen evidence of that."

When I told him I'd be heading to Amherst early in the morning, he invited himself along. I welcomed his company on the ride, a young man who'd listen and watch the people I talked with.

"You need me there." That made little sense, but I always liked his observations because they were intelligent. On the money.

We arrived at mid-morning, parked my car in a lot across from Emily Dickinson's ancestral home, and strolled up a busy Main Street, at the edge of Amherst College. I liked the place, a vibrant college town. Old New England stability mixing happily with breezy modern collegiate life. Two aging tie-dyed middle-aged radicals chatted with old friends in front of a Puritan church, a severe backdrop for the ponytailed spirits. A happy lesbian couple, arms linked, sipped sodas on sidewalk ice-cream chairs, oblivious of the November chill. Frantic Amherst students rushed across the green. UMass undergrads browsed in a video game store. Students with protest buttons, street corner advocates for world peace, a young man with a faded Free Tibet T-shirt. This was not Sinclair Lewis' *Main Street*.

"I used to come here with Liz," I told Hank. "Here—and over to Northampton. Once or twice we came with Vinnie and Marcie. We'd browse the old bookstores, eat at a new Thai or Mexican restaurant, watch the people, maybe drive over to the Iron Horse Café to catch a concert—we listened to Jackson Browne once—and then back to Hartford. For us, it was civilization. New York City without the wino's scowl and the freak's anxious hard-on."

"For God's sake!"

I shrugged.

So Hank and I were enjoying our easy, gentle stroll up and down Main Street, stopping at a coffee bar for strong espresso and a blueberry muffin. I smelled bittersweet incense and perfume—the intoxication of flowers for sale and the curious cloying scents that seemed obligatory in any college shop. I hadn't been here in a while, a long while, and I was loving it. Hank's head swung around, taking it all in.

"What do you think?" I asked.

"Cool."

It *was* cool.

We walked to the address the Farmington Boys' Academy records office provided. The careful, discriminating Joshua had located what I considered an ideal retirement village on a narrow side street off Main Street—quiet, tree-sheltered, a series of tiny clapboard cottages and two-or-three-room apartment complexes, weaving lanes and English boxwood hedges, thick shielding maples, an oasis removed from the bustle of the street. Yet everything was in walking distance for an old man—town library, college bookstores, benches in the park, theater, street fairs, restaurants. An old professor's paradise. Joshua would be at home here. Frankly, I'd be at home here, and joyous.

I rapped on the door of the small white-clapboard administrative building, labeled as such by the discreet sign over the door. No one answered so we walked in. I heard humming from the back room.

"Hello," I yelled. Still no response.

"Hello." Louder this time.

"Yep?" a voice responded. "I'll be right out."

I smelled pungent coffee brewing back there, and warm yeasty bread. Finally a man appeared, youngish, in his twenties, with a scrubby beard, wide flaring nostrils in a wide pale face. Full lips. Gold loop earrings in both ears. He nodded at me, raising a wide hand that held a Boston Red Sox mug of steaming coffee. He looked as if he'd just fallen out of bed. His blue-denim work shirt was half out of his pants.

"Help you?" He was smiling, and I saw shiny even teeth with braces.

I identified myself, showing him my laminated license with my picture on it, introduced Hank—who was staring at the coffee mug—and asked about Joshua Jennings.

"Yeah, I heard he died." He made his voice appropriately somber, running his tongue over his lips after a sip of the coffee.

"Do you remember him here?"

"Vaguely. I was new then. I'm a grad student at UMass in biotechnology, and this, well, pays some of the bills. We come and go—if you know what I mean. But him I remember."

"Were you here when he moved in?"

"No. Just afterwards, I guess. Quiet man, friendly. A little creaky and remote, but most are like that. They're either too talkative and in-your-business, or they hide away, like wounded animals."

"But you say you remember him?"

A long pause. He ran his fingers around the rim of the cup. "Hey, you want coffee by the way? I'm being rude."

I shook my head no. Hank did the same.

"I sort of remember him. One time he had these books and dropped them. I walked him back to his home. He never said thank you. His cottage was a rental unit in the back, near the lane just off Main Street and the park. A couple of times I saw him on Main Street, though, coming back from the library, arms loaded with books. A reader, he was. But he had trouble walking, stooped over and all. I think he used a cane. Now that it's cold, they all hide indoors. Summer's too short a season for the old folks. Once I nodded to him as he sat alone in a luncheonette, sipping tea and eating a sandwich. He looked old and tired. And, I guess, lonely."

"No visitors?"

"I wouldn't know."

"You don't keep a log?"

He laughed. "No, we don't. This is not, you know, a group home or something. These people have money. Lots of money. We have medical staff on call, but most have private doctors and private nurses and…"

"Could you check any records you have on him?"

He scratched the back of his hand. "Well, I don't know."

"He's dead," I stressed.

He strolled to a computer terminal and typed in Joshua's name. "He moved in on April 4. He asked that he have hired help in unloading and packing. Wanted special care for an old desk. We provide that service." He smiled. "He complained on June 2 that the air-conditioning wasn't working. He called again on June 3. Problem taken care of that afternoon." The young man looked up. "I came on board just about that time." He scrolled up the screen. "He'd paid for three months, didn't renew, and he moved out on July first.

"Does it say why?"

"Hold a sec." He disappeared into the back room, returning with an uncut loaf of warm bread. He cut off a slab. "No, but I remember. He was too lonely here. One of the kids who helped him pack for the move told me, I remember. He was moving to some place back in Connecticut for the summer. Then he planned to be back in Farmington. I guess he had his family or something. Like he had a niece, I remember, who was here that last day, helping him and all."

"Any forwarding address?"

He cut a slice of bread and handed it to me. Thick oatmeal bread with cinnamon. Delicious. I nodded toward his coffee, and he read my gesture, pouring me a cup. He grinned. "I knew you were someone who could be tempted." He nodded to Hank, then poured him a cup of coffee.

He returned to the computer and found an address for a place in Clinton, Connecticut, on the water. And the grand niece's name: Mary Powell.

"She packed him in blankets, I remember." A pause. "She didn't seem happy, like she wanted to get away from him."

"Ever see the niece here before?" I was sitting now, having my snack.

"That was the first I saw her, but she could have driven by me a hundred times. They're not required to stop, you know."

"Did he have any other visitors?"

"None I know of. As I say..."

I cut in. "I know, I know. They don't have to report."

"Exactly."

"On the weekend after this past Labor Day an older woman came to visit him—Marta…"

He cut me off. His hands slapped each other. He spilled coffee. "My God, I'd forgotten her. Can you believe it? Holy shit. I remember *that* visit, all right."

I smiled.

"I was in the office that day, and I remember it was hot. Real hot. Like August still. Blistering. This woman, all dressed up and with what my mom calls high perfume, she walks in looking for Joshua Jennings. I could tell she was nervous, fluttery, but she was also a little angry. I remember that I tried to calm her down, offered her something cold to drink, which she took. I said it was hot, even for September."

I leaned forward. "This was the weekend after Labor Day?"

"Positive. And I was sort of waiting for it."

"Meaning?"

"Old Joshua had stopped into the office one afternoon and told me some woman might try to reach him. He got this letter from her or something. It shook him up. I think he was mainly talking telephone—he had this unlisted number, they all do—but he also said she might show up. And he described her in detail. Down to this matronly hairdo and the old-lady perfume. He told me that she was hounding him, that I was to keep her away from him."

"Did he say why?"

"'Done him dirt.' That's what he said. I remember 'cause he didn't look like a guy who'd say it that way."

"Meaning?"

"Slang. The guy was like upper-crust." He chuckled. "Imagine—an old lady stalking him. Tell her anything, he said. But she never did show up."

"But she did."

"But she came way after he moved out. He left on July first. And I told her that. And I mean she flipped out. Raged around, then started crying. I mean, I read it as a lover's quarrel, like they were an old married couple way back when. He was an old-timer, wheezed when he talked. A weird, squeaky voice, a real old man. She was—well, lively as hell. I think it got to her that he was already gone *two* months and she thought he was still here. And him back in Connecticut. Then she left."

"Did you give her his new address?"

He nodded. "Bingo. I did. Sorry 'bout that." A sheepish grin. "It was my only way of getting her out of here. I figured he gave the same instructions wherever he moved to. Maybe the niece could put the brakes on her. She was real nice—the niece. Mary Powell. Imagine that—an old lady stalking an old dying man."

"How did you know he died?" Hank asked.

"He had a neighbor here—an old lady who collected his mail sometimes. She read about it in the Connecticut papers. She was originally from the Hartford area."

"What's her name?" I asked. "I'd like to talk to her."

He shook his head. "Sorry, man. She died a week or so back. Maybe a month ago."

"Of what?"

"Of being ninety-nine years old."

◇◇◇

Back in Connecticut, I called the Boys' Academy, but no one had information on Mary Powell. I checked Manhattan information, but there was none listed. Five Powells with first-name initial. "M." I made a list.

"How do you know she lives in Manhattan?" Hank asked.

I sighed. "Christ, it could be one of the other boroughs."

"A long list."

I groaned. "Thanks."

I dialed Hattie's number.

She answered on the second ring. "Who is it?"

"Rick Van Lam."

Her voice became wary. "Yes?"

"A quick question. I just got back from Amherst. The guard at the gate remembered that Marta went there to see Joshua."

"I told you she'd gone there. Came back in a huff."

"He wasn't even there. He'd already moved back to Connecticut."

Surprise in her voice. "You're kidding?"

"No, she never saw him."

"Can you beat that? No wonder she had nothing to say. Just fumed...cried." A barely suppressed giggle. "I stopped listening to her."

"Did she mention Clinton?"

"The president?"

I smiled. "No, the town on the Connecticut coast."

A long pause. "As a matter of fact, I think she did. But not then. One time. For some reason. Maybe not. I can't remember." There was a deep intake of breath. "What does that mean?"

"Joshua moved to Clinton to be with his niece."

"Really? A niece?"

"A great-niece."

I could tell she was lighting a cigarette because I heard the snap of a lighter, her words spoken through tightened lips.

"Whatever. I got tired of Marta talking about him—his life— so much. I just tuned her out after a while. She..." She inhaled.

"Did you know if Marta traveled to Clinton?"

"I can't remember—she was starting to get so secretive."

"Secretive?"

"You know, not answering questions, staring off into space. This was right near the end." Hattie grunted. "I do remember that she drove to New Haven, but she didn't ask me to go. Maybe she went to Clinton—it's nearby and all."

"When was that?"

"About the same time. Back in September."

"She never said why she went?"

Hattie was ready to end the conversation, her words running together. "Look, maybe Marta was a little overboard about Joshua. I tell you that outright. A silly woman dreaming about a silly man. I've been there, but not *that* silly. Joshua was a pompous fool who led her on. Old folks acting like spring chickens."

I waited, drumming my fingers.

"That," she added in a cackle, "and the fact that she was drinking too heavily after he left. I knew the woman—she was my friend, you know—but she could tip that elbow something fierce. I like my little cocktail now and then, but there's a limit. It may not have been suicide, young man."

"No?"

"No. Maybe she toppled off that bridge in a drunken stupor. Let me tell you this, sonny. I've seen her fall into the all-you-can-eat buffet at Caesar's Palace in Vegas."

Chapter Eighteen

I wandered into Zeke's Olde Tavern on a lazy Sunday afternoon, meeting up with Marcie and Vinnie. Manic laughter and loud backslapping assailed me. A crowd of folks, mostly college kids, watched a football game on TV, and the noise slammed me in the face.

This was not my favorite time of day at the Tavern. I liked it later at night, near closing time, a few regulars crowding the bar, the ancient jukebox filling the corners with early Motown and soft rock from, say, The Delfonics. Music to miss the old days you never really had.

Vinnie pushed a chair at me. "Have a seat, sleuth."

"You making fun of me?"

"Of course."

"I want to be taken seriously."

"No chance of that." Marcie leaned into me, drumming her fingers on my arm, flashing me a big smile.

"You both been drinking here a while?"

"Your tone suggests a new temperance campaign," Vinnie said soberly. "Carrie Nation lives."

"We're married to each other. He votes Republican," Marcie laughed. "I—we—have to drink."

Vinnie raised his glass in tribute.

Marcie smiled again. "Vinnie and I both have our pet theories on your little murder. You want to hear?"

"No." I waved the barmaid to the table. I wanted a long, cool scotch.

Marcie didn't stop. "Of course you do. There is absolutely no proof, but I know it was murder. It has to be. For one reason alone. Women don't throw themselves off bridges when they're on the way to a man's house. They throw themselves off bridges when they *leave* men's houses. Then they have reason to."

Vinnie scoffed. "And my theory. Simple desperation. Depression. She wanted a man to marry her, and he moved away—rejected her. Women die when men reject them." Of course, he pronounced this last bit of wisdom facing his wife.

They went back and forth, light-hearted, throwing frivolous barbs. But genially. It amazed me that they had been able to locate and settle into some middle ground where their marriage could survive and thrive. Humor, I guess, and genuine love. I envied them. But then I stopped because you don't envy friends. Buddha said: *Your true friend is only that part of you that is love.* I smiled.

Marcie was denouncing Vinnie as "deplorably sexist," adding, "Women no longer kill because of what men do to them. Women kill to get rid of men. Men are barnacles on the *H.M.S. Sisterhood.*"

Vinnie insisted women die for love. "In Victorian times they just pined away."

"Because," Marcie insisted, "men refused to bathe more than once a year."

"Women still die for love."

"Rick, look who's the romantic in the family. Vinnie, you should write Harlequin romances. E-books for the emotionally challenged. The supermarket shelves await your purple prose."

Finally, realizing I was sitting there silently, nursing a scotch in which the ice had melted, Marcie turned to me. "And what do you think?"

"Simple. She killed herself to get away from friends who never stopped talking about her private business."

"Well," both roared at once, looking at each other and laughing.

"Well," I concluded, "sometimes bridges look inviting."

Marcie sneered. "Then you should tell your girlfriends to keep their mouths wide open."

"That makes no sense," Vinnie told her.

The afternoon drifted by. Around seven o'clock—long after I'd planned on leaving—I stepped outside and dialed Karen. Marcie and Vinnie were headed off to get pizza in West Hartford after failing to persuade me to join them.

"Did something happen?" Karen asked.

"No, checking in."

"Come over. Rick. We can go for a ride or something. I'm going crazy here."

I deliberated. "All right."

"Just come over."

"I don't have anything new to tell you. A little, maybe. My trip to Amherst."

"I don't care. I need to talk to a human being."

"I don't know…"

Before she hung up she surprised me. "No talk of Aunt Marta. Not one word tonight. Promise me."

So we didn't. We caught the late movie at Trinity College, a French farce that bored me. Near the end Karen nudged me, and so we left. She smiled. "I couldn't follow the plot."

"I kept spotting grammatical errors in the subtitles."

She didn't want to stop for coffee and a snack—we'd munched on leftover pasta at her place just before leaving for the movies—but she didn't want to go home yet.

"No," she kept saying, "drive."

Drive, she said. So I drove. She fiddled with the radio dial and turned up the music. She settled for the Hartford retro seventies station, complete with inane disco patter and soft-rock musings. *Turn the beat around…like to hear percussion*. She twisted in her seat, but her movements didn't seem to be in time with the music's insistent rhythm: *in and out of love. This time, baby*. Karen mumbled the words. She ignored me.

"I was happy then." The joke I always made whenever some forgettable decade from the past intruded on my present life. People were always pulling me into their past lives. High times at the old high school. Or senior prom. Or sorority dance. It didn't matter what past event. I was happy then. Deliriously.

Of course, I was a rag-tag boy running the streets of Saigon during that decade. Ho Chi Minh City.

…boogie nights…

Karen faced me, alarmed. "Why did you stop being happy?"

I didn't answer her.

She turned the music louder when the Bee Gees suddenly somersaulted from the backseat into the front. I almost went off the road. *Stayin' Alive. Stayin' alive…ooh ooh ooh…*I thought of crisp white suits and black dress shirts.

Karen made me drive aimlessly for an hour. When I stopped to refill the tank, she bought junk food and soda. Then I took her home. Watching me closely, she invited me into the apartment, but I hesitated. I didn't know why.

"What's the matter?" she asked.

We stood for a moment on the sidewalk while she groped for keys. It was bone-marrow cold, with knife-like wind, and I suddenly felt the coming assault of winter. I got depressed standing in the ink-black night, the groaning wind rustling in the trees nearby. I was staring at Karen who looked helpless, fumbling in her purse, swearing, twitching her head in frustration. She looked ready to cry, her jaw tight, tucked into her neck.

Inside, she seemed relieved to be out of the cold. Taking her time, measuring and nodding, she made me delicious hot chocolate laced with real cream. I was still chilled, and my body shook from a cold spasm. I remembered a line my adopted mother used to say late at night when a chill went through her body: *Somebody just walked on my grave.* That was always a conversation stopper in the old New Jersey household.

But now I think I understood it. I slurped down the hot drink while Karen watched me, peering over her cup. She took the cup from me and refilled it. She poured herself some liqueur that looked sticky and smelled sweet. It seemed medicinal, so I refused the glass she offered me.

I hated her apartment, a sterile modern box, all angles and lines, none of them graceful, with redundant off-white walls. Everything was in block form, from the square windows to the boxy kitchen cabinets. The awful sameness was lightened, but only slightly, by her own huge abstract oil paintings gracing every wall. Phantasmagoric splashes of primary color. It was the stuff of serious nightmare. I tried to convince myself it all dated from an earlier, disturbed period, now happily past.

"Are you nervous?" she asked, sitting down near me, her arms folded against her chest.

"No."

"You look nervous."

But I wasn't. In fact, she looked nervous, squirming around, sitting, standing, folding and unfolding her arms, tossing her head back, pursing her lips. I sat stone-like, concentrating on my hot drink, happy with it, and my head swam a bit. I was relaxed now. I wasn't cold any longer.

"*You* look nervous," I told her.

"I'm not nervous." Too loud. She suddenly jumped up and walked behind me. Had I been some devotee of Hollywood's *Friday the 13th/Nightmare on Elm Street* horror flicks, I would have expected a brutal cleaver severing my fragile neck. That was really the way she moved. Instead I felt a soft hand on my shoulder and I smelled a hint of sweet perfume. Roses, I thought. And sweet powder. Her breath was hot with sweetness—that green liqueur. I closed my eyes.

She leaned over and kissed the nape of my neck, her hair brushing my cheek. She had her hands on my shoulders, so I reached back and covered them with mine. Her skin was soft but the hands, fluttery now, slid out from under mine and disappeared back into the folds of her dress. I turned to face her. Eyes closed, mouth open, she looked drugged, a face melting from its own warmth.

I left the chair and walked back to her, taking her hands into mine. She opened her eyes and for a moment looked startled, as if seeing me for the first time, as if coming out of a narcotic stupor. But then there was the slight sliver of a smile, the gray-blue of her eyes becoming dark and cloudy.

I kissed her and felt her mouth tighten. She didn't seem to want this, but then slowly, as though forcing herself, she slackened her mouth, her jaw.

"Yes," she whispered.

She kissed me, almost panicky, out of breath, and then stopped, afraid of something. She didn't move. A chill spread through me.

She said nothing but her hand lifted to her face, and she sighed.

"Karen."

Silence for an answer.

Surprising me, she walked into the unlit kitchen and stood in the darkness. She lit a cigarette in the dim light, and the match and cigarette lit the dark with such deliberate movement it seemed as if she were landing airplanes. She drew ambitious arcs in the darkness, ovals and circles and stabs at the night. Red-glow punctuation. She was starting to scare me.

"Yes, I wanted it like you," she said finally, talking to the wall in front of her, away from me.

"And?"

"But you have to leave. You can't stay."

"Karen," I began, but stopped.

She was shaking her head. I thought she might be crying, but no sound came from her. The dim light of the cigarette made her shadowy, ghostlike. The cigarette waved me out the door, pointing the way.

Buddha talked to me: *Abstain from sexual misconduct.*

I closed my eyes.

He had a point, that wise man. What had I missed here? I was never good at reading women, I knew that, always off-center, insecure, afraid my moves were—what?—too obvious, too boyish, too something. But Karen had played this her own way, and I couldn't follow. Suddenly I thought of Davey's line about her: *Karen runs from everything while she actually thinks she's running to it.*

I found myself thinking about Liz. Every woman I would ever meet would pale beside her.

In the parking lot, sweating in the cold wind, I looked up at the darkened window and I swear I saw a shadow fall away, behind the drawn curtain. Suddenly the window was dark again. No movement. I shivered. A ghost had walked into my shadow.

Chapter Nineteen

At five o'clock in the morning I was up for a run. The house was quiet except for the creaking of old Victorian woodwork, the breathing of loose-paned windows against dark morning wind. I ran the empty streets. A thick frost covered everything. Veins of white lace twisted on buildings and fences and cars. Wearing sweat shorts and a light parka and knit cap, I was numb with cold. So I ran and ran.

I ran until I exorcised the confusing night—Karen lovely in her fragile bones—out of my system. Sweating, exhilarated, eyes bright with the coming sunny day, I took a long hot shower, steamed my skin into reddish wrinkles, and settled down to hot, fresh coffee and a bran muffin from Whole Foods.

Hank knocked at eight. I was expecting him.

"You've been running."

"How'd you know?"

"You got that health-club glow."

"The body dutiful."

He poured himself coffee. "Is everything all right? You got a look on your face."

I ignored him. "You ready to go?"

"Yeah, that's why I'm here. I'm supposed to be studying at the Academy. Instead I follow you around like a puppy dog."

"I'm the Alpha dog."

"Clever."

"Let's move. You want to watch how a real PI functions, right?"

"If I did, I'd be in Hollywood on the set of *CSI: Special Victims Unit.*"

We headed for the town of Clinton, a town less than an hour away, down I-91 and over to I-95. I turned off the highway into the small shoreline village. I'd never been there before. Some shoreline towns like Branford and Guilford I knew—friends rented beach homes in summer. In November Clinton looked lazy and anonymous, a coastal town getting ready for winter, the tourists gone and permanent waterfront homes beginning to wear their drawn-in sheltered look. Beach cottages, with their bleached, blue-gray wood, lined narrow roads near the water, clustered together tight and cozy. We could smell the seaweed-laced salt water.

We drove around, found Main Street with its rustic coffee shops, antique shops, and clothing boutiques. We asked directions. Gusts of wind off the unseen ocean made walking difficult. The complex we sought was a few streets removed from the shore, tucked into a hidden cove, overlooking choppy water where hungry, swooping seagulls dipped and swooped. Only a few boats remained in the water now. A quiet secluded area, a hidden retreat for the very few.

"Looks like real money," I told Hank.

"Everything looks like money on the shore. A shack is money here."

The string of cottages circled the cove, but everything was closed now, off-season. A chain stretched across the entrance, blocking passage, a sign announcing it a private road. I copied down the realtor's name and address. But first I wanted to walk the grounds, despite the blustery cold. We ducked under the chain and strolled among the bleak, deserted tiny bungalows, smaller than I would expect, but carefully styled, all shuttered and shingled to look a hundred years old. I tried to imagine the place in summer, at the height of the season, but I realized it must have been isolated even then because towering white pines clustered around the edges, closing off the place from idle passersby.

"Money," Hank was muttering. "The rich ain't like we are."

I could easily see Joshua summering here during the long, lazy days, near to dying, the night breezes from the sea chilling his old bones. But I couldn't see it as a place a young person—say, his niece—would rent for herself. His money—yes. Her phone call—maybe. This had the feel of a retirement colony—old people with their private nurses, the *New York Times*, and their blissful reveries.

It took us most of the morning to locate the realtor, convince her that we were not troublemakers and simply investigators of the most benign sort—we smiled a lot and she frowned a lot—but she finally told us the name of a man who might help us, a Clinton old-timer who served as caretaker during the high season. After much prodding—and Hank's annoying questions about rental costs and possible student discounts—she provided me with Mary Powell's New York phone and address. Manhattan, Upper West Side. My old neighborhood near Columbia. Finally I had a definite lead on the elusive Mary Powell.

As we left the office, she gave me her card. "It's a good time to rent for the coming summer." She looked at Hank. "We have the best rental properties. You and your little brother would love it here."

Hank grinned. Little brother.

Hank and I stopped for lunch at a coffee shop in the center, munching on tuna salad sandwiches while we waited for Mr. Jared Peakes to answer his phone. It was busy whenever I dialed—no message clicked on—and we were waiting for him—or whoever—to hang up. The realtor had told us he was a retired man in his late seventies.

"Quite the eccentric in a town of lots of eccentric people. He used to be a *hardware* salesman." She had stressed the word and clicked her tongue as though he'd been in porno flicks. His son now ran the business. "If you know what I mean," she added.

I didn't but I also didn't want to know.

An hour later, Mr. Peakes answered grumpily, and when I said I'd been calling, he said, "So what?"

That stopped me cold.

"The dog knocked the phone off the cradle. Landed in the laundry basket. She's a mixed breed," he added, as though that explained the problem with the phone.

For some reason I was tempted to apologize.

"So what do you want? You'd better not be selling something. My home phone don't belong to the business community, and that includes the Lions Club and the selling of those light bulbs that go out..."

I cut into his rambling and mentioned the summer bungalows and his job as handyman. He agreed to meet us at the very coffee shop we were in.

"I live one street down back," he informed us. "Haven't eaten yet. Thank you."

"We're buying him lunch, I guess," I told Hank.

Mr. Peakes was not what I expected, one of those skinny, wiry old Down East cracker-barrel souls, one of those frizzled, wizened old New England types out of *Desire under the Elms* or an old *Yankee* magazine you see in a dentist's office. No, Mr. Peakes was a squat roly-poly man, with tired milky eyes and a pronounced asthmatic wheeze. He sat down across from us, adjusted his vast weight as though settling potatoes in a sack, and sighed.

He ordered four or five items, and I figured he had a crowd coming. He caught me glancing at Hank. "Retirement makes one hungry."

Hank chuckled.

"Your younger brother?" he asked.

Now Hank and I, both tall and lean, do not look alike, except for a dim Asian connection.

"Yes," said Hank. "But different mothers."

I stared at him.

I explained why we were there. What did he remember of Joshua or his niece? I held off mentioning Marta.

"Of course I remember them, though I have no idea what you're up to here. The niece was a beauty." He snickered. "Of course, at my age, what young woman ain't? Unless you're talking about those cows on afternoon TV talk shows, those…" He was ready to sweep off into some tirade.

"And Joshua?" I cut in before it was too late.

"Him I scarcely talked to. Maybe once or twice. Getting sicker by the minute. Old, old, skin and bones. One weekend there was a problem with a lock and I brought over a locksmith. Old man lying on the deck covered in blankets. Nodded to me. Mumbled something about being hungry for sunlight on his bones. Nonsense."

"He moved in the beginning of July?"

Mr. Peakes raised an eyebrow. "Exactly. His niece—Mary Powell, the name, a fine figure of a girl, dark hair like a crow's, but too much makeup, these women, you know—had rented the place in June. Out of the blue. She had called and we had a cancellation. We got a repeat crowd of older types. We are not cheap. We rent from May to September, but someone bailed out because of illness. That happens. Old people cancel. Some even die. It happens. Moved in sometime in June. Reduced rate. Her timing was great. We usually don't do such things."

"Did she say why she waited so late to rent?"

"Not unusual. First-time renters—like young people—think they can rent anytime, walk right in, not realizing things get booked up early. Or they discover they cannot stand the city in the summer. You know."

"She drove up from New York City?"

"Exactly. Weekends. Not much that I saw, at first. She always had mounds of paperwork with her. She whispered to me that her uncle demanded she get him someplace…balmy. He was a nuisance, she said, ruining her schedule. He had money, it seems. Young people have no respect."

Mr. Peakes was already digging into the second sandwich, an overstuffed roast beef on rye. Meals surrounded him. He surveyed them all, carefully choosing one over the other. He talked with his mouth full.

"She told me he was a problem. Oh, now I do remember

something. Yes, indeedy, I do. She said he had located her in New York. A long lost relative. He had no living relatives, so he thought, but during his stay in Amherst, the college library did some genealogical research on the Internet—Ancestry.com, some snoops, I imagine—and discovered a family line that ended in her. Some long-dead disinherited stepbrother's child. Something like that. Excited, he wrote to her. She was surprised, but I think she was a little annoyed."

"Why so?" From Hank.

I sipped my third cup of coffee and watched him answer.

"Demanding, he was. And the minute they met, he started to die and she had to take care of him."

"Don't you think it's odd that some distant relative would take care of an old man she just met—even family?"

He eyed me. "The girl had dollar signs in her eyes—you could see it. She was pissed off that he'd sold some mansion upstate. 'I'm always a day late,' she told me. Unpleasant."

"Unusual."

"I tactlessly mentioned a will to her and she laughed. 'He has lots of money, but it's going to some goddamn school.' I sensed she thought he'd make a few adjustments along the way—you know, lovey-dovey. Family blood, and all that. 'Who knows, I might still get a little something.' Then he got sick one weekend when she was here, and an ambulance took him out of here. She called and told someone he'd had a little stroke and was at Yale-New Haven Hospital."

"When was that?"

He bit into a sandwich. Mayonnaise oozed from its generous corners.

"Near the end of the month—August, that is. She came back to close up the place—the lease was ending anyway—and said he could walk but with difficulty. 'A matter of weeks,' she told me. I think she said he was going into some hospice."

I interrupted. "He died September 15 in New York City."

Mr. Peakes didn't miss a beat. "He lasted that long? He looked like death itself. There was a box waiting for that man, for sure."

"That's it?"

I waited while he sucked in a cheeseburger, a few French fries hanging off the melted cheese, dangling like icicles until, with a swoop of a large gray tongue, he dragged them into his mouth. I'd seen dogs perform such a feat, but never a human being.

"Guess so." He sipped his coffee. "The gal was charming, I must say. And clever. She always joked with me. He was—well, he was an old man far from home who was dying. Mentally, I think he was losing it. Him and me had one small conversation. He told me he missed home. Moving was a big, big mistake. 'Strangers around me.' That's what he said. 'I made a mistake. Got no home to die in.' That's all he did in the short stay here—he went about the business of dying. It's a full-time job, you know."

He was looking at the dessert menu.

"One other thing." I waited until he put down the menu. "Do you remember a visit from a woman named Marta Kowalski, sometime around the beginning of September, after Joshua was gone? A woman in her sixties?"

For a moment I thought he wasn't listening. Then a smile appeared on his glistening, mayonnaised lips. "A handsome woman. A truly handsome woman."

I sat up. "So you remember her?"

He took a sip of coffee, seemed to gargle it, and I expected him to spit it into the saucer. "Hard to forget that one. Appeared one day, one afternoon, by chance. The first chill of fall that morning, I remember, a quiet time, summer people all gone, the kids back in school. Quiet time. Shutting things down. Half the places cleared out. I work until the last ones leave—the middle of September. She appears with a piece of paper and says she wants to see Joshua Jennings. She's looking mighty attractive in a yellow summer dress and her hair up. A little lipstick. A classy woman, let me tell you. So I tell her it's too late. I mention the stroke and him gone to a hospice. I mentioned the niece."

"Did she know about the niece?"

He shifted in the chair, and the folds of fat moved, glacier-like.

"I dunno. All I know is that she stands there, rigid as steel, her face suddenly changing. I was expecting tears, hysterics, the breakdown of a woman in love. I've been through it myself many times. You can always see it coming. But no, the face became real hard. Her eyes on fire. And she screamed, real dramatic-like, 'People don't walk away from me and leave me like that.' Something like that. Real Joan Crawford. And then she walks away. Not even a good-bye. One mighty angry woman. I figured she headed to the hospital in New Haven."

"You didn't hear from her again?"

He pointed to custard pie on the menu, just pointed. I signaled the waitress.

"Why should I? Joshua was gone. That's who she wanted. Love has only one point of view, you know. Lovers only got one story, really. Yup, she was a mighty handsome woman. Handsome. But too steely for me. A scare, that one."

I left my card.

Getting into the car Hank mumbled, "A scare, that one."

We started laughing.

Sitting in the car, I made a note to check Yale-New Haven Hospital, some local hospices, as well as follow up on the address the realtor had given me for Mary Powell in Manhattan. I summed up my observations on the laptop, while Hank texted everybody he'd ever met in his life.

"So what have we learned?" I asked Hank.

"We learned Marta's timing was way off. She was always one destination too late."

"And then Joshua was dead."

"She was even late for that," Hank said.

"But I'm bothered by the niece, Mary Powell."

"Why?"

"How does she fit into the picture? What's her story? So he located her through Ancestry.com or something, and she's all over the place."

"Money."

"Sounds like it. But why rent this place here? Was that Joshua's idea? Or was she planning on bringing him here all along?"

"She got a summer vacation out of it. Out of the city."

"Did Marta know about her?" I asked.

"Joshua's a key, Rick."

"Yes. All of Marta's behavior in her last days centered on her pursuit of Joshua, anger at him, despair, and so on. She was onto something. He held some key. He knew something. Or he had told her something. Or she wanted to tell him something. I feel he had the answer to her death."

"Yet he died before she did," Hank summed up.

"But he's the cause of her death, one way or the other. I know it." At that moment Buddha talked to me. *The two do exist here because of the One.* I smiled. "Their deaths are one thing."

"What?"

"Each one's death is reflected in the other."

"He's in his grave."

"And she's in hers. Everyone with an answer is dead."

Buddha, again. *If One is all, the One is many.*

"Maybe not everyone." Hank stared into my face.

I nodded. "Someone knows something. 'One is all. All is part of One.' I have to believe someone alive understood what happened between them. Out there."

I pointed through a window at the chilly landscape.

Chapter Twenty

That evening, around five, I waited for Marcie and Vinnie on the sidewalk outside my apartment. Then the three of us strolled under umbrellas through the drizzly, raw twilight streets to Selena and Peter Canterbury's house for a small cocktail party. It was their first gathering since moving into the old Joshua Jennings homestead.

"Just a dozen close friends," Peter had said.

I told Marcie and Vinnie about my colorful morning in Clinton. "So I finally got Mary Powell's number and I call it."

"No answer?"

"Busy. All afternoon."

Marcie smirked, "The trials of the modern PI."

"It's…"

We stopped talking as the front door opened, almost on cue, and Selena stood there, a big grin on her face.

"I thought you weren't coming."

"Actually I thought we were early," Marcie told her, but Selena ignored her.

She took my hand and moved closer. I planted a kiss on her cheek and smelled hot whiskey breath. She wore the glazed look of an all-night reveler. Selena had started celebrating early.

Inside, she took our coats—hanging them in a hall closet larger than my kitchen—and directed us to a table with booze on it. Various members of the college faculty, glasses raised, waved to us. Peter was nowhere in sight, and Selena disappeared when the doorbell chimed.

The three of us stood in the center of the large living room, and Marcie whispered confidentially so that Vinnie and I had to bend into her, "It isn't the same. It can never be."

I knew what she was talking about. The old Federal Colonial home had been Joshua Jennings' splendid and cherished retreat. An exquisite house, with all the mannered charm of hand-hewn beam and dark, weathered woodwork. The word *elegant* always came to mind. Twelve-on-twelve windows, feathery cream wainscoting, floor-to-ceiling black walnut bookshelves with rippled hand-blown glass. A vast pink-and-black Italian marble fireplace filled one sweeping wall, a late Victorian addition to the room, Joshua once told me.

Filled with pride and glory, he had often volunteered his home for college functions when it seemed appropriate to have them off campus—that extra swagger of class—an opening for the Farmington College Art Show, the cocktail party for the annual fund raiser, receptions for visiting luminaries—I once met Jimmy Carter there. Joshua loved showing off the place. Over the years all of us became familiar with the lovely home, thrilled to be invited into the stately rooms.

But Marcie's *sotto voce* remark was apt because it was no longer the same. Gone was Joshua's heavy Victorian ambiance: the overstuffed chairs, the tufted sofas with the embroidered antimacassars, the deep bookcases filled with leather-bound collected works of the likes of Bulwer-Lytton and Shelley and George Eliot and Wordsworth. French doors had opened to a sumptuous private library that housed Joshua's favorite books, including his valuable collection, among them his prized early editions of Cooper, safely locked behind leaded-glass doors. When I glanced into the closed room now, I saw empty shelves. It saddened me, that room so starved for books.

One man had lived in a twelve-room mansion. I heard that he used to quip, "I really need more rooms." People didn't find it funny.

Joshua was forever selling the monstrous place, but his desire was only half-hearted until age and illness panicked him. The huge shell of a house scared him. We heard how he had fallen one night, almost toppling down the stairs, and that was it. A sprained ankle suggested worse problems in the future. I remember him hobbling on the sidewalk one day, and it was sad.

"Have to move," he whispered to me.

Suddenly he wanted out. He'd taken a liking to Selena and Peter, especially to flirtatious Selena, and he'd suggested that they buy the homestead. Peter had no interest—imagine the heating bill in winter, he'd told me. They had little money, of course, but Joshua got realistic when he had the place appraised. The house needed too much costly renovation, its electrical system archaic, its plumbing medieval. The old windows invited the heat to escape. Joshua had a white elephant on his hands.

Yet Selena and Peter finally wanted it, which surprised all of us. They'd been married less than a year. Joshua pleaded—told them he'd work out a deal, a workable down payment, realistic payments, and he'd possibly hold the mortgage. Seductive, the idea. So they were hooked. After all, it was the Farmington showplace, and Peter and Selena loved the image. One night we all met there to celebrate the sale, myself included, invited because I was part of Marcie and Vinnie's inner circle, and Joshua toasted the new owners with champagne.

"I feel like a ton of bricks is off my back," Joshua announced, a remark that made Peter twitch.

Selena got tipsy, Peter got nasty, and Joshua fell asleep.

We all knew it was a mistake. Marcie and Vinnie, close to the couple, had argued against it, warning. One time, at a college function held there in winter, pipes broke in the basement, the sound of rushing water thundered through the radiators, and we all went home.

Marcie had told Peter, "It's a land mine."

Peter had became indignant. "Yeah, but we love it."

Vinnie once hinted that Joshua was a cagey man, someone who suckered the young couple.

Young and foolish, they couldn't see beyond the wonderful ambiance. But once Joshua's old furnishings were gone, carted off to the college or the boys' academy, the huge rooms were suddenly cavernous and bare. They discovered the place needed major upgrading—not only the electrical and plumbing, but roofing and masonry repair. Walls were rotting, plaster flaking off—you could hear plaster falling in the night. The basement flooded regularly. Carpenter ants strolled across beams. Dry rot in the attic. It was worse than they had believed. The pretty shell disguised decay, lack of attention. The old-style wiring was dangerous and contrary. Bare bulbs hung in closets from frayed cords, and during thunderstorms, sizzling noises sputtered through the rooms. The sweet smell of run-amok electricity. It became, almost immediately, a nightmare. So I learned from a depressed Peter.

"She wanted it," he hissed, blaming Selena.

Other times she blamed him, even as he stood nearby. She fell into a frenzy, he into passivity. The fought their battles royal in front of all of us. The house ended their honeymoon.

Standing in the living room, I was disheartened. Selena and Peter had so little cash, and the large yawning rooms looked vacant. They'd stuffed their sleek, newlywed modern apartment furniture into the house, and it didn't look right. Isolated pieces of cut-rate Danish modern clashed with the elegant—though woefully faded—rose-cream brocade wallpaper. Everything looked on sale. Yard sale. They were renovating a room at a time, starting downstairs, we'd been told, and most of the house was still locked up, devoid of furniture and life, the radiators turned off. The front living and dining rooms were habitable now, which occasioned this party. The breakfast nook, the treasured library, the solarium—all were closed empty shells.

"Ugly," Vinnie mumbled to me. "They're unhappy here."

Selena found me and handed me a scotch and soda. Of course she'd remember what I drank.

"Did you see what Peter did to the kitchen?" she asked, dragging me away, leaving Marcie and Vinnie standing there.

I nodded dutifully at the new kitchen. He'd simply refinished the old glass-fronted cabinets, replaced rotted wood, and laid a new tile floor. The tile looked discount-house variety, and temporary. Several squares were askew, slapped down willy-nilly. The house deserved better.

Suddenly Peter was with us, up against Selena. He shook my hand.

"Rick." His hand swept across the room. "I actually learned to saw wood." He pointed to simple trim above the kitchen cabinets. It looked uneven and poorly stained, something out of middle-school shop class, but I congratulated him. Here was a twelve-room decaying house, jolted back to feeble life on a shoestring budget.

As we walked back into the living room, Selena touched my sleeve. "I overheard someone gossip that Joshua had better reading taste than we do." She was not smiling. Her lips were tight, her words slurred.

Buddha, I knew, wouldn't be happy: *Abstain from intoxicants that cloud the mind and the tongue.*

"What do you mean?"

She stopped in front of the floor-to-ceiling black walnut bookcase in the living room, with leaded glass panes and ornate gingerbread trim. Inside were textbooks, paperbacks, academic journals, the kind of collection a professor's office was filled with. An instructor's den in a split-level frame house.

"In time," I told her.

"We do know what it should look like," she said too loudly. "We're not stupid people."

I resigned myself to lying throughout the party, my only method of survival. "It's fine, Selena."

But as the evening unfolded and a group of junior faculty apologized for leaving early—I knew they were headed to the XL Center for a Josh Groben concert—Selena became more manic. Admittedly, she looked stunning in a pair of snug black slacks and an oversized ski sweater. Southwest-style turquoise earrings picked up the muted colors of the sweater. Sitting down, she crossed her legs—I saw an ankle bracelet of similar turquoise stone. Or was it a tattoo? Nothing would surprise me. She caught me looking.

"Rick." She stood and bowed. "I'm a walking craft show."

"Very nice." No need to lie that time.

Approaching me, she got serious. "You mean that?"

She had spilled a drink on the front of her sweater and the stain looked vaguely like the state of New Jersey. I thought of my adolescence.

She stood too close to me, her face inches from mine, and suddenly Peter shot over, maneuvering his body between us. I smiled at him, backed up to let my body language tell him he had nothing to worry about. He looked exhausted, as if he wished everyone would go home.

"Kitchen is nice, Peter."

He frowned. "Yeah, sure."

"I mean it."

Selena interrupted. "We're almost done with the library." She pointed behind her. That had been my favorite room, of course. Wall-to-wall bookcases with leaded glass panels, with beautiful wine-red mahogany crown molding, deep plush armchairs. But I knew Joshua's Italian Renaissance *Madonna and Child*—by a student of Raphael—was gone now. That lovely painting now hung, a spotlight illuminating it, in the boys' academy chapel.

"We'll have it ready for the college fall fund-raiser reception next week," she added. "Tonight's a trial run. We want to keep Joshua's tradition going." But the words came out haltingly, and she seemed surprised by her own slurred sentences.

When we'd dated—God, it seemed so long ago—she rarely drank. A social cocktail, if that. Usually something with an umbrella, a concept I never grasped. Yes, her quixotic mood swings alarmed me then, but never that much. Since her marriage I'd heard horrible stories. Quite frankly, she'd made a mistake. Peter, drone-like and manipulative in his own way, was no match for Serena's erratic intelligence and her wild, unfocused ambition. Peter's ambition centered on his career—Selena's crafty and shrewd behavior seemed simply manic.

I knew of one affair she'd had with a garage mechanic at the Texaco station on Route 10. One time Marcie swore she was driving by and saw them hugging while he was working on Selena's car.

"You're making that up," Vinnie had accused.

But I suspected the story was true, in one form or another. Selena *had* changed. A stupid marriage and a monstrosity of a house had made her sloppy at the edges, and downright mean at the core. I knew there'd be a time when I'd find an excuse to avoid these inelegant cocktail parties.

I couldn't deal with her brazen flirtations, so often in front of Peter.

She was doing it now, playing with the lapel of my sports jacket. Peter watched, red-faced.

I thought of something. "Did Joshua ever contact you after he moved?"

Selena looked surprised. "No, why would he? The bastard. He took the money and ran."

"He seems to have been manipulated by a great-niece."

Peter looked puzzled. "I thought he had no relatives."

I smiled. "So did he. But Ancestry.com changed that."

Selena shot a look at Peter. "That woman."

For a moment Peter looked baffled.

"What?" From me.

Then Peter spoke up. "Christ, yeah. In July we saw a woman parked in a car in front of the place. At one point she got out, walked up to the front door, peered into the windows."

"But then she was gone," Selena added.

"We didn't think anything of it." Peter didn't look happy. "Do you think...?"

"His niece?" Selena asked.

"Maybe," I said.

Selena leaned into me. "You got such a serious look on your face. Rick. Makes you look—sexy."

Peter grumbled.

I was cruel. "Are you friends with Karen Corcoran?" I asked her. Selena's gift shop was near Karen's art gallery in the arcade.

Selena tightened. "No, not really."

"We went to the movies Sunday."

"How high-school date night of you," she said sarcastically. No slurring now—harsh, direct. But she moved closer to me.

"How is she?" Peter wondered.

Selena sniffed, "At least you're not still working for her—that business with Marta. My God. I could think of a hundred better uses for an inheritance."

"Oh, but I am."

Selena gave a hoarse laugh and started hiccoughing. "Shit," she giggled. "Now I'll hiccough all night."

"Two weeks before she died," Peter ignored his wife's noises, "we hired Marta to clean here."

The news surprised me. "What?"

Now Peter looked sheepish. "My family was coming from Vermont to see the house and it was a mess. School was starting and all. She'd cleaned for everyone, knew the house. She was at the market, looking lost, so I asked her as a favor. She kept saying no, that she didn't want to return to this hateful house. I didn't know she had a problem with Joshua—had such a bitter feeling about the place. But she did it as a favor to me."

Selena grinned sloppily. "Peter charmed her." It wasn't said as a compliment. "She can't—couldn't—resist a pretty man."

"And?" I waited.

"Well," Peter went on, "nothing. Really." He pointed to the library. The door was open but the room was dark. In the dimness I could see a stepladder and paint cans, drop cloths. A huge cloth covered an object in the center. Peter pointed to it.

"Marta didn't know that the one thing Joshua left with the house was that grand piano of his." He frowned. "Out of tune, of course. Worthless, of course. A fortune to repair, of course." He shook his head. "Everything else was sold to antique dealers. Choice pieces were sent to the academy or the college. But he let us buy that. For a price—not a big one—but a price. Neither Selena nor I can play." He was shaking his head.

"But it looks great there," Selena said.

Peter ignored her. "So Marta comes one morning and starts to clean, does the front rooms, the bathrooms and kitchen, the guest room in back we're gonna use, but she's moping around. And then she opens the library door and sees the old grand piano—we'd pushed it in there from the music room, unfortunately scraping the French doors—and the tears start to fall. Wailing, I tell you. She never finished cleaning, and we had to take her home. She sat there on the piano bench, duster in one hand, bawling her eyes out. It was awful, like a slapped cat or something, a high-pitched wail of a cry, bone-chilling. We couldn't stop her."

"Did she say anything to you?"

"She kept saying he died on her. She said he didn't have to run away, that she didn't mean what she said to him."

I got interested. "She say what that was?"

"No, she was babbling. She looked real lonely, sitting there in that big empty room. I guess it was wrong of us to make her come back here. We just didn't *know*. She hadn't been here since long before he moved out last spring. Even before he sold the house they hadn't talked in a while. Some major blowout."

"Did she say anything else?"

"No. I almost had to carry her out to the car. I drove her home. In her car."

"Why haven't you told me this before?"

Peter looked dumbfounded. "It's important?"

I shrugged. Maybe it wasn't. True, it was a familiar variation of what I'd been hearing from everyone else.

"Sorry," he mumbled.

"Anything else?"

"No," he said. "I can't believe you think this is important."

I entertained a mental image of Marta draped over the piano, weeping for lost love. It made me sad, thinking about her in that cavernous room, but in that moment the face of Karen superimposed itself on her dead aunt's. The same melancholic, drawn face, the wasted blue eyes, the sagging mouth, the birdlike movement of the lips. I imagined Karen sitting at the piano, weeping. Karen touching me on the shoulders, her body hunched over, shaking, Karen motioning me out of her apartment.

I shook my head. Peter was standing there looking weepy himself, like a beaten dog. But I heard a syrupy dripping sound, and I turned to face a hiccoughing Selena. She was staring from Peter to me, as though unable to follow the conversation, a whiskey glass against her cheek, and she was trying unsuccessfully to suppress a fierce giggle.

Chapter Twenty-one

After the overheated packed room, the buzz of two stiff drinks in my head, and the groping fingers of Selena, the cold outdoors was a relief. As darkness fell, the streets became raw with icy air seeping into my bones. The earlier drizzle had ended, and I liked it. I bundled up, drew my collar tighter, and walked.

I didn't expect to bump into Charlie Safako, strolling along with a hesitant little pug. I was staring at the sidewalk, sloshing through accumulated fall leaves, enjoying the crunchy noises I was creating, when I heard a deep intake of breath. I looked up to see the professor standing still, gloved hand gripping a taut leash. He looked like an unsorted pile of clothes. Oversized parka with a tear in the sleeve, a wrinkled disheveled look about it. His hair was carelessly tucked under a wide-brimmed cap, the kind you see on men in summer golf carts. He hadn't shaved. He waited until I was near, and then he grunted at me. It was a sign, I knew, that he'd missed me.

"Well, well, Professor Safako of the history department, waiting on the heir apparent."

He half-turned away, as though to ignore me, but Charlie Safako liked to assail people. He'd practiced on generations of hapless students at the college.

"Rick Van Lam, PI. Please Irritate. Intimidate. Or is it Irrigate?" He chuckled, amused at himself. "Or Pesky Immigrant."

"You weren't invited to the Canterburys' party?"

"Oh please, that tiresome serial? The Bitch and the Beaten. Selena and I have a brief history. She wanted—well, never mind."

His smile was creepy. I waited. I couldn't imagine Selena wanting him. "Sounds like you're dying to tell me something."

"Are you still playing Jessica Fletcher for *Murder, She Wrote*? Or uploading a video onto You Tube—Mr. Lam's interviews? America's funniest videos—or some such crap. Little boy, what does your daddy say to your mommy at night? Giggle, giggle from America's TV living rooms."

"Doing my job."

He laughed, mimicking my voice in a deep growl. "*Doing my job.* Oh, Duke Wayne now. Lord, you do have those lines down pat. Thank God my charity dollars buy TVs for orphanages and resettlement camps in Guam. I consider it part of the Americanization process."

I cut in, not wanting to let him get the better of me this time. "I was wondering. What exactly was your relationship with Richard Wilcox and Joshua Jennings? I know what you said about Marta but…"

He bristled. "You just don't understand relationships, my young man."

Sarcastically, "Well, fill me in, Teacher."

"If you must know—and obviously you must—I was not part of *that* equation. I was there as bored Greek chorus. Those two pitiful men played out their game with each other. Richard, quite frankly, was jealous of Joshua and his money and name."

"And?"

"Well, Richard hated Joshua. Lied about him to Marta. Acting like pouting children. I watched it from Mount Olympus, imperious and cynical. For a while it was a good show. And then it got trivial and boring."

"Why was that?"

"Because neither Joshua nor Richard wanted resolution. *Denouement.* They wanted the game to keep going. A pleasant diversion for lonely old celibate men. Marta was, indeed, an attractive woman."

I nodded. "So I hear over and over. I still can't understand her appeal to such men."

"Do you mean because she wasn't an academic? Like them, covered in diplomas from Ivy League gin mills?"

"Perhaps."

"You know, she talked and talked, dreadful really, but in the end she always ended up *listening* to us. She had that...*talent.*"

"But you guys all have such negative things to say about her now."

"Well, we're just not nice people, after all."

"She was a friend."

"Yes, she was fun, most of the time."

"Patronizing?"

"So be it."

"But she wanted more from the little play she was acting in. She wanted that resolution you mention. She wanted conclusion."

"She wanted climax." He grinned, showing stained teeth. "It was all meandering complication. There was no turning point in this Elizabethan farce."

"But there *was.*"

For a moment he seemed out of focus, confused, on the verge of saying something. Then he started to walk away. Finally, he turned back, raising his voice against the wind. "But someone substituted a different script, Mr. Lam. Different play, new ending."

I yelled back to him. "Did you have a part in this play?"

"My boy, they didn't even invite me to the rehearsals."

◇◇◇

I phoned Richard Wilcox the next morning. "How are you doing, sir?" I began. "How was your trip to the hospital?"

A pause. I could hear short, quick breathing.

"If you must know, things have changed. Now I know the horrible truth. As Brecht said, 'Those who are still laughing have yet to hear the terrible news.' You see, I have months left, I'm told. Months. Not years. Months. Months are things you don't think about, things you throw away. We think about years—years are solid and long and in the future. Months end tomorrow. So I will end tomorrow."

"I'm so sorry, Mr. Wilcox." I waited. "Is there anything I can do for you?"

He wasn't listening to me. "I didn't think I'd be this frightened." Then, after a pause, "You're calling because of Marta."

"Yes."

"That all seems so far away now. Like I knew her and Joshua in another life. Not a better life, but another life."

"I still have found nothing."

"Nor will you, I'm afraid."

"I don't mean to bother you now."

"Oh, but you obviously do."

"I'll call back...."

"It was my fault," he blurted out. Another deep intake of breath.

"What?" Startled.

A sardonic chuckle. "Old, old people playing the youthful game of love and kisses. Old foolish men." I waited as he suffered through a coughing spell. "You see," he went on slowly, "I was a jealous man. Neither Joshua nor I had any sense when it came to Marta. I was jealous of the attention she gave him because I was so taken with her. I had a little infatuation. She was attractive, flirtatious, a deeply sensual woman, remarkably stupid, a woman whose dogmatic and shrill personality added to the...allure, and gave her, well, plebeian crispiness."

He chuckled, darkly.

"But she was taken with Joshua, and he with her. Somewhat. Of course, he had no intention of marrying at his age. Let's be realistic. He'd *never* married. Neither had I—no stomach for it. She was a diversion. He was so patrician in the awfulest sense, and she was pleasant company. Lord, I almost said—peasant company."

"Unfair to her, no?"

He chuckled again. "Oh, the facile judgments of the young. I can still make a snobbish joke. You know, she could make a lonely celibate feel like—well, like he was a handsome young man in a diet-soda commercial. Isn't that an odd thought? That kind of young-at-heart world. It was all game play. When I talked, she stared into my face as though I were dispensing the most cherished wisdom."

"Did she pressure Joshua for marriage?"

He laughed out loud. "It did come up. Joshua told me one time when we talked. She talked so openly about it—not to Joshua, but to me—and perhaps others. Joshua was getting sicker and sicker—he's older than I—*was* older than I—and she got more desperate."

"And you poisoned the well?"

His voice got stronger. "Smart man. It was easy. He had this elevated view of her—devout Catholic observant, you know, even though Joshua always held Catholics suspect, as we all do. My Lord, they eat wafers and think they're tasting God. Delightful primitivism. But her fervor did suggest goodness—of sorts. Christian faith, hope, and charity. You know."

"And?"

"And I took care of that."

"How?"

"I learned somehow—it may have been through Marta herself—or maybe her fickle friend Hattie, that hag—that Marta liked to frequent a place called Louie's in Unionville, a local bar or tavern, a little rough at the edges. Marta could bend the elbow if she wanted to. I'd never been there, of course, but Louie's has sort of a sleazy reputation."

"I know the place. And so you told Joshua?"

"And so I told Joshua. I couldn't wait. I think it led to some words because directly afterwards there was a shooting there—some lowlife I should have sent a check to in gratitude—and it made the local paper. Louie's on page one. Perfect timing. God must be a journalist—he so likes breaking news. And I think Joshua, always frightened of publicity and the world in general, backed off from her. He avoided her. Then that hissy fit with the gardener and a tracking of dirt or something. Then a bigger spat."

"About what?"

"I never knew because she clammed up. She got more strident—her true colors emerging—and Joshua backed off more."

"Is that why he moved?"

"Well, that surprised me. He talked about moving for years,
of course. A real bore about it. But I suppose so. That big house
was an albatross. Marta was huffing and puffing at the doorway,
ready to blow the house down. Life elsewhere probably seemed
desirable—and peaceful. She was smothering."

"Did Joshua understand your...sabotage?"

"Of course. I told him before he moved."

"And?"

"He shunned me after that."

"Were you bothered?"

"Yes, because I didn't expect silence. I expected—applause."

"Well, you can't blame yourself for the way things went down."

"I can do whatever I want, young man. I even told him she
went home with strangers. A complete lie. Oddly, Marta was
a virtuous woman who just liked to wander around the edges
of sensation. Gambling, but only slot machines. Bars, but only
appropriate mixed drinks with various garden produce in them.
Occasionally a late Saturday night, but home in time for early
Mass. After all, the Blessed Virgin was watching her from some
tree in Rochester or somewhere."

"Did she know about what you said to Joshua?"

"Of course. None of us could keep a secret. We didn't talk
for some time. But she came back. We missed each other. We
were, after all, friends."

"She was coming to see you the night she died?"

His voice tightened. "Yes. That was weird, I must say."

"Why?"

"I've already told you. She sounded...panicked. Frightened.
I never heard *that* before. Sad, depressed, angry, annoyed—but
this was different." He seemed to be holding the phone further
away, his voice fading.

"If she was panicky or frightened, wouldn't that suggest murder?"

He made a *tsk*ing sound. "All it suggests, I think, is…panic. Fear of the god Pan—that's the root of the word, you know. Fear of the unknown. She was frightened by loneliness."

"But…"

"And she was drunk as a skunk."

"Did she say anything else?"

"Well, she was babbling. Something about dying, but that was old stuff. She was always talking about her impending death. A fear of the grave. An old lady's aches and pains. That's why I wanted her to come visit—to calm her down. Do you know how I know it was suicide? Because she *told* me so. In all the babble she kept mumbling about me burying her. I just assumed she feared cremation, I don't know. We'd talked about it once—I guess Karen advised her to be cremated." A snicker. "Probably sooner than later. 'Can you bury me?' Me bury her! I had to step in. Imagine that. Slurring her words. Afraid her niece wouldn't tend to her sacred Catholic burial rites. She wanted some guarantee. It was all preposterous. A drunken conversation. Was I supposed to storm St. Augustine's—me, the old Protestant? A revisionist Martin Luther in a new Reformation?"

"You didn't tell me this before."

"Well, I…" Then nothing.

"It does sound like a suicide cry," I admitted, finally.

"Well, haven't we all been telling you that all along? Perhaps you should start listening."

Chapter Twenty-two

Hank knew all about Louie's Bar on South Road.

"It's a dump," he stressed, "a real hellhole. Guys from the college hit it, usually when they're already drunk and feeling daring. You know, wet T-shirt contests, spring-break stupors. St. Paddy's Day green beer. Jello shots. That kind of stuff."

"You've been there?"

"Once."

"And?"

"I didn't look American enough to survive."

"I'm going there tonight."

"And I'm right by your side."

"You sure?"

"Wouldn't miss it for the world."

"I don't know…"

"Hey, I've been there. You haven't. Who's the babe in the woods here?"

Hank insisted that underage college kids with phony IDs savored its seediness and its reputation for fistfights. The college kids assumed its tawdriness was calculated and cultivated. What they didn't realize—those errant kids who found themselves sitting in a dean's office with Mommy and Daddy flying in from Philadelphia or Atlanta—was that the place was a sewer, a real-life pit stop for hard drinkers. Mostly fringe people, ranging from lonely soggy sots who wandered in from the town's rural farm lanes, to the nervous druggies buying crack or weed in the dirt parking lot, to the young farm girls flirting with the welfare prostitution that would ultimately swallow them up on needle-strewn Hartford streets.

Louie's was Farmington's only real hellhole, tucked into sheltering trees far removed from the upper-crust sensibility of the Cotton Mather-seal-of-approval town center. Miss Porter's was symbolically light years away. It was a dirt-bag bar where Harley hogs lined up in front of the barn-red clapboard exterior.

"It sucks" was Hank's rhapsodic description of the place.

I couldn't wait to get there. Marta in such a wonderland? Hank warned me about what he called the tacit dress code—no slacks and loafers, no J.Crew sweater, no…

"Well, you get the idea," Hank said. "Your usual look."

But no one at Louie's cared, I discovered. It was too early, it was a slow weeknight and a workday, to boot, and only five or six mummified barflies drooped over the bar. Nobody even looked up at us.

"Maybe we should have come later." Hank sounded disappointed.

"Why? You looking for a date?" I asked. "Or a fight?"

The bartender was eyeing us, but then I saw him smile. With good reason—it turned out he was a former student from one of my night classes on Criminal Procedure, a part-time fireman with hopes of becoming a policeman. But his lack of serious motivation caused him to leave after one unsuccessful semester. Actually he left in the middle of a mid-term exam. That was how I remembered him. His phone went off loudly—appropriately, I thought—and he bellowed that there was a fire somewhere, startling everyone, and he was gone. He never returned to class. So here he was.

"Hello, Jamie," I began, stumbling on his name.

"Jonah," he corrected me. "Jonah Rivera."

"How Biblical," Hank muttered, and Jonah obviously heard him because the grin disappeared.

"You work here?" I said, displaying my usual acute insight.

He looked over his shoulder. "Yeah, that's why I'm behind the bar." But he was smiling again, and he shook my hand vigorously. "Good to see you, Professor."

He was a skinny hayseed, a milk-fed farm boy, lots of moist fiery acne on his impressive high cheekbones. His small eyes looked watery and dim, as if he were watching me through a fog. He treated us to our first drink. He was happy to see me. He repeated that over and over. Happy, happy. "Your class was cool."

"You're not coming back to the college?"

He shook his head. "Naw. I'm gonna be a fireman full time 'cause I'm getting married. No time for classes. This here"—he pointed around the barroom—"is real good spare change."

"I've never been here before."

"No surprise," he whispered. "Not exactly the Farmington Country Club. If you get my drift."

Hank and I sat at a rough-hewn table near the bar, and Hank, delighted as could be, leaned back, hands behind his head, and grinned at the ceiling. He was having a good time.

Jonah nodded at Hank. "Prof here is a good guy."

"Of course," Hank answered. "He's my friend."

Jonah looked perplexed. "Why did you two come here?" A grin. "Of all places."

"Well," I began, "I'm working on a case and I thought you— actually someone at this bar—might help me."

Jonah lit up, a trace of pink rising in the high cheeks, his eyes becoming less watery, more focused, pinpoints of pupil, hard as steel. "Wow." He breathed in. "Man. Cool."

I didn't know how cool it was, but I knew he'd be receptive to my questioning. He scooted from behind the bar, glancing for just a second at the barflies at the far end, and pulled up a chair. A spindly woman, eyes hidden behind owl eyeglasses, screamed for a drink, but Jonah ignored her. She shut up.

I took a sip from my Bud. "Marta Kowalski." And waited. Nothing. "She used to come in here—at least now and then. Or so we've heard. How long have you worked here?"

"A long time. Last year—over a year. Marta who?" His brow furrowed as he tilted his head.

I described her, but he interrupted me. "I always heard her name was Martha."

Hank jumped in, excited. "You knew her?"

"Sure, not really a regular. Once a month maybe, maybe more, maybe less. Actually less. Sometimes with this other old bat with too much makeup. They were a pair."

"I'm looking into her death. She killed herself."

Jonah tried to look grief-stricken, but it didn't work. I decided not to mention the possibility of murder. I didn't want him to experience a forensic orgasm.

"She didn't come that much, but when she did she made herself a presence, let me tell you."

"How so?"

He tapped the table with his index finger. "At first she'd be quiet, sitting at one of the tables against the wall, sipping some dumb lady drink, and you'd think she was in the wrong place. Always on a Saturday when it was packed with"—again he lowered his voice—"the usual lowlifes. But after four or five belts, she'd order straight vodkas, and then the voice got louder, she and the other bat, and their bodies start to shake and sometimes they even danced around like hotsy-totsy girls on TV or something." He grinned. "A sight and a half. Takes a lot to create a scene in this place—to make someone notice you—but they could do it. I'll tell you she was harmless. Let an old sleaze try to pick her up or say something sexy to her, and she'd haul off and slug him. Or, once, start to cry even. 'I'm a lady,' she'd scream."

"But she came here." Hank sounded baffled.

"Hey," he shrugged his bony shoulders, "it's a local bar. Ain't a crime, you know. We got a license. Maybe she lived in the neighborhood."

And suddenly I realized she actually did—three or four streets over in Unionville, so the place was really local for her, a gin mill round the corner from her house. It was probably the closest bar to her home.

"You ever see her with anybody besides that woman?"

"Nope. Most times by herself, in fact." He whistled, as though the news just arrived. "So she offed herself. Didn't seem the type."

"Why?"

"She was such a good Catholic."

Now that surprised me. "You picked that up from her behavior here?"

He laughed. "Yeah, I did. She never really talked me up, you know—just one time when I was rude or something, and then she hollered at me. After that she ignored me. Pushed up her shoulders as she strolled by. Like I'm gonna be a wreck because a grandma ain't taken with me. But sometimes when she got drunk—and she always did, sooner or later—she'd get this rigid look, jaw thrust out, eyes set, and she'd survey the room looking for lapses in moral conduct. And let me tell you, this place on Saturday is wall-to-wall moral lapse."

"Like what?"

"Like she'd see some mixed-race couple, like black and white, and she'd yell at them. Sometimes she'd get on this real Catholic kick—about the Virgin Mary loving her and us and living in all of us—Amen!—and she'd kiss this cross she wore around her neck. Not the best floor show for a bad-boy bar. 'Tomorrow is Sunday and you and I will all go to Mass.' That kind of thing. After a while people ignored her."

"So she was a racist?" Hank asked.

"She was everything. One time she accused some young guy of being a faggot and lit into him. 'You queers will burn in hell.' That sort of thing. He ran the hell outta here, followed—would you believe—by the guy's crying girlfriend, and we had to ask her to leave because she kept going on and on about queers."

He returned to the bar and brought back a couple of beers.

"She ever pick up anybody?"

He smirked. "I told you—she was a virtuous lady."

"So she never left with anyone?"

He looked around. "Like I said, man, would the Virgin Mary do a one-night stand?"

◇◇◇

Back at my apartment I leafed through a folder Gracie had slipped under the door. She always spelled my name wrong: *Rik van Lam, from Gracie. Info you asked for*. Inside was a pamphlet I'd asked her to pick up at Mass on Sunday, a brochure disseminated by the Brown Bonnets. It was similar to the one I'd found at Marta's home, a poorly printed rag, cheap tabloid paper and bleeding, smudged ink. Not exactly state-of-the-art desktop publication, it looked like some old PTA mimeographed bulletin. But I'd seen this sort of strident rag before—leaflets in Oklahoma City protesting the Vietnamese refugees there, anti-black propaganda on street corners. Down with 'Ricans. It grew out of the same world of frightened farm boys in their battered pickups who checked their gun-racks before the KKK rally in a dying Connecticut mill town.

"What do you know about the Brown Bonnets?" I asked Hank, waving the pamphlet at him.

"Well, we discussed them in my Social Problems class. One of the students did a research project for the class. They protested an exhibit at the Athenaeum—I mean, Jesus on the cross submerged in urine, I guess that's art I don't understand. You had to walk past their signs and their jeers to get in." He smiled innocently.

"Big group?"

"Bunch of tired old ladies. Only in Connecticut. Even the Catholic Church steers clear of them. Too fruitcake. They scare the parish priests. They publish this ad in the *Hartford Courant* each Saturday—a verbatim conversation with the Virgin Mary. Word for word. The Virgin appears in some tree in Albany or some place like that. Upstate New York."

I slipped off my shoes, put my feet on the coffee table. I'd seen their ads and was always mildly amused by them. But I never read them closely.

"What does the Virgin Mary have to say?"

"She makes a lot of grammatical errors, I hate to say. In need of a refresher course."

"New York accent?"

He smiled. "No accent that's detectable."

"What's her story?"

"She's on gays this week, last week abortion. 'Don't rip.' That's one of her favorite lines. She does have a way with words. Good image, no?"

"Hank, you sound like a faithful reader."

"Not really. After the class presentation, I found myself paying attention. They scare me."

The pamphlet I showed him was crammed with tightly printed columns of unabashed encomia to the Virgin—personal prayers of thanksgiving interspersed with pure unChristian venom against patsy liberal Democrats, the satanic pro-choice movement, and some local bogeymen whose names meant nothing to me. One article wept about the possibility of altar girls—"The ruination the church." Another told how, in China, baby-girl fetuses were bottled and sold for soup. I stopped reading. I didn't need another nightmare.

"I don't know if Marta was a member, but she had an interest in them."

"I'm not surprised."

"The pamphlet says they number in the hundreds."

"Probably twenty-five hysterical women. That's what the professor said when we discussed them."

I tossed the pamphlet on the table.

"But I got a problem here—no, a question," I told him. I yawned, ready for bed. "It's been coming up in lots of my interviews. Something that keeps coming back at me. If she was such a good Catholic, devout and observant, would she kill herself? Suicide is a mortal sin in the Church. Marta would not willingly condemn her soul to eternal damnation."

"You kill yourself when this place is no longer beautiful and that place—death—is." Hank looked very solemn.

"But we know that Marta was never a weak woman. You don't walk into Louie's by your lonesome and take swipes at biracial couples or suspected sissies. The woman had mettle."

Hank stood up. "I'm tired." He grabbed his coat. "You settle this yourself. Good night, Rick."

I followed him to the door. "And that mettle wouldn't let her kill herself—drunk or not. The Virgin Mary, looking down from that tree in Albany or wherever, would frown her into submission."

He tapped me on the shoulder. "Tomorrow."

"But what have we concluded?"

Hank flicked a finger at me. "Seems to me we just concluded that she was murdered."

Chapter Twenty-three

Early the next morning I jogged. Last night's bottles of beer had jumbled my thinking, slowed down my body. Stomach sick, I woke feeling the way I used to when I chain-smoked cigarettes or indulged in party weed at Columbia College, late night on the campus quad, sitting on the steps in the shadow of Low Library. The next morning I would stumble from my dorm room to class, hoping for rain to wake me up. So now I suited up, and jogged. Sweat suit, hood up against the fierce November day. The morning was clean and whole and crisp. It diminished the dark corners of Louie's and the slimy beer ache in my stomach.

Showered, refreshed, I fixed myself a light breakfast of scrambled eggs and whole-wheat toast, fresh-squeezed orange juice, and settled into the garage-sale leather armchair. Outside the wind blew. This was a morning for phone calls.

I was in search of Mary Powell, that Johnny-come-lately niece who provided such anonymity and possibility. I'd tried her number at various times since my morning in Clinton, but it rang and rang. Or was busy. Had she also moved? The old address, I knew, was a curious one. I knew New York streets. Her building was east of Broadway in the midst of a dense, noisy Spanish neighborhood. Bodegas busy with playful children and old women sitting outside in the cold on beat-up kitchen chairs. I couldn't imagine a relative of the aristocratic Joshua Jennings living there. But who knew? I might have to take a trip to New York.

I dialed the number and let the phone ring for a long time. Then, just when I was ready to hang up, a tentative, almost whispered voice said, "Hello."

"Mary Powell?"

Silence. I waited.

"Who's this?" she asked, keeping her voice barely above a whisper.

I told her my name, that I was a PI, that I was calling from Connecticut, trying to get information on someone recently dead. All matter of fact.

"I don't know…"

I thought I detected a slight accent in her voice.

She sounded ready to hang up. "Wait."

"I gotta go…"

"I got your name from a real estate agent in Clinton."

I could hear another voice behind her, a man's voice, sharp and edgy, but I couldn't make out the words. I sensed Mary Powell tightening up, breathing heavier.

"What did you say?" she whispered into the phone.

I explained again that I was looking for Mary Powell, blood relative of Joshua Jennings, now dead, and that I'd gotten her address from the realtor in Clinton. I might as well have spoken Farsi to her because I heard her mumbling to someone nearby, her hand covering the receiver.

"No, you got the wrong person."

But her words had something wrong with them. I didn't know whether she was lying because something else was there: wariness, uncertainty. I was scaring her. I also realized she sounded young.

A man's voice nearby. "Hang up."

"Wait, please. You are…"

"No, I don't…never been in Connecticut. Never." She whispered. "And I moved so…"

"Maybe someone else. Your mother? Is she Mary Powell?"

Hesitation. "Yes, but…"

"Maybe she…"

"Ma is in a home on Staten Island."

It was wrong, I knew. The manner, the voice, the carelessness, the confusion. The call caught her by surprise—and alarmed her. And that man with her—who?

"Joshua Jennings," I repeated.

"I never heard of him," she said, her voice shaky.

"Hang up now." The angry voice behind her.

"But…"

Somehow I believed her. She was never a part of Joshua's world. Not this Mary Powell.

"You got the wrong girl."

The voice behind her. "Now, baby."

"I gotta go." She hung up.

It made no sense.

Money.

All along I'd thought someone was in it for the money—someone Joshua contacted, perhaps by error, someone who saw a chance to cash in on the old man's loneliness. Maybe. It was still a possibility.

But was it money? I brought up the files on my laptop: Joshua's money—at least the money everyone knew about—had gone to the boys' school. All of it, and lots of it. Stock portfolios, money markets, bonds, even his simple savings account. All of it. But maybe there was other money that no one knew of. After all, Joshua was an old man, eccentric, a man willful and stubborn, a flirt and deceiver, a pain in the ass. Maybe there were assets removed from the security of a bank vault or a lawyer's office. Maybe Mary Powell had discovered—how?—something that Joshua owned that made it all worthwhile. Maybe that man with the gruff voice was somehow behind a scheme. Joshua and Mary. Maybe it was something she could steal away from him. Maybe they'd met somewhere. Joshua used to go into New York for museums, for theater. Of course, these excursions happened before he toppled over that last time. Maybe this Mary Powell, meeting him, was part of an elaborate rip-off scheme. A cagey waitress and her slimebag boyfriend, some con artists…

Maybe.

Who was Mary Powell?

I reread the local obit. My frayed photocopy of the obit mentioned that he'd died in New York City while visiting his niece. I couldn't imagine the venerable Joshua squirreled away in an apartment in a borderline neighborhood, the *bam bam boom* street noise wafting into his solitude, the aroma of burnt bacon and cheesy fries permeating the bland diet of his bland life.

I made myself a note to get hold of a death certificate. Perhaps there was information there to lead me to the lost and mysterious Mary Powell.

Chapter Twenty-four

I scheduled an appointment with Joshua Jennings' lawyer in New Haven late the next afternoon. Off Chapel Street, near the Yale Art Gallery, the nineteenth-century brownstone was a curious anachronism nestled in among a fast food restaurant, a frame-it-yourself art store, a faded luncheonette, a discount furniture store, and the milling hordes of laughing hip-hop kids who were hanging out on the bus benches under the high leaded-glass windows. Winslow, Winslow, Winslow, and Clay, Inc. I felt sorry for Clay.

I didn't need to feel sorry for Clay. William Clay, Esq., I discovered, was the only surviving senior partner. Clay, I realized, would soon be joining them. An old, leathery man, small and wiry, creaky as old wood, sort of like Joshua Jennings himself, but in an expensive suit, with a calculated haircut for the four strands that insisted on inhabiting his crusty scalp.

He was granting me ten-to-fifteen off-the-clock minutes, which must have cost him in the range of two thousand in billing time. So I calculated. He was doing it because he'd once liked Joshua. Those were his words: "I once liked him."

He nudged a file toward me. I took it.

"I met the niece once," he informed me. "A looker."

I tried to imagine the Mary Powell I spoke to in New York as a looker, but the only images I created were of a scared young woman. To the ninety-year-old Clay, with his Coke-glass eyeglasses, halitosis breath, and liver spots on his wrists as big as silver dollars—who knows what constituted a looker?

"A nervous woman," he told me. "But smiling. But jittery."

"Why was she here?"

"She said she had friends in New Haven. I had spoken with her by phone—she called from New York about Joshua—and then she was in Clinton with him. Then he was sick and in New York. It was hard to follow her movements."

"Did you see her again?"

"I spoke with her once on the phone. Then she sent a copy of the death certificate and a brief note he'd written to me before his death. It's there. A copy."

I leafed through the thin folder and read the death certificate. Fairly standard, dated September 15 in New York City. I started to jot down the doctor's signature.

"The folder is yours." He looked annoyed. I thanked him. Inside was a photocopy of the note Joshua wrote, a few painfully written, scribbled sentences saying hello, dated a week before his death. There was also a three-line typed note from Mary Powell that listed the legal documents enclosed.

"Nothing funny about the will?"

"Funny?" He didn't like the word. "It was years old, of course. I reviewed it, I remember, but an associate handled it. I spoke with him, and it was *pro forma*, actually. Old will on file, no codicils of any sort, fairly standard, no bequests other than to the school and college. All charity. A comfortable man. No property other than bank assets."

"But he left nothing to his niece."

"Nothing unusual there. I was told that he had only known her a short time. He'd located her online. That bothered him, of course. Some genealogical site. A distant relative. Who knows? She wasn't happy he found her—wanted to write an end to the whole business, she said." He locked eyes with mine. "She admitted that he gave her ten thousand dollars, a gift."

"I didn't know that."

"If she told me that, I imagine the amount was higher. But the will was ironclad. She'd have an uphill battle contesting, a point I made to her—in case she harbored such an idea."

"Had she mentioned the will?"

"She told me on the phone that she didn't want money from him—didn't expect it, in fact. I gather she found him a nuisance." The old man smiled. "She did say something amusing, I thought. 'Lovers take care of me,' she said, and I thought that a most frank and unnecessary admission."

"She didn't mention any lovers' names?"

He seemed surprised. "How would one respond to such a line, Mr. Lam?"

I could think of a dozen, but maybe I come out of a different time and place.

He raised his hand. The conference was over. We shook hands. "Intriguing," he said to my back.

"What is?" I looked back.

"Alive, Joshua was an uneventful man. Joshua has only become interesting after his death. It's what I hope for my own life."

I walked out. How would you respond to such a line?

◇◇◇

Leaving his office, I walked into darkness and bitter cold. The New Haven streets were filled with people headed home, huddled against the chill wind. I enjoyed being in the city, loving the aimless wandering, watching a storekeeper fighting with some resistant Christmas lights that refused to stay put. It wasn't even Thanksgiving yet. Americans, I discovered, like to rush the holidays, frantic to get them over with. Although I celebrated no holidays myself, Liz and I—in our fairy-tale honeymoon period in New York—had celebrated Christmas with a little real tree we bought on Carmine Street in the village, and Hanukkah candles. A mish-mash. She was (not is) Jewish. I was (not am) Buddhist. Somehow, though, we both remain Jewish and Buddhist. And oddly Christian. Happy holidays. Shalom. Feliz Navidad.

...like a Buddha in a dying lotus blossom
...like honey blanketed by swarms of bees...

I'd always hunger for order and balance. For calm, serenity.

I glared at the storekeeper. He kept fighting with the strings of lights.

I lingered in a deli over pastrami on rye and a Sam Adams ale.

Back on the street I found myself exhilarated. Yale students streamed through upper Chapel Street, bumping into one another, laughing, their faces bright against the cold. I recalled nights back at Columbia, jostling with buddies down Broadway toward Tom's Restaurant. We didn't give a damn about anything. So I wandered now. By the time I decided to head back to Hartford, it was after ten o'clock. My car sat on a side street, a ticket slapped on the windshield.

I fumbled for my keys, my fingers numb against the cold lock. Across the street I heard forced laughter, a man's reedy high-pitched warble in counterpoint to another man's deeper, more aggressive boom, and I suddenly realized that the laughter was familiar. Turning, I stared through the darkness, past the faltering neon of a kosher Chinese restaurant, past the art-deco neon of a corner bar. There were two men standing in front of the bar, and they were laughing.

I watched quietly as they moved off the sidewalk, coming closer to where I stood. The man nearest me, I realized, was Davey Corcoran. And he was gripping the sleeve of Ken Rodman, my upstairs neighbor.

I looked past them, back toward the bar, and through the half-lit window, I saw the press of dancing men. I may be slow when it comes to such things, but I did live in New York. I know a gay bar when I stumble onto one.

Davey and Ken were crossing the street. The laughter had stopped but not the intimacy. I wrestled with the scene—there was no way I could have connected Ken with Davey. Ken, freshly divorced and finding his way alone in the apartment above mine, seemed a placid insurance executive. Marta, Davey's aunt, had cleaned his apartment.

And Davey, that bitter isolato—or so I thought—locked away in that messy, littered apartment, dressed in his Mayberry

RFD flannels and hayseed mentality, was just a guy with a smart-alecky mouth. He was a lonely reader of books. Here he was, still dressed in flannel, with a camouflage vest over it, and jeans and boots. The way he always dressed, I guess. But now he was far from home—and in the company of men, as they said in Victorian novels. Sort of.

"Davey," I yelled. I regretted it immediately, but I knew he'd spot me within seconds.

He stopped in his tracks, literally locked in place, and stared across the street. When he saw me, his smile faded, his laughter ended.

Worse, he shuddered as though chilled, and looked left and right. He threw his large head back, almost melodramatically, as a character would in an old tearjerker, then bolted. That's the only word to describe his actions—he bolted. He ran, bouncing off the dark walls, careening around a couple of late-night partygoers leaving the Chinese restaurant, and then disappeared around the corner.

"Davey," I yelled to the empty black corner.

When I looked back at Ken, he was standing with his arms by his side, staring at me. But even across the street, under the purple haze of streetlight and November wind and neon garishness, even under that artificial light, I could see he was grinning.

◇◇◇

The next evening, unplanned, my friends showed up at my apartment. First Liz stopped in. I'd spoken to her earlier about Marta because she was wondering what was going on, and she told me she was a few streets over.

"Come on up," I told her.

Though she hesitated, she agreed, and promised to bring takeout from Triple Star. We'd finished our moo shu pork and sesame chicken when Jimmy dropped in, and Gracie soon followed. Jimmy was dressed in a bright sky-blue sweater with giant white cobwebs covering it. He looked ready for a ski slope. He made a grumpy sound when I told him this, and Gracie giggled, saying that Jimmy's only exercise was carrying a box of cigars from the car into his house. He beamed at her. She was, of course, the only person he ever grinned at. I mean, he smiled and charmed, and he laughed. But when Gracie was around—tonight she'd dipped herself into some potent hyacinth perfume and decked herself out in a go-to-bingo pants suit with sequins and sparkles—the two of them acted out their light and innocent romance, if that was what it was.

Liz and I served drinks—for a moment I experienced *déjà vu*, the two of us in our Manhattan apartment entertaining friends. We relaxed. Within minutes there was a knock and Hank wandered in. He'd shaved his head. He long sported a close-cropped haircut, but now he looked...bald.

"Christ, a skinhead," Jimmy sang out.

"This is how guys look now," Hank protested.

"I like it," Liz told him.

Then, just as I was remembering I had a batch of term papers I had to grade, my Criminal Justice students stumbling through their case-study reports, Vinnie and Marcie dropped in. They were coming home from dinner, driving by, saw Hank parking his car, and spotted the lights on in my apartment. Everyone was talking at once, everyone was laughing. I smiled at everyone, overjoyed, but I was tired.

Jimmy said he missed the days when he could have a cigarette with his beer—and I remembered Willie Do's declaration in his own apartment. Gracie teased Hank. She'd taken a real shine to him—"Such a cute boy, and quick"—and loved goofing on him. Liz gave him a bear hug. Hank always looked embarrassed by the attention, but I could tell he was pleased. Since Hank and I became buddies, he'd slowly worked his way into all my friends' affections. Now, with all my friends around me, Gracie kidded Hank about his shaved head ("a skinny Buddha") and his shadowing of my investigation.

"I want to learn from the master," Hank declared grandly.

Jimmy interrupted, "I'm not taking on any pupils, Hank."

We laughed.

There was a sudden rapping at the door, and we all jumped, guilty of something. It gave me pause. After all, my closest friends were at that moment huddled in the room with me, and the hour was late. Who? The police? I thought of Karen, but I knew she'd never drop in. Nobody came to the door around midnight. Everyone must have been thinking the same thing because we became quiet, very quiet.

I opened it. Ken Rodman looked sheepish and uncomfortable. He had on an overcoat, so I assumed he was coming home from somewhere. His face looked stiff with cold.

He looked over my shoulder at the crowd, all of them staring back with expressions ranging from accusation to curiosity.

"I didn't know you had company," he said.

That surprised me. We were raucous enough to warrant eviction—had the landlady herself not been a major culprit in the noise.

"Come in."

"Oh, no." He backed off. "I wanted to talk to you about last night."

"I want to talk to you."

"I have something to tell you." He mouthed the word *Davey* silently. "I should have told you before." But he was already backing off, fast now. "Later on. I'll catch you later." He backed off, headed up the stairwell.

I stared at my friends. An obligatory moment of silence, then the frantic Babel of insistent voices rose in awesome crescendo.

"I have nothing to say." I relished the moment.

They pushed into me, trapping me, all of them believing they'd seen a pivotal moment in the Case.

"I have nothing to say," I repeated.

No one believed me. Then, smiling, I quoted Buddha: "'Look for sand in your rice. Look for rice in your sand.'"

Everyone groaned.

Chapter Twenty-five

The next afternoon, after classes, I swam for an hour at the college, then headed to the shopping arcade to visit Karen. She had an hour till closing, she said, though she was restless and ready to leave. When I'd called, she told me to stop in.

"I'm bored," she'd said, "and we gotta talk."

I got there early, so I wandered down the sidewalk, window shopping. Lingering outside Farmington Books and Things, staring at a display of New England travel books, I felt a tap on my shoulder. I turned.

"Did you see Peter at the college today?" Selena asked.

"No. Why?"

She stood there, waiting.

"Does he have a late afternoon class?" I asked.

She shrugged her shoulders. "It doesn't matter." She smiled. "You shopping?"

I didn't answer. I looked over her shoulder, and her face tightened.

"You're here to see Karen." Her voice was flat.

"Yes."

"Wasn't I neurotic enough for you?"

I smiled. "You did a good job of it."

"All women get neurotic around men. You men train us to be that way. It's a form of slavery. Men want us off balance."

I kept my mouth shut. Karen, glancing out the doorway of her shop, spotted me, and waved. I nodded toward her. Selena followed my eye and frowned. She drew her fingernail down my lapel, applying pressure, and then without a word turned away. She disappeared into her shop.

"She still got it for you?" Karen said when I entered her store.

"I don't want to talk about it."

"She and I have this little thing—this tension—for a while now. I don't know where it came from, but the fact that you dated her adds to the fire."

I didn't say anything.

"She has no friends here." She waved her hand across the line of shops. Then, smiling, "Oh well. Some folks rub others the wrong way."

Her smugness bothered me, prompting me to defend Selena, whose childhood was as lost as my own. "You gotta remember where she came from, Karen. She never really fit in, you know, growing up with a crazy mother, a rotten father never around, Radcliffe on a scholarship, then meeting Peter who…"

Karen cut me off, angry. "I know the resumé. The whole goddamn town has heard it. The poor All-American girl meets the poor All-American boy. Fireworks. The pretty people. I need a rest from it."

"Sorry."

Almost closing time, we talked very little while she tended to the store, eyeing a young mother who kept frowning at a piece of art on the wall. When we were alone, she told me that she'd found another box of Marta's papers tucked into a clothes drawer that she was emptying out. Mostly old bills, but she wanted me to look through it. "Telephone receipts, that sort of thing. I don't know why she kept them."

"I'll check them out."

"Come for dinner. You can go through them."

I nodded.

"Look, it's just an excuse to see you."

I nodded again.

As we drove to her place—I'd walked to the arcade so I rode with her—I asked her when she planned on selling Marta's house.

"I hate that house. Way out there—so—well, so like Marta herself. Those fifties windows and that fifties kitchen with the black-and-white tile and the…" She stopped, waving her hand. "I don't want to live there because she once lived there. I'm going to sell it, but not right away. I want to take my time."

While she tossed a salad for dinner, I leafed through the cardboard box of papers. Elastic bands bound receipts from years back—household bills from the Connecticut Light and Power, Connecticut Gas, the sort of stuff anyone would have thrown out long ago. At one point Karen walked in. She'd changed her clothes, slipping out of her work outfit of a casual gray wool suit and into a pair of billowing fawn-colored slacks and that light yellow cashmere sweater I liked. She'd let her hair down and looked like a young girl, the autumn colors masking the stress in her face.

"You look happy," I told her, but she said nothing, returning to the kitchen. A cabinet door slammed. I'd just made her more uncomfortable. Davey's voice, again: *Karen runs from everything while she actually thinks she's running to it.* Why did that line stay with me?

Idly I sifted through another box she'd carried from Marta's home.

"Marta's attempt to mimic Joshua's collecting," she yelled to me.

I scanned some of the titles. A Thomas Hardy novel, a Robert W. Chambers romance, some faded and chipped leather volumes, odd genteel romances with embossed gilt covers. They were lined up in the bottom of a cardboard box.

"They remind me of her." Karen appeared behind me, looking over my shoulder.

"I like old books."

"I don't," Karen said. "Neither did Marta. She complained that she had to dust his walls of books. And every other professor's. Like Wilcox and Safako. Books and books and books. She hated books."

"You're hard on her, Karen."

"Am I?"

"I find it strange that this woman men wanted as a friend has such bad stuff said about her—after her death. Even Hattie."

"She wasn't a saint, you know."

I stared at her.

Throughout dinner we barely spoke, a faraway look in her eyes despite my attempts to generate conversation. I gabbed monotonously about Gracie and Jimmy, but she kept looking away.

"Your aunt saved a lot of junk." I struggled for a topic.

"You want to talk about the case?"

"I guess so. Is that why I'm here?"

"Yes. I mean, yes, but I also wanted to, you know, relax."

"But you want to discuss the case."

"You don't call me about it."

"I don't have much to tell you yet."

"But you will?"

I shrugged my shoulders. I noticed she barely touched her salad. For a few minutes, mechanically, I outlined what I'd done, everything chronological and matter of fact, ending with the Mary Powell question and my side trip to New Haven and Joshua's lawyer. I left out seeing her panicky brother outside that bar in New Haven. That was none of my business—at this point, at least.

"So," she concluded, "we are still nowhere."

I apologized, but she held up her hand. "It's okay. You're onto something."

That comment startled me. "What?"

"Joshua Jennings and Mary Powell. They hold some important answer. That Mary—she's hiding something. I can *sense* it."

As she spoke, her words so emphatic, without qualification, it suddenly rang true. Not so much the Mary Powell part—most likely that was a dead end—but Joshua held a key to this puzzle. The story of Joshua would lead me back to Marta's fateful night on that final stone-cold bridge.

Over coffee we relaxed, her easy-going mood returned. We sat together on the sofa, the box of Marta's papers between us, and she tossed canceled checks and useless papers into the wastebasket. Unused church collection envelopes. United Way appeals. Girl Scout cookie receipts. Marta's tight, constipated script appeared on lists of dollars and cents spent on little things: chewing gum, hair dye, a Sue Grafton paperback from an airport kiosk. What for? Tax deduction? I doubted that. Canceled airline receipts from many years back. Not the important Russian trip—I looked for that—but quick jaunts to Las Vegas, to the Mall of America, to New Orleans, to Atlantic City. US Airlines. American Airlines. Delta. Standard domestic carriers. We tossed it all away.

But I looked through it all first, every envelope, every receipt, and in one of the last airline packets, folded neatly in half, was a scribbled note definitely not in Marta's handwriting, dated two years back.

"Look at this." I handed it to Karen.

"That's Hattie's handwriting. I'd recognize it anywhere."

It was a short note, handwritten, torn from a school-style notepad, signed by Hattie Cozzins, acknowledging the loan of twenty-thousand dollars, some two years back, to be repaid in installments determined at a later time.

"Now that doesn't sound like my aunt at all," Karen insisted.

"Why not?"

"Generosity was not one of her strong points. And Hattie was a travel companion, not a bosom buddy. With me, she spent more time ranking on the poor woman than—well, celebrating their friendship."

I took the piece of paper. "I'll visit Hattie and see what she has to say about this."

Antsy now, she wandered the rooms, folding and unfolding her arms, leafing through papers, stopping, sniping at me.

"You're bothered by the note," I commented.

She glared. "It's *my* money that woman has."

I shut up. Money, Jimmy always told me. Most murders came down to money.

I suggested a ride to the 880 Club in Hartford to listen to some local jazz, a venue she knew nothing about.

"I don't know jazz."

"You don't have to."

When we got there, it was still early and the place was nearly empty. A few tables of veterans and regulars nodded and tapped feet to a small lively combo. But after a half hour Karen stood up and touched my shoulder.

"Could we leave now?"

She walked away. I followed her out, rushing to catch up with her.

"Everybody in there is too happy."

That amazed me because the combo was slinking around a downbeat improv of "St. James Infirmary." A mournful, low rider kind of night. The rent hadn't been paid and the band hadn't been laid. Nobody was happy.

"Rick. My God."

I heard a voice from the parking lot. Liz was stepping out of a car. She was with a woman I didn't know. Both were muffled in scarves and pullover hats. I smiled. Her silky voice gave her away.

I stopped to say hello, but Karen, wired now, face set, plunged ahead, standing by her car, waiting for me to get there. I nodded in Karen's direction and Liz, looking back at her, widened her eyes, tilted her head. I read the look—*You seem to be in some trouble here, and it's all your own doing.* A quick peck on the cheek, and she disappeared into the 880 Club. I joined Karen.

"That was Liz."

"I know who she is. Does your ex-wife follow you around, Rick?"

"A public place, Karen. Sometimes we bump into each other. Especially here. A favorite spot…" My voice trailed off.

Her voice dipped. "Like Selena today?"

"Selena found me—and her shop is right near yours."

"Christ, Rick. Women and you. You're cruel to them. That's why they want you."

Whatever that meant—I had no idea. The line came out of nowhere—and was preposterous. It had no basis in any fact I knew about. I might be a lot of things—a little vain sometimes, a whole lot insecure, a tad foolish at other times—but I don't really see myself as cruel. Not one of the deadly sins. I don't like it in others, so I don't want it in myself.

She refused to talk on the way back to Farmington. Sitting in the car outside my apartment, I started to say good night, but she turned her head away. For a moment I thought of Marta—the severe Puritan howling in the wilderness.

"Karen."

"You're on the time clock." Her voice broke at the end. "Tonight was business."

◇◇◇

I didn't feel like going into my apartment. So I went into the back, hopped into my car, and spun around for an hour, stopped in to see Jimmy, and eventually, late at night, walked into my apartment.

I had one blinking message. Liz, not surprisingly. The appropriate end to this evening's periodic sentence.

Her voice was jittery. "You two did not look happy tonight. Or—together. I'm sorry but it's true. And I hope she's not there listening to this message with you. If so, make me out to be the witch I am and call me a meddlesome ex-wife who doesn't know when the glow is over. Sorry I called but I can't take it back."

Her words rambled on. I smiled. It was the kind of dumb message she and I would have ended up laughing hysterically over many years before, as we held onto each other and howled. When, indeed, we were in love. We could laugh for hours over little things.

I sat in the chair, my eyes closed, smiling. It was times like this that I really regretted the end of our marriage. So much of us was so good. Maybe we were just too young then. She brought out the best in me, and I wasn't embarrassed by it. She could always make me smile at the absurdity of things. Like now.

Leave it to Liz to end my day with laughter.

Chapter Twenty-six

In the morning I slept late, too late, with no desire to jog or swim. The phone startled me awake at nine-thirty.

"You alone?" Liz again.

I wasn't smiling. "Liz…"

"You are. Good."

"Liz…"

"I'm sorry about last night, that message I left. It was stupid, but that's not why I'm calling so early in your day. I'm at the office. Some of us do go to offices."

I waited.

"I told you that I'd run all the names you gave me, and nothing came up. But a lot of the records aren't computerized yet, so I had an intern do a manual check. I made a few phone calls out of state. It's amazing the amount of info people are sitting on. I have a juicy tidbit for you. It has to do with Professor Charles Safako. Charlie Safako."

Liz took her time.

"In going over his file I noticed he'd lived in Massachusetts years back, but there were noticeable gaps in his history. Something seemed questionable. You know how you can tell when things seem a little too doctored in a resumé? After a few phone calls—I have a colleague with the Massachusetts State Police—I learned that the venerable Professor Safako was arrested for manslaughter when he was a young man. At age twenty-three, in fact. In Methuen, Massachusetts. He served five years of a fifteen-year sentence. Did parole, and disappeared, ended up, suddenly, on the faculty of Farmington College. A felon, mind you. He couldn't even vote for president. Talk about your phoenix rising from the ashes. None of this is in his college resumé, of course."

I was wide-awake. "Great work." I was pleased. "Fax me the file?"

"Will do."

"I knew he was hiding something."

"Somebody didn't ask some questions when he was hired at the college."

"Or somebody covered something up. Had to be. Somehow. That kind of conviction is hard to conceal. So I got some questions for him. Now I think he'll listen."

◇◇◇

When I arrived at Charlie Safako's office, a student was just leaving, opening the door slowly. She was grinning sheepishly as she walked by me. When he saw me standing there, he frowned, stood up, and looked as though he wanted to slam the door in my face. I held out my hand, a traffic cop.

"This hour is for students."

"Let's take a walk."

"Let's not." He sat down and fumbled with some papers on his desk.

"Let's. Methuen. Five years. Manslaughter." I mouthed the words slowly. "Shall I keep going?"

The minute I spat out the words he crumpled, his eyes blinking and pale. His body slumped in the chair. I shut the door behind me.

He looked up, dry-eyed, and forced himself to stay calm. When he spoke, his voice was clipped and crisp. "So you've come to stick a knife in my vulnerable ribs."

"No, I've come for some straight answers."

"That's what Joe McCarthy said as he ruined a life or two. Sit down."

"Look, I'm only concerned with how any of this relates to Marta Kowalski's death."

Again he looked surprised, as though he had forgotten what I was all about. For a second I saw relief in his eyes.

"What do you know?"

"No, you tell me."

I stared at him, an out-of-shape guy dressed in professorial corduroy, complete with the crinkly leather patches on the elbows. Yet the thinning hair was a little too long and uncombed. Whether he was affecting a classic Bohemian style or he thought he was a little too late for the Summer of Love, I couldn't tell. I didn't like him.

I sat still, saying nothing. Eventually, I knew, people talk. Vacuums are for cleaning rugs.

I waited. I had all day.

A deep sigh. "Okay, okay. So you know. I'd just like to know how you found this out." He smiled weakly. "Academics have no previous lives. Especially when we keep ourselves totally undistinguished in the profession." He took another deep breath. "It was a stupid barroom brawl and I smashed a guy over the head with a bottle. He died on me. Dumb luck. A local bar I hung out in. I suppose I was trying to kill him—I had a temper. Still do, I'm afraid. Five miserable, stinking years in jail. It was a young man's stupid indiscretion."

I thought murder occupied a category a little apart from indiscretion, but I let him talk.

"In jail I read and read, and when I got out I finished my Ph.D. at Tufts. Obviously I would have trouble getting a teaching job—murder doesn't look good on a *curriculum vitae*, shall we say, although it's preferable to most scholarly journal publications—but I had connections at Farmington College. Actually on the Board of Trustees, a distant cousin or something of my mother's. Favors owed, et cetera. All hush hush, to be sure. Records were falsified, and the Board appointed me—actually established a position for me. Trustees cavalierly usurp faculty power when the right connections are in place. So I was an assistant professor, without past or portfolio, and the rest was easy. Knee-jerk promotions by means of flattery and fakery. No one ever looked back. No reason to. Here I am. Until you snooped into my life, no one has ever discovered it. No one even *looked*." He lifted his arms into the air, as in surrender. "Now I've filled in your blanks."

"I'm not on a witch hunt."

A bitter smile. "So they all say."

"But I'm curious, Charlie. What about all those rumors about you? The affairs with students."

He lowered his voice into a whisper. "You mean that I fathered a child with a coed?"

"For one."

"Not true. I don't know where that started, but it got ugly for a while. That was a long time ago when I was first here. Then I stopped denying it, and a generation passed. On university campuses such rumors then take on a mythic life of their own— they actually contributed to my reputation. Undergraduates find nothing interesting these days, so legendary bed-hopping by balding professors who still make sexual remarks in class—all that passes for intrigue. The classroom itself is tedious. Legend rarely is."

"And somehow that baby rumor would keep people from your real past."

He smiled. "Precisely."

"So the legend of lady killer is just that."

He seemed piqued. "Well, women have loved me," he hissed.

"I mean students…"

He cut me off. "I repeat—women have loved me. Don't be so smug. We both shared the same woman, you and I."

That stunned me. "What?"

Then I remembered his throwaway remark about Selena.

"You make it seem like such an impossibility. She's always been rude to me—she actually sat in on a class of mine some time back and never shut up—but you do know she's a little bizarre."

"What happened?"

Charlie sat back, slipping into the present tense. "We're at this party, separately of course, and Selena's drinking and giggly.

I'm ready to leave when someone made a crack that I alone of our little Russian tour party will be the last survivor, once the aging Richard Wilcox is dead. Joshua, Marta, Richard—and me. I live. At the door there's little Selena, looking like an understudy for Martha in Albee's little domestic farce. Then, weird, she's all over me. We leave, get a bite, end up chatting like magpies, and then she comes to my place. Couldn't shut her up, and I'm wondering if she's insane. She unbuttons her blouse, and the minute my hand finds forbidden territory, she slaps me, bolts out the door." He shook his head.

"Why?"

"I guess the liquor wore off."

"When was this?"

"A few weeks back." He smiled. "I gather, from the rumor mills, that you did not have such a painful experience with the lovely woman."

"I don't care about that—or her. I'm here about Marta Kowalski."

He jumped, knocked over a folder of papers.

"You think because I killed someone at twenty-three I'd kill decades later?"

"It's been known to happen."

"Look, Marta was not even a friend. She was Joshua's friend, Richard's. I was *their* friend. We almost became friends at one point, but I didn't like her most of the time. Too judgmental. So am I, but frankly"—he smirked—"I'm usually right about things. She thought me a bitter, cynical man."

"I think the same thing."

His mouth curled for a second. "Well, the majority opinion is in then. We've heard from the disenfranchised."

I laughed. "You can't be nice, can you?"

He actually smiled. "Look, Marta at the end was all business with me. She cleaned my apartment. We talked. Damn it, she'd just dusted my apartment before she died. I wouldn't kill her because she left cobwebs on the light fixtures."

"No romance?"

"Please." He stretched the word out. "That Catholic crone. A woman who got her credo from a Walmart catalogue? Please."

"I still don't understand her power over men."

"There was no power, really. Some men, just a few lonely old souls. My God, man, she did something no one else will do for us."

"What?"

"No," he raised his voice, "not that. She paid attention to us. When we talked, she acted interested. Batted her eyes and made us think we were still important."

"But that came to an end."

"Well, even Joshua was getting sick of her. Of course, he was fickle. I'd see him at the town library. The last time I saw him he told me he missed Marta, even though—as he put it—she was imperious. He wanted her back, in fact. Imagine—that old fool. He started to say something else, but he stopped. They'd stopped talking, you know. Had a terrible row. A spat over the gardener, then *another* blow out, so I understand. He did say he was sick, but he was ambivalent about leaving Farmington. His home here. He'd changed his mind. Again. Again and again. Imagine my surprise at that. I tried to talk some sense into him. Colleague to colleague. Old guard to old guard. Told him to get out before his world fell down around him. Thank God he listened to me."

"And they never reconciled."

"The man had a brain, young man."

"But somehow you escaped her power?"

"That rumor about the baby has its genesis in one true fact. I like the young ones—like the one that just left my office. The curvaceous coeds whose blouses I look down in class. They know it and know I reward them. They brush against me in the office, so I reward them. It's real pathetic, my needs. The young ones, in the first flush of womanhood. Little girl red cheeks bathed in a harlot's perfume. My lord."

I stood up, ready to leave. He was making me squirm.

His sarcasm returned. "You're a prude, like all young men. You know nothing about nothing."

I opened the office door. "How do you know I'll keep your secret?"

He preened like an exultant bird. "But this is not the secret you care about. You'll keep quiet." He hardened his face. "You're a coward, like all young people. You're afraid of the consequences. Dangerous liability for a PI, no?"

"What about ethics?"

He laughed. "Mr. Lam, you probably can't spell the word."

Chapter Twenty-seven

The next afternoon, dressed in baggy slacks and a ripped-at-the-elbow sweater that always made me feel at home, I settled in with coffee and a grilled cheese sandwich. I took down all my note cards, shuffled them at random, spread them out. I checked them against the files on my laptop. Marta and Richard. Marta and Joshua. Marta and Davey. Marta and Karen. Marta and... On and on. Trying to make new connections.

Marta on her last day—the secret lay there, I knew. That last day. And somehow that last day involved the men she'd been friendly with. My gut instinct kept pushing me back to Joshua. Back to Russia, in fact. Even back to Atlantic City and the photo taken on the boardwalk, all of them vacationing together. But it was Russia where it all began, the professors getting to know one another for the first time, huddled against a dark Moscow skyline, beginning the friendship that shifted and altered and blossomed or declined in the years to follow. Marta's wooing of the resistant Joshua. Back to Joshua, buried with his secrets. Was the mysterious Mary Powell in New York City one of those secrets?

I repositioned the cards on the pegboard and scrolled through files on the Mac.

Marta on her last day. A conversation on the telephone with Richard Wilcox. Slurred drunken speech. An aborted stroll to his condo. Marta had something to tell him. She was *different* that last day. What did she know? Playing around with Richard

Wilcox's file, I was coming up with nothing. It was time to visit him again—to replay that final day. I started drawing correspondences of Richard with people other than Marta—with Joshua, for one, with Charlie Safako, with Hattie, with other faculty at the college. The old Farmington guard, rarefied patrician and discreetly removed from the hopelessly roustabout younger faculty members, that newer generation with their herbal teas, fat-free micro/macro lives, and lifetime memberships at Bally's Health Spa.

There was a knock at the door, which surprised me. It was midday and usually I wasn't home. The rapping continued, almost insistent now, and I paused the computer, debating. Then I heard a voice. "Rick?"

It was Ken Rodman. After his surprise visit the other night, he'd disappeared. Out of town, Gracie told me. I'd left a note on his door: "Call me when you get back." When I opened the door, he was ready to knock again, his face contorted, angry.

"Ken?"

"I saw your car."

That made no sense. My old Beamer often sat in the yard when I walked to the campus or into town. I waited.

"I just got back to town. Away on business. I had to see you." But he took a step backward.

I motioned him in. He stood inside the door, but didn't move.

"Does any of this relate somehow to the case, to Marta's death?"

"Wait," he cut me off. "Whoa." He actually said that—*Whoa*—like in an old Roy Rogers black-and-white western, recycled these days on Nick at Nite. "I don't think this has anything to do with *that* business."

"Then why come to see me?"

A long silence. "I didn't care for Davey's reaction to seeing you, you know, on that street in New Haven."

"And you think that doesn't relate to his aunt's case?"

"It never dawned on me. I thought it was, well, because of…"

"Is Davey gay?"

"He's like me," he faltered. "He's bisexual." Again, the silence.

"Your marriage?" I prodded.

He nodded. "We agreed it was best. It was a good marriage, and I love her, but I was seeing more and more men, and she was scared for my health, and there was tension, and we had kids and I wouldn't come home. I was a bastard, and suddenly I find myself alone at my age. Alone."

"And Davey?"

"Well, I knew him from town. For years, casually. From the garden shop. Nothing much. When I had a yard, I shopped there. I went to this bar in Hartford called Mirage and he was leaving. Actually I don't think he even went in, he was so scared. I think he was hanging out in the parking lot. But we talked and we went out just twice, but it was awful. He's a mess."

"Why?"

I had trouble hearing Ken because he was whispering.

"Davey doesn't want to be gay. He just is. He refuses to be. He, well—like now and then has sex with a guy but then he hates himself and he hates the guy and he goes back to Mass and prays. He's like his aunt, I guess, from what he told me. A devout Catholic yet he can't stand the sex thing—but he can't help himself. Like I said, we saw each other twice, I think, but he was so fucked up, I stopped."

"And that bar in New Haven?"

"Pure chance, let me tell you. I was in the bar and I saw him pacing in front, back and forth. He was going through one of his stepping-out periods. I went out and got him, dragged him inside where I bought him a drink. Christ, he spilled it, he was so nervous, and we were both leaving when we saw you. He was actually laughing and loosening up. It blew his mind—you right there and all—that's why he ran away."

"You see him since?"

"He called me and told me to keep quiet. If you said anything to me or anybody, to deny it. He was scared of his aunt—like she was still alive. It gave me the willies. He was crying and sputtering, and it was awful. He's told me he's praying a lot."

Standing there, I recalled a guy in New York City years ago, a weird perp I busted. A Jesus freak, a holy-roller type who wore huge crucifixes, prayed out loud on subways, and saw himself as God's faithful buddy. But every once in a while his dreaded sexuality drove him to cruise waterfront bars below Christopher Street, picking up young guys in alleys. Then, filled with self-hatred, he'd get violent. One time he beat a teenage boy to death in an alley. When I found him, he was praying in St. Patrick's, his fingers wet with holy water.

Thinking of Davey, I wondered how this bit of autobiography sat with the fiercely homophobic Aunt Marta.

"And his aunt," I asked Ken, "did she know?"

"Yeah, he talked about that. He was real bitter. He didn't tell me how she found out—but she hated faggots. They had a wild fight and that's why she cut him out of the will. He hated her." He stopped, listened to his own words. "But, come on, he's not gonna kill her for that. He's a devout Catholic."

"Catholics kill."

"Not Davey. He's just, well, fucked up about this gay thing."

"Okay, so Davey still has to deal with it."

"You can't mention this conversation."

"I can't promise that."

"I told you—he begged me. He doesn't want people to know."

"I can't promise you that. This opens up questions I might have to ask. I'm sorry."

He turned abruptly, making me jump. And as he did, the pleasant face crumbled, twisted, an unlovely face.

"You'll be sorry," he swore.

"What does that mean?"

"Davey is a ticking bomb." He stared at me for a second, and then left.

Chapter Twenty-eight

Davey and Aunt Marta. An explosive combination.

I waited until Karen was home from the shop before I phoned her. What did she know about this deadly equation? What fit of anger, bursting from Davey's repressed confusions, might have triggered an attack on a vicious, unsympathetic aunt? Here was a woman who would gladly curse him to the fires of the hell he already believed awaited him. I hadn't mentioned seeing Davey in New Haven to Karen, but I debated what choices I had.

Karen was surprised to hear from me. "Rick, this is pleasant."

"Karen, I have a question about Davey." I hesitated. "His private life."

She breathed in, a deep rasp. "I know what you're gonna say."

"You do?"

A long time before she answered. "I've been waiting for this. I suspected. I mean, my aunt hinted something once or twice. When she'd had a little too much wine at dinner. I knew she disliked him for something like that. But I didn't want to deal with it." She sighed. "I still don't want to deal with it."

"Tell me, did they fight about it?"

"This isn't important, Rick." Her voice rose. "I never cared who…he went with… *That* really wasn't his problem. No, it was the religious stuff that got him nuts. Not that other. He was receiving all these mixed messages about everything. He's never been…stable."

"But your aunt…"

Suddenly her voice hardened. "Rick, you're going in the wrong direction. Stop it. Just stop it. My aunt was nuts about issues like that. Sex like that—to her…When she thinks—suspects—her nephew might like, you know, guys…"

"Maybe she confronted him?"

"I don't know. Look," her voice got weary and faraway, "I think Davey has been hurt enough. Leave this one thing alone, okay?"

"But you hired me to look…"

She screamed at me. "Leave it alone, Rick. You hear me? Davey and I don't see the world the same way, but I'm not going to let him get hurt."

"What if he hurt your aunt?"

"Impossible." She spat out the word.

"She cut him out of the will because of it."

A rush of words. "How do you know that?"

"I heard."

Sarcastic, seething. "You're saying my brother murdered my aunt?"

"No, I'm not. When you hired me, you must have thought about suspects. Wouldn't you have thought—even for a second—about Davey, given what you knew?"

"No."

"Come on, Karen. You never did?"

"Damn you."

She hung up.

I sat back and shook my head. My temples throbbed, pain barreling toward the corners of my eyes. I shut them and saw stars. I needed exercise, I needed to run. To swim. A walk. I opened my eyes, rubbed them, and stared at the cluttered pegboard suspended over the computer, the rows of orderly index cards, all chronicling the strange death of Marta Kowalski and the world she left behind for me to deal with.

◇◇◇

Davey opened the door after I knocked, and he didn't look happy to see me. Dressed in a tired blue wool sweater—holes at the elbows, food stains at the collar—he looked like a morning-after campsite, hair in his eyes, the rancid breath of a steady drinker. He didn't motion me in. Instead, he stepped forward, forcing me to step backwards. He had the advantage, and I didn't like it.

"I was gonna call you," he said.

I was surprised at the softness of his voice, some of his words muffled.

"I was in the neighborhood." I immediately regretted my words—too smart-alecky. Davey looked worn to a frazzle.

"Come in." His head swiveled back and forth nervously.

He didn't invite me to sit down, so we stood close to each other, wary athletes on a playing field, sizing each other up. I looked past him, and the messy apartment looked worse than my last visit. More magazines, more newspapers, more detritus of a lonely man's disheveled life.

I stepped around him.

"Where you going?"

The last time I was there, he'd hidden something under a stack of magazines. I located that same spot and lifted yellowing stacks of the *Farmington News*. As I suspected, nothing had shifted in the apartment since my last visit, a packrat's inertia. A pile of pornographic male-to-male magazines, glossy covers revealing the vacant thrill of wiped-out sexuality that I always noticed in porn.

"Damn you," Davey stammered.

I faced him. "This is your business. Only yours. But I need to know what it has to do with your dead aunt."

An unfunny laugh, bitter. "That bitch."

"Tell me."

He slammed his fist against the back of a chair. It flipped over but landed in magazines, jarring a towering stack that now seemed ready to fall. "Damn you to hell."

I thought I heard the hissing of a teapot, the sound of steam against metal. Then it stopped.

"I'm not like—him. Ken. He thinks it's a good time."

"It's not a big deal these days, Davey. Nobody cares. Really."

"I can never be one of them."

I waited. Then, watching his face, "Tell me about your aunt."

He sat down, dumping himself into a chair so that he filled it, his arms draped over his knees, his head buried in his chest. When he looked up, he seemed old, old. A painful keening escaped from his chest, then stopped. Silence, raw. I watched him.

"That bitch." He looked up, not at me, but beyond me, talking to the wall, to the murky unwashed curtains. "She called me a sick faggot one night. We were eating somewhere, and her face turned—she could get real ugly—and the words just spilled out of her mouth."

I sat down across from him, sitting on newspapers.

"How did she know?"

"She kept hammering at me. I ran out of that restaurant, but she phoned me. Said the same thing. 'Do you think you won't burn in hell?' That's what she kept saying into the phone. I could hear it in my sleep. And then I knew I *would* burn in hell, but then I knew I *wouldn't.* I love my God. I go to Mass." He was talking to himself now, looking down into his hands.

"And your aunt?"

He looked up, startled, jerking his head back. His eyes got wide, the eyebrows bunched together. "Nothing."

"It never came up again?"

He gave that insincere horse laugh, but it caught in his throat. "How could it? She never spoke to me again."

"You never tried to talk to her?"

He stood up, his jaw tight. "It was a done deal. She was nuts. A crazy drunken old bitch."

"She kept your secret, though."

He paused, digesting the information. I saw hesitation.

"Who'd she tell?" I asked.

A sad voice. "She told Joshua, that's who."

"Joshua." I was surprised. "Why?"

Davey sighed. "No use keeping it a secret now, I guess. You want to know why Aunt Marta and Joshua stopped being friends? It wasn't her begging him for marriage. No, he took my side."

"You knew Joshua?"

"The shop had a contract to deliver fertilizer and mulch in the spring and fall. Every so often I dropped off the stuff. Once I'm leaving and Marta's driving in. This was after we stopped talking. Her face fell. Joshua didn't know I was her nephew. Now I got on with the old man—he liked me—and she tells him I'm a faggot and to throw me off the property. I'm standing right there. Joshua looked dumbfounded. He starts to say, 'Marta, leave the boy alone. It's his life.' I couldn't believe how decent he was about it. Marta flips out and calls him—Joshua, mind you—a faggot, too. Says maybe he likes me. I beat the hell out of there. Left the two of them screaming at each other."

"So that was their big fight?"

"It was the last straw. Joshua told me she'd called the cops on the yardman, Willie Do. He's the one I often dealt with. Joshua fought with her about the way she treated him—tracking dirt in or something. I think Joshua could have let that go—maybe not—but then, a day or so later, the brouhaha with me. Joshua— I mean, he *burned*."

"I heard all about the ruckus with Willie Do."

"I bet you did." Sarcastic. "You folks stick together, right?"

"Yeah, we're funny that way."

"But Willie didn't fight her. I did."

"So Joshua had had it?"

"Next time I go there, Joshua says Marta and he were, you know, kaput as friends. I heard through the grapevine that she was never the same." A slick grin. "Sad to say."

"They never spoke again."

"He was furious being called a queer on his own front lawn. In *this* town. But no, they never spoke again. Funny, though…"

"What?"

"Last time I saw him, he said he still missed her company. The house was nothing without her. Just before he moved, he told me he might reconcile with her. That was his word—reconcile. Even though she was dreadful at times—'I'm too old for battles,' he said."

"But he never did."

"Maybe he did. I don't know. I never saw him or her after that."

"And then she died."

He pointed a finger at my chest, like a kid aiming an imaginary gun. "Just a minute, buddy," he yelled. "This has nothing to do with her death. Nothing."

He crashed his fist down on the stack of newspapers, making a dull thud of noise.

"Damn it," he swore. "That fucking Ken."

He twisted around, his heavy body ungainly. He didn't know what to do in the tight space of his apartment.

"You know, he got off on that scene in the street. I begged him to keep still, but he just laughed. He got a kick out of it."

"I repeat, Davey. No one cares. It's your life."

"It's the life Jesus allows me."

"But it shouldn't…"

"You want to ruin my life. That's what it is."

"Davey."

He ran to the door, threw it open, and the hallway light showed a face streaked with tears. "You and my sister. I bet you're fucking her. Isn't that a conflict of interest or something? You're fucking her. You're gonna push her into a wall, too. She'll hide in a corner and hate you. She'll turn on you."

I followed the direction of his extended arm—out the door. As I walked by him, he bent his head toward me. His breath smelled, a mixture of anger and fear and excitement and decay. My stomach turned.

His breath covered my neck. "And you can tell that bastard Ken Rodman—you tell him he opens his mouth, I will kill him. I'll kill the motherfucker."

I took a step into the hallway. He shoved me. I started to topple, regained my balance, and looked back. He'd already slammed the door.

Chapter Twenty-nine

No one answered at Richard Wilcox's apartment. I phoned throughout the day. Late in the afternoon, when I'd come to expect the long, perpetual ringing, a woman picked up the phone on the first ring, announced in a loud, booming voice that she was Richard's housekeeper, and I became immediately confused. I immediately thought of Marta meticulously dusting that furniture, Marta whisking that vacuum across threadbare orientals.

This woman was young, with a singsong Jamaican accent, a deep voice, impatient. "Is not here." She had work to do, and I was interrupting. The man "that live here," she informed me, was at John Dempsey Hospital at the other end of town.

No, she knew nothing about his condition. "Is not my business."

She used no subjects in her sentences, which gave her speech an incomplete sensation, like hang-gliding through the English language. The service dropped her off and picked her up, she said. She'd only met him twice.

I visited Richard in his private room at the hospital. Tucked into crinkly white linen and enclosed in antiseptic curtains, he looked like an unwilling specimen in some lab experiment, curled up and frightened. Surprised to see me walking in, he squinted, trying to focus.

"Well, at least you're not the grim reaper."

I smiled. "Not in my job description."

He looked tired, and for a moment he nodded off. His eyes closed, his head dipped to his flabby chin. But then he opened his eyes, wide as coins, and shook his head.

"Don't tell me you're still pursuing that phantom. Murder, he didn't write."

"Afraid so."

"Any conclusions?"

"None."

He chuckled a little. "As I suspected."

"How are you feeling?"

"I'm dying. Simple as that. Declarative statement with all the force it is intended to have. Death is a blanket prognosis." His fingers twitched against his cheek. "A week, a month. I lived my life slowly, deliberately, conservatively. Never any speed. How ironic that the final cancer is raging through me as if my body is, well, a speedway. All deliberate speed."

"I'm sorry."

He interlocked his fingers, straightened his spine. "How can I help you?"

"You were the last person to talk to Marta—that we know of. Over the phone, at least."

"And I've told you…"

"I'd like to review it one more time."

"Why?"

"You may remember something."

He waved his hand in the air. "Well, I have nothing but time now."

"Thank you." I sat down in the chair next to his bed. "Are you sure you don't mind? I don't want to disturb…"

He cut me off. "I actually welcome a visitor." A thin grin. "Even you."

"Thank you. I'm trying to construct a picture of Marta's last day. You said at first she said she wouldn't visit, then she changed her mind."

He shook his head. "We'll never know, will we?"

"She came to a decision about something."

"Why?"

"Because originally she was coming to *tell* you something."

"Young man, she committed suicide. She asked me to bury her."

"But isn't that odd?"

"She was really drunk."

"Did she mention Joshua?"

"No, why?"

"She spent a lot of time tracking him down—only to have him die."

Wilcox smiled. "When Joshua died, I thought it was over. At last she could finally believe that he was never coming back to that house."

"No mention of his name?"

"No."

"He became her only obsession. Can you remember anything else?"

"No. I can't."

"What did you say when she asked you to bury her?"

"I was silent. After all, she was tipsy. And I knew that she visited her husband's grave all the time—placed flowers there." He shook his head. "I sort of resented her request that I be in charge of her burial. But what does one say to that? Of course? Can you bury me? Probably alongside Joshua's body. The poet all over again—I died for beauty but was scarce adjusted in the tomb when one who died for truth was laid in an adjoining room. A paraphrase, of course." He snickered. "I still remember."

"I doubt if we're talking about truth and beauty here."

"How crass!"

"I'm sorry."

"The apology of the unrepentant."

"So she said those words and headed to your place but never got there. She kills herself at the bridge."

I was talking but Richard was not looking at me. Something had happened. I was sure of it. His eyes closed tight, his lips quivered, I thought he would pass out. I was ready to call a nurse when he opened his eyes, and what I saw there was raw fright. He raised a slender hand to his temple, supporting his head, and closed his eyes again.

"What is it? You okay?"

He nodded.

"You want a nurse?"

"No, no."

I waited.

"I remembered something I said."

"To Marta?"

He mumbled, "I realized some awful truth. My own words. I told her—'No, no, no. Stop this nonsense.' I didn't listen to her. I was the one who murdered her. Yes, me. My words."

"Tell me."

He shook his head. "Why? It's over. I murdered her. My silly, happy mouth killed her."

"Tell me."

But he was shaking his head, closing me out. "I take the blame. I am the one who murdered her. I killed her."

I kept probing him but the conversation was over. His head rested against his chest. I stood up to leave, though he didn't look up. Something had happened and I hadn't a clue. In these few minutes he remembered words he spoke that—what? Words that led not to the suicide that he had believed in, demanded I believe in, but, instead, to the one thing he absolutely refused to accept—murder. His words: *I was the one who murdered her.* He didn't say—my words drove her to suicide. Of course, I realized, he could be assuming blame for *not* understanding something, and called himself her murderer. That was possible. But I left with the words echoing in my head: *I was the one who murdered her.*

Chapter Thirty

Back at home, replaying the conversation with Wilcox, I came up with nothing. I'd wait a day, then get back to him. He held part of the answer to the endgame I now had to maneuver. I checked my pegboard looking for loose ends to follow up on. I phoned Liz at her office. Her secretary had to call her out of a meeting.

"Let me guess. You need a favor."

"Of course."

I could hear laughter in her voice. Someone was speaking loudly near her, and I could sense her turning away from the shouted voice. Hers was a frantic, busy office.

I briefly mentioned Wilcox's comments, but she had no ideas.

"But that's not why I'm calling you. I had a thought."

I filled her in on Davey, the chance sighting with Ken, Ken's visit, the aborted confrontation with Davey himself. "Something happened with Marta, and I think it had to do with the law. How else would she know about him? He was so circumspect."

"I think the word you mean here is *repressed*."

"That, too. But something had to bring it into the open."

"But I checked the police reports on all the names you gave me. Nothing turned up on Davey, at least not locally."

"It would be local."

"Nothing."

"That's it. No arrest, no charges, no convictions. It doesn't mean nothing happened. This is a small town. Ask around. Cops on the beat. You know how these things get squelched. See what you can dig up from your side of things? I'd appreciate it. Okay?"

"Will do."

"But diplomatically. Quietly."

"The only way."

"I don't want him hurt any more."

"I understand."

"Thanks, Liz."

"You owe me."

"You always say that."

"And you never pay off." Laughter in her voice.

"That's why we split up."

"How quaint. Split up. Like we're Archie and Veronica in a malt shop."

"I wasn't around then. I wasn't in America. I was an idea in the mind of Buddha."

"I'm always around. Always." She was laughing as she hung up the phone.

◇◇◇

She called me back within the hour. "We got lucky, babe."

"How so?"

"Our little Davey is not the Christian camper he poses as."

"Arrested?"

"That's it."

"I knew it." I hit the table with my fist.

"I rechecked files. Nothing. As I suspected. But I ran it by a couple of the cops I'm friendly with. At first nothing, but then one of them called me back. He remembered something from a few years ago. He used to work as a rent-a-cop security guard before he joined the force. He was covering West Farms Mall. It seems a drunken Davey put his hands on some teenage boy, and the kid erupted, hit him, called the cops. Real messy."

"No arrest?"

"That's where it gets murky. Johnny—he's the cop—says nothing happened. He remembers the name because it was the first arrest he'd been a part of. He remembers because Davey started talking wildly about Jesus…and perdition."

"Damn it."

"Nothing came of it. Somebody knew somebody."

"Marta."

"My guess, too. Maybe that's how she knew—that's why she was so hard on him."

"And that's why she knocked him out of the will—and her life. The favored nephew consigned to auntie's purgatory."

I was making notes, trying to type with one hand into the laptop. It was coming out like hieroglyphics.

"She did a number on him, I guess," Liz said.

"That's why she confronted him on Joshua's lawn. Tried to get Joshua to throw him off the property. Joshua wouldn't, so she turned on Joshua."

"Poor guy. Needed counseling, not cover-up."

"Well, he hated her, and it ruined her friendship with Joshua."

"What are you gonna do?"

"I got to talk to Karen about this first. She's not happy with me going at Davey."

But suddenly I thought of Richard Wilcox: *I am the one who murdered her.*

I thanked her. Suddenly, as an afterthought, feeling a little bit lonely, I asked her if she wanted to come with me to Peter and Selena's cocktail party. Then we'd go to the college art show opening together. I'd treat her to a late supper in Hartford. She was quiet for a while.

When she spoke, her voice was thin, uncomfortable. "Is this a date?"

"Old friends?" The wrong thing to say.

"No," her voice a whisper, "I don't think so."

"I didn't mean it a bad way." I wanted to see her. "Come on."

She sighed. "If you pick me up and act like you are excited to be with me."

"I promise." A pause. "I won't have to act, Liz."

"I won't hold you to that promise. You'd have to break it. You have weak character."

"Not weak—undemonstrative."

"You're a shy boy."

"You know it."

She laughed a long time, enjoying this. "How distorted is the mirror we carry in our heads."

Smiling to myself, I thanked her again.

◇◇◇

When I called Karen, she told me I couldn't stop over.

"No, it's impossible." Her voice was metallic. "What do you want?"

The abruptness startled me. We were being strangers now? I was never ready for her volatile mood shifts, dark-laced. They bothered me.

"I've got something to discuss with you. Something has come up, and I'd like to see you face-to-face."

"No," she said, flat out. "No."

I hesitated.

"Tell me now. I'm paying you."

As quietly as possible, I filled her in about Davey, providing her with the skimpy details of his hushed-up sexual assault. I suggested that Aunt Marta was the instrument behind the dismissal of charges—for a housekeeper she obviously wielded considerable influence in various quarters in the old town—and that drunken incident was the reason for her banishing her favored nephew Davey.

She interrupted me. "I talked to Davey yesterday."

"About what?"

"I called him. I'm a little tired of being estranged from him. Of being his enemy. I have one relative left. He's my brother."

"How was he?"

"Surprised, I think, and friendly."

That was not the word I would have used for Davey these past few days. "Did he say anything about the case?"

"We didn't talk about the case."

"What did you talk about?"

"I told you"—her voice strident, clipped—"it was nothing. A sister calling her brother. We *are* allowed to talk, you know. Marta wanted us apart because she hated him. We have to rebuild."

Rebuild. I thought of fire sales, of houses of cards crashing onto a table.

"Did he sound bothered?"

"I told you—he was friendly. We're going to have lunch or dinner. I'm gonna give him some money. Share it. I feel guilty."

"Wait a bit," I broke in. "Hold off for a while. We don't know Davey's role in Marta's death, if any. Maybe nothing, but I have to see it through. I have to be blunt with you. Marta terrorized him. He's got this mixed-up confusion about sex and religion and..."

"He's not like that."

I sat back, overwhelmed with fatigue. Repression was the operative word in the Corcoran family.

"Karen..."

"Rick, I'm going to call him and ask him about that arrest. I never heard about it. This is ridiculous. Wouldn't I have heard of it? He'll tell me the truth now."

"Karen, that's not a good idea."

"And I'm his only living relative."

"Karen, let me come over for a while. Just to talk. Okay? I think we need to get some balance here. Davey is a wild card."

"I know what happens when you come over."

"Just to talk."

"No, I've seen men like you before. There's too much hunger in your eyes."

Inadvertently I glanced at a nearby mirror, caught my glance, looked into my tired eyes, the lazy slant that came from my Vietnamese mother, the bluish tint that came from my father. Liz's words—how distorted is the mirror. I was still staring into those eyes when I heard the click of the receiver on the other end. Exhausted, I closed my eyes. Lightning flashes in the darkness, humming in my ears. I knew it was time for a nap.

Chapter Thirty-one

The next day started out quiet, quiet. I spent most of the morning going through a computer print-out I'd gotten from an old cop buddy on the NYPD. An incomplete listing of Mary Powells in Manhattan. "There are thirty-four on the list, but that's probably not half of them," he told me. "These are culled from business indexes and street registers from a couple years back."

I didn't know what I hoped to accomplish. After all, I'd already spoken with *the* Mary Powell whose number I'd got in Clinton. *That's* the Mary Powell I had to deal with. But that seemed all wrong. So I asked for this new list.

It was something to go on. Most women in New York, especially single, do not list themselves by first name in directories. M. Powell was the most I could hope for. So my buddy's list was much better than nothing. I dialed. And dialed. Dead end. Disconnected numbers. Hang ups. Suspicious husbands. Suspicious Mary Powells. It was a stupid game, I told myself, but it came with the territory. Machines everywhere—after all, it was a weekday. And unanswered long ringing. The friendly Mary Powells were mostly old women, hidden away in fourth-floor walkups. Of course, they wanted to talk. I lingered a little, but eventually I had to break off. They always sounded disappointed.

I'd learned nothing from the morning.

Hank phoned, complained about my line being tied up. My cell phone went to voice immediately. He wanted to make certain I remembered his mother's invitation to supper. I'd been checking notes in my laptop, momentarily distracted, so he read my hesitation as ambivalence.

"You gotta come."

"I told you I would."

"Dad won't…"

I broke in. "Hank, enough. Your father and I have signed a peace treaty, brokered by your grandma."

"People at peace still go to war."

"Not when they're eating Happy Pancake."

He sighed. "Food is the answer."

"To almost everything, no?"

"Don't be late, Rick. Sometimes you float along, gape at the landscape like you just toppled off a turnip truck."

"Another wonderful food maligned by cliché."

"What?"

"I'll be there."

I grabbed a coat and drove to Hank's home. He greeted me at the door, his arms cradling the Criminal Justice text he'd used in my course.

"You checking some fine point of police procedure?" I asked.

"Naw," he said.

"No one reads these books twice." I pointed to the oversized textbook.

He grinned. "I'm reading it for the first time."

I quoted Buddha to him. "'Honest work—it's a great fortune.'"

He grunted.

He was dressed in baggy sweat pants, a faded, stained Tar Heels jersey, and was barefoot. His shaved head gleamed underneath the overhead light. I rubbed it. "Buddha."

"You're early. No one's home yet." He walked to the refrigerator. "Mom told me to ask if you wanted coffee." He laughed. "She thinks I lack social skills."

"Ah, where to begin…"

We sat with coffee—his instant version, dreadful—at the kitchen table, and I filled him in on the latest events, particularly Davey's secret life.

"I'm surprised that got by me," he noted.

"And why is that?"

"You see, I'm a different generation. We don't *have* sexual secrets, so I wasn't thinking in that direction."

"I wish your generation would keep some of its secrets—well, secret."

"We only try to hide our intelligence."

"How well I know that. You were my student."

I sat back, relaxed. "But I still don't know anything that relates back to Marta. It's like a spider's web. I keep learning new stories—like Davey knowing Joshua. I'm convinced Joshua is at the heart of this—somehow. What does that mean?"

The kitchen door opened, the sound of his mother and grandmother laughing at something. Hank jumped up to take a paper bag from his mother. Grandma smiled at me, but spoke to someone behind her.

Stepping into the kitchen, bundled up against the November cold, Aunt Marie did not look surprised to see me. We bowed to each other. Willie Do's wife.

Hank stammered, "Aunt Marie, I didn't know you were here." Hank threw a sidelong glance my way, confusion in his eyes.

His mother said in a soft voice, "You don't know everything, Tan."

"But…" He faltered.

Aunt Marie was watching me closely—something was going on here, I felt. She was in that kitchen—as was I—for a reason.

The women slipped off coats, hung by Hank's mother on a rack by the door. The whole time Aunt Marie watched me, nervous, stiff.

"You boys go into the living room," his mother said, slipping into Vietnamese, her hands making shooing gestures. "We need to make the Happy Pancakes."

Grandma stood near the table and pointed at Hank. "You give him sewage to drink." She kissed the top of my head. She took my instant coffee, and Hank's, and poured them down the sink drain, and proceeded to make me a cup of real Vietnamese coffee, a potent brew rich with condensed milk and powerful beans. The glass was hot to the touch. I could have hugged her.

"I know you like it extra sweet," she told me.

Hank grinned at her. "You spoil him, Grandma."

She looked at Hank with love. "Such a pretty boy better find a wife who cannot see that his looks are his only talent."

Hank grinned. "Thanks, Grandma."

She looked at her daughter. "Real coffee, then exile in the living room."

Aunt Marie smiled but didn't move.

"So," Grandma said to me, sitting down so close our sleeves touched. She pointed at Hank, referring to him by his Vietnamese name. "Tan tells me that you are looking into a murder."

"Well…"

"Grandma, I'm working closely with him."

"He tells me he's—essential."

"He is that. And more."

"Where do you look for this murderer?" she asked me.

"What do you mean?"

"You and Tan, you spend your lives looking in books for murderers." She pointed to the thick volume that Hank had rested on the kitchen table.

"Well, not really. I'm interviewing people and…"

"Books are conclusions days later." She nodded her head slowly.

"What do you mean?"

She smiled, her face getting wrinkled and gleeful. "Buddha is a book with pages you've already read."

I nodded.

"He said: 'When you are troubled, act. Be bold.'"

"I can't act until I have…" I stopped.

She leaned into me. "When you hold a book, you forget to look into someone's eyes."

"I do both."

She wasn't listening to me. "A book is only as good as the hand that holds it. When you close the book, what's missing?" She actually winked. "Buddha says, 'There are not holes in eternity. What is missing is already filled in.'"

"Grandma…" Hank began.

"You're telling me that I already have the answer?" I stared into her face.

"All you have to do is open your eyes—read the page you skipped over."

"Thank you." I bowed.

"More coffee now." She bowed back. "And sesame buns for sweetness."

Hank's mother pointed to the living room. "If you two stay here gabbing with Grandma, we will never eat."

Sitting in the living room, I faced Hank. "Aunt Marie?"

"You got me, Rick. Nobody tells me anything."

"You do know that she's here for a reason."

"Well, she does stop in to see Mom now and then. She doesn't drive, dropped off by Willie for the afternoon. They cook piles of rice cakes."

"But…" I pointed a finger toward the kitchen, a purposeful quizzical expression on my face.

He cut me off. "Yeah, I know. Something is going on." A slapdash grin covered his face. "This has all the hallmarks of a behind-the-scenes conspiracy."

So we sat quietly, listening to the three women bustling in the kitchen, laughing, gossiping. Pans banged against a counter, the sizzle of heated oil. But Aunt Marie was saying very little, a few, scattered monosyllabic responses, hesitant. Grandma and Hank's mother were chatting about some neighbor, a rambling tale of midnight indiscretion spotted by Grandma who'd gone into the kitchen for a glass of water and happened—"I am not one to peek from a window, you know that"—to spot the misalliance in the next-door driveway. A fresh round of wonderful laughter.

"Relax," I said to Hank, who was squirming.

The living room was a tight, square room, probably little-used because the family lived its life in the kitchen. Cluttered with too much overstuffed furniture, threadbare and draped in floral sheets, the room looked forbidding, a solemn place you brought strangers for coffee. Insurance salesmen, schoolteachers, folks you didn't know how to entertain. What jarred me, although pleasantly, was the collection of watercolors positioned on the walls, a display of schoolroom art executed by one of the younger children, Phoung, the thirteen-year-old girl, whose first name dominated the tops of each of the drawings. Hank spotted my eyes drifting from one to another.

"Phoung at summer art camp, sponsored by the *Hartford Courant*."

The young girl had fashioned clunky pastoral scenes of an imagined Vietnam, perhaps copied from travel guides, glossy photographs painstakingly rendered in watercolor paint that dripped onto and smudged the paper.

"Dad thinks she's Picasso, proud as hell." He pointed at one particularly horrid drawing and whispered, "A failed Rorschach ink blot."

Each drawing was encased in an oversized gilt frame. The effect was startling, true, but I found the drawings comforting. Perhaps a dozen of them hung lopsidedly, each in a garish gold frame. They held me, these childlike images, because there was about them a soft sentimentality—the land of her parents filtered now through the hazy lens of an American childhood. They spoke a real love, a family that celebrated their children. Touched by it, maybe stupidly envious, I told this to Hank now. "Devotion."

"At any price," he replied.

The bustle in the kitchen suddenly stopped, the hiss of the gas stove ceasing, quiet, quiet.

Aunt Marie stepped into the living room, her hands dangling at her side, her face drawn. A sweep of wind slammed the window, a branch banged against the siding, and she drew in her breath.

"What is it, Aunt Marie?" Hank asked, half-rising.

As she waved him away, she sat down next to me. "I am here for a reason," she said in a soft but carefully modulated English. A rehearsed speech practiced over the kitchen stove, probably edited by Grandma.

I nodded at her. "I guessed that."

She sucked in her breath. "My son Xinh…" she began slowly. Then, shaking her head, she used his American name. "My Tony…he…"

She folded her hands into her lap, a prim gesture, closed her eyes tightly but immediately snapped them wide open.

"Aunt Marie." Hank's voice quivered. He shot a confused look toward the kitchen. Silence there. Grandma and his mother probably listening at the door, now shut.

"Tell me," I said gently, though my heart raced.

Her voice trembled. "He cannot bring himself to talk to you. His pride." She gulped. "His fear."

"Of what?" Hank interrupted.

I faced Hank. "Hank, let me do this."

He nodded.

"Ever since you came to the apartment to talk to my husband Vuong—Willie—he worries. My Tony worries. Maybe a murder now, he thinks, and he is afraid of what he did." She bit her lip. "You are"—a long pause—"like the authority. Like looking into it all."

"Tell me." My voice even softer. A sliver of a smile. "I'm a friend, Aunt Marie."

She ignored that. The words spilled out of her. "Back in April when he had the fight with Marta Kowalski, I mean, when she said his look threatened her—it wasn't a fight because he will never fight…Before she called the police on him. I mean, *after* that…*After*, not before. I'm confused. But my Tony was so mad at her. He felt his father had been hurt too much already. Willie, you know, is a man you have to be careful with, so hurt, and so ready to break…a good man, a hard worker, talk nice to you, and friendly. Well, my Tony wanted to confront Marta. Maybe make her understand what she…do to that man."

Hank squirmed. Color rose in his cheeks.

"He drove to her house to talk to her. So dumb, yes. He didn't know what else to do."

"But why?"

She shrugged. "He got this anger and he felt…to yell at her… something to let her know what a horrible, mean woman she was. How the cops *looked* at Willie. The American police in the house, standing there."

"What happened?"

She looked away, then turned back. "Nothing. Tony—he sat in front of the house. Sat there. She was not home so he waited. An hour maybe. Stupid. He went home." She glanced at Hank, a helpless expression on her face. "Rick, he went back two or three more times, sitting there. One time he saw her drive in, the lights go on, nighttime, late. But he couldn't talk to her."

"No one will believe he did anything wrong, Aunt Marie," Hank began.

She shook her head vigorously. "But he's afraid neighbors saw him, remember his plate number, remember his face maybe. If Marta was murdered, if *you* find out she was murdered, then the cops will come back." She shuddered. "This time for him."

"But nothing happened." I stared into her face.

"The last time she came home with Karen, the niece, I guess. They drove in, and Karen spotted him sitting there. She kept staring at him. When they went into the house, she opened the front door and she ran out. I mean, she ran down the sidewalk. She was screaming and cursing. Waving her arms. Like a crazy person. He drove away."

Hank and I shared a quick look. Karen hadn't mentioned any encounter with Tony, but she might have paid it no mind—perhaps forgot it. I'd have to question her about that.

Her words finished, Aunt Marie sighed, settled into the sofa, her arms sagging by her side. It was as if she'd weathered some awful tempest and now, a surprised survivor, she had little energy to move. Her face caved in, deep wrinkles around her mouth, her eyes wet. She was gazing at the redundant watercolors of Vietnam done by Phoung, a child's delightful fantasy of a Vietnam she'd never seen. Aunt Marie's eyes moved from one to the next—a bamboo sway bridge, a cluttered market square in

Saigon, a towering banyan tree, and a yellow river surrounded by bamboo groves—and she started to cry.

Hank moved next to her, wrapped his arms around her.

"Thank you for telling me this," I told her. "But please don't worry about this. And tell your son it doesn't matter. Nothing happened. He simply sat there."

"But something did happen," she insisted, making eye contact. "The woman maybe was murdered."

"But not by your son," I answered. "Or husband."

"Who will believe that?"

"I do."

For the first time she showed a hint of a smile. "You do?" A tick in her voice.

I nodded—and I did. I saw question in Hank's eyes, but I smiled at Aunt Marie. "I do," I repeated.

She rose, bowed, and returned to the kitchen.

Hank was watching me closely. "That was nice of you."

"Maybe, maybe not. But I don't believe Tony or Willie could kill Marta. They come from a family that's seen too much grief from killing, no? What happened to his sister. The daughter. Other families in Saigon. I mean, it's possible, but my gut says no."

Hank whistled softly. "But if Marta was murdered, the authorities"—a flash of a grin—"authorities other than you, of course—won't be as understanding as you are."

"True. And that's the problem. Tony put himself in harm's way." I glanced toward the kitchen. "But Aunt Marie and the family don't need to know that part of the story yet."

"Let's hope they don't have to."

"That means I'd better identify a murderer soon."

Hank made a clicking sound and pointed a finger at me. "Well, what are you waiting for?"

I pointed back. "If I believe what epic tales you tell your grandmother, you are integral to the investigation."

The grin returned. "Perhaps I exaggerated my position a little."

"Really?"

A sudden rush of voices in the kitchen, the slamming of a door, a yelled greeting, boisterous. The men of the family had returned home, followed quickly by Hank's younger brother Vu and sister Phoung. Laughter, sputtering, the boy teasing his sister, but Hank's father suddenly yelled at his fifteen-year-old son, who'd not finished an earlier task. The kitchen got quiet for a moment, then erupted as the boy sputtered an apology that his father talked over, his voice harsh and nasty.

Hank caught me eye. "Christ, not now."

Sometimes, I knew, Tuan Nguyen came back from his factory job after stopping for a few beers and shots of whiskey at Meyers' Tavern, two streets over. There were nights when Hank, sitting with me somewhere, answered his cell phone and then bounded out the door, rushing home to rescue his mother from his father's angry and cruel hand.

Grandma opened the door to the living room and called us to supper, her tiny old hand waving us in. As Hank and I walked into the room, his father was still berating his sheepish and moody son, but the man stopped talking. He dropped into a chair, fingers tapping the table. It was Hank's grandfather who glared at me, ice in his eyes, as though I were the reason for the father-son spat. The old man, small and withered like a gnarled twig, sat in a chair, his arms folded. He called out his son's name—"Tuan!"—and shook his head. As his eyes went from my face to his son's, the expression communicated one thing—look who is violating our warm and loving Vietnamese kitchen. Our evening meal. The child of the dust from under a rock. But Grandma, watching the horrible tableau, began humming as she spooned rice batter into a skillet, a tune I did not recognize but was obviously some Vietnamese song they all knew. *Cay Truc Xinh.* She sang about a lovely girl who stood next to a lovely bamboo tree…so serene a snapshot.

Her daughter smiled broadly.

Hank heaved a sigh and muttered, "A hymn to beauty." He went on, "I think that I will never see a poem as lovely as a…"

He stopped when his father grunted at him. He whispered the last word: tree.

Grandma stopped humming but she was smiling at Hank.

The only one not happy was the grandfather.

But unlike the grandfather, Hank's father, Tuan, always distrustful of me, the visiting dust boy, had long ago made a separate peace in the household. Respecting his son's delivery into American culture—just as he celebrated his daughter Phoung's slavish imitation of Matisse—he acquiesced to the strange and serendipitous god that sent him into exile in America and then allowed someone of impure blood to break bread with him. Or, in this case, the cheerfully but ironically named Happy Pancake. What I knew might happen, of course, was that Tuan would initiate a conversation with me about his current hobby horse—the reinstituted trade relations between Vietnam and the United States—a diatribe that somehow blamed me for world events. I'd learned to keep my mouth shut.

Tuan savored the incendiary headlines of the day, gleaned from the yellow pulp tabloid newspapers printed on the West Coast. He culled tidbits about restored relations with Communist Vietnam and the death of the old life.

Now, occasionally hurling a sharp look at his younger son, he caught my eye. "*Time* magazine tells me that Vietnam is a favorite place of the wealthy American tourist these days. Cruises, tours."

I said nothing.

"Dad..." Hank began.

"Isn't it funny how a Communist country, one that slaughtered nearly forty-thousand American soldiers, not to mention millions of their own people, tortured them, beat their children, can now become a...a popular resort..." He pounded his fist on the table.

I kept my mouth shut.

"So we begin another Vietnamese-American Conflict. This time the bodies are the ghosts of those left behind, maybe unburied, during the first war. People who fell from helicopters, fleeing.

Unavenged, their spirits trampled on by the feet of laughing, rich Americans."

"Some of them are Vietnamese returning home—or their children." Hank spoke in an even voice, quiet.

"I spit on them all."

"Now, now," Grandma interjected.

I kept my mouth shut.

"What do you think?" he finally spat out at me.

A loaded question, for sure, because any answer I delivered would be twisted and mocked and derided. I was allowed to sit at the supper table, but there was a price I had to pay. Because, in effect, I was the nagging symbol of the bastardization of the homeland. I was the American metaphor that was paradoxically also the Vietnamese metaphor for failure. Both these metaphors—melded together—centered on a man who was determined to keep his mouth shut.

Luckily, I didn't have to answer, because Grandma delivered the first batch of crispy, savory Happy Pancakes to the table. The glorious *banh xeo*. A sizzling crepe, crisp and aromatic, filled with chunky pork, split shrimp, diced green onions, a generous handful of bean sprouts, all fried until the rice flour shell hardened into a saffron yellow, to be folded into fresh lettuce and basil and mint, then dipped into a savory fish sauce. *Nuoc mam*. Sloppy, chaotic, rich, but—happy. Hushed, expectant, we lifted our chopsticks, sipped from bowls of jasmine tea, bowed our heads over the sumptuous feast. Grandma kept replenishing the community dish on the table. The Happy Pancake—a peacemaker, that pancake, because we stopped fighting the war I was never a part of—and dug into the food. When we ate, we talked and laughed and slurped and whooped it up. Grandma winked at me, which Hank caught. He gave me the thumbs-up, as though he'd brokered my little entente.

Afterwards, the men disappeared outside to smoke Marlboros, while Hank and I sipped hot jasmine tea.

Hank belched, which made his mother frown.

"In Arabian countries," he explained, "a burp after a meal is a sign of satisfaction."

"Yeah," said his little brother, "in some cultures it's a sign of being a pig."

Hank laughed. "You hear that, Rick? Fifteen years old and a wisecracker."

"He's had a good teacher."

His mother smiled. "All my children speak before thinking. That's what comes of living in a world of twenty-four-hour cable and teachers who have tattoos on their arms."

"Mom," Hank said, "that makes no sense. All you watch on TV is the Cooking Network."

"I watch nothing." Aunt Marie was speaking for the first time. She seemed startled by her own words. She raised her hand to her white hair, then slid her hand over her jaw.

"Why?" Hank asked.

"America is a place that will always confuse me."

Her words served as a period to the meal because the women began clearing the dishes. Aunt Marie looked distracted and apologetic, as though she'd spoken out of turn. She picked up a greasy platter, but it almost slipped from her hands. She yelped, then smiled.

Grandma wagged an amused finger at her. "Dear Marie, you lie to us. I've been to your home and we've watched the American soap operas all afternoon." Grandma, tickled, leaned in and said something I didn't catch.

Aunt Marie nodded. "Watching those American women yell and scream and cry is like being hypnotized by a snake—as much as I try, I cannot turn away."

Hank guffawed in English, breaking the smooth Vietnamese rhythms. "Aunt Marie, you are something else."

She turned to him, puzzled. She started to say something but a staccato *wah wah wha* from a car horn made her jump.

"My Vuong is here to take me home."

Aunt Marie looked into my face. "He will not come in." Again the apologetic look. "He prefers…"

Hank leaned into me. "He never does."

The horn blared again, the same three sounds, each one longer in length.

I sat up. "I wonder if I could have a word with him?" I asked Aunt Marie.

Fright flashed across her face, caving it in. Watching her, protective, Hank's mother waved her hand wildly in the air, as if looking for a way out of this situation. Only Grandma, eyeing me closely, wore the sliver of a smile.

"You have questions?" she asked me.

"I just want a clearer picture of a few things that happened."

Hank spoke up. "Maybe I can…"

I interrupted. "No, Hank. Let me be alone with him."

Perhaps my abrupt request was a violation of something I could never fully understand, perhaps not. But I had been wondering about timelines, fragmented details, Marta's erratic behavior back in April, and now was an opportunity I might not have again. Violation or not, I had no choice. Willie's encounter with Marta back then, his final days working for Joshua Jennings—perhaps he might recall an anecdote or a few spoken words—maybe even something he'd spotted but didn't comprehend—that might provide me with a spark, a direction.

"I mean the man no harm." I smiled at Aunt Marie. "In fact, I want to help him. You do believe that, don't you?"

She stammered, "Yes."

"Good. Then let me do this."

Hank made a squeaky sound, irritated at his exclusion. But I understood that Willie had to be approached with delicacy, man-to-man conversation, direct, honest. Faced squarely, he'd talk to me. I recalled his comment about old man Joshua—how the patrician gentleman treated him fairly, a mutual respect, even conversation Willie welcomed. At heart here was a good man. I believed that to my core.

The kitchen froze, no one moving except for Hank who leaned back in his chair, two legs off the floor, rocking dangerously. When I looked into his face, I saw an enigmatic smile. He understood me.

"Go outside," Hank advised me. "If I know Uncle Willie, he's standing in the cold, shivering, back against his pickup, smoking a cigarette. Any minute now he'll lean in and blow the horn again."

Grandma bowed me out.

Willie looked startled to see me approaching him. His body stiffened, turned away, his collar buttoned up against the chilly November night, a faint hint of pale white smoke wreathing his head. The red tip of a cigarette glowed in the darkness. For a second he leaned into the pickup, as if to take shelter there, but, resigned, he faced me.

"What do you want?" In English.

"A minute of your time, Willie. Please. Some talk." I answered him in English, my words sounding harsh after the smooth rhythms of Vietnamese at suppertime.

"I ain't got nothing to say."

"I think you do."

"I told you everything."

"Your wife told me about Tony sitting at Marta's house."

"I told her not to." He swore under his breath.

"But she had to. It was unwise of him, yes, but innocent. He was thinking of you. A son defending his falsely accused father. Your son is not a killer."

His shoulders slumped as he dropped the cigarette to the ground. He raised his hand to tap the pack of Marlboros in his breast pocket, his fingers trembling.

"Yeah, I know that. But it ain't right."

"And neither are you a killer."

He nodded. "You know that?"

"Yes. That's not who you are."

"Then what do you want from me?"

"I have a few questions."

He nodded toward the Toyota pickup, still running. "Sit."

Inside the front seat I surveyed the messy truck, an ashtray stuffed with cigarette butts, spilling out. The stale scent of too much cigarette smoke and too much fast food. Vietnamese newspapers strewn on the floor. A white carton from old Chinese food, cheap wooden chopsticks jutting out. A crumpled McDonald's wrapper. A pair of work boots, the laces broken.

He lit another cigarette though he cracked the window a few inches. Smoke filled the car. I cracked my window. My throat fogged up.

"I don't know if I trust you," he began.

"Why?"

He was silent. He blew smoke into the air.

"Is it because of my white blood?"

The question embarrassed him and he turned away. Then, speaking rapidly, he faced me. "You have the bright blue eyes of an American soldier that I remember. On our street, fighting with us, but one who walked away, deserted, hurt…Never mind."

I smiled. "That wasn't me."

"I know." He breathed in. "This has to do with *me*, not you."

"I know."

A rush of words. "What do you want from me?"

"Willie, I'm trying to get a picture of Marta's last days, but now I want to go back to the time when she fought with you, last April, when Joshua Jennings broke off his friendship and moved away. Her reaction to everything. The events. I think something she did triggered something—I don't know what. But maybe it led to her murder."

"If it was murder, right?"

"Yeah, exactly. I could be on a wild goose chase."

He closed his eyes for a moment. "A woman easy to hate."

"But you didn't hate her."

"You know, I never thought about her until that day when she yelled at me, called me names, said I threatened her."

"Could something have happened there that set her off?"

"Maybe. I mean, it was like she was bruising for a fight. Like she had to take it out on someone."

"She might have been mad at Joshua, no?"

He nodded. "You know, I ain't seen her that much. I mean, I wasn't there when she cleaned the place, except now and then. But I know that after cleaning, she…well, in summer they sat on the back patio, sipping coffee, laughing. I'd walk by and Joshua would comment on the lawns or gardens. She never did. But I'd hear her…you know…flattering, giggling, teasing him. Like a show. But I was invisible to her."

"But when you tracked in the mud…"

"She went ballistic."

"Tell me about it again." I cracked the window some more, breathed in the brisk air. "Joshua got angry with her for talking to you that way."

"He was a good man, that Mr. Jennings." Willie locked eyes with mine. "You know, he and I sat on that same patio and talked. A kind man, Mr. Jennings. He looked into my face. He asked me about my family, my…" His voice trailed off. "He defended me that day—yelled at her."

"But that wasn't the reason he ended the friendship with her. At first I thought it was."

A fake laugh. "Yeah, like that would do it. It was only one piece of the puzzle he put together. He was…like a trusting man with so few friends. She was his friend, but she sucked up to him. I think he started seeing her different like. You know, she smiled at him and flattered and…you know. "

"But then he saw a different side of her."

"Maybe he saw it before but it didn't matter." He fumbled with a pack of cigarettes. "Her life was a lie."

"Do you think she got panicky because he was moving away?"

"He was always moving away." A wry laugh. "But then he didn't." He tapped the window nervously. "And then he did. Back and forth. Crazy. I joked that he would never move. No, one day I drove back to work, and Marta was in the yard screaming like a crazy woman. Something had happened. The man who dropped off the fertilizer and mulch from the garden center was standing there and she was yelling at him, then at Joshua. It scared me so I drove away."

"That was Davey, her nephew."

He looked surprised. "I don't know. I didn't know that."

"But you went back?"

"The next day. To work. The old man was still mad as hell. I mean, he told me that Marta had done something horrible to him, that she went nuts on the lawn, and that she could never return. He couldn't believe a friend—he said 'a lady I really liked, laughed with'—could show her true colors. I didn't know what to say."

"What next?"

"Well, it was that night the police came to see me. I thought it was all over, the thing about the mud, but maybe she was flipping out. Getting ready to be real mean to me. Call the cops. When Joshua called me to come and do the lawns, I told him about it. I told him I was afraid to come back—she was there. The cops. Then he told me she would never step foot in the place again. He swore that he was glad he was leaving Farmington behind. He told me he'd called Peter Canterbury. 'It's yours,' he says to him. I still didn't believe him."

"But he did leave."

"Yeah."

"That must have bothered you."

"Yeah, but he was old, sick. Everything changes—it has to. The house was too much. He invited me over to meet Peter and Selina Canterbury and told them in front of me that they should hire me to work the grounds."

"What did they say?"

"They smiled. Mr. Jennings said that he wanted the grounds to always look the way I kept them. He said to Peter, 'Promise me.' Peter looked confused. like he could buy a house and he had to still follow certain rules."

"So Marta never came back to the house?"

"How would I know?" A pause. "One time I drive up in my truck. This was after he told her to get out. I pull up, and she's sitting in the driveway in her car. Scared the shit outta me. I kept driving."

"Where was Joshua?"

"Dunno. But I remember watching a shade pull down in the front window."

"She stalked him?"

"She was a woman who didn't want to hear a no."

"That was the end of it?"

"I don't know."

"But didn't Joshua call you to straighten the grounds for the Canterburys, even after he sold the place. Your son Tony said…"

"Yeah, he called one night, late at night. I was almost asleep. I hadn't been there in a week or so, because I didn't know what to do. He was real proud of his house and yard. He laughed and said, 'My lovely spring gardens need your touch. Come back to work.'"

"Did you?"

He shook his head. "I drove by once, but I thought I saw Marta's car on the street, so I kept driving. I mean, she probably drove him crazy. I suppose he couldn't wait to get away from her. What the hell was wrong with her?"

"Rejected, and not happy about it."

"I ain't never seen a woman like that."

I grinned. "You're lucky."

"A few days later when I went back, the lawn was mowed. I never went back. There was a moving van in the yard."

"No Marta?"

"Not unless she was hiding in the bushes."

"The end of the story?"

"Yeah. The end of her story."

Chapter Thirty-two

Driving home, I swung by my office to collect mail. When I walked into the messy room, Jimmy grinned. He was surrounded by packed boxes.

"My partner," he said. "Come to see your old office—soon to be a fond memory?"

"Are we still moving?"

He pointed to a notice he'd stuck on my computer. "Yeah, now it's definite." He wagged a finger at me. "Your job is to find new quarters—cheap."

"I know. I'll get on it."

He grumbled. "I've heard that before."

He slapped me on the back and immediately poured me the turgid liquid he defined as coffee. I took it but didn't drink it. No one ever did—after that first numbing sip. I was still savoring Grandma's lusty and lush Vietnamese confection.

"You gonna wrap the Marta case up—if a case it is—by Thanksgiving?"

I counted on my fingers. "Yes," I said quickly. "Probably not."

I shook my head. Maybe it was the long morning phone marathon to the Mary Powells of Manhattan, my aimless stuttering through the ungainly list, getting nowhere. Maybe it was Grandma's cryptic words—those Buddhist abstractions that were poetry for my soul. Maybe it was that unsettling talk with Willie Do in his pickup. Marta's manic behavior, her obsession. But did such behavior bring about a reason for murder? How to connect the dots? I stood there with a gob-smacked look on my face.

Jimmy was staring at me. "If you get defeated, you won't see nothing right in front of you, Rick."

He was lighting one of those monstrous, barnyard-smelling, politically incorrect cigars, puffing smoke in my direction.

"True," I admitted, but my admission didn't help. I closed my eyes.

"Look." He walked near me, leaned in. "Here's the first rule of thumb for you to think about. The killer—if there is one—is most likely someone you've talked to since Karen hired you. This ain't no random murder—if, I repeat, it was murder. Think about it. You've talked to the killer."

"Not bad." I liked that idea.

"Right," Jimmy went on, puffing away. "Now go home and rethink everything. Sometimes too many details cloud your sight. Strip it down to essentials. You talked to the murderer. Remember that. You already talked to the murderer. Now put a name to him."

I thought of Grandma. "There are no holes in eternity. What's missing is already filled in."

◇◇◇

Back at my apartment, parking in the lot behind the house, I spotted Gracie pulling overstuffed trash barrels to the curb. "Come on, Gracie, let me do that."

"Most of the trash comes from you any way."

"You're making that up." But walking back from the curb, I stopped. "Let me treat you to a cocktail."

Her wrinkled face broke into a wide grin, and she loosened the thick scarf around her neck. She was wearing an old bulky sweater and a frayed lumberjack jacket.

We walked to Zeke's Olde Tavern. When I noticed her scanning the chalkboard menu, I suggested something warm. Hot soup—thick barley cream, with chunks of black bread. A Sam Adams lager ale for her, a scotch-and-soda for me.

Feeling mellow, I brought up an old topic. For some time

I'd been after her to donate her overflowing steamer trunk of vintage stage memorabilia—programs, autographs, letters, costumes, sheet music—to the Farmington College archives. Her glory days as a Rockette and a Korean War entertainer with Bob Hope left her with wonderfully rich memories she steadfastly refused to write down. But at least the college could catalog and safeguard her tangible memories.

She scoffed at the idea. "I was a gypsy hoofer who lived on peanuts. What kind of history is that?"

She tipped up her empty bottle, so I called out to the bartender. She giggled. "Me a part of history?"

"But…"

"Forget it."

Later, tucking her arm into my elbow, we had a leisurely stroll back to the apartment.

She leaned into me. "Maybe I will…if you help me."

"Of course."

But the minute we opened the front door, entering the large cluttered foyer where stacks of occupant mail and weekly advertising circulars littered the floor—Gracie would straighten it once a month—we heard a voice calling from the upper landing. Ken was leaning out his door.

"Rick," he yelled down, "that you?"

"Me and Gracie."

He bounded down the stairs and planted himself in front of us, his face drawn. He looked as if he'd just got out of bed, his shirt rumpled and unbuttoned, his hair uncombed.

"Bad news." A somber tone as he looked from me to Gracie. "A friend just called me. He heard it from a friend who's a cop."

"What?" I got impatient.

He sucked in his breath. "Davey Corcoran killed himself."

Gracie's hand flew to her mouth. I gasped, stunned.

"He hung himself. When he didn't come into work for his afternoon shift, somebody called, then went to his place. They found him hanging in the bathroom. The front door open."

My mind shot to Karen. I saw her pale face, nervous as a

squirrel's. Grief again. Marta, now Davey. In that kaleidoscopic moment I imagined her pale eyes losing all color, becoming dull. I heard an echoey scream, long and sharp, the wailing of a soul falling into chaos.

Upstairs I phoned Karen. No answer. Her cell phone. Nothing. I tried her store. The phone rang and rang. I tried her land line again. Finally her machine kicked on—her wispy voice, short and sweet. "Not here. Leave message." Words omitted so the message had a quirky urgency.

"Karen, it's Rick," I spoke into the machine. My voice hollow, strained. "Call me. Please."

Was she really at home tucked into an armchair and listening to my voice, her hands wrapped around her body, swaying with—with what emotion? Sitting in the dark room, maybe with the lights off, so weak and so cold, listening, November cold seeping under the windowsills. Listening, waiting, waiting. Perhaps mourning a brother she scarcely knew.

◇◇◇

Though it was late, I threw on my thick wool sweats, pullover cap, and scarf, and I hit the sidewalk. A shadowy night under a brilliant fall moon, though the raw chill and the biting breezes were awful harbingers of the long winter on its way. I craved the wind, hungered for it. Brown leaves swirled on the sidewalk, drifted down from the almost-bare trees.

Davey Davey Davey.

I ran and ran, furiously, breaking through my normal pace, hurling my body against the crisp wind and cold, plowing down and across new roads and lanes, weaving through cars, folks walking dogs, and young girls from Miss Porter's returning to their rooms, their girlish laughter high and wonderful. I drove myself till I couldn't breathe any more, wheezing, nearly crying from the pain. Wind needles pierced my lungs, my side ached, my head throbbed. Streetlights flashed before me, out of focus. Trees wavered. Buildings bent. Skies cracked. I threw my head back, exhausted, and yelled into the bare-bones tree limbs spread above me. I slumped over, felt the depression ooze out of my pores. Davey and Karen. And Marta. Suicides. Davey hanging himself in a bathroom. Murder. Karen, alone now.

Davey, hanging.

I walked home slowly, my body in real pain, and tossed off my sweaty clothes inside my hallway. Naked, I felt the heat of the radiators hit me like a harsh flame. Naked, I paced the room, my body cool, eerily calm.

Davey Davey Davey.

My face thrust into his, demanding answers. Pushing at him. Tell me tell me tell me. In that second I felt stripped of something. I don't know what—some childlike awe of things. His dying and the cold November air slapped at me.

I took a long, long shower, hot hot, my skin crinkling under the jets of shocking water. I gulped for air, breathless now. When I was done, I slowly dried my body, holding the fluffy warm towel lingeringly on my arms, chest, legs, hair. So much death around me. I wanted to feel alive.

I also wanted to crawl into bed.

When I checked my messages, I heard Liz backing out of my invitation to come with me to the Canterbury cocktail party. Something had come up, she said—she had to cancel. But I knew the tone of her voice.

"I can't do this with you just yet."

We'd been through this before. Last-minute squeamishness. Panic, dread. She'd glance at me with that look, and then the smile. *I thought for a minute we were still in love.*

No, she chose not to do that to herself.

I crawled into bed, wrapped myself in covers.

Almost asleep, the phone rang, and my machine picked up. Liz, again.

"Rick, I just heard. You must have heard by now. About Davey. Call me. You hear? Do you want me there? Call me when you get in. I'm so sorry about Davey."

I got drowsy from the steam heat.

I slept.

Buddha talks: *All man's words are but an echo.*

Chapter Thirty-three

Vinnie and Marcie rang my doorbell the next afternoon, but I was waiting for them, dressed, jacket over my arm, a weak smile on my face. They'd called earlier that morning because Liz had called them about Davey. I insisted I was fine.

"Leave me alone."

"No," Vinnie had said, "we'll come for you, walk with you to the party."

"Liz is worried about you," Marcie told me now.

"Psychologists worry about everyone." Too glib, smart-mouthed.

"That's not fair. She thinks you'll blame yourself."

"I do."

"She was right." Marcie tapped my shoulder. "Davey was a man who was already doomed."

Vinnie clicked his tongue. "Troubled."

But within minutes, tucked between Vinnie and Marcie like an invalid parent, I knew my going to the cocktail party at Peter and Selena's was a mistake. The party would be short—barely two hours before the art show opening—but I knew I'd be unable to lighten up. I'd spent the morning in bed or puttering around the apartment, my head fuzzy. Now, watching me, Marcie hovered like a mother hen, her eyes wary, watching.

We talked about the suicide, and that conversation led to Marta and her death.

"I feel sorry for Karen," Marcie whispered.

I got quiet.

"Liz might show up," Marcie told me.

"No," I said. "She doesn't want to be there."

"She's concerned about you, Rick."

"You did your job, Rick," Vinnie stressed.

"Yes, you did." From Marcie.

They exchanged glances.

I stopped walking. "Did I hound him into this?" My feet kicked fallen leaves.

Marcie touched my sleeve. "Stop this, Rick. Davey was consumed by his own self-loathing. God and sex—a collision course. You know that."

"You got a lead." Vinnie faced me. "You followed it. You didn't step over any bounds."

They kept talking, but I barely listened.

At the party, I expected someone to mention Davey, but no one did. Most of the faculty and staff, of course, didn't know him, but it was a small New England town. People gossiped. The circumstances would intrigue—Marta and Davey, two suicides? A matter of weeks apart. I wandered from small group to group, a tepid scotch-and-soda in my hand, avoiding conversation but listening to the grandfather clock count out fifteen-minute Westminster intervals. After an accumulation of such intervals, I could go home.

Charlie Safako was there, but he avoided me. He was with one of the junior faculty members, a young woman in the Fine Arts Department who was always in everybody's business. She had a lot to say about the art show we'd be experiencing shortly—it didn't compare to what she'd seen elsewhere. Widely disliked, she was cultivating all the wrong professors. She held onto Charlie's arm, intent on monopolizing him. One time, the two of them strutting by, I caught his eye, though I didn't want to talk to him.

He nodded toward an inexpensive Dali etching by the doorway. "Look how they've cheapened it. I bet Joshua's rolling in his grave now."

I waited to see how Charlie would act around Selena, but they avoided each other. Once I caught Selena frowning in his direction. Another time they walked near each other and I noticed two faculty members glance over at them. They, too, had probably heard Charlie's lurid and melodramatic version of Selena's visit to his apartment.

"Nobody here." Vinnie came from behind me and touched my shoulder. I looked around. He was right. The spacious living room area was sparsely filled. A few faculty members had already left. Selena was busy with drinks and platters of paté and crackers, but she looked anxious, a scowl on her face. This was not a successful evening. It was a dull cocktail party, the music—I swear it was a dreary, plodding Slavonic Mass—long and dull, inducing sleepiness.

Gazing out the front windows, I could see early snowflakes, wispy and faint, illuminated by the porch light, and I wanted to be out there. I wanted to be running again, my body hurled against the snow. Inside, people were looking at watches surreptitiously, waiting for signals to flee. Static filled the room. Selena moved faster, served more drinks, downed many of them herself. When he walked from the library, Peter looked ready for bed, eyes half-shut. Had he been dressed in pajamas, I wouldn't have been surprised.

I wanted to leave. Meekly, I followed Vinnie and Marcie into the renovated library. Marcie punched Vinnie in the side as I leaned on the old piano. I read her mind. She was remembering the room the way it had once been occupied by Joshua. The walls of leather-bound books, the bust of Charles Dickens on the mantel, the Victorian keyhole desk, Joshua's hanging green-tinted lights—all gone. This colorless room stunned. Folding chairs for guests who never arrived, an easel holding a painting Peter had executed in a college class—I remembered it from their old apartment downtown. Vases of rust-colored chrysanthemums only made the space seem funereal.

Idly I sat in an overstuffed chair tucked into a corner and fiddled with an ornate Elizabethan recorder.

"Play something." Vinnie grinning widely.

Peter came from behind me. "You shouldn't touch that. It's an antique. Selena brought it back from London. Late Victorian. A shopping expedition. She was going to sell it in the shop but it was too beautiful, she said."

Then he darted out of the room.

"Elizabethan," I mumbled. "I took a course…"

"Snob." From Marcie. "Peter's a law professor. What does he know about the Elizabethans? They were a lawless sort."

Marcie leaned into me, her back to a small cluster of folks in a corner. She mumbled in low, breathy tones about the room. I only heard part of it, but Marcie fashioned a satirical sketch of an army barracks, and, for sure, the room had a sharp-edged, clinical austerity about it. It was the way they'd painted the walls an institutional white, a sin against the natural beauty of the wood. I stayed by the books, lost in the titles, the floor-to-ceiling wall of bindings that looked out of place now in this echoey room.

Joshua's lovely rare books were now gone. Instead, the bookshelves displayed random collections of books. A vice of mine—I loved to examine other people's bookshelves. Running my fingers along the spines, I saw yard-sale collections of Book-of-the-Month volumes, and noticed names like Erle Stanley Gardner, Fannie Hurst, Taylor Caldwell, A. J. Cronin—names that always popped up when I rummaged through books at library or church sales. Walter Scott romances. More interesting were bound volumes of forgotten novelists like Mrs. E.D.E.N Southworth and Marie Corelli, worthless literature made graceful by pretty gilt bindings and dust-pocked age.

"Nice," I said to myself.

But textbooks and law reviews dominated. Dreadful.

"Snob." Vinnie stepped behind me, reading my thoughts.

Marcie was making light of the garish South American vases that held the flowers. I followed her gaze, but it wasn't funny because stark images of Davey and Karen surfaced. And suddenly, I didn't know why, I felt sorry for Selena and Peter who had struggled so hard and had failed so dismally. All the pain I had for Davey's aborted life—his battles with God and a sexuality he never understood, all culminating in a lonely, dark-night-of-the-soul suicide—haunted me now in this sad room. When Selena walked into the room, looking lost, her face worried and lined as she picked up an empty platter from a side table, I saw Davey's own haunted face. Somehow this dumb little party was thrusting me back to Davey's messy apartment and his final moments.

Davey's shadow covered this dreadful room.

I had to leave. I could only hide among books for so long. I said good-bye to Marcie and Vinnie, made a half-hearted excuse to Peter, and avoided Selena. Other than a quick nod of hello, I hadn't spent any time with her. But that seemed to suit her fine because she'd been skirting me, too.

On the sidewalk, bundled up, I looked to the sky for the snowflakes that had already stopped falling. I searched the dark blue sky, hungry for the taste of white flakes on my tongue. Nothing. Only the chill that went deep into my bones. I rushed home, pulling a scarf up across my face.

I knocked on Gracie's door, but she didn't answer. I thought of Ken upstairs, but he was the last person I needed to see now.

In my apartment I phoned Karen but the machine came on again. Nothing. "Call me, please." I repeated the message. "Call me, please."

I imagined her grieving, alone, in that apartment. The sound of the phone would jar her as she turned away from it.

I undressed and threw myself across the bed. I couldn't sleep at first, so bone weary that I was restless. I replayed images of pushing my way into Davey's apartment, rushing past him, ferreting out those pornographic magazines, holding up those glossy hardcore covers as though I'd unearthed gold.

I must have dozed off in spite of myself because I woke with a start, sat up on the bed. I was sweating. Something was bothering me. Something had happened. I knew something now, but I didn't know what it was. An answer, as hard and as clear as ice, lay somewhere in my unconsciousness. Grandma's comments—questions have answers. A hole in the universe, already filled. I already knew something. Suspected something. I rushed to the pegboard, stared at the index cards. Something had been said? Or done? Or seen? What? Charlie Safako, I told myself. Maybe. The look on his face? What?

I didn't know, except to know that I had the answer in me now. I thought of Ken yelling down the stairs about Davey's suicide. Karen's refusal to answer her phone. Willie Do and Marta back in April. Joshua leaving, Joshua dying. I turned on the computer, checked files again. The Mac hummed but yielded no answers. I started connecting unlikely people. I connected Ken with Charlie. Willie with Ken. Ken and Karen. Tony and Joshua. Selena and Tony. Maddening, all of it. But that led nowhere. Or did it?

For the next hour I made random, off-the-wall associations, hoping to trigger that kernel—that flickering dot—deep inside my head. I read Buddha. Tell me the answer. If I have a question, I have an answer. Grandma's humming words in my ear. Put the people and things together. Davey's suicide with Marta's death. With Joshua. With Richard Wilcox. Motive? Jimmy's voice came to me. Motive.

Nothing. Nothing at all. I sweated.

Missing. Space. Empty.

◇◇◇

At quarter to midnight, snuggled into my covers, wrapped like a mummy, I was jarred from a half-dream world of wild panicky chases and deadly falls from stone bridges by the phone ringing. My cell phone—I scrambled to locate it on the floor.

At first I couldn't hear the thin, slight voice on the other end. "Hello?"

"It's Karen."

I woke up.

"I'm Karen."

A strange way to begin.

"I've been trying to reach you, Karen. I heard about Davey

and I wanted to see if I could help." I paused because she was talking over my words. "What?"

"A mistake. It's all a mistake."

"What is?"

"Hiring you." Her voice was drawn out, flat. "It was stupid."

"No, you weren't. You did what you thought best."

"And Davey died."

"Not because of the investigation."

Her voice got louder. "You're wrong. Real dead wrong. We killed him, you and I."

"Karen, come on."

"First my Aunt Marta kills herself. Maybe because of me? Who knows? Then my brother. That's my whole family."

"Karen, do you want some company now? We'll go for a ride. We'll…"

"No." Harsh, lethal. "You are to blame."

That rattled me. "Karen."

"I'm firing you."

"What?"

"You heard me. I'm stopping this whole nonsense. You said a few weeks and I let you wander through my life and friends and smash things up. Pieces of debris surround me now. Bits and pieces of my life, like you dropped a vase and…"

"Stop, Karen. Stop it. Let me come over."

"No more work," she yelled. "Just when I wanted him back in my life again. No more. End this now. I'll send you a check but stop this."

She was rambling on and on, sobbing, little gasps of grief seeping between the angry words. As she spoke, I was becoming more and more awake. My mind focused—not on anything specific but on my sense that something was falling into place.

"I need more time," I told her.

"No." She screamed the word.

"I'm close to something."

"I have a right to fire you. You're delusional."

A strange word to throw at me. Delusional. What did that mean? I started to ask her what she meant, but then I changed my mind. "Can't I help you with arrangements?" I said at last. "With the funeral. With anything?"

"Isn't that a little like a hangman asking to wrap the body in a shroud? Like a killer wanting to dig the grave?"

When we hung up, I crawled back into bed, but I couldn't capture the soft warmth of my covers again. I shivered through the long night. In the morning I dreamed of the four horsemen of the Apocalypse but I couldn't remember them all. I got Disease and Death and Famine, and I wasn't even sure of those three. Only when I sat up, sweating, did I remember the last one. Despair.

Chapter Thirty-four

The next morning I texted Hank, who called back immediately. He was headed to classes at the Academy. I filled him in on what had happened, the particulars of Davey's suicide. That stunned him.

"Want me to come over? You sound down."

"No, I'm all right."

"Look, Rick. You got to realize something here. Actually two things. The first is that you had nothing to do with Davey's suicide. Nothing. You hear that? And the second thing is this. You got to realize you're family now. My family. When you're down, you drop in for food—and Grandma." He laughed. "You're Grandma's family. She keeps talking about you. I'm a little jealous about being replaced as number one on her list."

"But not on your grandfather's list." A stupid remark.

He clicked his tongue. "You can't worry about him. He's never going to like you." He paused. "What's on your plate today?"

"Why?"

"I thought I'd join you."

"I don't want you skipping class."

"What are you doing?"

"Loose ends."

"C'mon. I know everything already. Tell me."

"No."

"When's the funeral?"

"Tomorrow, according to the paper."

"I'll go with you."

"No. You don't even know these people."

"I know you."

"No, Hank."

"I'll stop by, okay?"

I was tired. "Okay." I thought of something. "A favor, Hank?"

"Yeah?"

"Could you call Aunt Marie for me? I have a delicate question, and you need to ask her."

Tension in his voice. "What?"

I told him.

"You serious?"

"Yes."

"Christ, Rick. Aunt Marie?"

"It's up to you."

"All right."

I hung up and thought about slipping back into bed. My body felt drained, empty.

I lingered over coffee, stale and cold, and found myself thinking about Hank. And smiling. He'd spoken to me as though he were the older one, the big brother. Family, he said—we're family. I thought of his big Vietnamese family, all loving and supportive. And I thought how hard it had been for Hank to usher me into that family—to go against so much that was hateful—his grandfather's unrelieved hatred of me because of my mixed blood, his hatred of the children of the dust. Me—*bui doi.*

Talking with him on the phone made me happy. It felt good that someone wanted to protect me.

◇◇◇

I started calling Karen, but her machine kept coming on. Its redundant message, mournful and solemn in the best of times, took on macabre overtones that alarmed me.

"Karen, call me. It's Rick."

But at one o'clock, idly dialing her number, she surprised me by picking up. "Hello." Brusque, businesslike.

I didn't answer at first.

"Hello." Again.

"It's Rick." I heard her sigh, unhappy. "I wanted to see if everything was all right. Do you need any help?"

"I'm really busy, Rick."

"I know. I'll help."

"I don't want your help."

"Karen, you can't do all this alone. It's not good."

She spat out her words. "I know what's good for me."

"I know, I know. But I'm a friend."

"You're not a friend. You're a hired boy I fired last night."

"I'll see you at the funeral."

She answered with the raucous, unfunny laugh bitter people make. "I suppose so. It's obviously open season on my family."

She hung up.

◇◇◇

I had to retrace my steps. Something boiled beneath the surface. What? I decided to follow up on one loose end—Hattie Cozzins' IOU for twenty grand borrowed from Marta some time back. That curious scribbled paper needed some explaining.

In the middle of the afternoon, unannounced, I knocked on Hattie's door, and stood there a long time. The hallway to her apartment was freshly painted, but the old walnut woodwork hadn't been scraped or sanded. A new layer of thick paint had been carelessly slapped on. Some splatter on the tile floor, drips of deck green paint on the doorknob. An old building, and successive generations of cheap paint lent the dim hallway a faded, spent look—all dressed up but nowhere to go.

I was running my finger over the glossy paint when the door opened slowly. Hattie watched me. She said nothing, her eyes squinting as though she were looking into the sun.

"Hattie," I blurted out.

She smiled dreamily.

I'd obviously wakened her from an afternoon nap, yet she also betrayed the drained, blowzy look of someone coming out of a hangover. Today she wore no makeup, missing that blatant layer of sweet-scented old-lady powder she'd worn the last time I met her. Her skin looked as crinkly and tender as snapped kindling.

"I remember you." She stood back and waved me into the room with a flip of her wrist and a slight nod. The small room smelled close and thick with old clothes and the cloying, fragrant aroma of spilt bourbon.

When I sat down, she began speaking, her whiskey voice raspy. "What do you want this time?" Blunt, a finger pointed at me. "You have to make it quick. I've been sick."

"I'm sorry. I just have one question."

She closed her eyes, as though bolstering herself for some unpleasant inevitability. "Shoot." Like she was at a gaming table.

I told her about the note Karen and I had found among Marta's possessions. "You were in her debt?"

She chuckled, low and throaty, lost for a second in her own thoughts. A heartbeat. "I hoped that damn note had got lost. But I should have known Marta would have tucked it somewhere. There were two, a typed one she made me sign. Me, a friend. A formal one, she said. The handwritten one wouldn't do."

"I didn't find that one."

She was still chuckling. "I managed to steal *that* one back one day when Marta wasn't looking. I knew where she'd hid it. The other—the one you found—she told me she'd thrown it out. She threw nothing out."

Buddha talked to me: *Abstain from taking what is not yours.*

I shook my head. "Well, she kept the paper because you hadn't repaid the loan, right?"

"True."

"Why not?" Looking around the cramped room, I wanted to open a window to let the cold November chill seep in, smother the cobwebs of the dank room.

"Look, mister. Marta lent me that money begrudgingly. She was a cheapskate—and a nuisance. We fought, but I was desperate. I had to blackmail her—I can admit that now because she's dead and it's all unimportant."

"About what?"

"Nothing important, at least now. She cherished this reputation as this devout Catholic woman, marching in anti-abortion protests, wooing the priest when she lied in the confessional, buying flowers for the altar at Easter. Mother Angelica with flowers in her hair. But drunk, the two of us, we could get crazy. I knew Marta's seamier side, the casino broad, hell to pay, and one time, hammered, she tried to perform a—well, a sex act on a man in an Atlantic City bar. She wasn't serious, of course. God, we were in a tavern, but the play-acting got a little too—how shall I put it?—risqué. He turned out to be a vacationing priest from New Haven—a little loose wire himself, I might add—but Marta's values clashed, as it were. She was always torn between being the Catholic angel and a hotsy-totsy devil in a red dress marinated in patchouli. So she was humiliated. She really wasn't like that, of course. A moral prig, most of the time. But, of course, I threw that in her face, threatened to tell Joshua and Richard Wilcox. Her niece Karen. It was cruel of me, but it had its effect because she lent me the money."

"But you didn't repay it."

"A gambling debt. I got in heavy with some guys. Something stupid. They're—what can I say?—unyielding. And I continued to gamble. I kept promising her, but I didn't *want* to. I actually couldn't. She was sitting on a pile of cash. She even plotted to get Joshua's treasure. Then she was dead."

"And you didn't have to."

"I thought I was free."

"You didn't like her, did you?"

She pursed her lips. "It's funny. She often irritated me—that I knew. But I didn't really know I hated her until after she died. I didn't kill her, by the way. Get that notion out of your pretty skull, young man. But when she died it hit me how much I *resented* her. She got so much damn attention by killing herself. Look at this—you're here talking about her long after she's dead. She was a cheap woman. With money, with men. You should have seen her and Joshua. Snotty, snobby. 'Joshua's instructing me in the classics.' What? I thought to myself. Classic positions?

Honey, you got them down pat. Kama sutra. At our age it's—kama suture." She screamed out a laugh. "Her and his books and art and shit. Irish shop girl. Slop girl. She pushed right in there and took what she wanted. I got leftovers, always. I was the church mouse, and she'd throw me crumbs. You know what she used to say? 'Good enough.' She always used that expression with me. 'He's good enough for you.' Or 'That dress is good enough for you, Hattie dear.' Second string. I was a fool."

"But now she'd dead."

"And I still can't pay that loan."

"It doesn't matter."

She smiled. "That's not the case you're hired for, is it, dearie?"

I smiled. "Exactly. It's your business."

"So it's over."

"Well…"

She cut me off. "So now you can leave. Tell Karen to stop this nonsense."

"She's busy with the funeral."

Hattie's expression shifted, her eyes danced. "What are you talking about?"

She didn't know, I realized. "Her brother Davey took his own life."

"You're kidding. Runs in the family, don't it? God, how Marta hated him."

"I heard."

"He got what he deserved."

"How so?"

"We all knew he was a filthy little faggot."

Chapter Thirty-five

The next morning Hank showed up as I got ready for the funeral. I opened my door to find him standing there in a double-breasted suit, something I'd never seen before. "I only dress up for the Vietnamese New Year's," he said.

"Tet trendy."

"Can I meet girls at funerals?"

"Yeah, catch them when they pass out from grief."

"I hadn't thought of that." A pause. "I spoke to Aunt Marie, Rick."

"And?"

"I'll call her again this afternoon. She said—maybe."

I nodded.

"You're making me nervous, Rick."

"I do that to a lot of people."

"C'mon. We don't wanna be late."

We were late. But there were few mourners at the funeral. There had been no calling hours, and a priest officiated at O'Brien Funeral Parlor, housed on a side street off Main in a rambling Victorian house. We arrived in the middle of it. The priest was counting a Rosary. *Hail Mary full of grace, the Lord is with thee...* The words fell in the empty room like rain echoing on a quiet street. Uncomfortable with the chanted words, I held back, staying in the anteroom, waiting, looking in. I signed the guest book. Hank didn't.

As we walked in, Hank whispered, "No Mass for a suicide, Rick. Mom told me that."

"I didn't know that."

Karen sat by the casket, alone, dressed in a black dress that looked too old for her, layers of lace draped around her neck and down her arms. She wore her hair up, pulled back, severe. For a second, approaching her, I was reminded of Aunt Marta. An old woman sat nearby but periodically sat in the empty seat next to Karen, holding her hand, smothering her neck with words. Karen stared straight ahead, unmoving, never looking at the coffin.

The folding chairs held perhaps ten people. Old people. There was a youngish man I recognized as a worker with Davey at the garden shop. I craned my neck around and in the corner, sitting with his back against the wall, his eyes closed, his legs stretched out in front of him, was Ken Rodman.

Hank slipped into a chair, out of the way. The room looked spartan, and I realized why. There were scarcely any flowers. One small bouquet rested on the coffin, red and white carnations. But none of the huge gaudy sprays I was accustomed to seeing at funerals. I hadn't sent flowers, as I had to Marta's funeral—I don't know why—but others obviously felt the same way.

"Karen, I'm sorry." I took her hand and leaned in to kiss her on the cheek. She was icy cold.

She mumbled thanks but didn't look into my face. I repeated myself until, awkward, I turned away. I passed by the coffin, not even stopping, but I glanced at the calm face. The Davey I knew was gone. None of the anger, none of the fierce confusion that colored his awful days and furious nights. This was a stranger.

Ken was motioning to me, so I sat down next to him. He shook my hand. "Terrible business."

I nodded.

We lapsed into painful silence. I didn't want to be sitting next to him. Hank glanced back at us, confused. He looked out of place, this lanky, young Vietnamese man sitting in his Sunday best, alone.

The funeral director entered, with obvious on-staff pallbearers lined up behind him, all with mask-like somber faces. Everyone stood to leave, the priest reappeared, and Karen seemed confused, turning left, then right, her hands against her face. She looked like a hurt child. Buddha talked to me: *Tears give us no peace of mind. We lose ourselves and lose our power.*

The director announced that there would be no service at the gravesite but friends were invited to Karen's apartment at one o'clock for a celebration of David Corcoran's life. That announcement took me by surprise. I didn't think she'd want that.

"You going?" Ken asked.

"I guess so."

"I *want* to. Davey and I were very close."

"I thought you saw each other a few times."

He gave me a weird look, as though baffled. "You don't understand."

He was right. I didn't. Outside I introduced him to Hank. He stared at Hank, not remembering that they'd met at the house. "This your brother?"

"Yes," I said.

Hank chose not to go to the apartment, which made sense, so I dropped him off at my apartment. "Call me later," he insisted. "I'll try to reach Aunt Marie again."

I nodded.

Greeting me at the door, Karen was smiling. "I'm glad you came."

Most of those in the apartment had not been at the funeral parlor. They were neighbors, I guessed, from the looks of them. Or acquaintances of Karen's from the shopping arcade. Some old friends of Marta's perhaps. Fifteen or so people, most of them old women dressed similarly in black dresses and white sweaters, slow-moving penguins of grief, patent leather purses gripped tightly. Marta's Brown Bonnet brigade? Maybe. For Davey—I doubted that. But I was pleased to see them there. Karen had plastic trays of supermarket cold-cuts, Palmer rolls, sheet cakes, a coffee urn, and a table with half a dozen liquor bottles. Ice melted in a soup bowl.

I watched Karen wherever she was in the room. She was buoyant, lively, embracing people, her smile constant. She bounced from person to person, sharing the same laughter with each one, so many seconds long, the same pitch. Curtain call.

Sitting in a chair by the window, I talked to no one. Karen passed by me, smiled down at me, and let her fingers graze my shoulder, not affectionately, but a simple acknowledgment of my presence. She turned her face away, widened her eyes as she greeted someone else. At that moment she looked like Marta. The few times I'd spent with Marta she'd been affectionate in that impersonal way, but I recalled the way she turned her head, twisted her neck, a thin show of teeth as her eyes brightened.

Dressed in matronly black, hair pulled into that Emily Dickinson bun, Karen moved like her dead aunt. It stunned me. A conversation came back to me—Karen talking about her childhood, a time when Marta wanted her to be some replica of herself—a severe teenage matron. Here was Marta again, resurrected, down to the morning-glory blue eyes with the gray cast in them. I didn't know why I was surprised. She was, after all, her niece. But the uncanny resemblance—the awful trappings borrowed from an old woman—unnerved me.

Pouring myself a cup of coffee, I realized something else I'd not spotted—so much of Marta now inhabited the apartment. Since I was last here, Karen had done what she told me she would never do. She'd carted so many of Marta's belongings to the apartment. All the things she despised were here. A floor lamp with a stained yellow fringe shade, a gaudy ceramic urn with ivy growing in it, a small plastic ottoman that was dyed a fifties turf green. On and on. Odds and ends, her aunt's garage sale world. All the stuff she should have thrown out, flea market inventory. It alarmed me, this behavior. Here was a lost Karen. Had she added Marta's sofa and chairs, the room would have been—Marta's. Now I wondered whether those stale, faded pieces would arrive soon. This was not the Karen I'd talked to at the beginning of my investigation. The room was a museum now. This was homage to a dead woman.

I sat down near a bookshelf that now held Marta's souvenirs, especially her Russian tourist relics, all crammed together. Karen had nailed Marta's fake Russian Orthodox icon of Jesus to the wall. Nearby was a fan labeled "Atlantic City," and a cup saying "What Happens in Vegas." Stacks of photographs in frames were piled on top of each other, yet to be displayed. This was Marta's scrapbook of her tourist junkets with Hattie. Marta's junk wall, and it had been moved here.

Suddenly now, turning around and surveying the room, I felt closed in. Karen was across the room, bending over an old woman, and I felt my skin get clammy. Karen was disappearing from this room, and Marta was coming back. Was I imagining it? I picked up a piece of embroidery from the shelf, some cutesy cat design, and I smelled it—Marta's smell, I imagined. Certainly not Karen's. The tablecloth on which the makeshift buffet was spread looked yellowed and old. It probably came from a closet in Marta's house. There was a patina of old sensibility here, of stale talcum power and the K-Mart perfume of blue-haired ladies. I swear to God—it gave me the willies.

Karen had placed Marta's small collection of books between plaster-of-Paris Virgin Mary bookends. The leather-bound books, the odd nineteenth-century volumes, cheap reprints mostly, a battered *Ivanhoe*, all looking out of place here. I ran my fingers over the spines. The delicious feel of old books, the dusty aroma of unturned, flaking pages.

And then, in that echoey room, I found myself thinking of Vietnam. I am a young boy, sitting in the barracks-like quarters, waiting to be taken to the airport—and America. A *cyclo* driver speeds by, and I wonder why my friend Vu had to disappear. I think of his beaten father—the frozen man. Tranh Xan Tan. I am wearing frayed dress pants, a couple of sizes too big, a blue-denim shirt with the smell of too many washings in lye soap, and a small bag, like a gym bag, but made of cardboard treated to look like old leather. Sitting there, quiet, nervous now, afraid of America,

I open the case. I want to be sure my *Sayings of Buddha* book is there, not because of what it says, but because I need something of my mother. I can see Sister Le Han Linh coming through the doorway, coming to gather me. I tuck the slim volume in my shirt pocket, and snap the bag shut. I wait. I am calm.

Now, sitting in Karen's crowded room, I felt the same calm the moment my mother's book rested against my bony chest. Peace—ease. Everything in harmony. Now Buddha talked to me:

Any object is an object for any subject.
Any subject is a subject for any object.
Buddha says that the relationship of all parts
Relies in the end on the one part that is missing.

Sitting there, in that magnified calm, I understood those words as though they'd been written on the spot for me. I thought of Grandma's words. "There are no holes in eternity. What's missing is already filled in."

...the one part that is missing...

I sat up, jolted by the words. Buddha. Buddha. The room suddenly got narrow, then large again. Space: empty: void.

I knew the meaning of the missing part. I *felt* it in my bones. Quietly, watching Karen out of the corner of my eye, I found my coat in the hall closet. I walked back into the living room. There was no one I wanted to say good-bye to, but I had another purpose for going back inside that room. No one was looking—I hid an object in the folds of my coat. A common thief. In a rush I was out the door, standing on the landing, my heart pounding. I could be wrong, but I didn't think I was. Pieces of a puzzle. I believed I had the one part that was missing. Everything is already complete because there can be no holes in eternity. I closed my eyes. I had the answer. Or at least I thought I did.

I felt it in my bones.

I'd been asking the right questions, but not all of them. In reconstructing Marta's last day, I had left out one crucial dimension. How did other people connect with others—and not just Marta—on that last day?

Even the dead in their graves.

I reached Richard Wilcox at the hospital.

He didn't seem surprised to hear from me.

This time I asked him the question I should have asked before. Whom did *he* talk to that last day of Marta's life? After all, she'd phoned to tell him she was walking over. All along, I assumed he'd stayed home, waiting for her visit. Had he left his apartment? Had he talked to anyone? Had he told anyone about her intended visit?

Silence from him.

He held the answer now, and somehow knew it. My last conversation with him had led him to the same conclusion I was grappling with now. That was why he'd changed—called himself a murderer. He'd come to his own conclusion, realizing he held a pivotal part of the puzzle. Yes, he had talked to someone that last day. He had, in fact, pointed the murderer toward Marta and that final bridge.

Suddenly I was seeing it all from his eyes.

I asked him again, "Who did you talk to?"

Silence—he wanted to die with the guilt he felt.

I mentioned a name, and it was as though he were waiting for it. A deep intake of breath, and I had my answer. As he recalled Marta's last slurred drunken words with him on the phone, he'd put the two pieces together. He'd made sense of her drunken words—the *reason* for her visit to see him. The murderer. She had named her own murderer.

Silence.

"Good-bye," I told him.

He was still on the line when I turned off my phone.

I needed a space to think. At McDonald's, I drank a cup of coffee. The place was crawling with school kids, teenagers, flirting and laughing and pushing. They sat across from me as I sipped my coffee. I took out my laptop and made some new connections, plugging in my new theory that at first seemed preposterous. A far-fetched hypothesis. Everything pointed in one direction now—Richard Wilcox, Charlie Safako, Hattie, even Davey himself. They all held parts of it. Not the *why* and not the *when* or *what* or *how*. But I had the *who...relies in the end on the one part that is missing....*

The problem was how to get to the rest of the answers.

Holes in eternity.

Finally, checking my watch, deliberate and calm, I left McDonald's, the boys and girls still cavorting and falling on each other. Time to ring a familiar doorbell.

Chapter Thirty-six

Peter answered on the fourth knock, and was surprised to see me. He looked tired, probably a little ragged from last night's failed cocktail party. Dressed in paint-stained sweats and a misshapen AMHERST COLLEGE sweater, he squinted and scratched his stomach, a dumb look on his unshaven face.

"Rick. A surprise."

"Can I come in, Peter?"

"Yeah, sure." He stepped back. I walked by him, and he looked over my shoulder. "We weren't expecting anybody. Selena's somewhere in the house but"—he laughed—"she won't want you to see her without her makeup."

"I've seen her without her makeup."

"What can I do you for?"

"I just came from Davey's funeral."

He bit his lip. "Christ, that was bad. I feel for Karen. Two in one family…" He stopped, shrugged. He shut the door behind me. "It's cold outside."

"I'm sorry to drop in like this, but I need some information from you. Only you can help me."

Peter's pale face turned parchment white with a slight tinge of pink on the cheeks, the face of an unhealthy baby.

"Glad to help but…"

We were standing there in the large foyer, three feet apart. "Could we sit down?"

"Sorry. Yes. Please. I'm not used to casual visits." He smiled. "Let me take your coat. Let's sit in the library. I was just having some coffee."

I slipped off my coat but kept it with me. He led me through the living room and into the library. They hadn't cleaned up since last night, and foggy glasses, stained plates, and crumpled napkins lay here and there, piled high, with that forsaken look a room has the morning after a party. In the old days ashtrays with cigarette butts would be everywhere, the rancid smell of day-old tobacco permeating the room. Not so any more because smokers were banished into the backyard or patio, purgatory for sinners. Peter motioned me to a settee, and he sat across from me in a wing chair. A cup of black coffee rested by his elbow.

"Sorry you left so soon last night, Rick." His fingers drummed a textbook on corporate law he'd been reading.

"Things to do."

He took a sip of coffee and then held onto the cup, cradling it in his two hands, as though warming them. "You sure you don't want coffee?"

"Yeah, Peter."

"Well…"

"You made a lot of changes here." I pointed around the room.

"Yes, but more to do. Lord, we never realized how costly this drafty house could be. And now with winter, the heating bills, the electricity, the…"

I stood up and walked to the wall of shelves. I pointed the Elizabethan recorder at him. "I was admiring this last night. It's a beautiful piece."

"Yes, I think I told you that Selena got it in London."

"Yes, and this?"

I pointed at random to a terra cotta vase, clumsily thrown, with some kind of South American Indian design painted sloppily on its finish. "That's from her shop."

I was making him jittery. When he sipped from the cup, I saw a finger twitch.

"I just came from Karen's apartment." I reached into one of the deep pockets of the overcoat and extracted a volume.

"What's that?"

I placed the old book on a table in front of him. My fingers tapped the book. "A wonderful book, really. And a rare one. One of a thousand copies of James Fenimore Cooper's novels, from the Leather-Stocking Edition of 1895. Putnam's out of New York. Thirty-two volumes bound in half-dark green morocco, gilt spine, raised boards..." I stopped. "As I say, rare. *The Last of the Mohicans*."

"Lovely. So what?"

"Joshua loved Cooper."

"I know. His collection is at..."

"They are missing this one. Did they count and reach thirty-two?"

"What are you talking about?"

"Joshua naively thought he'd instruct Marta Kowalski in the classics. In fact, he lent her books that she never read. But not, to be sure, his treasures, his one case of special treasures. When I was here, he was thrilled to show me his collection, but would not allow me to touch one. I remember the bound nineteenth-century sets, so perfect, elegant."

Peter twitched, reached for his coffee. "Everyone has old sets of the classics."

I tapped the book again. "I hazard a guess that Marta, for whatever reason, borrowed one of the volumes, probably planning to read it—and surprise Joshua. He probably never noticed one of the series missing from the glass case. Books she dusted so lovingly. But here it is. A lovely book. Karen told me he wanted her to read *The Last of the Mohicans* and lent her a cheap copy. Maybe he told her to take one from the shelf. But such a beautiful copy must have tempted her."

"So what?" His words sharper now.

"Joshua would not knowingly lend her this book."

"Well, obviously he did."

"But when he moved and packed his books, a sharp-eyed Joshua would notice it missing, no?"

"How do I know how his mind worked?" A pause as he swallowed his words. "Joshua left some of his books behind."

I smiled. "Buddha tells me that everything depends on the one part that is missing."

He babbled, "I mean, yeah, he left some sets behind." Finally, looking into my face, "What do you want?"

"Joshua wanted his rare books with him."

"So what are you saying?"

"When I first went to Marta's house with Karen, this book was resting on the kitchen table. It never registered with me that she had placed it there for a reason. She'd been thinking about it, I suspect. It was Joshua Jennings' book, and she still had it. She knew how crazy he was about books. She'd had a quarrel but wanted reconciliation. There's no way of knowing, but maybe he did spot the missing volume. Yes, he exiled her—a fight about Davey, a spat with Willie Do. But we'll never know—maybe they fought over *this* book."

"Ridiculous, Rick. He had so many."

"Maybe. But I talked to Richard Wilcox a short time ago. I asked him if he spoke to anyone about Marta coming to visit him that last day. A question I should have asked earlier. It was you, Peter. Richard met you in town. Excited, he blabbed the news to you about her visit, how she had something to tell him. She was bothered by something. All along it meant nothing to him because he believed her death was a suicide. But when I was with him the other day, he made a connection. I asked him about Joshua, if she'd mentioned him in that last conversation. Something dawned on him while we were talking. He was telling me about Marta's drunken phone call and her suicide plan—'Can you bury me?' Sounds like suicide, no? That's how he heard it all along. It seemed to fit."

Peter closed his eyes for a second. When he opened them, they were wet.

"I realized an hour ago what Richard understood at that moment he was talking to me—and why he called himself a murderer. She was talking about you, Peter. She was bothered by something that happened to her in this house. She must have been mumbling your name, Peter. Not 'Can you bury me?' but probably a slurred, garbled 'Canterbury.' Easy to confuse, no? An old man hearing sloppily spoken words. She was telling him your last name. She knew something was wrong in this house."

Peter picked up his coffee cup but put it down slowly. It rattled in the saucer.

"The other day he remembered talking to you the afternoon of her visit. So now he's a dying man who believes he set up a murder."

I waited.

"My name? Come on. This is nuts."

"Something was wrong, Marta knew, and it had to do with you. This house. Joshua. She'd cleaned here—you told me that yourself. She acted strange…"

"Rick."

"Confused, she couldn't put it all together. So she had to tell someone. She suspected you of something, Peter. When she was in this house, something happened to her."

"Nonsense."

"Why you, Peter? Why did she say your last name?"

A hollow chuckle. "You said she was drunk."

"Everything leads back to Joshua Jennings, to the house he loved. Charlie Safako told me that Joshua told him he'd changed his mind—that he wouldn't sell the place after all. He was definite about it—or, at least, he convinced Charlie. And even Davey, who gave me the answer to Marta's fight with Joshua, told me Joshua said he missed Marta, considered reconciliation. He was too lonely by himself. He had no one *but* Marta left. You know how Joshua was—afraid to leave this house. A hermit those last days. He was ready to resume his old life—visits from Marta especially. Die quietly in the town he loved."

"It was our house, Rick."

"Was it? The yardman, Willie Do, told me something interesting about those last days, not only Joshua banning Marta but a phone call from Joshua *after* the house sold. Joshua's words—'My gardens miss your touch. Come back to work." Interesting, no? 'Come back to work.' Joshua wanted his life to go back to the way things were. Not a goodwill gesture to the new owners."

"Of course, it was. But I did the lawn."

"You certainly did." I breathed in. "But Joshua, quite simply, was going nowhere. Leaving Farmington was just one more game he played. And that led me back again to this house—his house. Why would he disappear so completely? I was bothered by the suddenness of his leaving, and, as well, his out-of-state death. The mysterious Mary Powell, the niece from nowhere. Marta came back here to clean and she spotted something. What, Peter?"

Peter wasn't moving now. I was waiting for him to say something. "And another thing. You know, when I met Charlie Safako, he was crowing about Selena coming on to him, which got me thinking. Why? He's a repulsive scumbag. Even Selena wouldn't sink that low—her flirtations are with young men. She spent an evening with him after Marta died. Why? To see what he knew. She may have heard him talking of Joshua changing his mind. Charlie yammered to everyone. She had to find out what he knew. She discovered that was all he did know, so she fled his groping hands. But it gave him a juicy story to spread."

I stopped. Everything had led to Selena and Peter Canterbury and the lovely house, all triggered by my holding that volume of Cooper. Marta, confused by something she saw when she returned to dust the Canterbury home that last time, went home and sat in her kitchen and held Joshua's book. The pristine book, orphaned from its other volumes, suggested wrongdoing. Why had Joshua fled Farmington without good-bye? What did she see in the Canterbury house that fueled her final depression?

But this was all I *did* know.

"It all came back to you and this house." A deliberate pause. "Everything."

Silence.

Slowly, at last, Peter spoke, his eyes flickering. "Cooper. I never counted the volumes."

I didn't answer.

"She told me she would leave me." His voice a whisper. "She said it would be all right. You know, Rick, we're not that kind of people. We're not."

"Why?"

"It just—happened. An accident really." He waved his hand around the room. "We wanted this."

"But Peter…"

"I know, I know. But it was pure chance. Almost an accident. Believe me. It wasn't murder or anything. Never murder."

"Tell me."

Peter shook his head back and forth. "I'm glad it's over. You know, it's made us different people."

"Tell me, Peter. Marta discovered something about you and this house."

Peter nodded. "It was a mistake asking her back here."

"Marta. To clean?"

He nodded. "We asked her to clean the place. I told you that. My parents were coming to visit, my brother, and the place was a mess. A shambles from moving. At first she said no, but then she agreed. She was the only housekeeper we knew. She cleaned our friends' homes. She'd cleaned this home for years. She didn't want to come back here. Memories of Joshua and all. We *begged* her. Selena was swamped at her store. Me with classes. God, how stupid we were. How cocky. It was a horrible afternoon. She moped around, depressed, hanging over his goddamn piano. I swear—she'd been drinking. All she blabbed about was Joshua. He moved away so fast. She said she sent a letter to Amherst but it wasn't answered. He got it, she said, but refused to answer. She had no energy to clean, pushing things around. She was only doing downstairs, the front rooms, and a guest room off the mud room, but she went upstairs for some reason, opened a walk-in closet upstairs that I thought I'd locked. She wasn't supposed to go upstairs. We *told* her not to. I'd locked *everything*. We'd filled it with books."

"Joshua's rare books."

He nodded. "She called to me. I rushed up the stairs and told her he'd left them behind. Everyone knew he'd take his valuable books with him—he told everyone that. The rest to the school. Not the Coopers. Some bullshit like that. She opens that door, it's jammed with books. Every inch. She kept shaking her head. 'But he loved these books. I dusted them.' I knew there was trouble. It *looked* odd. The way they were jam-packed there—she knew they were hidden."

I pictured Marta at that chilling moment. It must have been frightening, spotting that long-cherished collection of books in that tight closet. All those chiseled, fine bindings, all the smooth hand-tooled leather. Rare volumes encased in plastic sleeves. One of them still at her home.

"She got disoriented," Peter said. "As I tried to shut the door, she touched the edition of Cooper's *Water Witch*, his rarest possession. Stupidly, with her cloth, she dusted it." Peter shook his head. "Dusting a book in a damn closet. 'Cooper,' she said. 'He loved Cooper.'"

"So she suspected something?"

"Maybe. I don't know. She was just confused. She was so mad at him, so hurt, that all her anger went to him. 'Bastard,' she called him. I mean, she started whimpering like some hurt animal, right there in the upstairs hallway. I could have kicked myself. All of the upstairs rooms were locked. Everything except that fucking closet. But she tried another locked door, and then stared at me. So she left after doing a sloppy job. We told her it was all right, but she agreed to return to clean up after the family left. When I called her later to tell her we didn't need her, she spoke before I did—she refused to come, too quiet on the phone. I mean, you could hear it in her voice. I asked her what was the matter, and she said she didn't want to talk. But her voice was real funny."

Peter looked down, his hands folded into his lap.

"She knew?"

A monotone. "She knew something was wrong. Something about Joshua leaving this house didn't sit well. She wasn't stupid."

"But why did you hire her, of all people, to come into this house?"

He looked up. "Everything seemed all right. She'd chased after him—wrote that damn letter and all—but when he was dead, what could she do? We never considered her a problem. A fucking cleaning lady? We were worried about it until Joshua was, well, dead."

I realized he didn't know about Marta's fanatical pursuit to Amherst and Clinton—those visits happened afterwards. All he knew was the letter.

"We thought she was nothing. A house cleaner with a stupid crush on an old man. She was—nothing. It never occurred to us that she was *that* important. When he talked about it, Joshua played it down—the relationship. His viewpoint. Not hers obviously. Then one night, walking home, I bumped into Richard Wilcox, and he was all crazy. Another old codger, smitten. He'd rushed out to get something and was rushing home to get ready for Marta's visit. He told me that she was walking over and had something important to tell him. He made it so secretive. 'What?' I asked, panicky. He didn't say anything. I knew there was trouble. She was going to tell him her suspicions. About us and the house. About Joshua and his books." His voice broke.

"And so you waited by the bridge. When she walked over, you pushed her?"

Peter gazed at me and shook his head. His lips trembled.

"No," he said. "I could never do that. I couldn't *kill* anyone."

Chapter Thirty-seven

"No." A voice from outside the room. "But I could."

Selena walked in from the living room. She pressed one hand against the doorframe, as though to steady herself, and my first thought was that she'd been drinking. She had a wild look in her eyes, a spitfire gleam.

"I did it." She was looking at Peter, angry now, fierce. "You fool. You pitiful fool."

Peter said nothing.

"He didn't know a damn thing, Peter. You gave it away. You didn't have to. You goddamn fool. He was guessing."

"Selena." I watched her turn toward me, her face hard.

"Well, well." She smiled at me, a grimace, really. "I didn't think Romeo boy would get to the bottom of this. I was convinced it was all dead end. God, we watched you stumble around. Running in circles. Nothing—no way to point an accusing finger at us. Nothing. You surprise me. Handsome and bright."

She stood behind Peter's chair and gripped the top of it. One hand brushed his hair, but he didn't move.

"You did it?"

We locked eyes. Selena shifted her gaze.

"It just happened. She knew—or sensed—about Joshua. I didn't, well, plan it, and it sort of happened. But yes, I did it."

"Where is Joshua?" I asked.

Silence.

Again. "Where's Joshua?"

Peter's voice was hollow. "He's buried in the backyard."

Selena shot him a contemptuous look. Her fingers pressed against his neck. He winced.

She smiled without humor. "Sort of like burying an old bone."

"For God's sake, Selena." From Peter.

She faced him but spoke to me. "Peter never thought he could break a law. Some lawyer, no? I married a man who still believes that law is sacred."

He spat out the words. "Yeah, and look where your horrible game got us."

"Rick, believe me, it wasn't supposed to be like this." A bittersweet sadness in her voice. "Not at all."

"Tell me," I demanded.

◇◇◇

Joshua had played with them, teased them, toyed with them about the magnificent house, enjoying the banter and the attention. He'd placed the house on the market so often, then always changed his mind. He canceled the deal with the local realtor, and sat back. The faded For Sale sign disappeared from the front lawn.

Selena and Peter attended so many school functions there, and loved the house. But they had little money. They became friendly with Joshua. He liked them, he said, and now and then they dropped in, bringing Indian or Chinese take-out. One night at dinner, he suggested that they should have the house.

"A young couple, good-looking, the future of the college. You look good in these rooms."

Joshua was looking into a retirement community in Amherst. Maybe it was time. He made them read the glossy pamphlet. Perhaps they could work out some deal, he told them, a private mortgage. A reasonable down payment—he wanted twenty grand, which made them wince because it was most of their savings—and then reasonable monthly payments. He wanted to unload the house.

He got them all excited, and they dreamed of the Federal Colonial with its Old World charms, its role as cynosure on Main Street, its affection held by the college and its faculty.

"Yours," he told them. "It should be yours."

Night after night they rhapsodized about the life they could live there, Peter promoted to professor, a high-profile private law practice on the side, the beautiful Selena assuming the role of hostess for those parties. The big-moneyed landed gentry of Farmington. A membership in the exclusive Farmington Country Club. That dream fired their early honeymoon days, made their anemic lovemaking sparkle. They visited much more often than they told their friends. Their friends supported them.

"Even you," Peter said to me now, "told us to go for it."

True. I suppose I did, a throwaway line at a dinner party. I didn't remember.

They could do it, Joshua told them. Each time they visited, Joshua tempted them.

"I'll throw in the grand piano."

Peter and Selena talked about it with family, who urged them to press on. Some friends like Vinnie and Marcie, unaware of the extent of their visits to Joshua, advised caution, warned of expensive renovations, but Selena and Peter were envisioning an illusionary homestead, not a rattletrap edifice. Joshua was a fickle man. He was stony as old Connecticut soil, a dangler of carrots before the horse. Peter and Selena pooh-poohed any negative comments, confident they would win over the irascible Joshua. Life in the grand house seemed inevitable. It was easy not to see the frayed electrical work, the leaking faucets, the worm-eaten windowsills. When they turned on the switch in the foyer, the burgundy Bavarian crystal chandelier created a wonderland.

"We told him yes."

Peter handled the straightforward legal work, orchestrating the quit-claim sale. When the announcement was made—Joshua agreeing—we had a little celebration for Peter and Selena at the house. Joshua smiled through it all.

"Signing our life away," Peter said at the time. "All our life savings."

"That's what we thought," Peter said now. "All we needed was his signature, a notary, and it was ours. We had a check made out for twenty grand."

"What happened?"

The afternoon following our little celebration, Peter met Joshua strolling on the sidewalk, and he mumbled about a change of heart, a plan to give the house—as well as his millions—to the boys' academy he so cherished. Joshua seemed out of focus, and Peter thought he was losing control of his mind.

"I'm righting things," he said to Peter.

That night Peter and Selena fought. They'd talked about the house so often that it seemed theirs already. That, Peter admitted, and the fact that their shaky marriage needed a foundation. The house promised to be the answer.

Panicked, Selena phoned Joshua and he confirmed his decision that a sale was unnecessary. He would give the house to the school. He would live in it until he died, but the school would own it. They'd maintain it. He could stop worrying. Eventually the house could be named in his honor. Joshua Jennings Conference Center. Immortality assured by the presence of a plaque on a well-mown lawn. No, he told Selena, he wouldn't change his mind. He was sorry.

"Then," Peter said in a low voice, "we started a dumb mind game."

Selena jokingly said that they should declare Joshua senile— he certainly acted strange a lot of the time, and he was reclusive— and force him to sign the papers. His signature was already on the initial agreement. Peter had orchestrated everything legally. A final signature was necessary, the quit-claim notarized.

Night after night, all that week, they played with silly notions of institutionalizing Joshua, of falsifying legal documents, of suddenly discovering blood kinship with him. Frivolous and implausible games borne out of frustration. But late-night conversation took on an eerie reality of possibility. The fanciful plans became more preposterous—snatched by a UFO. And those laughing, rollicking conversations were fun, verbal foreplay. They experienced a closeness they'd never had. But the conclusion of each of those bedtime stories was the ownership of that grand old house, plain and simple.

During the daytime, however, the nighttime game-playing seemed otherworldly. The house was moving away from them. Joshua stopped inviting them. At one time Selena had sought Joshua's confidence, used to drop in at various times, brought him things from her shop, things he disparaged. Claptrap, he'd called her offerings. Bored, sitting with him, she'd listen while he talked of his empty life. She learned the facts of his long but meager autobiography—the fact that he had no living relatives, that he was giving all his money to the boys' school. She knew where he kept his vital papers, not that she planned to snoop, but that was the way it happened. She learned the intricacies of his slow, retired life, his ornery ending of the friendship with Marta. At some point Marta had stopped phoning. Marta no longer mattered. The housekeeper with the stupid crush.

That Friday night after she closed her shop, Selena stopped in to see him. Surprised how friendly he was, she was convinced that he would sign the house over to them. Joshua, light-hearted, seemed excited. He flirted with her, something Selena had encouraged before. She wanted the house, so she let him. A repulsive man, all fingers and old-man fantasy. He liked to touch her, his fingers grazing her neck. But that day it rankled. Bitter about the house, she wasn't in the mood for his shenanigans.

"I asked him to stop," Selena said now. "He snapped back at me that I'd never get the house that way."

On Monday, he said, he would meet with the boys' school to make it final. He'd inform them of his intentions—he'd itemize exactly what he wanted them to have. His decision was ironclad—the house would go to the school.

"I hated him then."

When his hand slid to her hip, she slapped him hard, angry, and he backed up, stunned. No one had ever hit him before.

Sputtering, he went to hit her back, but she shoved him, disgusted, and he toppled over.

"He gasped, clutched his heart, and pleaded for help. He started making gagging sounds. There was spittle in the corners of his mouth."

Then he was dead.

"It was over so quickly. We were fighting, and then he was dead."

She hunched over his body, this withered old man dead at her feet. And the promise of the splendid house faded from her reach. Wild with fright, she stared around the vast room. "This was to be *my* home."

"It was then," Peter added, "the game-playing became real."

"Why not?" sputtered Selena, almost in tears. "It should have been our house. It *was* our house. He'd agreed. We'd even given notice at the apartment complex."

She called Peter, demanding that he get there, and a frightened Peter raced over.

"Why not just forge his name on the papers?" I asked.

Peter shook his head. "What? I file the papers on Monday morning. Joshua is found dead the previous Friday. Who'd believe it? There couldn't be any question. No doubts. No contesting the estate. We didn't know if the boys' academy knew of his intentions. Yes, we found a copy of a letter in his desk informing the headmaster that he'd be giving the school the cherished Renaissance painting, some antiques, and a volume of incunabula. But we didn't want them saying they were told the house should be theirs. No. Joshua had to be kept alive until we were in the house for months. There had to be…an interim of time."

"Time?"

"To make it seem believable. After all, he was dead."

Selena glared at Peter. "You wanted to call the coroner."

Peter looked miserable. "We should have."

"I had to push him." Selena pointed at Peter. "Threaten him. He finally agreed."

Everything shifted to slow motion. Peter and Selena became a bizarre couple dragging a dead body across the floor. A cheap horror movie on TV. Other peoples' lives. Trancelike. "We didn't stop to think what we were doing. We just kept moving."

Under cover of darkness, Peter dug in the muddy eighteenth-century gardens behind the house. Joshua's body disappeared under the wet sod. Peter stared into my face. "When the last shovelful of dirt was thrown and the original sod replaced, I knew there was no turning back."

Back in the house, they stared silently at each other, both grimy with dirt and sweat and tears. "It was like we'd walked out of a movie," Peter said. But the horror of it made them tremble. "We sat on the floor and cried and cried. There was no going back now."

They needed to buy time—a couple months. On Monday Peter filed the papers, forged. For years he'd had a silly flirtation with Myrtle Banks, the aged librarian at the college. Luckily also a notary. He wore his lawyer's face, exaggerated, as she did his bidding without so much as a question. He promised her lunch. He deposited twenty grand in Joshua's account. No one saw Joshua around because he rarely went out. Marcie and Vinnie took Selena and Peter to dinner that night. Everyone celebrated.

"They toasted us," Selena told me.

They read the glossy pamphlet on the Amherst retirement village. Selena did a short-term rental, using forged checks from Joshua's household account, and the game plan grew. Peter knew Amherst because he'd been an undergraduate there. Posing as Joshua in a careful letter, they terminated the services of his accountant—just in case. They stopped other services—oil delivery, the *Hartford Courant*. In New Haven they bought theatrical makeup at a shop near the Yale School of Drama, and at night they practiced transforming Peter—who had acted bit parts in college—into a feeble, squeaky Joshua. They created a voice for him.

"Remember how everyone made fun of my performance as King Lear?" Peter said. "The reviewer in the college newspaper mocked me." A pause. "Well, King Lear was reborn."

Peter-as-Joshua moved into his quiet place in Amherst. "People don't pay attention to old folks. They walk around them. So it was easy."

That part was easy. They used Joshua's money to pay for expensive short-term rentals, for removal of his furniture to Goodwill. The promised Renaissance painting, antiques, and cherished incunabula delivered safely to the boys' school. A thank-you note sent from the Board of Trustees with an invitation for Joshua to visit when the painting was unveiled in a ceremony. He declined, claiming illness.

At night, still frightened, they plotted the long sequence of events—from Amherst to Clinton to death in anonymous New York. To leave no trail. There'd be no question. They suffered waves of panic, but it was too late to stop. Joshua lay in the garden.

"We were afraid Willie Do would come back to work the back gardens, so I mowed the lawn, trimmed the bushes. He never came back."

"He did come back."

"Really?"

"But he went away."

"Everyone went away."

"But not Marta."

He winced. "Yeah, we'd spot her car on the street. That bothered us."

They became obsessed. There was always something else to think of. A new expense. Letters that surprised. Keep going.

Peter, in disguise, established a life in Amherst, visible on occasional weekends, returning by bus to Hartford during the week. Back and forth. Luckily he was on summer break from the college. Selena played niece when she had to, dealing with the New Haven estate lawyer, the people in Clinton. Rental cars and highly-visible visits but rare stopovers. Joshua was a hermit. They wanted a trail that would end in sudden death in New York.

"Why New York? Why Mary Powell?"

Peter smirked. "A mistake."

In New York one time for business, Peter had talked up a waitress in a West Side bar. Mary Powell, single and lonely, in a bad relationship she couldn't shut up about. He flirted with her, promised her a call, and she gave him her number and address.

"I was feeling low." Peter avoided looking at Selena. "My ego needed stroking."

"Ass," Selena snarled.

"The name on the paper became the niece." Peter sighed. "That was a mistake."

"I told him to make up a New York name and address, something bogus. But, oh no—not my Peter with that slip of paper tucked into his wallet." Selena shook her head.

"That was a stupid error," Peter went on. "I got careless. My mind wasn't working. I just felt that—what if someone tried to call—at least they'd hear a real voice, a real Mary Powell. It would confuse people." A sob escaped his throat. "I wanted everything to go away."

"Weak." Selena wagged a finger at him. "It would have worked. Joshua had moved away."

"Except for Marta," Peter said, his tone mournful.

"Yes, Marta," Selena echoed. "Marta. That witch."

They ended the Amherst rental on schedule, sublet the Clinton beach cottage—they actually made *that* into a vacation for themselves because they'd talked about a summer rental all winter—and then orchestrated his sudden death in New York.

"Everything like clockwork. A bogus death certificate sent to Joshua's lawyer was no problem."

In his files Peter found the death certificate of a former client. Scanned, Photoshopped, cut and pasted by a diligent Selena, the document, printed, became an official declaration. Who would investigate? He was the lawyer involved—he'd talk his way through any questions. But there were none.

Routine papers, a few phone calls, letting one part of New York's bureaucracy work against another part. Orchestrated with Peter's careful attention, the estate was probated without problem, the New Haven lawyer routinely signing off on it, without question. After all, he hadn't seen Joshua in years. An obit to the newspapers. The school got his millions. His rare Renaissance painting and the rare volume of incunabula, the items promised by him in that discovered letter, were already on display at the boys' school. Supposedly he'd moved with his rare Coopers. No one would wonder about those books. The Canterburys were already the owners of the house, which was, of course, no longer an asset.

"A mortgage paid in full on paper."

Joshua had suggested he'd hold the mortgage, and now, conveniently, it was paid off. No questions asked.

Slowly they refurbished the rooms in their own way, covering up Joshua's life in the house. People knew they'd spent most of their money buying the house so no one expected much inside. They did that purposely—to make people forget Joshua's awesome presence in the vast house. They wanted it to look—poor. The piano stayed—they'd mentioned to friends that Joshua said they could have it.

"No problem. Clockwork."

"We all knew about the piano," I noted.

"Life went on," Selena said matter-of-factly.

The body in the summer garden.

Yes, I thought—and the toll was your fragile marriage.

Peter sat back. "It was a game that got too easy. We owned the house. Legal. Fair and square. Paid for. We didn't kill him, Rick. He died of a heart attack."

"Marta." I waited. "Marta."

"Marta," Peter sighed. "Christ, we thought that she was out of the picture. But the day before Joshua—well, moved—she left a message at the house. And that letter to Amherst scared us. We knew she might go up there, so we prepared stories for the guard there to keep her away. So much of our planning had to do with her. But after that one letter—nothing. Silence. She gave up. The summer went by. We were free."

"And then months later you asked her to clean your house."

"Fools," Selena spat out. Her eyes got bright, fiery. "Can you believe we never gave her a thought? She was a cleaning lady."

"His cherished books." Peter glanced toward the staircase. "I didn't want to get rid of them. So wonderful. A pristine collection. Lovely. In an unused closet."

"Upstairs." Selena bit her lip. "Peter was supposed to lock the closet."

"So you had to kill her?"

"The look on her face when she opened that door," Peter mumbled.

Selena watched me closely. "Marta was a silly old woman, but Richard Wilcox isn't. Too dangerous. We couldn't risk it."

Selena waited by the sheltered stone bridge, standing in the shadows, knowing it was the route Marta would take from her home.

"All I wanted to do was talk to her, get some sense of…" Her voice trailed off. "Nothing more, I swear. Just convince her that Joshua had moved. I didn't go there to harm her."

But Marta, spotting her, turned, backed off. Selena ran at her, grabbed her shoulder, and the older woman, already tipsy, struggled.

"She fell." Selena raised her voice.

"No," I insisted. "She couldn't fall like that. The wall was too high."

"Well, we fought."

"You pushed her."

Selena got quiet. "It was so simple. She was a little plastered, but I had to fight her, lift her…" She sighed.

"Everything got out of hand. It was crazy." Peter was crying. "We're not that kind of people. You know us, Rick. You're our friend. We're not that kind of people."

Buddha talks. *Abstain from taking the life of everything that lives.*

Epilogue

Buddha, Lord, he says: What must be completely known, I have completely known.

When I called Karen about the arrests of Peter and Selena, she mumbled a thank-you and hung up. That was it. She sent me a generous check. She'd forgotten that she'd already paid me, so I sent it back with a note. She sent it again. Both times there was no note to me. The second time I tore it in half. I called her every day, leaving messages. Dinner, I suggested. Let's talk about what happened. When I finally stopped at her store, she refused to speak to me. Embarrassed, I left.

I avoided her shop. Marcie told me the rumors floating around. Karen was increasingly cranky and miserable some days, happy and spirited others. She started attending Mass, she cut her hair, she wore glasses now, and she handed out pamphlets in her store. Leaflets about God and man. Not Brown Bonnet stuff, thank God, but little New Age sermons on life. People were staying away.

One day, shopping, Marcie watched movers emptying out Selena's gift shop. Karen stood outside, a smile on her face. Thanksgiving arrived, a holiday from classes, but little else. I never ran anymore. I ate too much, drank too much, hung out with Jimmy and Gracie too much. Ken moved out one night and said no good-byes. Marcie still insisted he was involved. Vinnie said that Marcie had to indulge conspiracy theories that could never be proven—like the Kennedy assassination, like the disappearance of Judge Crater, like Amelia Earhart and Jimmy Hoffa. Somehow she connected Ken to Selena and Peter. Ken moved out of state, I heard.

For a while everyone at the college talked of Selena and Peter, but then they were talking about Charlie Safako whose pug died suddenly. He fell apart in class and wept.

I received a short note from Richard Wilcox, a card really, and in it he wrote this sentence: "I'm sorry for the way I spoke to you. I treated you shabbily."

That was all. It was a decent gesture. When I called to thank him, I learned he'd died the day before.

Jimmy and I finally had to move our office out of the South End of Hartford. Though he grumbled and fumed, he finally agreed to a space I located. "About time." The second floor of a converted three-family Victorian home on Farmington Avenue, tiny rooms that looked out on an all-night Shell station, fast food restaurants, and a Hair Today beauty parlor. Jimmy could walk to work—his studio apartment was down the street. The first floor held law offices of an old Hartford stalwart, a feisty lawyer named Praleen Johnson, though I doubted anyone mocked that first name when confronted by the bulldog in court. The third floor held a helter-skelter video production office run by Praleen's bohemian and unfocused son, Marcus, a haven for off-the-wall characters. The only money they made was from taping court depositions for Daddy—and most likely drug sales, along with the offbeat avant-garde short films they showed at film festivals.

Jimmy, sizing up the house situation, remarked, "I'm afraid there's gonna be at least one murder in this building. Have you seen the characters?"

But he acquiesced to the move when he realized that Pizza Parlor next door delivered at all hours. Not only pizza but also Buffalo wings with hot sauce.

"A new chapter for us," he summarized. "You better like it here."

I sighed. "Jimmy, I'm the one who found the place, no?"

"Believe what you want."

◇◇◇

A day later Hank and I visited Aunt Marie, who had trouble looking into my face. I thanked her, and we drove an hour down to Stamford. We had lunch with Dan Fowler, an old roommate of mine from Columbia, once an FBI specialist and now an archivist with the Smithsonian. I repeated what I'd told him on the phone.

"Tomorrow," I told him.

He grinned. "You ask the impossible, Rick."

"That's because I know you can do the impossible."

He flicked his head toward Hank. "Do you believe this guy?"

Hank smiled back. "A man of surprises."

We drove back home, but we had to return the following afternoon.

That night, nervous, I met Hank outside and we drove to Willie Do's apartment. We walked into his living room, and I caught my breath—everyone was there. Willie, Marie, Tony and his wife, even the fifteen-year-old boy called Big Nose. They stared at me, wary, tense.

I cleared my throat. "With great respect, Vuong Ky Do," I began, looking into his face. "I want to thank you for helping to solve a murder."

Willie raised his hand. "No, I want nothing."

I glanced at Hank, who sputtered, "But Uncle Willie, Rick had an idea."

Willie stood up, his face hardened, ready to leave the room, but his wife touched his sleeve. He looked down at her face and drew in his breath. She had tears in her eyes,

"What?" Nervous, twisting his body around.

I held out a manila envelope to him, but he didn't take it.

His wife touched his sleeve again, nodded at him. "Vuong." Her voice a whisper.

Willie slipped an eight-by-ten photograph from the envelope and sank back into a seat. He gripped it in both hands. Frozen. His eyes never moved off the photograph. Beads of sweat on his brow, his lips quivered.

What I'd done—with Hank's and Aunt Marie's imprimatur—was to take the torn, faded, stained photograph Willie had carried with him as he fled Vietnam, the precious relic he looked at once a month in Tony's apartment—*that* photograph. The one with the faded hint of his dead little girl, the girl smiling under her father's touch. An image almost entirely disappeared. I delivered the photograph to my friend in Stamford with the proviso that I return to retrieve it the next day. With his state-of-the-art technology, Dan had performed a miracle. The reconstituted photograph was crisp and vibrant. But what mattered was that Willie and Marie's little girl was no longer washed out, a dim suggestion of a pretty child. No, that girl with her innocent smile, her father's loving hand on her shoulder—that girl was alive now.

Willie moved the photograph closer to his face. His fingers trembled on his dead daughter's lovely face.

He stood up, as if in a panic, his eyes darting from one member of his family to the next. A low groan came from the back of his throat. Finally he stared long and hard at me. Uncomfortable, I looked away.

"Rick Van Lam."

The whole name.

I shivered.

He left the room, taking the photograph with him.

We sat still, all of us.

Suddenly we could hear Willie's difficult wailing, an awful keening for the dead, beautiful daughter whose ghost walked the earth and could not come home to her father.

Hank and I stood up, ready to leave.

Aunt Marie grabbed me and hugged me. She whispered in my ear:

"*Toi la hoa binh.*"

He is at peace.

◇◇◇

One night, lying on the sofa, the phone rang and the machine picked up. It was Liz. We'd spoken right after the sensational arrests, rehashing the details. I'd thanked her for her help with roses and a dinner at an Italian restaurant in the South End of Hartford. A failed evening because she talked about a man pursuing her, an Aetna vice president who sounded dull as dry bread. I got angry and that made her angry. But tonight she left a message asking me to have dinner.

"It's almost Christmas. I'm alone again."

I was going to call her back. In fact, I had the phone in my hand, but I changed my mind. Instead I went to bed early. The old radiators clanged and hissed and popped. Music to my ears. Outside the wind picked up, whistling through the naked limbs of the towering oaks that slammed against my windows. There would be snow that night. I wanted lots of snow. I wanted it as high as the windowsills.

In the morning I'd get back to the gym. It had been a while. I was out of shape. Yes, I'd see Jimmy and Gracie. Marcie and Vinnie. Hank. Yes, I finally smiled. Especially Liz. I wanted my old self back again. Somehow I'd lost it during the long and unhappy autumn.

I slept well.

To receive a free catalog of Poisoned Pen Press titles, please provide your name, address, and email address in one of the following ways:

Phone: 1-800-421-3976
Facsimile: 1-480-949-1707
Email: info@poisonedpenpress.com
Website: www.poisonedpenpress.com

Poisoned Pen Press
6962 E. First Ave. Ste 103
Scottsdale, AZ 85251